She clung as the roan raced faster through the trees. She craned for one look over her shoulder. Beck was in the lead, his face pale beneath the bound leather strips.

"There!" he shouted. "It's just a boy! Get him!"

The roan broke into a panicked gallop. Bramble suddenly knew who had been responsible for those welts and scars on his hide. But they were going too fast... They were too close to the chasm: they'd never be able to stop in time.

The roan didn't falter as they broke from the trees and headed wildly toward the abyss. Bramble considered tumbling from the horse's back before he reached the edge. Then she heard Beck's voice calling. There were worse things than death. There would be a leap and a moment suspended, and then a long hopeless curve to the rocks and the river below. They would fall like leaves between the clouds of swifts and then be washed away by the thundering rapids. Bramble clung to that thought. If their bodies were washed away, then there could be no identification, no danger of reprisals on her family. She hung on tighter. The roan's hindquarters bunched under her and they were in the air.

It was like she had imagined: the leap, and then the moment suspended in the air that seemed to last forever. Below her the swifts boiled up through the river mist, swerving and swooping while she and the roan seemed to stay frozen above them. Bramble felt, like a rush of air, the presence of the gods surround her. The shock made her lose her balance and begin to slide sideways. She felt herself falling. With an impossible flick of both legs, the roan shrugged her back onto his shoulders. Then the long curve down started and she braced herself to see the cliffs rushing past as they fell.

BLOOD TIES

The Castings Trilogy
Book One

PAMELA FREEMAN

www.orbitbooks.net
New York London

Orbit
Hachette Book Group USA
237 Park Avenue, New York, NY 10017
Visit our Web site at www.HachetteBookGroupUSA.com

First North American Orbit edition: April 2008
Originally published in paperback
by Hachette Australia, 2007

Orbit is an imprint of Hachette Book Group USA.
The Orbit name and logo are trademarks of Little, Brown
Book Group Limited.

The characters and events in this book are fictitious.
Any similarity to real persons, living or dead, is coincidental
and not intended by the author.

Library of Congress Cataloging-in-Publication Data
Freeman, Pamela.
Blood ties / Pamela Freeman.
p. cm.—(The castings trilogy ; bk. 1)
ISBN 978-0-316-03346-6
I. Title.
PR9619.4.F78B66 2008
823'.92—dc22   2007043687

10 9 8 7 6 5 4 3 2 1

RRD-IN

Printed in the United States of America

To Stephen

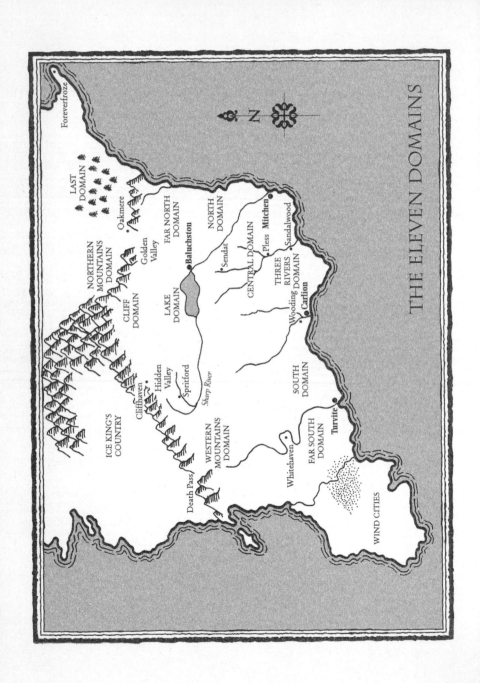

THE ELEVEN DOMAINS

BLOOD TIES

THE STONECASTER'S STORY

THE DESIRE TO KNOW the future gnaws at our bones. That is where it started, and might have ended, years ago.

I had cast the stones, seeing their faces flick over and fall: Death, Love, Murder, Treachery, Hope. We are a treacherous people—half of our stones show betrayal and violence and death from those close, death from those far away. It is not so with other peoples. I have seen other sets of stones that show only natural disasters: death from sickness, from age, the pain of a broken heart, loss in childbirth. And those stones are more than half full with pleasure and joy and plain, solid warnings like "You reap what you sow" and "Victory is not the same as satisfaction."

Of course, we live in a land taken by force, by battle and murder and invasion. It is not so surprising, perhaps, that our stones reflect our history.

So. I cast the stones again, wondering. How much of our future do we call to ourselves through this scrying? How much of it do we make happen because the stones give us a pattern to fulfill?

I have seen the stones cast too many times to doubt them. When I see Murder in the stones, I know someone will die. But would they have died without my foretelling? Perhaps merely saying the word, even in a whisper, brings the thought to the surface of a mind, allows the mind to shape it, give it substance, when otherwise it might have remained nothing more than vague murmurings, easily ignored.

1

Death recurred again and again in my castings that night. I did not ask whose. Perhaps it was mine, perhaps not. I had no one left to lose, and therefore did not fear to lose myself.

There was someone at the door, breathing heavily outside, afraid to come in. But he did, as they always do, driven by love or fear or greed or pain, or simple curiosity, a desire to giggle with friends.

This one came in shyly: young, eighteen or nineteen, brown hair, green trousers and blue boots. He squatted across the cloth from me with the ease of near-childhood. I held out my left hand, searching his face. He had hazel eyes, but the shape of his face showed he had old blood, from the people who lived in this land before the landtaken, the invasion. There was old pain, too, old anger stoked up high.

He knew what to do. He spat in his own palm, a palm criss-crossed by scars, as though it had been cut many times, and clapped it to mine. I held him tightly and reached for the pouch with my right hand. He was strong enough to stay silent as I dug in the pouch for five stones and threw them across the cloth between us. He was even strong enough not to follow their fall with his eyes, to hold my gaze until I nodded at him and looked down.

He saw it in my face.

"Bad?"

I nodded. One by one I touched the stones lying faceup. "Death. Bereavement. Chaos. This is the surface. This is what all will see." Delicately I turned the other two stones over. "Revenge and Rejoicing. This is what is hidden." An odd mixture, one I had never before seen.

He brooded over them, not asking anything more. The stones did not speak to me as they often do; all I could tell him were their names. It seemed to be enough for him.

2

"You know what this refers to?" I asked.

He nodded, absently, staring at Rejoicing. He let go of my hand and slid smoothly to his feet, then tugged some coins out of a pocket and let them fall on the rug.

"My thanks, stonecaster." Then he was gone.

Who was I to set Death on the march? I know my stones by their feel, even in the darkness of the pouch. I could have fumbled and selected him a happy dream: Love Requited, Troubles Over, Patience. I could have soothed the anger in his eyes, the pain in his heart.

But who am I to cheat the stones?

After he left, I cast them again. This time, Death did not appear. She had gone out the door with the young one and his scars.

SAKER

SAKER REMEMBERED the first time he had tried to raise the dead. It was the night after Freite, the enchanter, had finally died. By then he had been her apprentice for thirteen long years, but only in the last two had she shared any real secrets with him, and only then because he had threatened to leave her if she withheld.

Freite had wept for her great age and his refusal to any longer give his power for her extended life. She had no more to offer him. He had learned everything she had to teach of her Wind City magic, and it had not included pity, or generosity. So he refused to touch her in her extremity, knowing she would drain the power out of him to give herself another day, another week, a month if she was lucky...She had died cursing him, but he was cursed already, so he disregarded it.

After she was buried, the Voice of Whitehaven had pronounced Freite's bequests and he had found that her house had passed into his hands, along with her savings, which were much greater than he had imagined. So there he was, rich but without a plan. He had gone to the stonecaster to find out what the gods wanted him to do next. And the stonecaster had sent him out the door with Revenge and Rejoicing awaiting him.

That first time, he hadn't even known he needed the actual bones for the spell to work. The enchanter had told him half-truths, half-spells, trying to hoard her knowledge as though it could ward off death. Saker knew, certain sure, nothing kept Death away for good. That Lady tapped everyone on the shoul-

4

der, sooner or later. But sometimes, just sometimes, she could be tricked.

He raised the black stone knife level with his palm, forcing his hand not to shake. *This must work.* Now, finally, he had the means, seven years since the stonecaster had set him on his path...

"I am Saker, son of Alder and Linnet of the village of Cliffhaven. I seek justice."

He began to shake with memory, with yearning, sorrow, righteous rage. There lay the strength of his spell. He touched the never-closing wound in his mind, drew on the pain and set it to work. The rest of the spell wasn't in words, but in memories, complex and distressing: colors, phrases of music, a particular scent, the sound of a scream...

When he had gathered them all he looked down at his father's bones on the table, his father's skull staring emptily. He pressed the knife to his palm then drew it down hard. The blood surged out in time with his heart and splashed in gouts on the chalk-white bones.

"Alder," he said. "Arise."

BRAMBLE

THE BLOOD TRAIL was plain. Every few steps a splotch showed brilliantly red. There were tracks, too. In summer it would have been harder, but in this earliest part of spring the grasses and ferns were thin on the ground, and the ground was soft enough to show the wolf's spoor.

Even the warlord's man would have been able to track this much blood; for Bramble it was like following a clearly marked highway, through new fern fronds and old leaf mold, down past the granite rocks, through the stand of mountain ash, blood marking the trail at every step, so fresh she could smell it. The prints on the right were lighter; it was favoring the wounded side.

It wasn't sensible to go after a hurt wolf with just a boot knife in her hand. She'd be lucky to get home without serious injury. She'd be lucky to get home at all. But she couldn't leave a wounded animal to die in pain, even if she hadn't shot it.

The brown wolf had limped across the far end of the clearing where she had been collecting early spring sorrel at the edge of a small stream, too intent on its own pain to even notice Bramble.

The forest had seemed to hush the moment she saw the arrow, the wolf, the blood dripping from its side. The glade glowed in the afternoon sunlight. Rich and heady, the smell of awakening earth, that special smell that came after the snow-melt was over, rose in drifts around her. She heard chats quarreling far overhead. The trickle of the stream. A squirrel leaping from branch to branch of an elm, rattling the still-bare twigs. It paused. The wolf stopped and looked back over his shoulder, seeing her for the first time. She waited, barely breathing, feeling as if the whole forest waited with her.

"There he is! See him? Don't lose him!"

"Quiet, idiot!"

The voices broke the moment. The wolf slipped into the shadow of some pine trees. The squirrel, scolding, skipped from elm to willow to alder and was gone. Bramble looked around quickly. The warlord's men were close. Nowhere to hide except up a tree. She dropped the sorrel and sprang for the lowest branch of a yew. Its dark branches would hide her, unlike the easier-to-climb willow next to it whose branches were still showing catkins, but no leaves.

She climbed fast, without worrying about scratches, so she was bleeding in a dozen places by the time she had reached a safe perch. She grabbed some of the yew leaves and crushed them in her hands, wringing them to release the bitter-smelling sap, then rubbed it on the trunk as far down as she could reach, to confuse the scent in case they had hounds, who would sniff out the blood for sure and certain.

She wondered who they were chasing. An actual criminal? Or just someone who'd looked at them the wrong way? Someone old Ceouf, the warlord, had taken against, maybe, or someone who had complained? Bramble smiled wryly. At least it wasn't a woman. Everyone knew what happened to a woman found alone by the warlord's men.

It angered her, as it always did. More than that, it enraged her. The warlords claimed that they protected the people in their Domain, from other warlords, of course, and in earlier days from invaders. Perhaps they had, once. But a couple of generations ago the warlords of the Eleven Domains had made peace, and there hadn't been more than a border skirmish since. The warlord's men weren't soldiers anymore, just thugs and bullies. You stayed out of their way, didn't draw their attention, and spat in the dust of their footprints after they'd gone.

It's not meant to be like this, she thought. *No one should have to hide in fear of the people who are supposed to protect them.*

Today she had been happy, happier than she had been for months, since her sister had married and moved away to Carlion, the nearest free town. She had been out in her forest again, rejoicing in the returning spring, giving thanks for new life. And they had brought death and fear with them, as they did everywhere. Her chest burned with resentment. Some part of her had always refused to be sensible about it, as her parents demanded. "The world's not going to change just because you don't like it," they'd said, time after time. She knew they were right. Of course she knew it, she wasn't a child or a fool. And yet, some part of her insisted, *It's not meant to be like this.*

"This way!"

The voice came again. Bramble parted the needles in front of her until she could see the clearing below. There were two men, one blond, one red-haired, in warlord's gear, with a blue crest on their shoulders to show their allegiance to this, the South Domain. They were young, about her age. Their horses were tethered near the trail that led into the clearing. One was a thin dark bay, the other a well-muscled roan. The trail ended there, she knew, and the forest, even in early spring, was too dense from here in for mounted men to ride.

"I know I got it," the blond said. "I winged it, at least."

"If you want to finish it off, you'll have to go on foot," the redhead said. They looked at the undergrowth consideringly, and then the blond looked down at his shiny riding boots.

"I just bought these," he complained. He had a sharp voice, as though it were the other man's fault that his boots were new.

"Leave it," the redhead said, clearly bored now.

"I wanted the skin. I've always wanted a wolf skin." The blond frowned, then shrugged. "Another day."

They turned and went back to their horses, mounted, and rode away without a backward glance.

Bramble sat appalled and even angrier. He had left a wounded animal to die in agony so he wouldn't get scratches on his boots! *Oh, isn't that typical!* she thought. *They're the animals, the greedy, heedless, bloody shagging bastards!*

She waited until she was sure they weren't coming back, then swung down from the tree, pulled her knife from her boot, and went to look for the wolf.

She followed the blood trail until it disappeared into the big holly thicket. She skirted the sharp leaves and picked up the trail on the other side. It finally came to an end near the stream in the center of the forest.

The wolf had staggered down to drink and stood, legs shaking, near the water's edge. Then it saw Bramble, and froze with fear. But it was foaming at the mouth, desperate for water, and she stayed very still, as still as a wild creature in the presence of humans, until it took the last few steps to the water and drank. The black-fletched arrow, a warlord's man's arrow, stuck out from its side.

After drinking, it collapsed on the muddy edge of the stream and panted in pain, looking up at her with great brown eyes, pleading wordlessly.

Bramble came to it gently, making no sudden move that might startle it. "There now, there now, everything's all right now..." she crooned, as she did to the orphan kids she raised, or the nannies she helped give birth. She lowered her hand slowly, softly onto its forehead and the wolf whined like a pup. "Not long now, not long," she said softly, stroking back to grip its ears. She gazed into its eyes steadily until it looked away, as all wild animals will look away from the gaze of anything they do not wish to fight, and then she cut its throat, as quickly and painlessly as she could.

Bramble sat waiting, her hand still on its head, ignoring the tears on her cheeks, while the blood pulsed out into the stream, swirling red. There wasn't much blood. It had bled a lot already. Her fingers gentled its ears as though it could still feel, then she stood up.

She hesitated, looking at the caked blood on its side, then stripped off her jacket, shirt, skirt and leggings, so she wouldn't stain them. She had to hope that the warlord's men wouldn't change their minds and come back. She could just imagine *that* scene.

Her knife was only sharp enough to slit through the hide. She had to heave the carcass over to peel the skin off and it was much heavier than she thought. There was blood all over her. She wrinkled her nose, but kept going. It was a good, winter-thick pelt and besides, taking it gave the death of the wolf some purpose, instead of it being a complete waste of life. She cut the pelt off at the base of the skull. It was worth more with head attached, but Bramble had always felt that tanning the head of the animal was a kind of insult.

She would have left the carcass for the crows and the foxes, but she didn't want the warlord's men to find it, if they came looking for the hide later. Let him think that he had missed. She dragged it up the hill to a rock outcropping, and piled stones on it. At least it would make a meal for the ants and the worms.

She washed the blood off both her and the hide, put her

clothes back on, tied up the hide and hoisted it over her shoulder. It weighed her down heavily, but she could manage it easily enough. She set off home.

The way was through the black elm and pine forest, and normally she would have lingered to admire the spring-green leaves that were beginning to bud, and listen to the white-backed woodpeckers frantically drilling for food after their long migration. She had been observing a red-breasted flycatcher pair build their nest, but today she passed it by without noticing, although she stopped to collect some wild thyme and sallet greens, and to empty one of her snares. She found a rabbit, thin after winter but good enough for a stew, and the pelt still winter-lush. Her hands did the work of resetting the snare but her mind was elsewhere.

The forest was ostensibly the warlord's domain, but was traditionally the hunting or grazing ground for a range of people, from foragers like Bramble to charcoal burners, coppicers, chair makers, withiers, pig farmers and woodcutters. It was a rare day that Bramble didn't meet someone in the forest; depending on the season, sometimes she saw as many people there as in the village street. It was just her bad luck that today she had seen the warlord's men.

She came out of the forest near the crossroads just outside Wooding and realized that it hadn't been just bad luck. There had been an execution today.

Her village of Wooding saw a lot of executions, because it was on the direct road from Carlion to the warlord's fort at Thornhill. For centuries the South Domain warlords had used the crossroads just outside Wooding as the site for their punishments. There was a scaffold set up for when the warlord felt merciful. And for when he wasn't there was the rock press, a sturdy wooden box the size of a coffin, but deeper, where the condemned were piled with heavy stones until their bones broke and they suffocated, slowly.

Today they had used the rock press. There was blood seeping out of the box at the corners. The condemned often bled from the nose and mouth in the final stages of pressing. Bramble slowed as she walked past the punishment site. Did she want to know who they had killed this time? What was the point?

She went over to the box and looked in. No one she knew, thank the gods. Some stranger—the Domain was large, and criminals were brought to the warlord from miles away. Then she looked closer. A stranger, but just a boy. Fourteen, perhaps. A baby. Probably accused of something like "disrespect to the warlord." Her heart burned again, as it had in the woods. Anger, indignation, pity. She would have to make sure she was nowhere near the village the next morning, when the warlord's men rounded up the villagers to see the boy's corpse removed from the box and placed in the gibbet. She doubted she could applaud and cheer for the warlord over this execution, as the villagers were expected to do.

Some did so gladly. There were always a few who enjoyed a killing, like the crows that nested in the tree next to the scaffold and descended on the corpses with real enthusiasm. But the rest of the villagers had seen too many people die who looked just like them. Ordinary people. People who couldn't pay their taxes, or hadn't bowed low enough to the warlord. Or who had objected to their daughter being dragged away to the fort by the warlord's men. It was important to attend the executions, and to cheer loudly. The warlord's men were always watching. Bramble had cheered as loudly as anyone, in the past, and had been sick later, every time.

So the warlord's men would have done their job today and gone home as soon as the boy stopped breathing. The blond had probably taken the shortcut through the woods and had seen the wolf by accident. He couldn't resist tracking it a little way. Couldn't resist killing again.

A hunter who didn't care if the animal he shot suffered deserved nothing but contempt. He certainly didn't deserve the hide of the animal he had abandoned to pain and slow death.

But the *sensible* thing to do would be to take the skin to the warlord's fort, say it had one of the warlord's arrows in it when she found it, and let the blond claim it. Let him have his prize for killing.

Bramble looked at the boy in the box, whose face was still contorted in pain. "Well, no one ever said I was sensible," she said.

She skirted the village and came to the back of her parents' house, through the alders that fringed the stream. She dumped the wolf skin behind the privy, then went the whole way back so she would be seen to come home through the main street with nothing in her hands but rabbit and greens.

Bramble passed the inn and ignored the stares of the old men who sat on the bench outside the door, tankards in hand, until one of them called out, "Got your nose stuck in the air, I see! Too high and mighty to tell us how that sister of yours is doing off in Carlion!"

It was Swith, the leatherworker's father, both hands cramped around his mug. He was a terrible gossip, but that wasn't why he had called Bramble over. He wanted her to notice his hands. The arthritis that kept him sitting here in the mild sun had swelled his knuckles up like a goat's full udder.

"She's well, she says," Bramble replied. "They're building a new house, on the lot next to his parents'."

"Ah, she's done well for herself, that Maryrose!" cackled Swith's crony, old Aden, the most lecherous man in the village

13

in his day, and still not to be trusted within arm's reach. "She wasn't an eye-catcher like you, lass. But he got a good hot bed to go to, I'll say that, her town clerk's son!"

The other men frowned. Maryrose had been liked by everyone in the village, and she was certainly no light-skirt.

"That's enough of that, Aden," Swith said reprovingly. "Your mam and da will be missing her," he said with a cunning sideways look. "She was their favorite, wasn't she?"

It was an old match of his, trying to get Bramble to give him back a short answer. It kept him amused, and it didn't do her any harm. Everyone knew that Maryrose was the favorite.

"They are missing her, of course, Swith," Bramble said. Then, feeling she had given Aden and the others enough entertainment, she said, "I notice your hands are bothering you. Could I be helping? Give them a rub, maybe?"

"If you want to help a man by rubbing something—"

"Close that dirty mouth, Aden!" Swith bellowed then glanced a bit shamefacedly at Bramble. "Well, lass, now you mention it..."

She smiled at him. "I'll come by after supper."

It was a more or less regular thing she did, massaging goose grease and comfrey into the old people's hands and feet. Not all of them, of course. Just the cross-grained ones who couldn't find anyone else to help them. She was glad Aden didn't have arthritis; she wasn't about to get within groping distance of him.

She hefted the rabbit and greens in one hand. "I have to get these to Mam." None of them had mentioned the rabbit, though they had eyed it and no doubt would have liked to hear all the details on where she had trapped it and what kind of snare she had used, the kind of talk that kept them occupied for hours. To ask would have been against custom, since they all knew Swith had called her over to ask her a favor, which she was granting.

If she wanted to tell them about her hunting, she would, in her own good time.

If she hadn't offered to help Swith, it would have been a different story, she thought with amusement as she walked up the street, exchanging greetings with Mill the charcoal burner, home at his grandparents' until after the snowmelt and spring rains, and ignoring the tribe of dogs that swirled around her heels as they always did. But she had made the offer, so the old men couldn't cross-question her without being unforgivably rude.

"I have a doe ready to drop twins, Bramble," called Sigi, the new young brewster who had doubled the inn's clientele after she had married its owner, Eril. Sigi's three toddlers, who ran around her feet as she brought in her washing, were screaming with excitement about a maggot one of them had plucked from the rubbish pile. "If she doesn't have enough milk for both, can I bring one to you?"

"Of course, and welcome," Bramble called back. "I've no orphans this season so far."

When Sigi had first met Bramble, she had reacted as many people did, with suspicion at Bramble's dark hair and eyes. In this land of blonds and redheads, a dark-haired person was assumed to be a Traveler, a descendant of the original inhabitants of the Domains, who had been invaded and dispossessed a thousand years ago. Old history. But no one trusted Travelers. They were thieves, liars, perverts, bad luck bringers. Bramble had heard all the insults over the years, mostly (though not always) by people who didn't know her, like ordinary travelers on the road through Wooding to Carlion.

Sigi had finally overcome her suspicion, and Bramble was trying hard to forget the insult. It would be nice to have a friend in the village, now Maryrose was gone, and Sigi was the best candidate. The other girls had long ago shut her out after she had made it clear that she didn't have any interest in the things that obsessed them, like boys and hair ribbons and sewing for their glory boxes. Not that boys weren't a pleasure, now and then.

Sigi's oldest child grabbed the maggot and dropped it down her brother's back and the resultant wailing distracted Sigi completely. Bramble laughed and went on to her own home, following Gred, the goose girl, as she shepherded her waddling, squabbling, hissing flock back to their night pasture outside the mill.

Bramble's family lived in an old cottage, a house really, bigger than it looked from the street, as it ran far back toward the stream. It was built of the local bluestone, all except for the chimney, which was rounded river stones in every shade of gray and brown and dark blue. It was thatched with the herringbone pattern you found on every roof around here, although in Carlion they thatched a fish-scale pattern, when they didn't tile in slate. The front garden caught the morning light, so it was full of early herbs just pushing through the soil. The vine over one corner was still a bare skeleton, but the house had a cheerful, open look with its shutters wide and its door ajar.

The door was ajar because her mother was in the road sweeping up the droppings the geese had left behind. The Widow Farli was doing the same thing outside her cottage a little farther down. Goose droppings were good fertilizer, and for someone like Widow Farli, who only kept a couple of scraggly hens, they were important. Bramble's mother, Summer, kept pigs, as well as goats and hens, and really didn't need them.

"No use wasting them," her mam said as Bramble came up. She swept the droppings onto an old piece of bag. "Here, go and give them to Widow Farli." She held the bag out.

Bramble took the droppings and handed the wild thyme and the sallet greens and the rabbit carcass to her mother.

Farli had a face you could cut cheese with, and the tip of her nose was always white, as if with anger, but at what, Bramble had never figured out. She stared past Bramble and said snidely, "Nice of your *mother* to take the trouble. *She*'s not one to go off gallivanting and leave all her work to others."

"Just as well," Bramble said, smiling sweetly, "or what would become of you?"

Farli's face flushed dark red. "Your tongue'll get you into mischief one day, young lady, you mark my words! Mischief or worse!"

She turned on her heel and flounced toward her back garden, keeping a tight hold of the bag of droppings.

Bramble grinned and went home. She had a pelt to cure. She fetched it from behind the privy and went to the kitchen door to ask her mother for a loan of the good knife to scrape the skin down.

"A *wolf?*" her mam said, that note in her voice that meant "what will the girl do next?" She had her frown on, too, the "what have I done to deserve this?" frown.

Bramble had grown up knowing she'd never be the daughter her parents wanted—never be like her sister, Maryrose, who was a crafter born, responsible, hard-working, loving in the way they understood. Maryrose looked like her mother, tawny-haired and blue-eyed, clearly one of Acton's people, while Bramble looked like her granda, who had started life a Traveler. He looked like the people who'd lived here before Acton's people had come over the mountains. Along with her coloring—or perhaps due to the way people looked askance at her because of it—Bramble had inherited the Traveler restlessness, the hatred of being enclosed. Where Maryrose was positively happy to stay seated all day at the loom with her mother, or stand in the workshop shaping and smoothing a beech table with her father, Bramble yearned to be in the forest, for the green luxuriance of summer growth, the sharp tracery of bare branches in winter, the damp mold and mushroom smell of autumn.

She had spent all her free time there as a child, and a lot of time when she should have been learning a trade. While she never did learn to weave or carpenter, by the time she was old enough to marry, a good proportion of the family food came to the table from her hands, and a few luxuries as well. Their flock of goats came from Bramble's nursing of orphan kids or the runty twin of a dropping. If she raised a kid successfully, she got either half the meat if it was a billy, or the first kid if it was a nanny. She had a knack with sick animals, and sick people, too. In the forest, she set snares, gathered greens, fruits and nuts, herbs and bulbs. In early spring, the hard time, it was her sallets and snowberries that kept the family from the scurvy, her rabbit and squirrel that fed them when the bacon ran out and the corn-meal ran low. They could have bought extra supplies, of course, but the money they saved, then and all through the year, from Bramble's gathering, made the difference between survival and prosperity, between living from day to day and having a nest egg behind them. And her furs brought in silver, too, although they weren't the thick, expensive kind you got from the colder areas up north near Foreverfroze. And old Ceouf, the warlord, took a full half of what she made on them, for a "luxury" tax.

There was always someone in the village ready to spy for the warlord. At Wooding's yearly Tax Day in autumn, it was amazing how the warlord's steward seemed to know everything that had been grown or raised or sold or bought in the last year. Bramble suspected Widow Farli of being an informer, but she couldn't blame her. A woman alone needed some way of buying the warlord's protection.

Bramble had never brought home a wolf skin before, but her mam thought poorly of it for one of those "it isn't respectable" reasons that she could never quite follow.

"The gods alone know what'll become of you, my girl," Mam said. That wasn't so bad; it was said with a kind of exasperated affection. But then she sighed and couldn't resist adding, "If only you were more like your sister!"

When Bramble was six, and seven, and eight, that sigh and that sentence had made her stomach clench with anguish and bewilderment. At nineteen, she just raised an eyebrow at her mother and smiled. It did no good to let it hurt; neither she nor her parents were going to change. *Could* change. And if there was still a cold stone, an empty hollow, under her ribs left over from when she was little, it was so familiar she didn't even feel it anymore.

"I'll make you a gorgeous coat out of it, Mam," she said, and winked. "Just think how impressed they'll be at the Winterfest dance."

Her mother smiled reluctantly. "Oh, yes, of course you will. I can just see myself in a wolf-skin coat. A lovely sight I'd be. No, thank you." She looked down at the rabbit and greens. "Well, these'll make a good meal."

Bramble nodded at the implied thanks, took the good knife her mother held out and went down to the stream to scrape the hide down thoroughly.

Every so often she couldn't help looking up to where flocks of pigeons and rooks, coming home for summer, circled the sky. High above them in the uplands of the air, a blue heron glided, like the old song said, free from care. It came from beyond the

Great Forest, from up near Foreverfroze. She longed to see what it had seen. One day, but not yet, because the gods forbade it.

"Time and past to milk the goats, Bramble!" her mother called from the back door.

Bramble groaned and trudged off toward the goat shed. She lingered for a moment at the gate, watching the sky turn that pale, pale blue that wasn't quite gray, as it did on these spring evenings, just before it darkened. She wondered, for the hundredth time, or maybe the thousandth, where the birds had been. She had wanted to take the Road all her life. When she was a child, listening to her grandfather's Traveling stories, she had promised herself that one day she would. Just go. But as she grew older she watched the Travelers who came to Wooding and realized that they all had trades. Skills. Tinkering, music, singing, tumbling, mural and sign painting, horse breaking... Bramble had no skills worth anything to anyone else. She could hunt and forage, but on the Road, far from the forest, what good would that be to her?

So she laid her plan: she would save her coppers and head north, to the Great Forest in the Last Domain, where the mink and the weasel and the fox furs were so thick that the city folk would pay good silver for them. She would not Travel, but travel, to where her skills were useful and could earn her bread. She would see the oldest forest in the world and learn its secrets and there, in its green darkness, she would be rid of this yearning.

When she came back to the house with a pail of frothy milk, her mam had warmed water for her to wash in, and had laid out cheese and bread and some dried apple, "to keep the wolf from the door until the stew is ready." Bramble smiled—it was her mother's way of making a joke, and making amends for maybe speaking too sharply. She never said sorry, but the dried apple was running low this side of winter, and to bring some out just for a snack was the only apology Bramble needed.

A while later, her da and granda came in from the workshop smelling of cedar and sat down eagerly to the rabbit stew.

"What are you working on?" Bramble asked.

"A blanket chest for the innkeeper. I told him that camphor laurel would do as well as cedar to keep away the moths, but he thinks that town-bred Sigi of his deserves the very best," Da said, smiling.

"She's the reason he can afford a new chest," Granda said. "She's a better brewer than he ever was."

"Wouldn't be hard," Mam said, sniffing. Mam, rather surprisingly, liked a good strong brown ale, though, less surprisingly, she never had more than one.

The meal went on as normal; they discussed the day's events and the village gossip, and wondered, as always, how Maryrose and Merrick were doing and when there'd be news of a grandchild on the way. Mam said nothing of the wolf skin and Bramble kept silent, too, not sure how much of the story to share. None, maybe. If there was trouble, she knew her family would be safer if they knew nothing.

Again she felt impatient, itching with annoyance. It was wrong that they had to go in fear of the warlord's men all their lives. Sitting at the table as she'd done every night of her life, she was overcome by a familiar rush of feeling: the desire to get away, somewhere, *anywhere*, anywhere but here. It was so familiar that she knew what to do about it. Nothing. The next thing that would happen would be the voice of the local gods in her ear saying *Not yet*. They'd said it every time she'd felt like this, from the time she could understand the words. And every time she thought back to them: *When?* But they never answered.

But this time, when she was filled with impatience and the desire to fly away like the wild geese in autumn, there was no message from the gods. Nothing but silence. It sent a chill through her, to have one of the deep patterns of her life broken without warning, but it sped up her heart as well. She breathed more deeply, thinking about it.

After supper she went out into the windy, cold dark and made her way unerringly to the black rock altar in the wood near the village. Not the deep forest, this, but a beech wood of skeleton branches, floor clear of everything but last year's leaves and a frail flush of new ferns. The altar was close to the burial caves, as it should be, in a clearing surrounded by other trees: oak, ash, hawthorn bushes, rowan, and willows near the stream that provided the gods with music. Bramble came to the rock at moonrise. It was a thin sliver of moon, on the wane, with the evening star underneath the crescent: a bad-luck moon, but beautiful.

She knelt at the rock and felt the presence of the gods lift the hair on her neck, as it always did. She didn't pray, or offer sacrifice. She had just come to ask a question.

"When?"

The wind stilled. The glade filled with the presence of the gods, like pressure, like swimming deep down into the quarry pool until she could feel the weight of the water begin to push against her chest and eyes, like being smothered in strength.

Soon.

They spoke into her head, as they always did, and then left. The glade was now empty, the pressure was gone.

Soon.

What, she wondered, had changed?

She went home via Swith's and massaged his hands, but she was so quiet he actually apologized for Aden's crudity that afternoon. She laughed it off, but that night in her dreams she was a wild goose, flying forever across a gold-leafed forest.

The next morning she asked Gerda, the tanner, for advice about how to treat the hide, in case there was anything different about wolf skin from weasel and fox. There wasn't, but she paid for the advice with a basket of tiny sweet strawberries that she'd collected from the deep glade where an old oak had fallen.

It was a lovely pelt, thick and glossy. Bramble slung it over the chair in her room and ran her hand over it every time she passed. The fur sprang back against her hand as though the living body had leaped and a small fillip of pleasure went through her each time she felt it. She didn't want to flaunt it, but risked wearing it out anyway. Looking back, she was sorry she hadn't hidden it in the forest and brought it back home after dark, sorry that she'd asked Gerda for advice.

The warlord's man tracked her down in the clearing near the Springtree. She wasn't gathering hawthorn, like the other girls were doing this day before the Springtree dance, but checking that the beehive she'd found last autumn had survived the winter. The hive was in the fork of a linden tree just breaking into leaf. The tree was one she'd climbed often as a child, playing a game with Maryrose where they had to get from village to home without touching the ground. It had been tricky but possible to jump from tree to tree to fence to tree all the way.

The hive was in good order, buzzing companionably. She sat on the limb a safe distance away, and talked to the bees awhile. She resolved to come back often enough through the summer so they'd get used to the sound of her voice, and not attack her when she came to smoke them and steal their honey.

A rider appeared from behind the big willow. It was the blond. Seen closer, he was a stocky, broad-shouldered man with the pale hair and blue eyes of Acton's people, mounted on a powerful-looking roan gelding. She grew wary, but he was far enough off that she could be out of the tree before he could get to her. The linden boughs intermeshed with a big willow; she could be away and into the forest before he could get off his horse. She stood up on the bough, one hand on the trunk.

"Greetings, mistress," he said, smiling the smile men so often used, the one that was meant to charm but never did. She nodded, not minded to give him any more than that until she knew what he wanted. Even smiling, he had a mean mouth and narrow eyes, for all that he was no older than her.

He was annoyed that she hadn't given him greetings. He frowned, then she saw his frown soften as he looked at her breasts. She knew that look, too. It wasn't desire, but lust, and took no account of what she thought or felt. Men who looked at you like that never met your eyes.

"Why not come down and talk?" He held out his hand invitingly.

"No, thank you."

He looked at her face then and she saw him register her black hair and eyes, saw the contempt in his face. She could see it made him angrier that a Traveler was resisting him. He drew himself up in the saddle, puffed out his chest like a ten-year-old boy trying to impress. She nearly laughed, but he was no less dangerous for that.

"Stop playing games, missy. You know why I'm here. Give me the wolf skin and I'll forget about your stealing it from me."

"If you've got a claim on something of mine you can take it to the village voice and he'll settle the dispute," Bramble said.

A voice was elected by each village and made decisions in disputes between villagers, as well as representing them in dealings with the warlord. The warlord's men never showed much respect to them. She didn't think the man would like to submit to the voice's ruling, but it was worth a try. The roan was fidget-ing, ears back; Bramble could see it getting nervous as the man grew impatient. She refused to let her own nerves take over. It was better to be annoyed than afraid.

"We don't ask favors of villagers," he said with derision. "Where did you get it?"

"From a wolf."

"From *my* wolf." He swept a black-fletched arrow out of the quiver at his back and shook it at her. "It had a black arrow in it, didn't it, when you found it?" He shot the arrow back into the quiver with a thump that made the roan flinch. Bramble felt a quick surge of fellow feeling for it. "You found the carcass and skinned it...well, there's no harm in that. But it's my skin and I want it."

"Did you kill the wolf?" she asked quietly.

He hesitated. "I shot it."

"But *I* killed it. If you won't go to the village voice, perhaps the warlord should decide it?"

He didn't like that idea, having to admit to his overlord that he'd failed to finish off the wolf. The roan jumped as he put in the spurs. It took a step forward, only to be reined in hard.

"Just give it here or you'll be sorry." He loosened his sword in his scabbard deliberately.

Her toes gripped the bark firmly. She was suddenly angry past common sense or reason at his arrogance. It was typical of the warlord's men, of all the men who carried sword and shield. Typical that he hadn't followed the wolf and finished him off, as any compassionate hunter would do. That wolf had looked at her with pleading in its eyes, and she knew enough of animals to know when it was for help, and when it was for a quick end to pain. She had done this man's job for him, and she would keep the results.

"I think I'd rather go to the warlord."

It had been a mistake to stand up. She saw him looking up at her legs, bare under her skirt. Her stomach turned over with revulsion at the thought of him touching her and there was a flutter of panic beneath her breastbone. She pushed it down. Men like him lived for the fear in others.

The intention to hurt was in his eyes and in the hands hard on the reins, but he hesitated. The warlord allowed his men great license, but there were limits. He couldn't just beat her and take the skin. She might go to the warlord and say that she had been happy to accept his judgment on the matter. If the blond just took things into his own hands, he knew he'd be in trouble. The roan snorted and backed away a little. He curbed it savagely but otherwise ignored it. She could see the thoughts move behind his eyes, saw him looking for a way to discredit her before the warlord. It chilled her.

"Black hair and black eyes," he sneered. "You're a Traveler wench, aren't you? Is it true what they say, that you'll go with anyone?"

"No." Her voice was as cold and firm as she could make it.

She saw some flicker of reaction on his face and the spark of warning inside her grew stronger. Old Ceouf was famed for allowing his men to get away with rape. If she complained to him later about the way his man had dealt with the wolf, the blond would deny it, and accuse her of trying to revenge her rape. And he'd be believed. She would have to give him the wolf skin and then go straight to the warlord and lay it all before him. It was her only chance. Her hand moved slowly to the skin, but he misinterpreted, thought she was taking hold of it in ownership.

"You'd better do as you're told, girl. You don't want anything to happen to your family, do you?" His hand moved again to his sword hilt.

Of course he would threaten like that, the coward. She felt the contempt take over her face and saw his reaction to it. But she wasn't prepared for the speed with which he moved.

He kicked the horse forward and reached to pull her down. She drew back one foot, tough as an old boot from seasons of barefoot running, and kicked him in the head. Her heel connected with his face and he fell backward off the horse. She turned to run, but from the corner of her eye she saw that he lay very still. As still as death.

She looked back slowly. As the roan shifted uneasily sideways, she saw that he lay on his back, eyes wide, his face with a curious crumpled look. His long nose was shortened like a pig's. She realized that she had kicked him flat on the nose, that the bone had gone back and entered his brain like a spear. She had killed him.

She'd meant to run, she'd *planned* to run. But in the moment when he reached for her, an instinct stronger than reason had taken over. Her leg had seemed to move of its own accord, but it had, she realized, been guided by some dark, bone-deep refusal to run: a rejection of fear, of the surrender that comes with fear, an inability to accept that he was worth her fear.

She hoped that when the warlord's men found the body it would look as though he had ridden thoughtlessly fast under the low linden bough and been hit in the face, and the horse had ridden to the forest. Would it look like an accident? She didn't know enough to predict their reaction, so she shrugged the worry away.

She'd killed a lot of things—the wolf, rabbits, weasels and stoats, fish and fawns. It was a job that had to be done. But she'd always meant to do it. To kill without meaning seemed... well, it seemed a waste. A waste of what, she wasn't sure. Life? Purpose? Or something harder to name, though she could feel it. Her own soul? She couldn't look away from his face. He seemed improved by death; his face had lost its scowl. It felt odd to have interrupted the life of someone she knew nothing about, to kill someone she had only just met, as though killing needed intimacy, deep knowledge of the other, to make it all right. She forced herself to look away from him, and immediately realized that she had better get away, and fast.

Her heart was racing, her stomach clenched, her skin was clammy. Fear or the exaltation of escape? She didn't know. But although fear was as good a name as any, the same impulse that had sent her foot against his face now prevented her from naming her racing heart as fearful. Excitement, the need to get moving, were better reasons.

She slid onto the broad back of the roan and gathered up the reins with clumsy hands. She couldn't reach the stirrups and it seemed somehow impolite to just kick the horse, so she clicked with her tongue, as plowmen did to draft horses, and the roan willingly moved off toward the trees. Even then, in the first moment of riding him, she wanted to keep him, felt that they had already become attached by fellow feeling against the man.

It was the first time Bramble had been on a horse since old Cuthbert, a Traveling tinker, had given her rides on his cart horse when she was six. It was a long way to the ground. She swallowed as the horse's swaying walk seemed to poise her over a long drop twice at each stride. The stirrups thumped against his side as he moved and he quickened his pace to a bumpy trot, and then to a canter.

She grasped the pommel and held her breath, feeling for the first time the intoxicating sense of power under her, the sense of being extended, that the horse's speed and strength and agility were all hers, even if only temporarily. It was an uncomfortable, unsteady passage, but by the end of it she was in love with riding.

She took him to a narrow gully in the depths of the wood, to her cave. It was less a cave than a cleft between two huge rocks that formed the end of the gully. She had come here since she was a child, whenever she wanted somewhere cool and quiet, somewhere to think or to pray. The rocks were covered with moss at the base and their cracked faces were shaded even in the middle of summer, since the trees around them were mostly evergreen, cedar and yew. It was a strange place, always quiet. Birds calling in the trees above sounded far away; water from a tiny spring where the two rock faces met trickled down gently, constantly, even when all the streams were frozen. It felt holy, but there were no gods here, just silence.

With a long tether made of strips of her underskirt, Bramble staked out the horse at the end of the cleft. It wouldn't stop him if he wanted to run, but nothing she had could. The cleft was just big enough to hold him. If wolves came the horse could retreat into it and protect himself with his front hooves. He was safe enough. She unsaddled and unbridled him, wiped off his sweat with a bunch of grass then leaned her back against the cool rock and watched him graze all afternoon. She went home with the memory of the warlord's man buried under thoughts of the roan.

The memory came back that night, though, in her dreams, where she endlessly kicked at his face, but he kept reaching for her anyway, over and over. She woke awash with sweat in the bed that she and Maryrose had shared, and wished that Maryrose was still here. If the warlord's men came to arrest her, she would go with them quietly and they'd have no excuse to bully her mother or father. But no one came except Eril, the innkeeper, to pick up the blanket chest in his handcart. He was full of the news that one of the warlord's men had been found dead.

"A riding accident," he said, shaking his head. "One of these harum-scarum young lads, it was, rode right into a linden bough and—phut!—dead! The warlord's not too pleased, they say, and the horse is missing, too, though that's not a loss to him up yonder, for it was the lad's own horse, they say. Keep an eye out for it, lassie," he said. "You might get a reward."

She didn't even consider turning the roan in for a reward.

That morning, before dawn, she had gone to the black rock altar in the forest. She approached silently, hiding in the thick growth of alders along the stream. She didn't want any of the villagers to see her and start asking questions about what she might be praying for.

There was no one there; she had come early enough. She stepped toward the rock, quietly, as she had always felt the local gods preferred. The villagers often laughed and joked as soon as they'd backed away from their prayers here, but she'd never understood that. Couldn't they feel the presence of the gods, that hair-raising, spine-chilling stroke along the skin, *beneath* the skin? Perhaps they couldn't. Perhaps that was part of the Traveler blood she'd inherited from her granda, just as she'd inherited his black eyes and black hair.

She sat down carefully, cross-legged in front of the rock, and bowed her head. Today she had a favor to ask, and there were time-honored ways of doing that.

"Gods of field and stream, hear your daughter. Gods of sky and wind, hear your daughter. Gods of earth and stone, hear your daughter."

Perhaps she should have brought a sacrifice; one of her goats had dropped a kid the night before. They liked young sacrifices, it was said. But the blood would have been noticed. The village snoops wouldn't have stopped until they'd found out who had made the sacrifice, and why. She forced her thoughts back to her petition.

"Gods of fire and storm, hear your daughter. Of your kindness, keep my family safe. Keep the warlord's men from them, keep them whole and happy."

She took out her knife and cut off a lock of her hair at the roots near her nape and laid it on the rock.

"Take this offering as a symbol of my reverence. Use it to bind safety around my family. Use it to bind me more surely to your service."

The hair stirred in a breath of air that Bramble couldn't feel. The gods were testing her sacrifice. The eddy of air turned and ruffled the hair on her head. In her mind she felt the tickle that meant the touch of the gods and, as always, the world spun around her as they tasted her thoughts. She rocked between joy and a holy terror that was completely different—cleaner—than the fear she had refused to the warlord's man. When her sight was clear again she saw that the hair on the rock had disappeared. The gods had accepted her sacrifice.

She let out a long breath of relief. There was nothing more she could do. Slowly, she got up and backed away. It was probably just superstition that said it was bad luck to turn your back on the gods, but she wasn't willing to risk bad luck just now.

She realized the gods had listened when at home she found her mam and da reading a letter from Maryrose and her husband, Merrick, inviting them all to come and live in Carlion. Mam had learned to read from her mother, who had been a waiting woman to the old warlord's wife, and she had taught her husband and both the girls.

They had talked about moving before, in a casual way, during the preparations for Maryrose's wedding, but now it was time to decide.

"They say they're building the new house big enough to fit all of us," her da said. "Merrick must be doing well."

"You should go," Bramble said. The memory of the warlord's man came up to confront her—his threats and the menace she'd read in his eyes—and it had made her voice harsh. She thumped some rabbit carcasses down on the table. "Get yourselves into a free town, where you're safe from the warlord's men."

They were startled.

"They've never bothered us," her father said.

"But they could. Anytime they want to. In Carlion you only have to worry about the town council." She tried to smile, to turn it into a joke. "Who knows, maybe you'll end up a councillor yourself!"

"It's a big shift, to leave everyone we know. All our friends," her father said, but he sounded excited by the idea of change. Mam sniffed.

"There's a few I'll not miss," she said, then paused. "And a few I will. But Maryrose is there…and any grandchildren we're likely to have will be Carlion born and bred."

From that moment, Bramble knew it was decided, although her mother wondered aloud how Bramble would cope with town life.

"For you're always in the forest," her mam said.

Bramble felt herself start to shrug, always her answer to that old complaint, but stopped. It was probably the last time she would ever hear it. "Don't worry about me," she said, eyes passing from her mam to her da.

But of course they did. They kept discussing it endlessly over breakfast. Bramble wished her grandmother was still alive. She would have forced them to admit they all wanted to go. No patience for dithering, her grandam. Bramble sighed. It was clear to her that the only thing holding them back was the thought that she would be unhappy in Carlion. She knew that as soon as she left they'd be packing up to make the move. She didn't try to explain that she probably wouldn't be with them. That would just lead to more questions, which she knew she couldn't answer.

After breakfast she went to her room and rolled her bag of silver, the wolf skin and some clothes in a blanket, to make a bedroll. It seemed to her that the gods' "soon" might mean very soon, and she had better be ready. She kissed her parents good-bye before she went to the forest. They were surprised; kisses were for bedtime.

She grinned at them reassuringly. "Just felt like it."

They were so surprised they didn't think to ask where she was going with her blanket. She crossed the stream at the bottom of their garden and headed for the forest. The roan was waiting for her, or at least waiting at the end of his tether, with his head high and his ears pricked. She stashed the bedroll and silver inside the cave then greeted him gently, stroking her hand down his neck, feeling very fragile next to his warm strength.

"Gods," she said, looking at his broad back and powerful rump. "Let's hope you're a good-natured fellow, because you'll have to be patient with me."

She contemplated the saddle. Not only did it look complicated, but it was branded with the warlord's mark. If she was found on the roan, she could claim that she had found it wandering in the forest, but if it had the warlord's saddle on it, she would be branded herself, as a thief. Or worse. Horse stealing was a garoting crime. So she left it aside with a feeling of relief. She didn't like the idea of having straps and buckles and harness on the roan. It felt wrong to tie up a fellow creature that way, like putting him in prison.

The blanket from under his saddle wasn't marked, so she slid that over him and then looked at the bit and bridle. It had a nasty look, all steel and sharp edges. The roan's mouth had calluses at the edges, marks of old wounds. She remembered the arrow in the wolf's side and threw the bridle away. The horse startled back a little when it hit the ground with a jingle.

"Shh, shh, now," she said, using the same tone she used with the sick lambs and kids she nursed back to health. "It's all right, everything's all right…"

She ran her hands over him, noting the marks beneath the hair and hating the warlord's man even more when she realized they were scars from whip and spur.

"Nothing to fear here, sweetheart," she crooned. She undid the tether and gathered it up. It was tied loosely around his neck and she used it to pull him over to a large rock.

"Now I know you could get rid of me with just a shake of your rump," she said, climbing on top of the rock, "but how about you don't? Let's see what we can do together, you and I."

She mounted carefully and adjusted herself on the blanket, pulling up the skirt she had worn over her breeches so that she sat comfortably. Then she leaned forward and undid the tether, stuffed it in a pocket and took a deep breath. How high she was! How far it seemed to the ground. The roan's hide was warm, even through the blanket. He seemed as solid as the rock she had climbed from.

And here I sit, she thought, smiling, *looking like a frog on a stone, with no idea what I'm supposed to do.*

"Up to you, horse," she said. "Let's go."

She clicked her tongue as she had before. The roan's ears flicked back in response. She did it again and squeezed his sides, very gently, with her legs. It felt like trying to squeeze a tree trunk, but the roan walked forward, then stopped. She squeezed again, a little harder, and he began to walk with more confidence, down the hill.

Excitement spiraled up from her stomach. She squeezed again. The roan broke into a trot. Bramble could feel her balance going and windmilled her arms, but she slid off sideways, anyway, right into a patch of nettles. She wanted to shout and curse, but she bit it back in case she frightened the horse, the completely untethered horse, into running.

She dragged herself up, thanking the gods for her breeches. The roan was standing, looking at her with amused, knowing eyes. He whickered to her softly.

"Yes, very funny," she said. "Perhaps we'll just stick to walking today, eh?"

He waited calmly while Bramble walked up to him. She took him by the forelock and led him uphill to the mounting rock. He nuzzled her shoulder. Up until that moment, she had seen him as a creature from the warlord's world that she could use, a living thing, yes, but like the goats and the chickens that she cared for at home. A domestic animal.

But the way he looked at her with amusement, she was sure, the way he greeted her with affection, the realization that he was here because he had chosen to wait for her, made her feel that he was more than that, that he was something she had never really had before. A companion.

It felt just as wrong to give him a name as to use a bit and bridle. Owners gave names. She wasn't the owner, not in any sense. It wasn't like she had any real control over him: they were just fellow creatures, spending time together. If he thought of her at all, it was probably as "the human," and so she would think of him as "the horse," or maybe, "the roan."

She practiced walking him around all day and by the time she went home, she could hardly walk, her thighs were rubbed raw and her hips ached. But nothing could have kept her away the next day.

When she groomed him—she had watched ostlers at the inn attend to horses—she found more scars from the spurs and whip, and thought with satisfaction of the warlord's man going down under her foot. The next moment she made a sign of warding, because of the nightmares. She had forced herself to shake them off as soon as she woke. She wondered if she'd have the nightmares as long as she kept the horse, the spoils of her murder, but even if that were true, the roan was worth it.

She had laughed at the other girls when they breathlessly waited for one of the lads to glance their way, or dreamed over him through their chores, planning what to say when they next met. But she was just as bad with riding. That night, in between the nightmares, she dreamed about riding, about the surge as the horse set off, the muscles sliding beneath her. All the next morning she daydreamed about the wind in her hair, forgot to water the beans because she was planning their next excursion, and was abstracted when her parents spoke to her. They lifted eyebrows at each other and nodded wisely when she blushed. She thought they were relieved to have her acting like an ordinary girl for once, but couldn't tell them the truth. If the warlord's men ever found out what had happened, everyone who knew the truth would be killed.

She distracted them with talk about the move to Carlion, pretending enthusiasm so well that they actually started planning the move. Her father went out, then and there, to book the carrier's cart, and they even started packing. The house was dismantled slowly around them and every blanket and piece of cloth was commandeered to wrap around breakables.

"We'll have to leave the loom until last," her mother said,

and started to make lists of all the things they would have to do before they left.

Bramble took the chance to escape and went to the roan. His breath snuffled in her face in greeting as he came to meet her at the end of his tether. She watered him and then rode him again, despite the pain in her thighs. She guided him with touches on the neck or a tug on his mane, but didn't take him far for fear the warlord's men would recognize him. So she rode as much as she dared around the confines of the deep forest. They rode that day as far as the chasm.

Wooding was in a valley around a small river that fed the much larger Fallen River, which flowed all the way to Carlion and the sea. Just outside Wooding, the Fallen curved around and dropped suddenly into a deep chasm, an abyss so far down it took a day to climb down and another to climb back up. There was one wooden bridge slung precariously across the drop, on the main road that a little farther on led through the village. The bridge was one of the reasons Wooding was more prosperous than most villages: there was no other way to get to Carlion. Unlike the bridge site, here in the forest the chasm was much narrower and the rock on both edges was soft and crumbling.

Bramble didn't take the roan too close to the edge, but they stood there for a while in the mist and moisture that rose from the wild turbulence of the river below, where the water leaped and spouted over huge boulders which had fallen from the cliffs. The noise of the falls, just out of sight around the bend upstream, shook the ground and made the roan uneasy. Bramble slid down from his back to soothe him.

"Nothing to frighten you here, sweetheart," she said.

She loved this place. She loved the sudden drop that seemed to entice her to fly out and fall, loved the raging of the river below, the clouds of foam that boiled over the edge of the falls and along the rocks. In the clouds and mists of the chasm, there were swarms of swifts that lived their whole lives on the wing, landing only to build nests and lay their eggs in the crevices of the cliff face. Peering over, it was as if the birds were emerging from the water, their curves and turns in the air like the splashes of white foam. Stunted trees clung to the ledges and crevices and there were ferns in every tiny niche: the cliff wall was itself a waterfall of green and golden stone.

Unexpected and dangerous and beautiful, the chasm was the wildest thing she knew, and she had come here all her life when she felt too enclosed in the village. The roan quieted under her hands and voice, and even put his head forward to inspect the chasm with interest.

Bramble took him back to the cave and groomed him thoroughly, reluctant to leave him. She finally tethered him for the night and ran home.

After dinner, the third evening after she'd killed the man, she leaned on the gate next to her granda and looked down the road that led out of the village.

"Don't you miss it?" she asked him, meaning what Travelers called the Road, the wandering life. She meant all the things she yearned for but couldn't describe.

"Why would I, with all that I love right here?" Granda replied.

It was the same answer to that question that she'd heard all her life. She'd been ten or eleven before she realized that he never answered her straight, but always with another question. And was thirteen, maybe, before she could read the look in his eyes when he stood at that gate and looked down the road to the horizon.

Tonight she wasn't minded to accept his answer.

"If you had things to do over again," she said, "would you have settled?"

He turned to look at her. Though his pate was bald, he still had a rim of dark hair around his scalp. He still walked strongly upright. Bramble could see the man he had been at eighteen, when he'd broken his hip and couldn't walk for a season. His parents, who were drystone fencers, had paid for Bramble's great-granny to board him until he could travel to meet them. But long before that, he and Bramble's gran had snuck off to the haystack and made her da, so he ended up staying and learning to be a carpenter from her great-granda.

He searched her eyes. "You're thinking of taking the Road," he said with certainty.

"Been thinking of that all my life," she said cheerfully, surprised by how well she could hide it. "No change there."

He looked relieved. "It's a hard life for a young girl, all alone. Travelers aren't liked anywhere. Well, you know that."

"I know it, but I've never understood why."

"Some Travelers say the sight of us reminds them that they don't really belong here, that what they have they stole. And that makes them angry. But I reckon it's just that everyone likes to have someone to look down on. When the warlord rides roughshod over you, it's good to be able to curse or hit or kick someone else, someone weaker. Makes you feel strong."

"And the strong hate the weak," Bramble said.

Her grandfather looked sideways at her, his brows lifted.

"That may be. No matter what the way of it, Traveling alone is dangerous. No warlord will give justice to a Traveler. Theft, beatings, even murder, it seems it doesn't count if it's a Traveler who's hurt. That's the worst of it. Even at the best, we're treated like foreigners. Like we don't belong anywhere. That can be hard, to be told you don't belong in your own land. Especially if you love it." His voice grew reminiscent. "You can't help but love it. From the cold north to the southern deserts, it's all beautiful. Travelers love the whole of it, not just the part they were born in."

"You do miss it."

"Sometimes." He paused. "But in the end, it's the people you love that matter. Traveling—it doesn't keep your heart warm. Remember that, sweetheart. It may make your heart beat faster, but it doesn't keep it warm. So, yes, I reckon I would settle, if I had to do it over again. Your gran was worth it, and I pray the gods give her rest until I join her, so we can be reborn together."

It wasn't, in a way, what she had wanted to hear, but it was reassuring nonetheless.

In the morning, Bramble washed and dressed carefully. She fed the goats and the chickens, carried water from the stream to the kitchen, swept out the cottage, laid her room straight and tidy, even weeded the front herb bed. At last it was time to go.

She walked down to the stream and turned east to follow it to the linden tree where his ghost would rise. Udall, the old thatcher, was gathering reeds in the stream and he nodded politely to her, though he didn't speak. He only spoke when he needed to: a silent, gray man, who lived alone and liked it. No need to worry about him gossiping with the neighbors about where she was off to at lunchtime. He looked at her with no curiosity at all, just recognition, and she wondered what he could see in her face.

It wasn't merriment, that was for sure and certain. She had a job to do, and the least she could do was show some respect. Just before noon, it would be three full days since she had kicked the warlord's man. Killed the warlord's man. And as his killer, it was up to her to lay his ghost when it quickened.

UDALL'S STORY

IT BEGAN on Sylvie's roof. My hands were cold. I blew on them to warm them, then gripped the ladder with my right hand, hoisted the third yelm of reeds onto my left shoulder and began to climb. My back was aching, low down, as it did those autumn mornings.

"Past my prime," I said to the reeds, and the reeds whispered back, as they always did.

Balanced carefully, I walked along the ridge pole of the roof to the southern end of the gable, the high end where the ladder didn't reach, and laid down the bundles of reed. My lashing awl was in my pocket. I sat astride the ridge pole and began to place the yelms so the reed lay snug and watertight, yelm over yelm. Then I lashed them with the crisscross herringbone pattern of the thatchers of Laagway.

"Getting too old for this," I said to the reeds. "They'll be cutting you and drying you and lashing you, too, for a long time yet, but I'm not sure I'll be doing it."

"Do they talk back?" A voice came from below me.

The stonecaster was standing in the room under me, looking up. She grinned. "It's an odd thing, to have your home open to the sky. I think I like it," she said.

"You always were an odd magpie, Sylvie. You wouldn't like it open when the winter rains set in."

"That's why I'm paying you, old man."

She stepped up onto a chest by the wall and stuck her head

through the empty rafters to face me. "If you're feeling old, Udall," she said, "you should take an apprentice."

"Pot calling the kettle black."

"Ahah! But I'm taking a youngling on, soon."

This was news. Sylvie had refused to take an apprentice for all the time I had known her. "Who is it?" I asked.

She shrugged. "I don't know. Someone's due to turn up any day now. That's why I thought I'd get the thatch done. So it'll be over and done with by the time he comes."

"So... it's a he. What else do the stones say?"

"You don't want to know." Sylvie shook her gray hair over her eyes and peered up at me, like a storyteller pretending to be a stonecaster, and spoke in a long, wavering voice. "Oh, good sir, you don't want to know the future! It's too terrible."

I smiled. It was a very good impersonation of Piselea, a storyteller who'd drunk his way through the inn's beer all summer. "Tell me anyway."

"They say it's time you got married," she said briskly, shaking back her hair. "I did a casting for you this morning. I had a feeling in my bones."

"Married. Me—married." I smiled wider. "Very funny."

But she was serious.

"The stones say it, and they mean it, my friend. Married before Midwinter's Eve."

Well, it was a shock. I'd lived alone for four years, since Niwe, my sister, had died. Married. Who? There was no one in the village, and though I traveled for my work throughout the district, still, I'd not met anyone who'd taken my fancy for... well, not since Merris married Foegen the butcher, over at Connay. And that was six years since. No, seven.

Married. Who?

I lashed and hooked the reed all day, and if Sylvie had a

watertight roof come winter, it was because my hands knew their job better than I did, at times, and I could tie my herring-bone lashing blind drunk and three parts asleep, if I had to. For certain, my mind was elsewhere.

All day on the ladder I went over the roll of women I knew, talking each one over with the reed and dismissing each. For Mathe was as ill-tempered as a vixen, and Sel was too young, and Aedwina much too old, besides having that young bull of a son living with her. I puzzled over it mightily, I can tell you, and as the short autumn dusk closed in, I climbed down the ladder and knocked at Sylvie's door to ask for a casting. She sat me down on the rug.

"Who is it?" I asked, and spat in my palm.

She spat in hers and joined hands with me. As our hands locked I looked at Sylvie with new eyes, feeling the strength in her grip and the softness of her palm. Not her, surely?

She drew the five stones from her bag and cast them out. They were all faceup, plain as day.

"The Familiar," she said, and raised her eyebrows. "Woman. Well, no surprise there. Child. Love. Death." She brooded over them, touching them lightly. "So. A woman you know, with one or more children, someone you love or will love, brought to you by death. Accidental death, I think." Her eyes grew compassionate. "It may not be who you think, Udall."

"No?" I broke the handhold, and sat back on my heels. "Someone I love, or will love, with a child. It has to be Merris. Who else? So Foegen dies?"

"It may be. It may be not so. Don't try to look further than the stones show you. Don't try to change your future."

"Are you saying the future's fixed? That I don't have any say in what happens to me at all?"

"Udall, I sit on this rug and cast the future. And I see folk try to avert what's to happen to them. I see them frantic, trying to change what's been foretold. And every time, the very thing they do to try to change things is what brings their fate to them. This is the way of it. Act selfishly, to change your fate, and it brings that fate rushing to your door."

So I got up and walked out. I packed up the thatch and left all tidy, and next morning I was back to finish the job, though I'd had little sleep the night before. The lashing straw went over and under, around and between, and so did my thoughts. If I went to warn Foegen, would I merely arrive in time to comfort Merris in her grief, to have her turn to me at last? Or worse, would me being there actually cause the accident to happen? Would I have to bear the guilt of Foegen's death and Merris's love the rest of my life?

I had a job starting two days later in Pank, thatching a mill house. It was three months to midwinter. I could think about it later.

I spent the next day bundling reed into yelms and tying them firmly, ready for the mill. Each knot I tied made me think of Merris, whom I had taken for apprentice ten years before. I had taught her to tie each of these knots, her brown fingers fumbling at first and then surer, her soft hazel eyes intent on the reed so I could watch her unawares.

My sister had liked her, too. Niwe was always telling me to make a move, to say something to Merris. "Court the girl properly," she'd said, and every time she said it something curled up tighter inside me, for the truth was that Merris was a girl, and I was too old for her. Too old, too set in my ways, too boring. I went to Sylvie for advice, and she had refused to cast for me.

"You know perfectly well what you should do, Udall," she had scolded. "You're just afraid."

So I had been, and very afraid, too. I'd been afraid to shatter the growing pleasure of working with Merris, the rhythmic, side-by-side movements of bundling, laying, lashing, hooking, netting. Afraid of seeing pity or disgust in her eyes.

That hadn't changed.

But—I thought secretly, and did not even say it to the reeds—she'd be a woman with two children to keep. She might be glad of a husband with a good craft, someone who would love her and be good to her and the children.

I stopped bundling in disgust at myself. To think that I'd take advantage of a woman's grief, just to have her sitting at my table. Lying in my bed. I twisted the lashing straw so hard it cut my hand, but the thought remained, all the long night, and left me sleepless again.

I set out for Connay at daybreak. If Merris was going to be a widow and in need of comfort, it wouldn't be because I hadn't tried to warn Foegen.

The road to Connay ran along the side of a brown stream, bordered with rushes and reeds, so that their familiar whispering soothed me as I walked. I even whistled through the brisk autumn morning, and lopped the heads off milk thistles with my ash stick as I went.

It was dinnertime when I came into Connay, and the street was quiet. Foegen and Merris lived at the other edge of town, where the steers could be pastured until killing time, away from the shop in the main street and its charnel stink.

"I'll just stop in the shop and have a quick word with Foegen," I told the reeds growing by the stream. "Then I'll turn back again. I don't think I'll see Merris this visit." I stopped whistling at the thought of Merris's smile.

The shop was closed. So I walked reluctantly to the house, past ten or more houses thatched with my own pattern of herringbone and Merris's special under-and-over netting, and knocked on the door.

It was Merris's oldest, Beals, who opened the door, but the others crowded around fast enough: Merris, her face alight, Broc, the toddler, grabbing my boot and trying to eat the ash stick, and Foegen, saying, "Udall, welcome, well come! We're just sitting to dinner, come and eat!"

I didn't want to worry Merris, so I said nothing, just sat at the table with Broc in my lap and ate as little as I could without it causing comment. My gut was clenched tight and I felt a kind of terror at what I was about to do. But in the babble of talk and questions from Beals—"Uncle, why is it always an ash stick? Why not some other wood? Uncle, how far is it to Pank? Why is it called Pank? What does Connay mean?"—my silence went unnoticed.

After dinner I grabbed the chance when Foegen said, "Come and I'll show you the new draft of steers arrived yesterday. I've got them settling in the barn until I can get that stream fence mended. I wanted to take a look at them anyway."

We went out alone, Merris calling Beals back softly, "Come help your mam."

The animal barn, behind the vegetable garden, was a lofty wooden building with, of all things, a slate roof. It had been built by the last butcher, whose brother was a roof tiler. On the lookout for accidents, I foresaw a slate sliding off that roof and crushing Foegen's head. Or one of the steers goring him, or...I decided I would warn him as soon as we got inside.

Foegen stumbled. I put out my hand without thought, steadying him upright.

"Swith the strong!" Foegen said, his voice shaking. "Look what you saved me from."

On the path in front of him, half hidden by the seed-heavy autumn grass, a scythe lay, blade up and glinting.

"If I'd fallen I'd have cut my throat open on that. I was working here yesterday when the steers arrived. I meant to come back for it but..." Foegen was shaking, knowing too well what blade did to flesh. "Gods, if you hadn't been here, Udall..."

We went back to the house, steers forgotten, and Merris made much of us both, but more of Foegen.

She kissed my cheek goodbye as I left, and thanked me. On the way home, I told the reeds, "Ah, it wouldn't have worked, anyway. I'm too old for her." But when the reeds whispered back, they didn't sound convinced.

At the next casting, there was no sign of the Marriage stone. I tried to be glad, for Merris's sake. And Foegen's, too. He made her happy, after all.

"Try to avoid your fate and it rushes to you," Sylvie said to me. "Selfishness draws disaster, they say. Me, I've never known a case where a man tried to avert another's fate, for no better reason than love. But then, love breaks all fates."

ASH

THERE WAS BLOOD on the wall. Ash could smell it. Steam rose from the body at his feet. He thought briefly of warming his hands at the open wound, but realized that the thought was the thin edge of hysteria, part of the shocked giggles he could feel working their way up his throat. He didn't have time for hysteria.

Ash wiped his dagger on the corpse's sleeve, and ran. He ran like a fit, sober young man, not the drunken sot he'd pretended to be as he had entered the alley, reeling from wall to wall, and talking to himself loudly about how it was definitely time to go home now that he'd won so much at three-card draw. He'd made himself bait and the bait had been taken. The girl had come at him with a cosh and a hidden knife, and she'd intended to kill him right from the start. She'd been skilled, too. He barely escaped the knife after he'd hit the cosh from her hand.

As he ran, he listened. His footsteps pounded like the muffled drums at a funeral, but they were the only footfalls. The others who had been following him had gone. They had thought he was an easy mark and when he proved differently they had melted away.

He ran out of the dark alleys and into a street he knew was respectable, safe, rich, because the householders had paid to have torches set at each street corner. Around the fifth corner he found himself back in Acton Square, with late-night strollers coming in bunches toward him, from behind him, and a slew of restaurant tables in front of him. He pretended to cough and turned aside, then slid his dagger back into his belt unobtrusively. He wasn't even breathing hard, and that seemed impossible. He felt as though he should be panting, sweating—showing *something.*

When Ash had first come to Turvite, Acton Square had astounded him. A large cobbled space between two-storied brick houses, it was always full of people. During the day, it was the market square, and the ground was covered by stalls and barrows and blankets spread with wares from every corner of the world. And unlike every other market he had ever seen, it didn't smell, because the fish market was down by the docks, where the fishing fleet came in. In the evening, when the market was packed away, the eating houses and restaurants that surrounded the square put out chairs and trestle tables—some even with tablecloths!—and the rich of Turvite came to eat and stroll and be seen.

On this fine early summer night the square was full of people dining on freshly caught fish and salted beef, eels in aspic, grilled squab and fried finches wrapped in spinach leaves, with the waiters sliding like snakes between the tables. The smell of food turned Ash's stomach.

Doronit had followed Ash unnoticed all the way through the "exercise." She watched him for a moment before she made herself known. He was flushed and a little walleyed, like a spooked horse, as she had expected, but he was not out of control. His dark hair was even darker with sweat, but it was a warm night so no one would think anything amiss. She saw him take a deep breath and turn pale with the smell of food. It was time to bring him back to earth. She slid around the alley corner and approached him from behind so that she would seem to have come from nowhere.

"Good," she said softly. "Almost perfect, sweetheart."

He had done better than she had hoped. It was always hard to predict how the softhearted ones would react afterward, even when she had trained them twice as hard as this one. His hand started a fine tremor, which was always the first sign of panic. Time to take control. There was nothing like sex to distract a young man from moral scruples.

She smiled at him and patted his cheek lingeringly. "You should have slowed a little before the square and put your dagger away. But that's a small fault."

Ash stared at her. She was dressed like a well-to-do city woman, with wide navy trousers tucked into soft yellow boots, dark brown hair neatly braided, and a shawl pinned at the shoulder by a brooch set with sapphires. To match her eyes, he thought. Even dressed demurely, she was so beautiful that men stared as they went by, and women glanced sideways with a mixture of envy and rueful acceptance. Doronit was all curves, smoothly rounded; there wasn't a hard line anywhere on her, from crown to toe. The girl in the alley had been curved, too, although skinny. He felt himself begin to shake.

Doronit tucked her hand into his elbow. "A nice hot cha, that's what you need. Come."

Ash tried not to react to the touch. Doronit thought his shakes were a reaction to the killing, and maybe they were, but he had never wanted her so badly. He couldn't believe that he could feel so aroused, so alive, just after killing someone. Did that mean he was mind-sick—a killer at heart, who enjoyed it? He took his cloak off as though he were hot, and held it in front of him. Doronit smiled as though she knew why, and he flushed more. She always made him feel like an unschooled virgin, which he hadn't been since he was fourteen. With Doronit any confidence he had disappeared and he was left, like now, holding his cloak in front of him and feeling like a fool. He clung to that feeling as a bulwark against the memory of the girl sliding down the wall, against the smell of her blood still in his nostrils.

They went to an eating house at the side of the square, sat on the bench in the farthest corner ("Never expose your back" had been one of his first lessons) and Doronit ordered cha and honey cakes. There was a piper outside the eating house playing "The Long Way Home." Badly. It grated on his nerves, but the words rolled out inside his head, automatically. *It's a long, long way, and I'll be dead before I get there...*

Ash forced the words from his mind and sat still, as Doronit had taught him, drew his breath down, down farther, let it out slowly, allowing the shakes go with it until he was calm again.

"Well done," she said. "You are ready to talk it over now?"

Her voice, as always, was soft, with a slight lisp, that faint hint of accent.

He shivered and nodded, losing some of his calm. "I killed her."

"Yes," Doronit mused. "A shame you had to use two strikes. That one to the shoulder left blood on the wall where she fell back against it. In this situation it doesn't matter, but if you wished to dispose of the body without anyone knowing whether death had occurred, you would have found that awkward."

Her words were a cold wind and steadied him faster than anything else could.

She sipped her cha and stroked his hand. "But I'm sure you won't do it again."

Silently, he shook his head. He hadn't expected this—that she would analyze this exercise as she had every other lesson she had taught him. Surely killing was different from weapons practice or scribing?

"Good." She held his hand lightly for a moment. He could feel the softness of her skin.

Trying to seem oblivious to her, he looked around at the activity in the square.

It was as busy as it always was in midevening. The swirl and chatter of people made no impression on Ash—but he was sharply aware of the safeguarders standing at the open doors of moneylenders, singlestaves in one hand and the other not far from their daggers. Ash looked at them with envy. Soon he'd be fully trained and one of them. Then he wondered if *they* had had to kill someone as part of their training. From where he stood he could see a good twenty safeguarders outside private offices and the Moot Hall. That was a lot of dead people.

Doronit tapped his arm to regain his attention. "Tonight you acted in self-defense. So. Killing is easy that way. Perhaps the time will come when you will have to kill someone who is not trying to kill you. What will you do then?"

He sipped his cha, playing for time. "If they were trying to kill—hurt someone else...I'd protect them..."

She smiled, for once, truly pleased. "Well, and that is what a safeguarder does, after all," she said reassuringly. "They protect."

The first step was killing to protect oneself. The second would be killing to protect someone else, an innocent. The third, to protect someone who'd paid for protection precisely because they weren't innocent. In a year he'd be slitting the throat of anyone she told him to, and sleeping twice as well as normal afterward.

She woke him before dawn, when he was in the middle of a dream about her. He blushed, thinking she might have realized (what had he said or done while she was watching?). But she merely nodded to the door.

"Sometimes," Doronit said, "you will have to go without sleep for days. This is a talent that can be developed. So. Run."

Ash ran. He would have done anything for her. He knew how much he owed her. He had known from the first day, when his parents had brought him to Doronit, not really believing that she would take him on as an apprentice, not when the baker and the butcher and even the slaughterhouse had refused, because he was a Traveler and therefore not to be trusted. Why would a safeguarder house take on someone who was traitorous by blood, he had wondered, when its very business was being trustworthy?

But they had tried Doronit because she had the dark hair of the old blood, and, Ash realized now, because his parents had probably known that she placed little importance on the opinions of others, being so sure of her own. He found that surety comforting, particularly because she seemed certain he could be valuable to her. Once he was trained. At the moment, he knew that all he was doing was eating her food and using up her time with no return for her. And at nineteen, he was old for an apprentice, although Doronit had said that she had no use for the usual fourteen- and fifteen-year-olds.

"Not strong enough," she had said, moving her hand admiringly down his arm. "Not mature enough to deal with the work we do."

So he ran through the thickening heat of the morning, trying as hard as he could. The skills he did have amounted to nothing off the Road: being a mediocre drummer and knowing hundreds of songs by heart (but not being able to sing them) weren't much use to anyone. If Doronit was prepared to take him on with nothing, no skills, no silver, no family with business contacts, he would burst his heart trying to please her.

Mountain girls are mighty kind
And river girls are pretty

Round the yard first, then down to the docks. His feet hit the hard stones of the street and slipped on the morning dew.

But Turvite girls are kinder still
To a smart boy from the city...

As always, he ran to the rhythm of "Turvite Girls," a rousing drinking song. The song, he had discovered, was most popular with the Turvite women themselves. Singing it in his head kept his feet moving fast enough to make him sweat, but not so fast he became breathless.

He turned the corner onto the drumming wooden planks of the docks. The fishing boats weren't home yet. The merchanters raised their single masts brown against the gray clouds, and the shrouds rattled down from the mastheads like dice in a cup, tantalizingly just out of rhythm. Behind him the hills stretched up, blocking out half the sky.

Turvite rose from its harbor in tier upon tier of houses, ascending in a semicircle of hills between two sheer cliff headlands. Down here near the harbor—immersed in the smells of old fish heads, rotten mud and bilges—the houses were wooden or wattled, with the occasional brown-brick inn.

Ash looked up and back, toward Doronit's house, wondering what she was doing, who she was seeing. Her house was amid the whitewashed brick buildings, halfway up the hills, with balconies out over the street. Farther up, on the highest tiers, the houses were golden stone mansions set in gardens full of small shrubs.

He stopped for a moment at the lowest part of the harbor to get his breath before he began the long climb. This was the best part of the day in Turvite, the only quiet time. The gulls were off chasing the fishing boats and the only sound was the wind moaning through the rigging.

For Carlion girls like salted flesh
And Pisay girls like bulls
But the Turvite girls love a city boy
Who'll fill their cup to full.
Bodgers and todgers and sailors all know
Yes, the fellows all agree
There's no finer girls in the wide, wide world
It's a Turvite girl for me.

He remembered asking his mother why everyone laughed at the chorus — he must have been five, or six. She'd said that the words were just clever, and that was why people laughed. He was twelve or so before he found out what the "sailors knew." He'd known there was another meaning, even at five, and he'd tucked it away in his mind, determined to find out the truth. He'd felt great satisfaction when he'd finally understood. Doronit said that only the truly determined survived, but he didn't know the difference between "determined" and "truly determined." He guessed he'd find out.

The first time he came to Turvite he had been a child. They had gone to the harbor to find lodgings, of course; it was in the old part of the city where Travelers, if not welcome, were tolerated. Coming down the hill on the main road that cuts the town in two, moving from the rich to the poorer quarters, Ash had been overwhelmed by the noise and bustle: pedlars shouting their wares, spruikers calling for shops and breweries, delivery wagons and handcarts trundling over the cobbles and, above him, the neighbors gossiping over their washing, strung between the balconies that almost met over the street. And down by the harbor, there had been more to marvel at: shouts and whistles from the stevedores, the slap of the tide against the wooden docks, and above everything, like a clean descant to a muddy melody, the calls of the gulls. His ears had rung for days after they arrived.

That first day, down at the harbor and almost onto the wharves, his father had turned him around to show him the city they had just walked through. It rose in layers of brown and white and gold.

"There's no green," Ash had said, feeling stupid. How could there be no green? The whole world was green, except in the snow country.

His mother sniffed. "Turviters think trees suck up the goodness from the air."

"It looks like a layer cake," Ash said, awestruck, and was thinking, Sweet. Rich. Delicious.

"Like old stale cake," his mother said. "And full of maggots and weevils."

A group of women in bright shawls and dresses without trousers underneath had walked past, laughing loudly.

"A few butterflies and ladybirds around, too," his father said drily.

"Where you get sailors you get butterflies," his mother retorted, then her face softened and they both laughed.

For years afterward Ash had looked for butterflies near any harbor they went to, but he had discovered they were few and far between.

Ash put the memory away from him and kept running. He rounded the Customshouse near the docks and began to climb the hill, past the swaying ghost of the drunk bosun's mate loitering on the steps where he'd broken his neck, and past darkened taverns and brothels where only a single torch hung outside. The whores were asleep. Even the Sailor's Rest, which never closed, had its door shut against the early morning chill.

He wanted to slacken off, to slow down as he breasted the hill, but he forced himself on, muttering the chorus once again. His feet slapped the cobbles a little faster. There was a drunk asleep in front of the Watering Hole. Probably asleep. Perhaps dead.

The girl's face leaped to his mind: young, she had been, fourteen maybe, with pale hair and quick hands. She'd have had him, if he'd been the sozzled young merchant she'd taken him for. She'd have slit him from balls to throat and smiled while she was doing it.

But after she died—*after he'd killed her*—her face had been washed clean of all the greed and hatred. She had lain like a child fallen asleep, waiting for her parents to come home.

Ash threw up in the road. Bile burned his throat. He stayed for a moment, bent over with his hands on his knees, panting. He forced down the memories of the girl, of the smell of her blood, the heat of her body against his hand as he slammed her against the wall, the soft sigh as her last breath escaped her. He pushed them all back down and his gorge with them. Then he straightened up and began to run again. Doronit was waiting.

His memory flashed back three months to the first time he had seen her. It was early in the morning. The day before had been very long, very dispiriting. No matter where they went, no one had been interested in employing a Traveler boy with no skills and no references. Most tradesmen and merchants had refused to even see him, and those who had were scathing. "Wouldn't sleep safe in my bed with one of you lot in the house!" said the butcher, who had been their last hope. Ash hadn't been sure whether to be disappointed or relieved. He had dreaded the charnel house and the dismembering, the constant stench of blood. But at least, he had thought, butchers ate well.

They had gone back to their lodgings and sat slumped at the table. Even his mother had been diminished by a full day of hatred and distrust.

"Perhaps we could find a Traveler to take you on. A tinker or farrier, or someone like that," his father had said.

"No," his mother said. "There's one more person left to try. Tomorrow."

"Who?" Ash asked.

"Her name is Doronit. She's settled. She hires out safeguarders."

"Swallow!" his father protested.

"I know it can be dangerous. But it's a trade that will never go short of work. And it is . . . respectable."

His father fell silent, passing his hand over his head in tiredness or uncertainty.

"I don't mind," Ash said. "There've been times I would have liked to know how to fight."

His mother nodded. "That's true. There's always times for a Traveler when it would be good to know how to fight."

His father stared at him. "If you fight, they kill you."

"Worse things than death," his mother replied.

His father smiled at that, the wide, wondering smile he kept for her. "They should have named you Hawk instead of Swallow," he said, and kissed her.

The next morning, early, they'd gone to Doronit's house, halfway up the thoroughfare leading to the most exclusive street in the city, a brick building painted pale yellow to mimic the golden stones of the rich. They had been impressed. But Ash knew now that she hungered to live at the very top, in one of the solid stone mansions.

She'd come to the door to answer their knock herself, dressed as most women in the city dressed: wide trousers tucked into boots, with a soft three-quarter skirt over the top, a wool shawl around her shoulders over a simple shirt. Her clothes had combined different hues of the same green. It was a modest, sensible, reassuring outfit. It should have made him feel that he was applying to work in a respectable, comforting, solid enterprise.

But he had been nineteen so he'd looked straight through the clothes to the body beneath, which was curved and full and promising; he'd looked at the face, with red mouth, even teeth, long, dark lashes and something about the sapphire eyes that was neither respectable nor comforting. Their eyes met and he saw hers widen, but he'd been overtaken by breathlessness and he still wasn't sure if it had been simple desire or something else, something like the pressure he felt when he knelt at the gods' altars. He had coughed with embarrassment and turned aside a little, shuffling his feet, and he'd seen out of the corner of his eye that she was smiling at him in amusement. That he had made a fool of himself. He'd flushed. Had thought that she'd never take him on. He'd suddenly burned to work for her, to prove himself to her, to wipe out this first impression of gaucheness and adolescent stupidity. He had been following his parents around for days trying to find a job because he needed to eat; because he had to leave them; because there was no place for him on the Road. He hadn't cared where he ended up if he couldn't make music. But he'd desperately wanted a place with Doronit.

His father had explained that they'd been looking to apprentice Ash. Ash had again been aware of her assessing stare and then a smile. But this time the smile had been fixed with pleasure, not amusement.

"Come in," Doronit had said, her voice as beguiling as a tenor flute. "I would be happy to take this young man."

From that moment he had dedicated himself to pleasing her.

Doronit owned a complicated business, the simplest part of which was the hire of safeguarders to other merchants. From protecting people who had been threatened, to guarding valuable shipments going from one town to another, to just standing around menacingly when large sums of money were being exchanged, safeguarders were as central to the merchants' business as their own staff. But unlike their own staff, merchants didn't need them every day, yet didn't like hiring them off the streets or out of the taverns. So Doronit had seen an opportunity, a service that supplied safeguarders only when they were needed. She had a core staff of six and could call on another twenty or so at need. Of them all, only Ash was boarded in her house. That was part of the articles of apprenticeship, of course, and nothing to be proud of, but it still gave him a small satisfaction every time the others went home and he turned indoors with her.

By the time Ash reached the yard again, panting and sweating, the other six had arrived. Aylmer was sandy-haired and blue-eyed with broad shoulders and slightly long arms. He had taught Ash to stand absolutely still: he was the stillest person Ash had ever met. He was quick when he needed to move, but when he came to a stop—he just stopped. There was Hildie, tiny and fast, who was teaching him to spot pickpockets—mostly by teaching him how to pick pockets himself. Elfrida, who usually posed as a waitress, with long blond braids and rosy cheeks, had once knocked him backward clear through a window with one swipe of her singlestick.

And then there were the three others: large, alike, fair-haired, and with faces scarred and scowling. Their last job had been as night-soil carters and they were known, collectively, as the Dung Brothers. Ash could never tell them apart and no one ever used their real names. They didn't seem to mind and, since they preferred to work together, an order to one was an order to all three. They were slower than the others at singlestave, but were so strong that one blow was all they needed to knock an opponent unconscious.

They practiced singlestave all morning, until Ash's head was swimming with hunger and fatigue and the Dung Brothers hit him across the room once each, three in a row. They grinned, identical grins, and turned their backs on him dismissively. He was too tired even to feel angry. Then Doronit let him eat.

She led the way to the front room. Her room. The pale cream walls, unlike the bright colors most Turviters painted their houses, were just a backdrop for the other colors in the room. Margolin rugs on the floor, traded across the desert and then over the mountains, sang indigo and russet in the cool darkness. Blue silk curtains embroidered with dark green butterflies dressed the window. A line of matching glasses sat on the high shelf to the left—clear glass, worth a warlord's ransom—with a bronze lamp kept alight underneath them to call up their multicolored fire.

The table, with a centerpiece of indigo linen, had been laid for a formal dinner: two knives, two spoons, a long spoonlike thing with a narrow cup on the end, like a tiny ladle. There were glazed ceramic plates instead of wooden trenchers and a piece of sea sponge floating in a pottery bowl.

"So. We begin the next phase," Doronit said. "In order to be most useful, you will need to blend in with your customers. Sit down." She picked up the tiny ladle. "This is for eating marrow bone."

A month later, Ash carefully wiped his fingers and mouth with a sponge, and dropped it back into the bowl.

The town clerk was about to speak. Ash angled on his bench so that he could see down the room, as well as to the center table. He gave half an ear to the speech, and all of his sight to scanning the room for trouble. It was the main chamber of the Moot Hall, with a gilded ceiling and huge wrought-iron candle-rings on the walls. The tables were set with Caranese pottery and glass goblets. He'd seen rooms like these many times before, when his parents performed at feasts, but he'd never imagined himself being a guest in one of them. Well, perhaps not a guest. He was here to work. But he sat at the same table as the guests, and ate the same food; the serving staff spoke to him with the same respect. He felt warmth spread in his chest. His parents, for all their skill, had never sat at a waxed wood table and been offered food and drink by servants in livery. And thanks to Doronit, his table manners were as good as any merchant's.

He brought his attention back to the present with a frown for his woolgathering, although he didn't expect any trouble. The Annual Gifting Dinners were hardly dangerous. Everyone already knew what they were getting from the city profits for the year. The infighting was over. The grudges were being nursed. But there wasn't likely to be any...

At the back of the room a door curtain waved in a draft. The councillor's ghost standing beside it turned her head to look through the gap. Ash stood up and made his way quietly toward the door. That door led deeper into the Moot Hall, not out. There should be no draft. The Dung Brothers, on the other side of the room, watched him impassively.

He flicked the curtain aside, his hand on his dagger. Doronit was behind it, smiling.

"Good," she said. "Very good."

She patted his cheek, then looked through the doorway to where the merchants sat. Doronit was dressed in blond lace and dark rose silk, cut low across her breasts. Her dark hair with its touch of red was dressed high with sapphire pins. More beautiful than any woman there. More desirable. But not exactly an honored guest; only the most important merchant families were given grants at the Gifting Dinners. She was there to work, like him. He could read in the tension in her arms and the set of her cheek her desire to be in the select company at the high table.

"You deserve to be at the high table more than any of them," he said. "Whatever I can do... You should have everything. You know I want to help... I could... I mean..."

What did he mean? That he was a prattling fool was what he meant. She would despise him, turn away from him. But although she had stiffened, displeased by his perceptiveness when he first spoke, by the end of the muddled speech she was smiling.

"I know I can trust you. It is good to know I have someone who cares for my interests," she said warmly. But she gave him a little push, like one you would give a child. "Go back to your place, sweetheart."

He went, the feeling of Doronit's hand on his back, on his cheek, still warm, not knowing if she laughed at him or valued him, turning her words from this way to that in his mind. But because he wanted her to value him more than he wanted anything else, on the way back to his seat, he watched for signs of trouble. The councillor's ghost watched Doronit out of the corner of her eye.

Ash knew Doronit was training others. She disappeared, sometimes for days. She had other houses in the city, other businesses apart from hiring out safeguarders. He didn't even know how many. It disturbed him, if he let himself think about it.

Were her other employees better than he was? Quicker, smarter? Better at killing? He needed to be indispensable to her.

And when she was gone, maybe she was meeting a lover... someone more her own age, more sophisticated, more intelligent, more charming... She was twice his age, he knew; he couldn't think of any reason why she would be interested in him. Yet she had taken him to live in her house; she was kind to him, buying him clothes, teaching him herself rather than leaving it to one of the others. She touched him... He remembered every touch, every glance, every smile. Surely she wouldn't act like that if she didn't like him? If he worked hard, learned quickly, became polished and strong, maybe then...?

At the town clerk's dinners and the Merchant House settling days, when merchants and creditors came together in the house's settling room, to pay their debts and strike new bargains, he kept a lookout for others she favored. But he couldn't, even using her training on how to read people's eyes and faces, find anyone she smiled at with more warmth than him. She employed many other safeguarders, but no young ones, like him. No one who lived in her house, ate at her table. He let that comfort him. And finally her lessons turned to areas where he was not entirely ignorant.

Doronit had timed it carefully. She needed, she thought, to bring him closer to her before Midwinter's Eve, so she called him into

her office one morning in early autumn. The office was a plain
room at the front of the house where she organized contracts with
her customers. No glass or silk curtains here, she thought with
satisfaction. The workmanlike wood and leather and painted
shutters were a kind of disguise to reassure the merchants, who
were about to entrust their treasures to her staff, that she was
efficient, businesslike, although in an unusual trade for a woman.
Her office looked organized, which she was, and simple, which
she was not. There was a big slate on the desk, with chalk laid
ready.

She gestured him to it. "Geography. I suppose you know the
main trade routes, but can you draw a map?"

He grabbed the chalk and began to draw confidently, marking the outlines of the Domains, all eleven of them, and then the
main rivers and towns, barely hesitating, whispering under his
breath as he marked each one.

"What's that?" Doronit asked.

"It's a teaching song from Foreverfroze," he said, "about
Domain rivers."

He was clearly embarrassed, using a child's song to aid his
memory, but Doronit nodded. "Useful."

It didn't take him long to finish the map. "Those are the main
routes," he said, dusting the chalk from his fingers. "I could put
in the secondary roads if you wanted…"

She smiled. "So. In this I think the student knows more than
the teacher. I will come to you when I want information about
secondary roads."

Doronit was more than pleased, and not just at his skill, but
at the strength and surety with which he'd completed the task.
For a while, while he concentrated, he had been a man instead
of a boy. She sighed a little inside, imagining what it would be
like to have someone she could trust, a strong man, at her back.

She'd never found anyone she could rely on, but perhaps this boy would become what she needed.

"I suppose you know your history, too?" she said, and gave him a flirting smile.

He reddened a little, but sat up straight, looking her in the eyes. "Yes."

"Are you sure?" A strong man sometime in the future was all very well, she thought, but she couldn't afford to have him become cocky right now. "Tell me about the war between the Western Mountains and the Central Domains."

"Which one?" She paused, unsure for once, and he smiled at her, but it was a happy smile, not a cocky one. "There have been three, in the last thousand years."

Her first impulse was to slap him down, but she restrained herself. This could be another moment to bind him to her, to make him love her as well as want her. She laughed, making it clear she was laughing at herself, not at him.

"And I thought I knew my history!" she said. "How do you know all this?"

He shrugged, clearly pleased but trying not to show it. "There are songs. Just about every important moment in time has its own song. At least one."

"But you can't know them all!" This time she really was astonished.

"Maybe not *all*," he said, being modest. "But most."

He was close to cockiness now, buoyed up by his first sense of superiority over her. She couldn't allow that.

"But you never sing," she said, and watched the knife go home.

He paled, picked up the chalk and fiddled with it, marking an unimportant tributary of the Knife River.

"No," he said quietly. "I can't sing. But I know the songs."

There it was, the sense of uselessness that his parents had

drummed into him, the fools! But it was helpful to her. He'd soon be at the point where only her opinion mattered.

"How wonderful," she said warmly, and he looked at her in surprise, taking self-respect from her and drawing himself up. She patted his hand and then waved dismissively at the map. "None of my other safeguarders care about the past. They probably don't even know that there used to be only six Domains instead of eleven."

He smiled tentatively. "North and South, Far North and Far South, Western Mountains and Central."

She patted him on the shoulder. "Acton may have been a great war leader, but he didn't have much imagination when it came to naming things, did he?"

They laughed together and then she sent him out to deliver a message. It was to Hildie, who had been hired out for the day to a jeweler expecting a big shipment of rubies.

The jeweler's workshop was a simple shopfront in the middle tier of the city, two streets above Acton Square: close enough to the houses of the rich that they wouldn't think it a trouble to walk there, but low enough down to have a reasonable rent. When Ash arrived, the counter had been drawn up and locked, so he knew that the rubies had arrived. He went in cautiously, whistling his identity code so that Hildie wouldn't jump him as he came through the door. He didn't see her as he entered, then felt her breath on his neck and spun around.

"Gotcha!" she said, and laughed at him. "Ya shoulda waited till I whistled back, young'un."

He blushed. He'd never get the feel for this constant suspicion and caution. "At least I remembered to whistle."

"Aye," she nodded, and showed him the knife in her hand. "Otherwise you'da been whistling through a new hole in your windpipe."

67

She smiled as she said it, and he wasn't sure how true it was. She was probably just trying to make him feel even younger and stupider.

The jeweler was examining the rubies before signing the receipt. She was a big woman, tall and solid, beginning to run to fat, with gray eyes and light brown hair plaited down her back. She wore blue trousers and black boots with a gray work smock—simple, inexpensive, misleading clothes—and showed a placid face to the world, although Ash knew she was considered one of the sharpest traders in the city. The ruby seller, a thin, sharp-nosed man with an enormous mustache, was fidgeting from one foot to the other, anxious to have the gems off his hands. If they were stolen before he got a receipt, it would be his loss, Ash knew.

"Well, you're a welcome sight," Hildie said to him. "Better two sets of eyes and hands right now—we's at the sharp moment now." She grinned. "Even your eyes might be useful."

He rolled his eyes in acknowledgment of her right to tease him, but he kept his face to the door and his eyes on the street.

"You're to report to the town clerk at eight tomorrow," he said, "for a meeting with some merchants from the Wind Cities."

"Why does the old fart need safeguarding from foreign merchants?"

Ash shrugged, but the jeweler chipped in, looking up from the lens she had suspended over the tray of rubies. "Because last time they threatened to cut his balls off if he substituted second-grade iron ore for the top grade they'd paid for."

"Ah..." Hildie nodded wisely, "and he's afeared they'll really try it this time and find out he don't have any, right?"

They all laughed, even the nervous ruby seller.

"All correct and accounted for," the jeweler said.

She packed the gems away into her strongbox and put it aside, then handed up a pouch of money.

The mustachioed vendor accepted the pouch and pulled something from his pocket with a flourish, all his nervous energy released once the jewels were safely paid for. "Something special," he said. "Unique."

He laid it out on the jeweler's tray—a big cloak brooch that mimicked a shield in intricate metal- and enamelwork. Bronze wire turned like hearts, or maybe faces, around a central circle with three curving enamel—*What?* Ash wondered. *Claws, birds' heads, scythes?*—coming out from the center. There was something about it that caught the eye. On one glance it looked calm, balanced, pretty; on another look it was packed with threatening shapes in a whirling dance. Unsettling.

"It's old," Ash said, and moved to see it better.

"Ancient," the man said, smoothing one end of his mustache into a curling tip. "As old as the Domains."

"I deal in gemstones," the jeweler said dismissively. "This isn't even gold, it's just bronze."

"They say—" The man paused dramatically. "That it belonged to Acton."

"And my grandmother's still alive and dancing the hornpipe every night at the Drunken Sailor."

"No, really! I got it in the west, near where Acton's people first came over the mountains. He gave it to some woman's ancestor."

"Why?"

The man shrugged. "Because she was a good shag, I guess. It was usually something like that with Acton, wasn't it?"

"And this woman gave it to you?" the jeweler said. "Because *you* were a good shag?"

He sniffed, which made the mustache bounce. "Because the

warlord there's a right bastard and she needed to pay her taxes. But if you're not interested, I'll take it elsewhere."

"It may be old, but it's not in my line—Acton's or not. I'll just keep the rubies, thanks."

The man turned to Ash and Hildie. Hildie hadn't taken her eyes from the street the entire time.

"What about you two?"

"Not interested in anything of Acton's," Hildie said, her voice flat. Ash saw the man register Hildie's Traveler accent and sneer a little.

"What about you, lad?"

"He's an apprentice," Hildie cut in. "He couldn't afford a *fake* bronze brooch."

"Too bad," the man said.

"Yes," Ash said, his eyes still on the curving bronze. "Too bad." He was drawn to it; he wanted to pick it up and run his fingers across the intricate scrolling. What if this *had* belonged to Acton? The man who'd invaded this country and disinherited Ash's people, turned them off their land and made them into Travelers—the man who'd changed everything. The first warlord.

Half the old songs were about Acton—about his courage and leadership and humor and, of course, his love life, which by all accounts had been prodigious. He loomed larger than life in the minds of everyone in the Domains, perhaps all the more because no one knew what had happened to him. He had ridden out one day from a camp up near the Western Mountains and disappeared. The legend said that his last words had been, "I'll be back before you need me"; and in the countryside a surprising number of people believed he *would* come back one day, from wherever he had ridden away to, if the country was in deadly peril.

The brooch seemed to shimmer in front of Ash's eyes, speaking of choices long made and chances long forfeited. Perhaps there had been a moment when his ancestors could have united and fought Acton off; but they hadn't. Their settlements had been too widely scattered, the people living in the central lands had depended on the mountain people to repel any raids, so when Acton broke through that defense there was no one to stop him. There was no one who really knew how to fight and no one to rally the far-flung villages and make a stand.

So Ash stood here in a jeweler's shop in Turvite, which had been founded by those ancestors but was a city of Acton's people now, and he didn't even know what the birthright was that had been stolen from him. It was so far in the past — a thousand years! — that no Traveler alive today knew the history of their people before Acton came. Not for sure and certain, although Ash's father had taught him what was known of the old language. All they had were a few scraps of songs and stories, some of the traditions and habits and superstitions... and the casting stones, which predated not only Acton but Ash's ancestors as well, and had come, they said, straight from the gods.

The man wrapped the brooch up again, tucked his purse securely inside his shirt and did up his coat over it. Ash blinked; it seemed the shop was darker than before.

"Any more business for me?" the man asked the jeweler.

She shook her head. "I'll let you know if I have another order."

The trader still had his hand over his pocket. It seemed to occur to him for the first time that a money pouch could be stolen as easily as a pouch of rubies. "Walk me back to my lodgings, young'un?" he asked. "Standard rate?"

"Danger rate," Ash said. "They could be waiting for you to make the trade — most thieves prefer money to gems."

The man sniffed, then nodded and waited for Ash to go out the door before him.

"'Acton, lucky under the sword, lucky under the sheets, favored by gods and by all the unseen...'" Ash murmured.

"Huh?" Hildie said.

"An old song," Ash shrugged. "I'll see you later."

He went quietly, carefully, out the door and escorted the trader to his inn with no trouble. But on the way back to Doronit's he had the rest of that song singing in his head: *Acton, brother of horses, Acton, brother of wolves, Acton, father of hundreds, Acton, father of us!*

It made him feel a bit sick. Acton, the killer. Ash had always despised him. But he was a killer himself, now. The girl's face rose in his mind, as it sometimes did before he went to sleep or, worse, in his dreams. Such a young face. So concentrated on him, on his death. The knife in her hand, held low. Her pale hair, her pale face, relaxed after she fell, her thin chest still, her hand letting go of its clutch on the knife. What he felt wasn't exactly guilt, more sharp regret; he regretted whatever it was—circumstance, fate, bad luck—that had brought them both to that alleyway.

MARVEL'S STORY

THE WORLD'S full of easy marks, but I never took myself for one of them, not me, not little Marvel. That's what they called me in the back alleyways of Turvite, a marvel 'cause I was so fast with my hands and light with my fingers. It's not a bad life, pickpocket and thief. Gods, why should I lie? It's shagging horrible — scary and dirty and hand-to-mouth and always scrounging. Better off dead, they say in other towns, but in Turvite we've too many ghosts to believe that. Not many neck themselves around here. No use complaining, that's what I say, not when you might get an easy mark around the next corner, with a fat purse and a yellow heart.

And I was lucky enough, though I'd had to kill a few times to get that purse. Life's not worth much in the alleyways. "Gutter" they called me, as well as Marvel. I'm not tall, see, and I can't reach a grown man's throat at the right angle to slit it neatly and quietly. Putting a shiv into the heart's tricky business, no matter what you've heard, specially if they're fat, so my best bet was to put the blade in just over their pubes and slit them from fork to gullet. The other thing is, if they're wearing a winter coat, most of the time it doesn't get much blood on it, so you can fence that, too.

It's good, when you're little and young, to have a reputation as a gutter. Keeps the thugs off you. Keeps the pimps away and the girlers who heave a woman or two aboard ships bound for the Wind Cities, to keep the sailors happy and sell to the brothels at the other end. One girler who tried that on me ended

73

up with his balls in his throat, and they didn't get there through his mouth.

Never had to shag for my supper. Not once. My brother used to earn his bread that way before the poppy juice got to him and I swore I'd never let anyone do that to me. Better kill fifty men than have one of them on top of me like that.

Life got easier after my brother died and I didn't have to find enough silver to buy his juice. I started saving up for...something, I didn't know what. To learn a trade? Start a business of my own? I thought I could maybe sell fish down at the harbor market, or make candles. It wasn't so far-fetched. Look at Doronit. She arrived in Turvite as poor as me and now she gets invited to the Merchants' Banquets! I wanted to be like her. Makes you laugh, doesn't it?

Sometimes, when I was washing my hands afterward, I thought about going to the Valuers' Plantation. I liked Valuer thinking: that there shouldn't be any warlords or high families, that no one's life is worth more than another's—all valued alike—and that the rich should share with the poor so no one goes hungry. They say anyone is welcomed at the plantation, anyone at all. But I wondered what they'd say to me—I lived as though no one's life had any value at all.

I thought, sometimes, in the early morning before I went to sleep, *I'll save up and go to the Well of Secrets, and confess.* She can magic the blood off your hands, they reckon. *Then I'll go to the Valuers and maybe, if I have clean hands, they'll take me in.* It got so I was thinking about that night as well as morning, thinking through the journey up through Carlion and then inland to Pless and farther up, imagining the welcome at the end of it. I went out more than I should have, maybe, to find fat purses and yellow hearts. Took risks, like going after young men as well as old. Should have known better.

I should have smelled a rat when I saw that drunk young cully reel down the alley where I kept watch, his fat purse clinking against his side. Looking back, I realize he was a bit too young, he moved a bit too well to be a stumbling sot of a merchant's son, no matter how he was dressed. But Shiv and Dimple had seen him, too, and started to follow him, and I thought, *Got to get to him first, got to get that juicy purse.*

So I ran and I leaped, and when he turned suddenly, sharp as the knife he cocked at me, it was too late. I almost had him—I was quick, I was bloody quick. But he was quicker. I recognized him as he took me in the shoulder—Doronit's new boy, the Traveler. His eyes were wide with fear and horror. *He doesn't have a taste for killing,* I thought, as though it mattered to me. Not yet he didn't. Then his knife went in again and it was over.

Surprising, there's not so much pain when the knife goes in; it's when it comes out again that it hurts. Wasn't a bad death, all things considered. Quick. Clean. Over. And that was a relief. Seemed to me—at the moment when I stopped seeing anything and felt myself, my *self,* still go on—that maybe I owed Doronit's boy for setting me free.

I'd like to get to the Valuers' one day, though. If not in this life, maybe the next.

SAKER

H E NEEDED bones. The right bones, restless in the earth. He went to his workroom, to the big map spread out on the table, the most complete map of the Domains that he had been able to buy. There were a few massacre sites marked in red — Death Pass, Turvite, Carlion. But too few. So many more had been slaughtered. Carefully stored scrolls filled the shelves around him, but so little of their information was useful. What did he care about the names of the killers, or who their fathers had been? Why should he want to know how they had held their weapons, how they had swung them against his people — his peaceful, gentle people? The poems and histories had been written by the invaders, and gave no details about those killed, least of all where to find their bones.

Saker slumped at the table, head in hands, another night's study ending in frustration. There must be other scrolls, other histories... He felt the bag of stones at his waist. At least Friete, the enchanter, had taught him how to cast, had given him a way of supporting himself. It was useless to cast for oneself, every stonecaster knew that. Either useless or dangerous — one or the other. But sometimes the temptation was irresistible. He dug his hand in the pouch and drew out the necessary five stones, cast them with a practiced flick of the wrist. But they landed, not spread out across the table in an arc, but in a huddle on one spot, facedown. Right on top of Connay, north of Whitehaven. Two days' walk away.

He didn't bother to turn the stones over. Their position was enough. *Connay.* The gods had spoken. He would find what he needed in Connay. He packed, and then picked the stones up almost reluctantly: Revenge and Rejoicing, Death and Bereavement, and the Chaos stone lying on top of them all. His spirits rose. They were exactly the same stones as that first stonecasting after Friete's death. Saker wondered why Death, Bereavement and Chaos were now facedown. *Secrecy,* he thought. *I must work secretly. That is the message of the stones.* He went out whistling, headed for Connay.

BRAMBLE

BRAMBLE WANTED to arrive at the linden tree early, just in case. Ghosts rise, if they rise, three days after death, but not to the minute. It might be an hour earlier or two hours later. Some ghosts never came — those who had died slowly, and knew they were dying and had said all their farewells. "May you have no quickening" was a blessing, a wish that the gods would give you a good death, where you had no need to come back to say goodbye or ask for forgiveness or confront your killer, where you went straight on to new life. "May you quicken and never be reborn" was a curse.

It was hard to see ghosts in daylight. Most ghosts were just a pale waver in the air, like heat shimmer above paving, but some were more substantial, blobs of white in the shape of the dead person. Travelers, it was said, could see ghosts better than other people, but Bramble had never found it so. Maybe she didn't have enough Traveler blood in her. But she had attended a few quickenings in her time, as most people had, and she knew she would recognize the chill of the flesh as the ghost arrived.

As she approached the linden tree, she heard men's voices. She stopped behind a yew and watched. *So he had some friends,* she thought. There were three men in warlord's uniform, sitting at the base of the tree, on the other side from where the blond had fallen. They were talking idly. One was throwing pebbles at the nearby willow; another, an older man with brown hair and a beard, had his head tipped back to look at the leaves above him; the third — the redhead who had been with the blond in the forest when the wolf had been shot—was sharpening his dagger with a small whetstone. He spat on the stone as she watched and honed the blade with deep concentration, as though preparing it for someone's flesh.

Bramble couldn't decide whether to leave immediately, or wait. If the blond quickened—and he would, she knew it in her bones—she should know what happened. His friends were here because he had died suddenly, but they thought it was by accident. If the ghost was strong enough to be seen clearly, it could let them know the truth. On the other hand, if they found her here, at this place, at this time, death was the best she could hope for.

The ghost decided for her. It took form, shimmering and pale gray, lying on the ground just as the warlord's man had lain three days ago. Bramble felt her skin chill and grow goose bumps, even from so far away. The three men jumped to their feet, and the ghost did too. They confronted each other. The dead man was just a blur, but it was clear enough for his friends.

"You're dead," the redhead said, gently enough. "You rode into the tree limb." He pointed to the branch above their heads. "Three days ago. This is your quickening."

The ghost put out his pale arms and waved negatingly.

"Yes, yes," the redhead said soothingly. "I know it's a shock. But you really are dead."

The ghost pointed to the tree limb and waved both arms again.

"Yes, that's the branch," the older man said. His voice was very deep, and hard. He sounded bored. "Just accept it, Swith. You're dead. No use going on about it."

Swith. Somehow it troubled Bramble that the blond should have the same name as her crotchety old friend. She didn't want to think of him as a real person, with a name and friends who cared about him.

79

The ghost waved an arm, shook a fist in the direction of the tree branch.

"He's not acting like it was an accident," the redhead said uneasily. "He's not being reasonable."

"You expect him to be different now from when he was alive?" the older man said scathingly. "Come on, we've done what we came for. Let's get back to Thornhill. I've got work to do even if you haven't."

The redhead looked troubled. "What if it wasn't an accident?"

The ghost pointed his arms at his friend and seemed to nod, although it was hard for Bramble to see.

"It wasn't an accident?" the redhead said. The ghost made a victory gesture above his head.

"Oh, shagging gods!" the older man said. "Of course it was an accident. Swith just doesn't want to be remembered as the idiot he was."

The youngest of the three, a man with big ears, sniggered.

The ghost fell down upon his knees. It sobered even the sniggerer.

"They never found his horse, Beck," the redhead said quietly.

Beck, Bramble thought, *that's the warlord's second in command.*

"That was a good horse," Beck said thoughtfully. "I trained him myself. Worth killing for, if you had somewhere safe to take him."

"I think we'd better talk to the warlord. Try to find the horse. If it's still out in the forest, well, then it's an accident. If not..."

The older man sniffed, then nodded. "All right. I'll talk to him. Let's go."

She waited until the three men had mounted and left. The

redhead clearly felt awkward about riding away from the ghost, just leaving it standing there by the tree. He tried to wave good-bye to it, but halfway through caught the eye of the older man and he turned the movement into a fumble on the reins.

They went west up the slope, toward Thornhill, without looking back. When they were out of sight, Bramble slowly came forward, her knife tight in her hand. When the ghost caught sight of her, he pointed one long pale arm at her head, turned as though to call back the men, then realized he couldn't. Bramble swallowed. Up close, the chill was much worse. She took a deep breath. Words had been laid down for this, words that had to be said.

"I am your killer," she said to him, trying to look him in the eye. "Lo, I proclaim it, it was I who took your life from you. I am here to offer reparation, blood for blood."

She cut her wrist with a sure flick of the knife and offered it to him, her whole body tensed against what was to come. But the ghost backed away and waved his arms: *No.* She could almost see his mouth, a slightly darker shape, form the word.

"If you do not forgive me, you will be caught here in this place, with no chance of rebirth," Bramble said.

He lunged forward, his hands out for her throat, forgetting for a moment that he no longer had a body to do damage with. His pale form passed right through her; she felt a horrible chilly wave. The burial cave smell enveloped her and she fought to stop herself vomiting.

The ghost turned, furious, unappeased, and raised its fists to the sky in anger.

It was enough. Bramble turned and ran back toward the stream. *Now,* the gods said in her mind. *Now.* She ran home, straight to her mother's workshop.

She fetched up at the side of the loom, panting. "I'm leaving.

I—I'll go to Maryrose. I'm going now. Don't worry. And if you're asked, you know nothing of where I am or why I've gone. You all come soon."

Her mother sat with her mouth open, astonished. Bramble moved around the corner of the loom, hugged her briefly, kissed her cheek, and ran out headed for her father's workshop before her mother could recover her breath.

Her da and granda were standing at the workbench, looking at some plans. As she ran to them they turned to face her. She reached up to kiss each of them on the cheek—*NOW,* the gods insisted—then ran out without speaking. She ran for the forest as though she were a wild goose flying.

She found the roan waiting for her. He nuzzled her shoulder while she tried to calm herself. His warm breath steadied her nerves, brought her back down to earth. She found that she had cut her forearm on the wild dash through the trees; it had ripped against a branch. Without thinking, she took her skirt off in haste and staunched the blood flow, then realized the stains she was making on the fabric. *Rot it,* she thought, *I could have used this skirt.* She tore enough off to make a bandage then tossed it aside. Her breeches would be enough. It would probably be better if she looked like a boy anyway. She pinned up her braid and put on a tight-fitting leather hood that she usually wore against the winter snow, and retrieved the carefully packed bundle from the rear of the cave and tied it to her back. Then she led the roan to the mounting block and climbed on his back.

"Come on, then," she said. "Go."

She found that her mind had been working on its own these past three days. There was a plan all ready in her head, though she hadn't been conscious of working it out. She would head for

Carlion immediately, but through the forest, not on the road where the warlord's men would be sure to find her. It would take longer, because she would have to go up beyond the waterfall, beyond the chasm, to find a ford where she could cross the river, so she could circle down to the road through the forest on the other side. Longer but safer. The warlord's men would start their search from the linden tree, so she had time.

She knew the forest better than anyone, but the roan couldn't move through the undergrowth as she could, so they kept to the track, as they had the day before. The roan recognized the way and went happily enough. It was a warm day, with sun filtering down to her where the trees were less dense. They moved from shade to sun and back again, warmth and coolness, like the rhythm of the roan's soft hoofbeats. It had lulled her, so the sound of men's voices at a distance, the jingling of harness, caught her by surprise.

They had started their search from Thornhill, not from the linden tree. And they were coming steadily from the west. She turned to head more directly for the chasm. There were rocks near the waterfall, with caves...Perhaps she and the roan could hide there. These men didn't know the forest the way she did. She was confident that she could outsmart them in her own territory. Then she heard the baying of the hounds.

The roan's head went up, too, and he took a breath to whinny. She leaned forward quickly and held his nostrils closed. He looked at her reproachfully and she stared back at his enormous eyes.

"No noise, my friend," she whispered.

He let his breath out slowly, and she let go, then urged him to a quick walk.

The hounds' note changed. Bramble had watched the hunt go by too many times not to recognize it: "We are on the scent!"

The roan quickened his pace when he heard men's voices urging on the hounds. He jumped at one voice in particular. A deep, hard voice. *Beck's*, Bramble thought. *The older man. The clever one.* The roan almost stumbled, then began to move faster, taking the rough ground in his stride, ignoring Bramble completely. She lay down low and clung to his neck with both hands as they moved rapidly through the undergrowth.

Behind them the hounds were belling furiously. Bramble tried desperately to think what to do. There was no time to hide. No way to get up above the chasm in time to cross the river and confuse the scent. She tried to think of other streams nearby, but there weren't any. She could probably climb a tree and let the roan go—the hounds would follow the horse scent. That would be the sensible thing to do. But she couldn't. She couldn't abandon him to the chase. What if the hounds' master didn't whip them back in time? What if the bloodlust got too much for them? What if they brought him down? These hounds were used to hunting people and horses as well as deer: they would leap for the throat. If she was still on the roan, at least she could help fight them off until Beck controlled them. He had admired the roan; he would save him. She decided that they would stand at bay at the chasm—a bad place but it was all they had.

She clung on as the roan raced faster through the trees. She craned for one look over her shoulder. Beck was in the lead, his face pale beneath the beard, his eyes intense.

"There!" he shouted. "It's just a boy! Get him!"

The roan broke into a panicked gallop. Bramble suddenly knew who had been responsible for those welts and scars on his hide. But they were going too fast...They were too close to the chasm: they'd never be able to stop in time.

The roan didn't falter as they broke from the trees and headed wildly toward the abyss. Bramble considered tumbling from his back before he reached the edge. Then she heard Beck's voice calling.

There were worse things than death.

There would be a leap and a moment suspended, and then a long hopeless curve to the rocks and the river below. They would fall like leaves between the clouds of swifts and then be washed away by the thundering rapids. Bramble clung to that thought. If their bodies were washed away then there could be no identification, no danger of reprisals on her family.

She hung on tighter.

The roan's hindquarters bunched under her and they were in the air.

It was like she had imagined: the leap, and then the moment suspended in the air that seemed to last forever.

Below her the swifts boiled up through the river mist, swerving and swooping while she and the roan seemed to stay frozen above them. Bramble felt, like a rush of air, the presence of the gods surround her. The shock made her lose her balance and begin to slide sideways.

She felt herself falling.

With an impossible flick of both legs, the roan shrugged her back onto his shoulders. Then the long curve down started and she braced herself to see the cliffs rushing past as they fell.

Time to die.

Instead, she felt a thumping jolt that flung her from the roan's back and tossed her among the rocks at the cliff's edge on the other side.

On the other side.

The roan slowed down and turned to head back for her. She stood slowly, muddled and shaken. She couldn't see properly, everything was in shadow, as though it were night. She reached out to touch the roan's shoulder. She knew she was touching him, but she could barely feel the warmth of his hide. She could barely hear; everything seemed distant, dull. She was breathing, but the breaths gave her no life. She felt like a dead woman breathing out of habit, as ghosts do when they first quicken, before they realize they are dead.

Her sight cleared, although the light still seemed dim. Her hearing came back a little. On the other side of the abyss a jumble of men and horses and hounds were milling, shouting, astonished, and very angry.

"You can't *do* that!" one yelled. "It's impossible!"

"Well, he shagging did it!" another said. "Can't be impossible!"

"Head for the bridge!" Beck shouted. "We can still get him. I want that horse!"

That got her moving, got her onto the roan's back and riding. The world still felt distant, but the roan, once she was on his back, was as sharp and clear to her as ever, each hair in his coat distinct, each movement warm and vital beneath her. Around her the forest was like a dream, but he was real. The need to keep him safe drove her on.

She didn't know this part of the forest quite as well, but well enough. She made her way as fast as they could go, cantering where the trees thinned out, walking quickly when they closed in. The roan was pleased with himself, she could tell; he cantered with his ears pricked up and almost pranced through the clearings. She showered lavish praises on him and he took it all in and pranced some more, until she almost laughed aloud.

She thought back to the leap. That moment in the air had been...magnificent. But once was enough. She wasn't sure, now, if the gods had merely surrounded her to taste the moment, as they sometimes did, or if they had actually held her and the roan up in the air for one crucial heartbeat.

Whether they had or not, she felt an obscure certainty that she had been meant to die in that chasm—that her time had been up. She should be tumbling in the white water of the river right now, being swept to sea, the roan beside her. It was only because the roan had made that extraordinary midair shrug that she hadn't fallen.

The fact that she was still alive felt wrong, out of balance. She didn't feel special, or protected, or gods-bound. She thought that the gods had acted to protect the roan, and she had just been along for the ride. It was the roan who was special, not she.

I should be dead, she thought. If she was dead, then it would all be settled. The warlord's men would have been satisfied to see her body swept away, the roan would have been safe from Beck's whip, the ghost of the man she had killed could have gone to his rest. There was a rounding off—a justice—in her death. But alive, no one was satisfied and no one was safe.

She looked ahead in her life and saw emptiness. If she should be dead, then there was no hole in the world she was destined to fill, no home, no place for her to find and claim. It was only now that she realized, when she had thought of the Road, her underlying assumption had been that she would travel until she found where she belonged. But if she belonged in the burial caves, then...

It seemed as though she was looking at the world through clouded glass. Noises were still muted in her ears. Was it shock? Maybe it meant something else. She didn't know. The only thing she was sure of was that the roan had saved her life, and she was in his debt. She murmured thanks to him as they rode, gave thanks and endearments and pats and encouragement, and he took it all as his due.

She would think about this again once they were past the Second River and farther away from the South Domain. Beck and his men *might* make it to the bridge and cut across to intercept her, but they were well behind.

She came to the Second at sunset, hearing the hounds far behind them. It took her a little while to find a place to ford, but the noise of the hounds grew no louder. They were on a false scent. She sighed with relief as they crossed the river. Once she had forded the Second she was in Three Rivers Domain, and they couldn't touch her or the roan without formal application to the Three Rivers warlord. Now it was an easy ride to Carlion, and Maryrose.

She knew that once she reached Carlion, she would be completely safe. There were arrangements for criminals to be sent back to the Domain they had come from but the free towns demanded a very high degree of proof before they would surrender anyone to a warlord's punishment, and Beck just didn't have any proof against her. In their own Domain, that wouldn't matter: he could act with the warlord's authority and no one could object. But the free towns were truly free, and because they were the centers of trade across the Eleven Domains, their councils were rich and powerful.

She rode through the night despite the lack of moon, trusting to the gods who had seen them safe thus far. The road was good, anyway, being the main road between the warlord's fort near Wooding, and Carlion, the second biggest free town in the world. The city was set on a natural harbor, almost as big as Turvite's, but the space between the harbor and the encircling hills was small and steep, so the buildings were crammed in tightly and the town huddled on the rim of the sea.

Bramble could smell the brine as she came down the hill to the first houses, and hear the rhythmic shushing of the waves against the rocks. But both smell and sound were muted by the fog in her head. The sharp salt smell only reached her nose, and didn't lift her spirits as it had on her last visit. The sound of the waves was dull instead of soothing.

She rode between the high, narrow brick houses, and the stones of the street were dark and slippery with sea spray. She clopped her way down Maryrose's street and into her yard before even the starlings were stirring.

She had first come to Carlion when Maryrose had married Merrick, who was a carpenter, like their da and Maryrose. Merrick's mother was the town clerk and he was well established, so Maryrose's new house was substantial, with a yard and stable, although they kept no horses yet. Quietly, Bramble let herself and the roan into the stable. She rubbed him down, fetched him water, then rolled herself in her blanket and slept until the town noises became too loud to be ignored.

Outside the kitchen door she hesitated. What if Maryrose looked at her and saw a walking corpse instead of a living sister? What if she really was dead and just didn't know it? It occurred to her for the first time that perhaps her body *was* lying in the bottom of the chasm, and the men had been chasing the roan, not her. What if she was a ghost who had quickened too soon? There was only one way to find out.

She popped her head around Maryrose's back door. "Any breakfast for a starving sister?"

Maryrose dropped the ladle into the porridge pot with a splash. She swept across the kitchen and enfolded Bramble in a hug. She smelled of woodsmoke and wool and wood, with a hint of lavender underneath, as she always did. Bramble was glad marriage hadn't changed that, at least. But even Maryrose's familiar scent seemed lost to her, somehow distant. A smell remembered rather than lived. But she definitely had a solid body that Maryrose could see and touch. Bramble returned the hug, her heart lifting and settling all at once, so that she was calmer than she had been since she killed the warlord's man. It was foolish, because it had been years since Maryrose could do anything for her that she couldn't do for herself. Come to think of it, she thought, there were a score of things Maryrose could do that she couldn't—weave, carpenter and cook in a hearth among them.

"How did you get here? Where are Mam and Da and Granda? What are you doing here?"

"Can I eat first and talk later?" Bramble said. "I'm starving."

It was true that she hadn't eaten since the day before, but the sensation of emptiness that filled her was stronger than hunger. She sat at the table and took the bowl of porridge that Maryrose handed her. It smelled nutty and sweet, but very faintly, as though she were smelling it from another room. She sprinkled on a bit of salt from the salt pig on the table and took a good mouthful. The taste was also muted. Like a damped-down fire, she thought, or sun behind clouds. She ate anyway. Maybe if she kept acting as though she were alive, the fog would burn off and she would be normal again. She didn't really believe that, but what else could she do? Lie down and die for real and true? Who would look after the roan then? She took another mouthful of porridge.

"Mam and Da and Granda are at home. I came on a horse overnight—he's in your stable. I'm —" Bramble hesitated.

She had come to Maryrose instinctively, but now she was here, she knew she couldn't stay. Already, after less than an hour, the solid walls of the town seemed to lean in on her, with a much more unpleasant pressure than when the local gods were present. She couldn't live in this comfortable, secure house. She'd go mad. It was time to put her original plan into action, and head for the Great Forest.

"I'm Traveling," she said at last.

Maryrose quieted immediately, served herself a bowl and sat opposite Bramble, gazing at her as though she could search her mind, or at least her emotions. Bramble endured it patiently. Maryrose had looked at her like that often enough before.

Maryrose was opening her mouth to speak when Merrick came in. He was as surprised as Maryrose had been, but a lot quieter about it.

"Hullo. Come to visit?"

She'd always liked Merrick, and this quiet welcome, complete with smile and pat on her shoulder, confirmed that regard.

She nodded. "Just a couple of days."

Maryrose was eating her porridge thoughtfully. She went, as she always did, to the heart of things.

"Where did you get a horse?" she asked.

So Bramble told them the whole story, nothing left out, although she found it difficult to explain the way she felt about the roan, about riding. It was a relief to tell Maryrose what had happened. If her sister had been at home Bramble would have shared it with her long ago. The only thing she kept back from them was her conviction that she had been meant to die. They listened with growing concern and astonishment.

"You jumped the *chasm?*" Maryrose kept saying.

"The roan jumped the chasm," Bramble corrected her drily. "I just hung on."

"They thought you were a boy...?"

"Yes, but they might start asking questions...So it's a good thing Mam and Dad and Granda are coming here to live with you. Just in case."

"They're coming? Good." Maryrose spoke absently, turning the story over in her mind. "Yes, it's reassuring to live in a free town. One good thing Acton did, anyway."

91

"What do you mean?" Merrick asked.

Maryrose lifted an eyebrow at him. "Acton established the free towns so that people would have a place to go where no warlord could follow them or have power over them. I love the fact that within the walls of Carlion we're out of their control! It was Acton's idea to make the main towns of the Domains subject only to their town councils."

"Well, I know *that*," Merrick said. "It was a stroke of genius — trade between the free towns keeps the Domains linked as they would never be if the warlords controlled everything. But why was that 'one good thing'? You talk as though Acton didn't do anything else good."

They both stared at him. Bramble saw, as if for the first time, his brown hair and hazel eyes, a legacy of the second wave of Acton's people who had come over the mountains after Acton's death. They had hoped to take land while the first tribe of invaders were leaderless, but Acton's son had dealt with them — done deals, traded, apportioned out land to the west and south. But even though a thousand years ago Acton would have been an enemy of his ancestors, Merrick still hero-worshipped him. That was plain in his indignation. Bramble looked at Merrick and Maryrose, sitting side by side but now with an indefinable distance between them. She hoped it wouldn't last.

"Our granda was a Traveler," Maryrose said slowly, as if thinking it through for the first time. "I suppose we were raised to...to think of Acton differently. As the man who had headed an invasion force that killed off almost all of this land's people."

"And forced the rest onto the roads as Travelers," Bramble added. "Except for the Lake People, of course, and he tried with them, but the Lake stopped him. A stone-cold, bullying murderer, that was Acton."

"No…" Merrick paused and looked from one to the other, from dark Bramble to red-haired Maryrose.

People often looked from one of them to the other, wondering how they could be sisters. But Merrick's eyes weren't suspicious or harsh when he looked at her. Merrick was a logical man, as well as kindly—*almost* good enough for Maryrose.

"Well…of course a lot of people were killed," he continued. "But he established our civilization, our whole way of life. And you—you're both three-quarters Acton's blood."

Bramble laughed. "Not me—not according to anyone who's ever met me. They take one look and think 'Traveler' and that's how they treat me."

"You can't reject your heritage because of a bit of prejudice."

"Be sure I can," Bramble said. "I'm taking to the Road, where I belong."

Merrick turned to Maryrose. "What about you, love?"

She smiled tenderly at him, kissed his cheek and twined her hand in his. "I'm no Traveler, Ric. I'm a crafter, through and through. But I can't just sing Acton's praises when I know how much pain he caused—and all for greed."

"Greed?" Merrick protested again. "His people were being attacked from the north, squeezed back into uninhabitable lands. They would have starved."

"So they attacked other innocent people in turn. And they'd been raiding over the mountains for years," Maryrose said, a little exhausted.

Bramble waved her hand dismissively. "Oh, it doesn't matter, Maryrose. We have to live in the present. It's ridiculous, anyway—what happened a thousand years ago can't touch us now."

She was glad to see both Merrick's and Maryrose's faces

lighten and their shoulders lean together to touch again. But she had shivered as she said those last words, the same kind of shiver that she felt when she sat by the black rock and opened her mind to the local gods. It was the first strong feeling she had experienced since she landed on the other side of the abyss, and she welcomed it even while it frightened her.

"Will you stay?" Maryrose asked, hesitantly.

Bramble shook her head. She could see her parents being happy enough here, but she knew she couldn't stay. She needed open air—field or forest or mountain. And underneath her breastbone, in that hollow place, there still lurked a fear that she was dead, was in some way just a ghost moving a body around, and that she should avoid all the people she loved, for their sakes. Even talking to Maryrose, a cloudy glass was between them, an insuperable barrier between life and death, and she was lucky to have been granted this chance to say her goodbyes before death caught up with her.

"No," she said to them. "I'm no city girl. I'm heading north."

She stayed another day, pretending everything was fine, chatting and currying the roan—while her sister looked on, astonished—and sitting in the big front room where Maryrose had her loom and Merrick his carpenter's bench.

They didn't mention Acton again, or Travelers, or warlords. Instead, Bramble told funny stories about the lambs she had hand-reared, the squirrels who scolded her in the forest as she watched at their nut store, about her first fumbling efforts to ride the roan, and the pain she'd been in afterward.

"I swear," she said, "I was walking like a woman who's just given birth, with my legs as far apart as they could go so the chafing didn't kill me. And Widow Farli comes out of the potter's and takes one look at me—reeling from side to side—and shouts 'the falling sickness, the falling sickness!' and runs to get the village voice. So I straightened up—and believe me, it hurt, every step—and when she dragged the voice out to see me, there I was, walking quietly along like a little lady, smiling kindly at the poor, deluded thing. So he turns to look at her as though *she's* got the sickness and she gets all in a snit and says, 'Don't you look at *me* in that tone of voice!'"

Maryrose giggled helplessly, her shuttle faltering halfway across the warp, and Ric shook his head, smiling as he planed a piece of sweet-smelling cedar. Bramble was happy, simply happy, but it was the happiness you feel when you remember a good memory, or as a ghost might smile, recalling the life that was over.

As she was packing to leave, Merrick brought her a present, a pair of horse bags that didn't need a saddle to hang off.

She was touched, and kissed his cheek. "Thanks, Ric."

She packed them evenly—one side for her gear, the other for the roan's feed and hobbles and curry combs that she had bought at Carlion market—then slung them across his withers. He was eager to be off, too; she could feel it.

She kissed them both goodbye, hugged Maryrose a couple of times, then used the mounting block in the yard to climb onto the roan. She grinned determinedly, nudged the roan through the gates, and took the Road. It was a beautiful morning, with gulls wheeling in the sky and a fresh salt breeze blowing. Bramble moved through it without truly feeling anything, as though only her body were present, not her soul.

Three-quarters of the way up the hill on which Carlion was built, she passed a house with a red leather pouch hung outside the door to show it was a stonecaster's. She rode past, but then stopped the roan and turned back. It was better to know than to wonder, she thought.

She put a loose strap around the roan's neck so that any passersby would think he was tethered to the bootscraper by the door, and knocked.

"Come, come," a brusque voice told her.

She found herself in a square green room with a white ceiling and furnished only with a dark blue rug. A middle-aged man sat slouched on the rug, running his fingers through a leather pouch the exact red of the one hung outside. She couldn't tell if he was a Traveler or one of Acton's people, because he was completely bald and kept his eyes on the pouch.

"Sit, sit, girl," he said.

She sat down cross-legged and spat in her left palm. The stonecaster did the same and they clasped hands.

"Do you want to say your question out loud?" he asked, as if he didn't care one way or the other. Bramble knew that the more specific the question, the better the results, so she thought carefully.

"What happened to me during the jump over the chasm?"

The stonecaster looked up at that, but his eyes told her nothing. They were nothing eyes — not blue, not brown, not green — that seemed to change color depending on what he was looking at. He brought out the stones, cast them across the rug and looked down.

"Death," he said. "Destiny. Rescue. All facing up. Spirit, facing down. And Confusion."

"What do they mean?"

He cocked his head, as though listening, as she had known other stonecasters to do. They said the stones talked to them, but she had never felt the presence of the gods at a casting.

The stonecaster sat upright, startled, and let go of her hand.

"They say you died," he said. "That it was your time to die and you died. Your spirit should have moved on to rebirth. But your body — was saved?"

"Yes," Bramble said. "My horse saved me."

This time the stonecaster looked at her with compassion. "I have never heard of something like this, where someone's destiny has been broken."

"Love breaks all fates," Bramble said.

"Love from a horse?" the stonecaster said. "Well, maybe, it may be... However it happened, body and mind are alive, spirit is — not yet gone, but not really here. Ready to be reborn but unable to because it's still tied loosely to the body."

"Like a ghost who has quickened but not been laid to rest?"

"Perhaps. Perhaps, yes. It may be so."

"I have another question."

"Of course," he said. "What should you do, yes?"

She nodded.

They clasped hands again and with his right hand he gathered the stones from the rug and cast again. Bramble found herself concentrating on the stones as they fell, as though she could change their message. Casting stones were all natural, not shaped, and they came in every color of rock imaginable. These five were a pattern of ocher, gray, brown and black on the dark rug.

Destiny again, she recognized. And she knew the Rebirth stone. The others were strange to her.

"Love," the stonecaster said, touching the ocher one lightly. "Endurance through trials. And the blank stone, which means anything is possible."

"What do they mean?

He cocked his head again, then shrugged. "What you see is all I can tell you. Destiny, Rebirth, Endurance... There is a way through for you, but it's not one the stones can easily describe."

"And in the meantime I'm dead?"

"Not dead, exactly. Detached from your spirit, which is your connection to the living world."

Detached, Bramble thought. Yes, that was how she felt. Detached and unfeeling. Even this casting, horrific though it was, left her with only a mild sensation of shock and despair, like an echo.

"Endurance," she said.

"Yes," said the stonecaster. "You must endure." He would accept no payment. "Not for news such as that," he said, his changeable eyes reflecting the green walls and reminding her of the forest she was heading toward. "Remember, there was love in the reading."

Riding out of Carlion east along the coast, Bramble almost felt calm. She knew the worst. She merely had to endure. At some point her body would die, as every body did in time, and her spirit would be free to be reborn. She might have to endure a very long time. If that were so, the forest was even more the place she should be. It would be easier to endure death surrounded by the myriad life of the woods. She turned the roan's nose and urged him to a canter.

MARYROSE'S STORY

BEFORE YOU were born and after the sun first shone, there was a girl. She was a young girl, a wild girl: there has been a girl like her in every village and town since the world was born. The girl whose first word is "No!," the girl who runs away from parents and sisters and rolls in the dust with dogs, who throws stones at boys and breaks the pots she is set to wash. The girl who can soothe a colicky baby or a frightened doe rabbit, the girl whose grandfather shakes his head over her but slips her honey cake under the table, the girl wreathed in flowers with bare feet and big eyes, the girl called Bramble, the interesting one.

Well, this is a story about me, her sister Maryrose, who had to stay home and milk the goats while Bramble roamed over the hillsides. Who held the timber still for our father, the carpenter, to saw, while Bramble hunted wild honey. Who threaded the loom for our mother, the weaver, while Bramble waded in the cool green creek. Who learned both to weave and carpenter, because there were only the two of us, and our parents had to teach someone—and Bramble was never there. Except at mealtimes.

Oh, believe me, I didn't dislike Bramble, not at all. Because, truth be told, I liked having my parents all to myself. And I liked weaving and carpentering and the cool green of the creek didn't tempt me at all, with the good wood whispering under my plane, with the bright wool whispering between my fingers and the sharp *clack, clack* of the shuttle flicking across the warp like a dragonfly.

But I worried about Bramble. For how was she to care for herself when she grew up, who knew nothing and could do nothing useful except gather wild food from the forest? I could see a time, after our parents' deaths, when Bramble would be forced into the cold, cold world unless I myself wove enough cloth and shaped enough wood to support both of us. And that, for I was only human after all, I was determined not to do.

So I looked at Bramble and I considered her, and I came to a conclusion that the one thing that she had in abundance, and which I lacked, was looks. She was a true briar flower: curly black hair, black sloe eyes and smooth skin, a pink flush in her cheeks, and the grace of a fawn. It occurred to me that some good man might not mind that Bramble could not even bake bread, if he was bewitched enough by her beauty and her charm (for Bramble, when she cared to, could charm the birds down out of the trees and onto her fingers). Then the man could take care of Bramble, and I wouldn't need to worry about her, ever again.

So I decided to look for a man for Bramble. A man who was hardworking, where Bramble was shiftless. A man who was prosperous, where Bramble had nothing. A man who was young and good-looking, or else Bramble would never look twice, let alone marry. A man who was merry and good-tempered, who wouldn't be irritated by the many things Bramble didn't know, but would value the wild spirit in her. A man who was strong—for somewhere, sometime, Bramble must be tamed. Maybe love could do it where everything else had failed.

I started looking in our own village. But there was no man there to fit the bill. For Wilf was sweet but ugly. Carl was hardworking, but timid as a mouse, and quailed whenever Bramble cast him a scornful look. Neither Aelred nor Eric, Ralf nor Martin were even-tempered enough, for Bramble could try the patience of a stone, when she came home singing late in the long summer evenings, when the dinner was cold and dried out, when the chores had all been done.

The other boys had parents who glared hard-eyed at Bramble when she danced (the lightest, the merriest of all) round the Springtree, and held back their sons from her light feet and shining hair. And none of the boys had strength enough to gainsay them.

So I looked elsewhere. When I was nineteen and Bramble a year younger, I took the cloth to market for the first time on my own, to the Winterfair in the city. It was good cloth—my mother and I wove so alike that no one could tell where one left off and the other began. We had dyed it a serviceable dark brown, a good yeoman color for jerkin or capuchin or cloak. As well I took a piece I'd woven all myself, on the lap loom, from scraps and scourings of wool, with a pattern of autumn leaves, bright as fire and gold as sun against the color of evergreens.

I set out my wares in the great trade hall, on a trestle table I had rented from the organizer of the fair, the town clerk. I spread out the good solid brown lengths and then, across the front of the table, I laid the bright piece. I watched the craftsmen and the craftswomen set up their tables around me; but mostly I watched the craftsmen, thinking, "No, he's too old for Bramble, that one's too young, that one's too short, he's too skinny, too mean a mouth, too flighty..." I turned them over in my mind as my customers turned over the lengths of wool on my table. I would have bought none of them for Bramble.

Many people approached, drawn by the swathe of autumn fabric, but I liked that piece and had no real wish to sell it, so I put a high price on it, and many who came to finger the red and gold and green I sent away with sensible brown. Then the town clerk came, with her husband the silversmith, her daughter the jeweler, and her son the woodcarver. The town clerk wanted the bright piece as a Winterfest present for her husband, to make a fine waistcoat and scarf. What could I do? For all traders know that the town clerk can make or mar your Winterfair, this one or next, by where she put your table and how much rent she charges for it.

So I named my price and gave the town clerk a good discount. I reluctantly handed the piece to the husband, and the family moved away. But the son, the woodcarver, lingered behind.

"It's hard," he said, "giving up something you've made, something you love, to a stranger."

I looked at him properly for the first time, and I liked what I saw. For he was comely, with autumn hair the color of turning oak leaves, and warm brown eyes, and good hands with calluses from chisel and saw. They were the same calluses as I had on my hands, the same as my father's. So I knew that he was hardworking at his trade, and I knew by his smile that he was merry. I set myself to find out more about him, for here at last was someone who might do for Bramble.

"It is hard," I acknowledged.

"My name is Merrick," he said. "What's yours?"

The more I knew him, the more I was sure. He was hardworking and prosperous, young and good-looking, merry and even-tempered, and strong—all the things I had wanted for Bramble. For the length of that Winterfair we were together, even after I'd sold all my cloth, for there was a heavy snowfall and the roads were blocked. So we walked together and talked together, and mostly what we talked about was Bramble. I told him about my sister: her beauty, her wildness, how she had never cared for a man, nor deigned to even smile at a suitor. For my grandmother had once told me that men love to hunt what they cannot have, so I made Bramble seem aloof and uncatchable—like a pure white hind in the forest—and that was the truth, after all.

Perhaps Grandam was right, for when the snow stopped and the roads were cleared, Merrick asked my permission to journey back to the village with me, to meet my family. The town clerk beamed and Merrick's sister kissed me on the cheek, and filled my knapsack with freshly baked bread and russet apples.

It was a happy journey. Merrick kept me laughing all the way, and when we were not laughing, we talked, comfortably, about timber: oak and ash and beech, pale, smooth lime, and rare, fragrant cedar. Then we laughed again.

But oddly, the closer I came to the village, the heavier my heart became. When finally we stood outside our front gate, and the door opened and Bramble came flying down the path to meet us with bare feet and black eyes and red cheeks, I couldn't bear to look at Merrick in case my plan had worked after all, and he was bewitched by her beauty and charm.

And maybe he would have been if he'd met Bramble first, black hair bright against the snow and red lips smiling. For Bramble, there was no doubt, was intrigued by him. She sat at his feet in front of the fire and made him laugh, and pelted him with questions about the city, and being the town clerk's son, and traveling as a journeyman, and seeing the wide world, and about life and death and even, once, about love. It seemed to me that we all stopped, breathless, to hear his answer.

He shook his head, laughing. "My mother always said I had a heart of oak," he said. "No softness in it for any maid." He reached out and brushed a flake of ash, casually, from my shoulder.

That was the moment when I realized that, Bramble or no Bramble, I was going to marry Merrick, and if I had to support her for the rest of my life to pay for it, then I would.

So we married and I moved to town, but underneath my joy was always the nagging worry—what would happen to Bramble? And then she went on the Road and my worry grew, for who knew what might happen to her out there? But there was no use trying to stop her, for nothing and no one ever has, nor ever will.

ASH

A WEEK AFTER their visit to the jeweler's, Doronit called Hildie and Ash into her office from the training floor.

Hildie slipped through the door without knocking and Ash, looming over her, followed, carrying his knives and staves. He was coming along well, Doronit thought. Improving rapidly at singlestave and knifework, and learning to read and write surprisingly quickly. He'd actually be making her real money soon. And then there were his *special* gifts...though it wasn't time for those yet. He had to be bound even more firmly to her. And this assignment might be another knot in that rope.

She smiled at them impartially, the boss's smile. "You know Martine, the stonecaster?"

Hildie nodded, Ash shook his head.

"Lives down near the shambles," Hildie said to him. "Got a good name. Accurate, like."

"She has the Sight, apparently," Doronit said, "and has Seen a...an attempt on her life. Soon."

"Ranny?" Hildie said sharply.

Doronit shrugged. "It doesn't matter who's behind it. Martine wants us to provide protection. You two can take the first watch. And no staves. We don't carry staves through the city without good cause. Knives will do. Off you go."

She let them turn to the door, then she called Ash back. "There will be death tonight, Ash. The stonecaster saw it. Make sure it isn't yours."

He nodded, grave-faced, and followed Hildie.

Doronit was only a little worried. She'd made the caster check that he'd be safe and, though no casting could be relied upon entirely, Martine had said that Ash should come through the encounter intact. She was less sure about Hildie. Doronit wasn't so concerned; risk was the nature of her business, and anyway, Hildie didn't have the same gifts as Ash. Those were... well, not irreplaceable, but rare. Very rare.

She went to the corner of the room where a concealed panel in the floor hid her cashbox, and deposited Martine's payment. She smiled, as always, at the sight of her treasures. She had hiding places all through the house and outbuildings, and in other places too, and she felt safe every time she looked at them. They reassured her that she'd never go without a meal or decent clothes, even if she lived to be a hundred. She'd been dressed in castoffs and rags for too long when she first came to Turvite. She smoothed the fine wool of her trousers under her hands and smiled again, then closed the panel and went to inspect the Dung brothers' attempts at archery.

Hildie led the way to Martine's through part of the city Ash had rarely visited, the oldest part, which predated Acton's invasion. They went through a small open space not far from the docks, which Ash had never seen before, but it set his nerves strumming. He had heard of this place: Doronit had mentioned it, laughing. His father had once taught him a song about it, a song of melancholy chords and dying cadences. In a past so long ago that even the stone-dwellers who live under the cliffs had forgotten, the place was once a ford over an open stream, the song said, and next to the stream was a black rock, a sky-born rock, where the local gods came to meet their worshippers.

The tip of the black rock still jutted through the cobbles

and gravel of modern Turvite, no more than two hands' width showing above the ground. Next to it, encircled by roots, stood the only full-grown tree in the city, throwing around it in summer an umbrella of green. It looked both incongruous and right, that oak tree, Ash thought. It towered over the cottages around it, out of place, out of scale. Yet if he looked only at the tree, he could see its shapeliness. The sweep of its branches had grace, and the yellowing leaves were pale flames against the sky.

Even in the heat of summer, though, Turviters did not sit under that tree. As Ash and Hildie went through, he noticed that others passed by almost as though they hadn't seen it. The song had said that Turviters never spoke of the place to each other nor mentioned it to visitors. The open space had no name, although every other crumb of the busy cake had a label, every crooked alley and dead-end street in the city had a name.

Ash could feel the tree at his back as they went into a small side street, could sense the black rock sitting there, its power seething. How could the Turviters ignore it? It called him back with a whisper of many voices saying his name. The voices were cajoling, inviting, familiar, like the voice he had heard in the cradle, the voice he heard in his own head. He had to force himself to go on with Hildie, feeling a cold sweat crawl down his back.

As they disappeared into the winding streets, the voices died, disappointed, like a wind dropping. He found himself walking more briskly, as though while he had heard the voices they had drained him, but now his energy returned. What would have happened if he'd gone back? *I won't go back,* he thought, *not ever.* But a part of him, a small trickle of desire, sent his thoughts back to the tree and the rock. He knew he would be able to point in its direction no matter where he was in the city, as though it were a lodestone and he a compass needle.

"Were you talking about Ranny of Highmark?" he asked Hildie, to take his mind off the altar stone.

"Mmmm."

Ash had never met Ranny. He'd heard stories: she was wild, profligate, ruthless, intelligent enough to know when others were more intelligent and to hire the best minds she could find. She was the head of a large merchant family that spread over half the world.

"She wants Martine dead. Tried to hire Dufe to kill her."

Dufe was a safeguarder Ash met occasionally in the taverns. He had worked for Doronit briefly before Ash had come to Turvite.

"Why?"

Hildie shrugged. "Goes back to a reading Martine did for her, they say. Told her she knew the day and the time of her death, and the cause of it, but wouldn't tell her anything more. Said it were against her code."

"It is," Ash nodded. "There's no stonecaster born will tell you the time you're to die. They say it takes all the joy out of living."

"Ranny reckoned she'd avoid her death altogether. Be somewhere else. She offered Martine...well, she offered her a lot, just to tell her *where* she was going to die. So she could avoid the place. But Martine wouldn't do it."

Ash grinned. "Traveler's proverb: 'He who runs away from Death has Her as a traveling companion.'"

"Tell Ranny that."

"I still don't understand why Ranny wants Martine dead."

"Because if Ranny can't know the time of her death, no one's going to know. That's what she said."

"How do you know?"

"Dufe told me."

Ash laughed to himself. Ranny had picked the wrong man there. Dufe was as far from a killer for hire as a safeguarder could be, which made him wonder if he'd ever gone through one of Doronit's tests in the back alleys of Turvite. Would he have killed the girl thief? Somehow Ash didn't think he would have walked down the alley in the first place. Maybe that was why Doronit had fired him.

They reached the stonecaster's house at dusk. It was a small house in the middle of the old part of town, with the caster's sign outside: an outsize canvas pouch hanging from the balcony, which jutted out over the street. He would have known anyway—there was a ragged circle of ghosts standing back from the door, waiting to be let in. Most of them were standing in the middle of the road, but they didn't care—ghosts in Turvite were used to being walked through without so much as a by-your-leave.

Martine was on the balcony looking down at them, so the first sight he had of her was her face upside down, with long dark hair falling either side so that it was like looking up a tunnel, with her pale face the light at the end. She seemed very tall.

"Push it," she said. "It's always open." Her voice was strong, but with an undertone of sweetness, like fresh mead.

The ghosts eddied and moved forward, but only one came to the door with them. The stonecaster must have spelled the door. It was often done. A ghost could only enter if it had some connection with the human visitor.

Hildie held the door open for Ash but he waited for the ghost to go ahead of him. Ash swallowed hard, to stop his gorge rising. It was the girl he had killed, clear as day, with the strong paleness of the newly dead, as though someone had drawn her with white wax on a black slate. He could see through her, of course, but it was like seeing through mist, or through a cobweb. He hung back, but she gestured him forward and he realized that the spell meant that he had to go in first, with the ghost following behind him in a wave of cold and burial cave stench.

He went past her with that chill that he always felt passing a spirit, and stepped through the door with all the prickles raised on his spine. They didn't seem to affect the Turviters. He supposed that if you were surrounded by ghosts from the time you were born, you got used to them. He'd been pleased, when he first came to Turvite, to find that everyone could see the ghosts. In most places he'd been the only one, he and his mother, although she always acted as if she couldn't see them. In Turvite the ghosts were so strong that everyone knew they were there—they were proud of them.

He turned in time to see the ghost slide in behind him. Hildie kept the door open for a moment more before following, as though she wasn't quite sure if the ghost were entering or not, then closed it with the snap of a good latch.

The room was bright with lamplight and firelight shining on pale yellow walls and bright blue painted woodwork. There was a frieze of leaping fish against the yellow around the ceiling. It was like coming into daylight after the dim dusk of the street. Ash blinked and looked away from the ghost.

The stonecaster had come down to meet them. She *was* tall, with very white skin and long green eyes. A strange, foreign face in this city of yellow hair and blue eyes, but beautiful in its own way. She held her head very high. Ash was reminded of the stories of the Lake People, the only people of the old blood who had withstood Acton's invasion. They were said to hold their heads like that, proud and undefeated. Most Travelers looked down, not up, in case their glance was seen as insolence and invited a curse or a blow. Ash had been taught by his parents to look, not down, but sideways, to keep his chin pointed ahead rather than up. "No need to invite trouble," his father had said, and his mother had been in a dark mood all that day.

The stonecaster looked at the ghost and sighed. "Well? What is this?" she asked Hildie.

"I killed her," Ash answered.

The stonecaster turned to look at him, and as her green eyes met his, he felt the same churning in his stomach that he felt with Doronit, and the same confusion, and a kind of recognition. These, like Doronit's, were eyes that he knew, and more, she had a pattern of speech and lilting voice almost completely obscured by Turviter inflection, but still there—a palimpsest of an earlier tale. That voice brought back nights on the Road around the fire circle, and stories and songs in a language the Turviters would not have understood.

"She was trying to kill me," he added, carefully suppressing everything but the business at hand. He turned to the ghost. "Weren't you?"

The ghost looked at him blankly.

He wasn't going to let her get away with that. His voice sharpened. *"Weren't you?"*

Reluctantly, the ghost opened her mouth. "Aye."

As always, it was a deep, scraping voice like rock on steel, a sound that sent shivers down to the fingertips. The three humans shuddered as one, and Hildie looked shocked and a little worried. She looked at Ash as if she'd never seen him before.

"Didn't know they could talk," she said.

The stonecaster raised an eyebrow, not at the ghost, but at Ash. She didn't seem surprised. "Well. Sit, then."

The ghost, Martine and Ash sat on the rug. He could faintly see the yellow and blue of the wool through the ghost's body.

Hildie took a breath, recovering her normal calm. "Naught to do with me," she shrugged. "I'm here to keep watch." She dropped the bar across the door and produced a wooden wedge from her pouch to fix it firmly in place, then moved to the window that gave onto the street. She settled into the window seat, turning her head from left to right and back again in a slow, steady scan.

Martine spat in her left palm and held it out to the ghost, who laid her own hand into it. Ash could see the shudder go through Martine at the touch; he knew that feeling, that sudden scent of earth and touch of cold stone.

The caster produced her pouch of stones and with her right hand threw five of them on the rug. The stones fell across the pattern, and every one of them landed on the yellow. And every one of them was facedown.

Ash stared at them as she turned them over.

"Death. Hidden Death. That's yours," she said to the ghost. The ghost nodded.

"Then Flight. Danger. Liberation." She turned the last stone over and hesitated.

"What is it?" he asked.

"Death of the soul," Martine said softly. She looked up into the empty eyes of the ghost. "This is him, not you."

"I don't understand," Ash said.

Martine became brisk. "These stones tell the story of her death: Death, Flight—that's you running away—and Liberation. I would say that this young woman is finding death more pleasant than life."

The ghost nodded. Ash felt a stab of pity go through him.

"I'm...sorry," he ventured, and looked for a moment too deeply into the ghost's eyes and grew dizzy.

"So," Martine said. "She has come to pay her debt to you by warning you. You are in danger—danger of losing your soul, losing who the gods want you to be. Do you understand?"

"But...from what?"

The ghost shook her head at him, smiling in derision.

He got angry. Even the ghosts were laughing at him now. *"From what?"* he shouted at her.

The dead voice came again, reluctantly. "From who, cully," it said. And that was all. The pale, young face faded away, still smiling.

Martine let her left hand fall back into her lap. "That one is gone for good," she said. "She's paid her debt and left. It was well done." She looked at him curiously. "It seems you lead an interesting life, young man."

Hildie, standing beside the window, whistled sharply. Ash was on his feet with his dagger out, his back flat to the wall behind the door, before his mind even registered the danger signal.

"Three of 'em," Hildie said. "They was keeping watch behind the baker's. Man and a boy, at the door. One's gone round the back, quick as bedamned. He's the one to ware of."

Hildie had never tried to sound like a Turviter, Ash thought, then shook his head. *"Irrelevant,"* he could hear Doronit say. "Concentrate or die."

There was a knock at the door. Martine moved toward it, looking questioningly at Hildie. Hildie signaled for her to stay still. Ash heard the faint shuffle of feet behind the door. He nodded to Hildie and she slipped out to the back room.

Martine collected the cast stones and put them back into her pouch. She hesitated, then sat back cross-legged on the rug and cast the stones again. All were facedown. She didn't bother to turn them over, simply collected them, dropped them into the pouch and reached in for five more. She seemed too calm.

Ash pulled his attention away from her. The knock came again, harder.

"Stonecaster, ho!" a deep voice called. A hand tried the door latch then jiggled it impatiently.

Poor training, he thought, one ear cocked for sounds from the back room. Then he heard the muffled scratch of boots on the roof. On the balcony. He whistled low to Hildie, *watch out,* and went to the stairs, flattening himself against the wall so he would be invisible from above.

The rattling of the latch grew louder. The bar began to lift a little with each jerk. The wedge that Hildie had jammed in would soon bounce out of its socket. He wanted to call to Martine, but it was too late. There were feet on the stairs. Almost silent. And fast.

Ash moved as the man hesitated at the bottom of the stairs, looking through the doorway to where Martine sat, casting the stones, her dark head bent. The men in the street were swinging the door latch as hard as they could. He knew what the man on the stairs was considering: do it now or wait until the others break in?

Ash moved. He slammed against the man shoulder to shoulder and sent him sprawling across the floor. But the man was quick, and rolled and came back to his feet in an instant, dagger ready. Martine retreated to the hearth, holding a white-handled dagger behind her skirt, and the pouch in her other hand ready, it seemed, to throw in the fire.

Ash felt his concentration narrowing, as it always did in a knife fight, blocking out everything except the other's blade, the muscles of his chest where movement would first be seen, the play of his feet. In this circle of tension it was curiously silent. "Don't look at the face," he heard Doronit say in his head. "Don't engage until you're ready to kill. If you're not ready to kill, don't fight with a knife."

The other man was cautious, too, but all he had to do was

delay until the others broke the latch. Ash had to move fast. He feinted right, dropped to one knee and struck up as the man moved to block him. The dagger went up under the ribs. Doronit had shown him the spot, had traced it on his bare skin with one finger.

The door latch broke as he pulled the dagger out and blood splashed over the blue and yellow rug. The man fell.

The two from the street charged in. The boy headed toward Martine but halted when she raised her knife. The man centered on Ash, his dagger poised. There was no sound but hard breathing. The man was bigger than him, huskier, and with a much longer reach. That was bad.

They faced each other across the corpse. Ash crouched, dagger edge out and ready. The other gazed at his face. *Mistake,* Ash thought, as he reversed the knife and threw it. *Bad mistake, cully.* "When you throw to kill," Doronit had said, "aim for the throat. It's the only spot you can be sure the knife will go in." She was always right.

The dagger went in through the voice box and the man was choking to death, clawing at his throat and turning blue, taking final gasping breaths. Ash knelt on the man's chest and drew out the knife, cutting the big artery as he went. His hand was quite steady. He had time to wonder at that.

Behind him he heard scuffling as Hildie sprang from the stairs to deal with the boy.

"No!" Martine said. "Just hold him."

Ash turned. Hildie was about to cut the boy's throat. Martine's knife was already in his shoulder, the hilt sticking out stark white against the blood. The boy was in his twenties, pale-haired, like most Turviters, but with large dark eyes that spoke of other blood, and a face all smooth skin and fine bones. Ash swallowed against the sudden block in his throat. The boy's eyes were searching everywhere for an escape and flinched away from the bodies of his two colleagues.

"Now," Martine said, and pulled the dagger out from his shoulder. The blood flowed after it, sluggishly, and the boy turned as white as the hilt. "Who sent you?"

There were two corpses on her floor, but her voice was calm. Too calm, her breath too even. It was the voice of someone who had seen events so terrible that nothing would ever be able to shock her again. He was reminded of Doronit, and the thought surprised him. What had Doronit seen that was so terrible?

The boy was silent.

"The mootstaff will not care if I have three corpses instead of two," Martine said. "Who sent you?"

Hildie pricked his throat with the knife.

"Ranny," the boy whispered.

Martine relaxed. "Thank you," she said.

Hildie tightened her grip on the knife and looked to Martine for instructions. Martine jerked her head toward the door. Hildie loosened her grip. The boy bolted for the street, rushing through the crowd of mingled ghosts and neighbors who were staring at them through the doorway.

There was nothing left but the cleaning up. The bright yellow and blue rug was ruined. Ash helped roll it up with shaking hands. ("A reaction, and perfectly normal," came Doronit's voice in his memory, "but try not to let the customer see — it undermines their confidence in us.") He thought he managed to hide them from Martine, though Hildie cocked an eye at him. Once he was used to scenes like this, as she was, the shaking wouldn't happen. He hoped. He was almost sure he hoped it.

Hildie fetched the mootstaff leader, Boc, who came with a handcart to take the bodies out to the graveyard (no burial caves for these ones). Boc was relieved to know there was no problem with the deaths. "Housebreakers coming by their just deserts," he said, nodding, as Martine explained, and asked Hildie to give his regards to Doronit. Doronit kept in well with Boc.

The mootstaff were supposed to keep the peace, but there was far too much crime on the streets of Turvite for a handful of men to control. That was why safeguarders were needed. And Turvite lived by the old laws, as did all of the free towns: you could—you *should*—defend your home to the death against all comers, even if all they had in mind was a little pilfering. Ash had sometimes wondered if it dated back to the invasion, when, if you didn't defend your home, you were dead.

Boc left with a helper trundling the handcart along the cobbles. And that was all. Hildie nodded to Martine and made for the door, but Martine put her hand out to stop Ash from following her.

"Three days' time," she said. "Be here."

He nodded and followed Hildie.

Doronit was pleased with them, he knew by the way she smiled gently at him. She was less pleased when she heard he would need to go back in three nights.

"That's the festival. We're booked at the Town Moot." She shrugged. "Well, get it over with early and join us there. We can't get a reputation for failing to clean up after ourselves."

The next day, Doronit sent Ash back to Martine to escort her on a visit to Ranny of Highmark.

"Ranny makes a bad enemy and we don't want to antagonize her," Doronit said to Ash before he left. "Just be businesslike toward Martine, not friendly, you understand?"

The Highmarks were a smallish, tight clan, Doronit had explained. Ranny had two brothers, younger than she and not as bright. Her father was dead, and her mother remarried to a Reacher from the mansion next door, a good marriage with fine trade concessions attached. Ranny ruled Highmark under the eyes of her grandparents, both physically hale and still sharp-minded but disinclined to continue running the business day-to-day.

Highmark ancestors included four mayors and eighteen town clerks—the family knew where power resided and preferred it to pomp and ceremony. They took their name from the golden mansion at the very top of the hill overlooking Turvite, the first to be built at that height and still the second biggest.

It seemed to Ash, as they stood outside Highmark, that Martine was unimpressed. "This won't take long, I just need to talk to her," she said. "What is your name, anyway?"

"Ash," he said, startled to realize that after all that had happened, they were still virtually strangers. He felt as though they had known each other much longer than a single day.

"Well, Ash, maybe we can sort this out without more killing."

Ash stood to one side as Martine knocked at the door and asked to see Ranny. They were let in straightaway by a young woman with chestnut hair and hard eyes who kept her hand near her belt knife and made them walk down the corridor ahead of her to the office.

Ranny was a slight, fair-haired woman with the pale blue eyes you only got when there was no Traveler blood at all in the family. She looked the opposite to Martine in every way.

Ash took up the standard safeguarder position just inside the room. The chestnut-haired girl stood on the other side of the door in the same position. They nodded to each other, the careful, deliberate nod that said, "Neither of us wants any trouble here but we're both ready for it." Her hand kept going to her knife and Ash realized that she was nervous of him. Then he remembered that he had killed two of her…what, colleagues? Either way, to her he was dangerous. A part of him was pleased to be thought dangerous by a pretty girl, but he brought his attention back to Martine and Ranny.

They were facing each other. Martine seemed to radiate calm over the desk to the other woman. It didn't work.

Ranny glared at her, her hands fidgeting with a stick of sealing wax. "What's the point of you coming here?" she demanded.

"I hoped to negotiate a truce."

Ranny snorted. "Fine. Tell me what I want to know and we'll have a truce."

Martine had considered it, she had told Ash on the walk there. But to tell someone the date of their death was to blight their life. And surely Ranny deserved it now, Ash thought, had invited it, even, by trying to kill her? Still, a swift death and rebirth was one thing; a living death, tormented, was another…

Martine shook her head and made her voice gentle. "You won't believe me, but I keep that secret out of a wish to not hurt you more than I have done so far."

"You should never have told me that you knew!"

Martine bowed her head so that the curtain of black hair hid her face. "That is true. I should have concealed it from you. But I was surprised it was there, so clear in the stones."

Ranny scowled at her. "Hypocrite!" she hissed. "No decent stonecaster would ever let someone know that they had discovered the date of a death."

"That is true," Martine said.

"Well then!" Ranny exclaimed. She got up from the desk and paced around the room. "Just tell me *when*. If I knew when, I could plan."

Ash could see Ranny's dilemma: should she have children if she wouldn't live long enough to bring them up? Should she have them immediately so that her bloodline would continue? Should she train one of her brothers to take over so the family wouldn't suffer when she died? Or, if she outlived them, would training one to rule, when he would never get a chance, sour and embitter him?

"I need to *know*," she said. "You owe it to me."

"You tried to kill me," Martine replied.

"You ruined my life. I can't sleep, I can't work... With you dead, I could at least be back where everyone else is, with no way of finding out."

"Ah..." Martine was startled at that explanation, but it was one Ash understood. Yes, there was a logic and even a justice in it. Martine nodded, also understanding.

"You think you can choose for me, but I should be able to choose for myself," Ranny said. "You are treating me like a child because you have the Gift and I don't."

There was enough truth in that, too, to give Martine pause. Stonecasters did tend to look on their clients like children to be guided, but not by them—by the stones. Had Martine allowed herself to become arrogant, to make choices that rightfully belonged to Ranny?

Ash looked into the pretty blue eyes and saw ambition, anger, ruthlessness, but not much wisdom. Perhaps Martine was treating Ranny like a child, but it might be that it was safer to do so.

"I need to know *when*," Ranny said.

Martine shook her head.

"Then you're going to die."

Ranny walked out of the room and the girl escorted them silently to the front door.

Ash was on full alert the whole way back to Martine's, wish-

120

ing that Doronit had sent Hildie or Aelred as well, to guard their backs. It was a relief to shut the door of Martine's house behind them.

"Do you think I did the right thing?" Martine asked, handing Ash his payment.

Ash paused. "I don't know," he said eventually. "I would probably have told her, but—she doesn't look like a woman who would accept any fate. If you told her, you'd be setting her off on a path to avoid her death, and then…"

"'She who runs away from Death has Her as a traveling companion,'" Martine said.

Ash nodded. "You know that's true."

"Yes," Martine said, relaxing a little. "I know less every day, but that I do know." She smiled. "Thank you, Ash. I'll see you in two days."

After Ash had killed the men at Martine's, he found his mind returning to one point of the night: the moment when Hildie had pressed the point of the knife against the boy's throat, and looked at Martine for instructions. If Martine had said, "Kill him," what would Hildie have done? He shied away from the thought, not wanting to imagine himself in Hildie's place, but it drew him back, time and again, during singlestave practice, on his runs along the sea cliffs, at night. Was that expected of safeguarders? To kill if the client said so?

It was autumn. The days were bright and crisp, the sea was glowing ultramarine, as it did near festival time, and crashing higher against the cliffs at the full of each tide. It seemed a time of clarity and light. But his mind kept returning to that yellow and blue room.

Other thoughts of the boy kept coming back—of his dark

eyes and smooth skin. They were eyes like his own. Ash slept badly and, when he did sleep, he dreamed of Doronit standing by smiling while he killed the boy. By festival night he was twitchy and couldn't concentrate. Doronit dismissed him to the stonecaster's with a frown that made his stomach drop into his boots.

"Go on, then, get yourself quit of these spirits. Come to the Town Moot as soon as you can."

She was dressed for the festival, her face painted with expensive silver tint, her clothes ghost-pale and flowing. She looked very beautiful, he thought, staring helplessly at her. She ran her hand down his arm, making his skin tickle and his eyes burn.

"Come soon," she said.

He walked through the streets to Martine's, resenting that he couldn't go with Doronit. He walked with desire running through him and no end to it in sight. *Very well,* he thought. After he finished at Martine's, he'd find himself a brothel and do something about it. If he couldn't have Doronit tonight, he'd have someone else. She didn't have to know. Then he thought of all the things Doronit knew that you didn't expect. All the people who sold her information, or owed her favors. She *would* find out. And then what? Either she'd laugh at him or be angry—he didn't know which was worse.

The streets were full of people enjoying themselves, painted like ghosts, wearing white, or silver if they could afford it. It was a city of happy ghosts. He hadn't wanted to dress up. It wouldn't have been very respectful to the ghosts he was going to meet. Of course, that was the point of the festival, held on the anniversary of Acton's victory over the city, to show the ghosts that no one was afraid of them.

He had been to the festival once before, when he was seven and his parents came to Turvite to perform for the merchants.

He remembered that night vividly. The whole city was full of ghosts, it had seemed to him. He hadn't realized that some silver shapes were actually people in costume. He hadn't understood why he could see through some and not others, why some made so much noise, laughing and singing the "Fly Away Spirit" song, while others drifted silently, shrinking into corners as the revelers careered by.

He remembered his parents practicing in the courtyard of Merchant House earlier in the day. His mother had sung "The Taking of Turvite," while his father played the flute.

Acton killed them all, she chanted.
All on the streets of Turvite
Their spirits rose up with a soundless cry
Their spirits rose up to cry to their gods
The faces of death stalked the streets of Turvite
The faces of death haunted the killers

Then she swung into the chorus, with Alured, their drummer, picking up the beat so that Ash hopped from foot to foot in time.

And the killers laughed!
Yes, they laughed!
And Acton laughed loudest of all.

He had tried to sing along, but, as always, his mother had laid a finger across her lips, not before he had seen a spasm of pain pass over his father's face. Looking back, he realized that that was the last time he had tried to sing for his parents. It was the day he had understood that he would never be a singer, as he yearned to be. If he was going to be a musician, he would have to play the flute like his father.

The sun was setting when he reached the stonecaster's house.

There was only one ghost left there, a thin, old wraith who looked as if he had seen a thousand festivals. Ash nodded to him and the ghost nodded back. Behind the ghost, the sky was a mixture of orange and gold, a real autumn sunset. It cheered him and he knocked at the door with more energy than he'd felt for days.

Martine let him in. The bloodstained rug had been replaced by a mat of lambskins, gleaming white in the lamplight. Martine sat cross-legged on the edge of the mat, and gestured for him to sit beside her. He sat aware of her long hands and hooded eyes. There was a darkness in the way her blood moved in her veins, as though she carried a secret.

"It's not always three days to the minute," she said. "Sometimes it takes a few hours. But then, this isn't the first quickening you've been to, is it?"

Ash shook his head and was aware, by the lift of Martine's eyebrow, that the answer had made him seem more of a killer than he really was, but didn't want to explain his past any further. He didn't want to talk about his parents. Musicians were often asked to quickenings in the far west of the country. There, the people believed that soft music helped the spirit on its way, especially the spirits of those killed by accident or violence or sudden illness. These were the ones who quickened back into the waking world. His mother had taught him that the other spirits, who had nothing left unsaid, went on to be reborn straightaway. Although the ghost was said to quicken three days after its death, his parents had often played through the night or through the day before the ghost had appeared. Outside Turvite, a quickening was the only time that most people could see a ghost, not that those spirits had been as...vivid as they were in Turvite. Turvite had the strongest ghosts in the world.

"You have old blood in your face," Martine said, studying

him. For a moment he thought she meant real blood, branding him a killer. She saw his confusion. "I mean, you have the look of the ones who were in this land before—the original inhabitants."

He felt forced into an explanation. "I'm a Trav—my parents was, were, Travelers. Musicians. They say that when Acton and his men came, a lot of the old people took the road, having no land of their own left to them."

"Yes," Martine said, brooding. "That is so. Did you know that that is why you can see the ghosts?"

"Everyone can see them here!" he protested. He had no mind to be any more set apart than he already was by his dark hair and eyes.

Martine smiled at him and shook her head. "No. In Turvite, where the ghosts are strong, everyone can detect...something. A shimmer in the air, a scent on the wind, a paleness where there should be darkness. Sometimes they catch a glimpse of eyes, hair, a hand. They feel cold as they pass. That's all."

"But the Turviters talk about the ghosts all the time. They're so clear here! It's like looking at...at white people."

"That is so for me, for you. I think for Doronit. For one in a thousand, perhaps. And only one in a thousand thousand can make them speak, as you did three nights ago. I cannot."

Ash believed her and was saddened. One of the things he loved about Turvite was that everyone else could see ghosts; he'd spent his whole life seeing things that others couldn't. But he had never understood how the people of Turvite could just walk straight through ghosts as if they weren't there. They seemed proud of their ghosts and proud of their indifference to them. The children of Acton, they called themselves. Acton, who had been faced by the ghosts—thousands upon thousands of the slaughtered Turviters whom he and his men had killed—and had laughed them down. "If we could vanquish you alive," he had said, "why should we be frightened of you dead?" And his people had moved into Turvite and taken it over from cellars to attics, had lived ham by haunch with the spirits of the dispossessed and had grown proud of it.

Ever since then, those who died in Turvite, even Acton's people, had strong ghosts. Ash's father had told him that it was a relic of the spell used to call up the Turviters' ghosts after the battle with Acton and his men. An enchanter who lived in Turvite had tried to give the ghosts physical strength, so that they could continue to fight. "She failed," his father had said, "but the ghosts became strong in other ways—they persisted, they could be seen or sensed by everyone." Acton's men cornered her on the cliffs north of the harbor, but Acton forbade anyone to kill her, in case that made the ghosts fade. He wanted his people to live with a reminder of their victory. He laughed as he said it, and she cursed him—he would never have what he most wanted—but he shrugged and said that he already had it, and gestured to the city. Then she shook her head and smiled a smile of sweet revenge and jumped off the cliffs.

No one knew her name now, and Ash supposed it didn't matter anyhow, because she was wrong. Acton lived for years afterward and by all accounts was a happy man. It was he who started the Ghost Begone Festival at the autumn equinox, when they found that the enchanter's death hadn't made the ghosts go away after all, and there were more every day as Acton's own people died, until there was no corner of Turvite inhabited by more people than ghosts.

Outside Martine's, the sound of the festival was growing louder. A party of young women went by singing "Fly Away Spirit" in high, sweet voices. Ash thought of his mother, who could see spirits just as he could, and sang higher and sweeter than any other voice on the Road. His throat tightened. He wondered where she was singing tonight, what accompaniment his father was providing. He wondered if they felt freer, happier, without him...and thought they probably did.

Then the ghosts quickened.

The big man roused first, solidifying on the floor as he had lain in the first moment after death. Ash saw the pale shape grow before him: white, transparent, but recognizably the same burly, hairy figure who had crashed through Martine's door. He sat up and struggled to his feet as though he still had a body. New ghosts were always like that. They acted as though they still had muscles and bones attached to their will. The older ones just floated, drifted wherever they chose, from floor to ceiling.

The ghost looked around, searching for his friend. The new rug confused him. He tried to touch it, saw his hand pass through the white tufts, and screamed. His mouth opened, the muscles of his face in a rictus of horror. But no sound came out.

Ash was crying hard, hot tears. There was too much pain in this face. He forgot, for a moment, that this man had been a killer for hire and had tried to kill him.

The ghost saw them. He stilled then moved for his dagger. It was gone. He held up his hands to show them he was unarmed. It seemed he thought they were still in the middle of the fight.

"It is three days later," Martine said quietly to him. "You are dead. This is your quickening."

"*No,*" he mouthed, and shook his head.

"Yes," Martine answered. "This is your killer."

Remembrance flooded over his face as he looked at Ash—remembrance and hate and grief. He looked again, frantically, for his colleague, then turned to Martine with pleading hands.

"He will come. Wait."

So they waited, Martine and Ash sitting still, the ghost rubbing his face against his hands, shaking his head, crying without sound, mouthing *no,* and what looked like *Dukka,* over and over.

Dukka came. He formed and solidified just like the first, but then rolled and jumped to his feet, his dagger ready in his hand. They had not been able to pry it from his grasp before the moot-staff took him away.

"Wait," Martine said. She rose and confronted him, pointed to his friend. "Look. He is dead. You are dead."

Dukka turned slowly to his friend.

"Speak to him, oh gods, *speak,*" Ash whispered to himself. He couldn't bear any more silent screaming.

"Hwit," Dukka said, the harsh ghost voice grating on the nerves as it always did. "Oh, my boy."

The two spirits moved toward each other and attempted to touch. But even a ghost cannot touch another ghost. Their hands passed through each other's faces. They cried aloud.

They turned to him.

"You," Dukka spat. "You killed him."

Martine intervened. "You were, if you remember, trying to kill him."

Astonishingly, Hwit let out a laugh. "True for you," he said, and his voice was the same, exactly the same, as the dead voice of the smaller man. Even though Ash was expecting it, it was always hard to hear that the voices of the dead were all alike, as though identity could not survive past the door of death.

Hwit grinned at Dukka. "Fair's fair," he said. "At least we're together."

For a moment Hwit held his friend's gaze, and the anger seemed to drain out of him. "Fair's fair. Knife cuts knife," he said.

They both turned to Ash. He had been to enough quickenings, so he knew what to do.

"I am your killer," he said to them. "Lo, I proclaim it, it were I who took your lives from you. I am here to offer reparation—blood for blood."

He pushed up his left sleeve and held out his arm, then took his dagger and cut the skin just above his wrist. His hands were steady, but his body was shaking as though with cold. The blood welled out slowly, dark red. It caught the lamplight.

Dukka moved forward and bent his head to the cut. Hwit laughed and joined him so that the two pale tongues reached his flesh and touched, granting their bodies only enough solidity at this moment to taste the blood of their killer, and enough to touch each other, once more.

The burial cave smell arose around Ash and he almost choked. The touch of the ghosts' tongues was ice, hot ice, cold fire. He trembled.

The ghosts raised their heads. As soon as they left contact with his blood they were wraiths again and the final drops of blood fell from their lips straight through their bodies to the rug.

"I release you," Dukka said.

"And I." Hwit leaned forward. "One day you'll follow us, lad."

The dead voice made it sound like a threat, but was it? Martine bared her arm and raised her dagger, but Dukka shook his head.

"It was because of me Ash was here. I am responsible," she said.

Dukka shrugged.

She snapped at Ash, "Get him to *speak* to me."

"Speak," Ash whispered.

"We release you," Hwit said. "We don't need any more. Blood must be spilled, but one killer's blood is enough."

And they faded.

"Just like that?" Ash squeaked, and then coughed to clear his voice. "That's it?"

"That's all," she said. "They were generous, those two. I suppose they recognized a fellow professional. Knife cuts knife, as he said."

That made him feel worse than anything else he had done. "Those *voices*," he said, shuddering. "I hate those voices worst of all."

Martine looked at him and repeated the Traveler proverb, "From the grave, all speak alike."

"Well, they shouldn't," Ash said.

Ash stood at the bottom of the Moot Hall steps looking up. The Moot glowed orange at every window with lamp- and firelight. The music was loudest here, drums thumped out a jig-and-spin, an old one that he recognized, the "Drunken Tailor." There were very few songs or dances that he didn't know, though he couldn't play any of them himself. He'd been no better a flautist than a singer. He could feel the music in him, but he couldn't bring it out. He couldn't even dance in time.

His parents had tried to make the best of it by getting him to drum for them. He'd been able to do it, barely, but not by feeling it. He had to watch his father's hands on the strings or the note holes and match his own hands to their stroke. It had been good enough for taverns and country towns, but not for places like Turvite and Carlion, not for warlords' courts, where they made a good deal of their money.

Then one night, not far from Turvite, the three of them had met up with another Traveler, a drummer, who was camped at the site they had planned to use, a common with a stream and a copse nearby for firewood.

His parents had hesitated as they caught sight of the stranger already encamped, but he had looked up and smiled and said, "Fire and water" — the Travelers' greeting. "Fire and water and a roof in the rain," Ash's mother had said. So they moved down to the campfire and shared their food and some stories as well. Inevitably, after dinner his father had drawn out the flute, and the other drummer, after waiting politely for Ash to find his drum, had pulled out a small tambour.

They had started with songs everyone knew: ballads and drinking songs, cradle and teaching songs. The drummer had played with his blood and his soul, and Ash had known by the end of the second song that his parents needed someone who could play like this, who could lay down the dark heart of the song behind the melody, could call out the dancing feet. By the third song he had known that he would never play the drum again, never pretend that he might be good enough someday, with enough practice. By the fourth song they had forgotten him altogether, and after the fifth they had started talking excitedly of where they could go next, to play together.

Ash had gone off, away from the fire, and fallen asleep wrapped in his blanket, as he had almost every night of his life, but this time knowing that the next day would be the end of the only life he had known.

Over breakfast, his mother had noted his quietness and hesitated, clearly weighing what to say. He hadn't wanted to hear it.

"I'd better find something else to do with my life, right?" he said. Though he had tried to keep the bitterness out of his voice, he hadn't quite succeeded. It had banished any softness from his mother's face.

"You heard. You have ears, even if you can't play," she said. "He's what we need."

"It will free you to do something else," his father said. "After all, lad, how can you be happy doing something you don't love?"

Ash had stared at him, astonished that he hadn't understood, that he mustn't have understood Ash at all to be able to say that.

"I do love it," he said. "I just can't do it as well as you."

It had taken both mother and father aback—they were musicians born, not made, and although they practiced daily, obsessively, it had never occurred to them that someone could love the actual making of music and yet not be good at it. To love music was the basis of being human, of course, but to love the making, the crafting—they had thought the love and the skill went together.

Typically, his mother had been the first ro recover. "We'll find you another trade that you can love," she said.

But they hadn't, of course, because no one except Doronit had wanted a gangly nineteen-year-old whose only skills were a poor hand on a drum and a memory crammed with every song known on the Road. So Ash had learned to be a killer, and wondered, now, if this was a craft that those who practiced it loved.

He stopped on the first step of the Moot as a rush of warm air and perfume and food smells swept over him. It was packed; latecomers spilled down the steps and out onto the street, all dancing and singing along. Silver and red and blue painted faces grinned and kissed and warbled, *"He was drunker than a wine vat, drunker than a rotten fart, ooooh, he was the drunken tailor of Pii-ii-say..."*

"An' I loved her, Arvid, I really did," a man wept on his

friend's shoulder at the bottom of the steps. "But she was a lying vixen, just like her mother."

The silver paint was rubbing off on Arvid's jacket. He stroked the man's hair, hand curiously tender, then looked up and met Ash's eyes, and blushed. He stuck his hand back into his pocket.

"Don't worry about her, Braden," he said. "Come inside and get drunk."

"You're my best friend, Arv, my very best friend in the world..."

They turned back up the steps, arms around each other, and blundered into a couple who were kissing as they came down. For a moment Ash thought it was Doronit; she had the same dark hair, the same kind of silver floating dress. He felt as though he'd been kicked in the stomach. Then he realized it wasn't her, but was still awash with his reaction: pounding heart, churning gut, sweating and cold at the same time.

He ran. He kept to the back streets, where there were fewer people, and he ran as hard as he did in training sessions when Doronit was waiting for him. He ran through the markets, alive with food vendors' and winesellers' calls, away from the shouts of those he brushed past, unheeding, and through the curling streets of private houses, with light and ghost pennants streaming from each window. He kept running until he reached the long hill that led to the cliffs outside town.

Everywhere he ran, he saw ghosts.

On the cliff tops they huddled in groups near the edge, waiting for morning. They watched the city lights. Some of them were fading already, although it was nowhere near dawn. That was the purpose of the festival, to cull out the city ghosts, to scare away the weak and insult the strong so they left forever. Without the festival, his father had told him, there would be many more ghosts than people in Turvite. He wondered now what his father saw when he looked at a ghost.

Old and young, big and small, they clung together. There seemed to be nowhere he could go to get away from them, no place he could be alone to think things through. It wasn't fair. It never had been.

He had come to Doronit as though to a safe harbor, a place in the world he could finally make his own. But if it meant he had to be a stone-cold killer, like Dukka and his friend, he wasn't sure he wanted it. Not even for Doronit. He didn't want to be the knife that cuts the knife. But if he didn't become that, what else could he become? There were no doors open to him except this one. He wanted to shout, or protest, but what good would it do? He was a Traveler who had lost the Road, and there was nowhere and nothing else in Acton's land for him.

His mother had taught him never to compel a spirit to speak unless it was really necessary, but that night he didn't care. He faced the multitude of pale forms and threw up his arms. He could feel the power to make them speak flood through him. He had never opened himself to it like this before; it was like a thousand drums beating together, like the crash of the waves on the rocks below, thunderous, overwhelming.

"*Speak!*" he conjured them. "*Speak.*"

Instantly a great moan went up from them. It was the strangest sound he had ever heard, for though it came from a thousand mouths, each made the same sound: dead, grating, harsh as stone on stone, it was a cry of pain. Silence followed as each ghost realized that it had made a true sound, that its screams were no longer silent.

"Speak," he conjured them again, at that moment hating everything, everyone, himself, wanting to hit back, wanting the ghosts to scream his own protests. "Speak all the night through!"

The ghosts cried out again, then turned to the city and began to move toward it. Slowly, then faster. They rushed past him in a wind of cold air, and as they gained speed they made a deep, screeching moan, repeated and modulated. It was the sound of desperation.

He sank down and clasped his hands around his knees. He giggled so that he wouldn't cry. He felt drunk, crazy, lost.

"Hah!" he said. "It may be I shouldn't have done that." And stubbornly, though he knew his voice was harsh, he began to sing "Fly Away Spirit."

BRAMBLE

*S*O IN MY *next life I'm going to get the gods to make me a big blond man,* Bramble thought. *Really big. Really blond. Maybe really stupid, too. Big, blond, stupid men seem to have a good time around here.*

The four big, blond and, quite possibly, stupid men were certainly having a good time standing in the middle of the road and not letting her pass. They were having a good time yelling things, too.

"Show us your teats!" was the favorite of the youngest and stupidest. His big brothers—or his inbred cousins—had other ideas.

"Gods, I love taking it from Traveler bitches!" the oldest said with a smirk.

The other two sniggered.

"Come on down, slut, and we'll show you what real men are like."

"Wait till you try a taste of my sausage, girlie!"

"Nah, not him, try me!"

"She'll have us all, and like it," the oldest said.

The others had just been having fun, but he meant it. His eyes never left her face; he was waiting for fear to show. There was a part of her that wondered what it mattered. She was dead anyway. But another, deeper part answered: *He can wait until hell melts.* The thought and the feeling cut through the fog she had been riding in and sharpened her attention.

"Get her down, Than. Grab her bridle first." He pushed the youngest forward.

The boy, no more than fifteen, hesitated. "She's not got a bridle, Cal."

They blinked, uncertain for a moment. Bramble drove her heels into the roan's sides and thundered forward. Cal made a grab for her, but she kicked him on the side of the head and was almost unseated when the roan kicked his back legs at the same time to knock over two more of them. *He's battle trained,* she thought with a chill. Then they were through and galloping. The men were left swearing and cursing her as they picked themselves up.

She let the roan slow, but kept him to a canter until they had passed two more villages. At the next stream she let him drink, and then walked him to cool down while her own trembling subsided.

She hadn't expected this sort of thing. Oh, from warlords' men, yes, of course. But not from ordinary men. Those big yokels were just like boys from her own village. She shuddered to think of Carl or Wilf or Eric treating some chance-met Traveler girl like that. Would they? Not Wilf, surely? She remembered lying with Wilf in the shade of a big willow tree last summer, his hands gentle on her, his body a pleasure. They had not been in love, but it had been lovely. Surely Wilf couldn't act like that?

But another voice, just as strong, reminded her: *To them, you're just a Traveler. They can do anything they like to Travelers.*

In the many full moons since she had left Carlion moving slowly along the coast toward Central Domain, she'd learned a bit about how Acton's people treated Travelers. She looked the part, of course, except for the horse. On close inspection her clothes were crafter clothes, even if she was wearing breeches. But at first glance she was just another Traveler girl. And that was the way she was treated.

When she'd asked for a room at the inn on the first night, they'd shouted her out of doors. "The kitchen door next time for you, girlie, and the stable's the best your kind'll get anywhere in this Domain!" the innkeeper had yelled, then set the boys in the village to throw stones at her as she left.

She had slept in the woods after that; she couldn't bring herself to go to the kitchen door, not while the spring and summer nights were warm.

She had food. Shops would serve her, she'd found, if she waited at the back until everyone else had been served first. They charged her more though, and if she protested they took back the food.

"Go hungry, then," the baker had said.

She was tired of being tensed, ready for a harsh word or a thrown stone, tired of being hated for no reason at all. Quite a few people in Wooding hadn't liked her, partly because she looked like a Traveler, but more, she realized now with a wry smile, because she had been wild to a fault. But even Aelred's mother hadn't looked at her with the blank eyes of hate, the eyes that don't see what's really there, don't see a person but only a Traveler. The warlord's man had looked at her like that before she killed him, but she hadn't recognized it then. She had thought it was more personal than it really was.

At night she dreamed of the blank eyes and sometimes she kicked out as she had kicked the warlord's man, and woke sweating and swearing and exhausted. She would turn to the roan for comfort, leaning her face against his warm side while he snuffled curiously at her hair. She dreamed, too, of the dark after death, from where she would be reborn. Those dreams were comforting, reassuring her that even if she were meant to be dead, even if she *felt* dead, there would be a new life someday.

The haze only lifted when the sun was on her back, the track seemed endless in front of her, or when she smelled the hedgerows at dawn as the wildflowers released their fragrance to the new warmth. She loved the sense that no one was waiting for her, that there was nowhere she *had* to be: no goats to be milked, no garden to be weeded, no orphan kid to be fed, nothing needed her except the roan. The idea of freedom was the only thing that seemed real to her. She was still looking through a cloudy glass, and was trying to accept that she might stay like this forever. But thoughts of the Great Forest kept her going.

She came toward Sandalwood halfway through the early autumn afternoon, with the wild geese practicing their flights overhead, calling as they went. In the past, Bramble had listened to those calls with a longing to be off, on the Road, going who knew where. Now the call did nothing to her heart except remind her that the year was turning.

There was a party of pilgrims waiting for the ferry by the river. Sandalwood was a big town, but there were no houses near the dock, just flat green fields. Their leader was carrying the traditional staff with its bunch of green leaves tied to the top, and saw her looking.

"Floodplain this side," he said. He smiled expansively. "I'm Marp. Used to be a trader, selling rugs and suchlike up from the Wind Cities. Know all of this Domain and a good few others."

"Not many people as well traveled who aren't Travelers," Bramble remarked.

"True, that is, true enough." He glanced quickly at her black hair and away again. "I take people as I find them, no matter what they are. The Wind Cities is full of people who look like Travelers, and they're just the same as anybody else, I reckon."

"What do you do now?"

"Why, guiding pilgrims, guiding pilgrims is my life's work now, lass." He beamed beatifically. "Well of Secrets, she told me that's my life's work. What she says, you know is true."

How do you know? Bramble asked herself. She'd heard the same thing said by people who'd never met the Well of Secrets, and doubted it as she doubted most things. But Marp seemed an intelligent, sensible man who'd thrown up his old life on the say-so of a stranger. Why? They said she could forgive, too, for sins and worse, but sometimes she demanded more changes than people were willing to make.

Bramble wondered if the Well of Secrets could lead her to rebirth or at least tell her how long she had to endure this half life.

The Well of Secrets was living in the far north at that time, in Oakmere, Marp told her, a small village on the road to End-holme, in the Last Domain. It had been a small village, but what it was after a couple of years of pilgrimages was anyone's guess. Bramble could imagine what would have happened if the Well of Secrets had moved to her village, Wooding. She could see the hastily built inns, the brothels, the shops with expensive food, the eating houses, the souvenir sellers...There was greed enough to go around, even among their handful of families.

The ferry was a flat barge, good for horses and carts as well as people. It wasn't rowed, but pulled along by a rope between two huge pulleys on either bank. The ferryman and his helper simply heaved on the rope and the ferry moved across as the rope moved around in an endless circle. The ferryman took Bramble over last, even though it was clear that she had been first to the dock. Marp tried to protest on her behalf, but she waved him to not bother. There was no point complaining. The pilgrims walked on through the town, but by the time Bramble and the roan arrived, she was tired and thirsty and headed for the nearest inn.

She wondered if the innkeeper would throw her out, but no one paid any attention to her as she sat down at a small table in the corner. She saw, looking around, that there were other Travelers drinking there. Two, at least, were unmistakable: young men with jet hair and sloe eyes, good-looking and all the more striking because they were twins.

The afternoon had turned a little cool, so she had the wolf skin around her shoulders. It, or maybe something else about her, attracted the twins' attention and they came over with their drinks.

"Mind if we sit here?" one of them asked. He had a nice smile. She could see that he was the cheeky one of the two, the one who liked excitement and a bit of risk. No wonder he was interested in a girl in a wolf's skin. A Traveler girl, too. He was someone she might have had a yen for in the days before the abyss. But the part of her that felt desire seemed dead too.

She shrugged and moved down to make room for them.

"I'm Ber," the young man said, "and that's Eldwin." He was nodding his head toward his twin.

"Bramble," she said.

"So, tell me all about yourself," he said softly, sliding his hand near hers so the backs of their fingers touched.

She had to laugh, it was so transparent, and he laughed with her, confident in his charm.

Then she shivered as the air suddenly turned cold. All around them it grew quiet and dark, like something was absorbing all the light. Ber grew pale and sweat popped out on his forehead.

The others at the table edged away from him. Bramble wondered if a fever had taken him suddenly. His eyes were blank and he started to shake. A fit, maybe. She took hold of his arm to steady him, and saw his brother do the same on the other side. Her hair lifted on her neck, but it wasn't the presence of the gods. The gods had nothing to do with this. Then he spoke.

"Born wild," he said, and it was like his voice, and yet not quite the same. "Born wild and died wild, and not fit for this young man," he continued. "No one will ever tame thee, woman, and thou wilt love no man never. Give over. Begone."

Bramble snatched her hand away. Ber's eyes closed and he toppled over sideways. Without thinking, because she didn't want to think about what he had said, she helped his brother lay him out on the bench. She patted his cheek and, when he roused, his eyes focused but bemused, she gave him water to sip.

Then she slipped away. Still not allowing herself to think, she rode straight through the town, and only when she was on the open road, between fields of ripening oats, did she let herself remember. It had not been the gods who spoke. She knew that, knew their presence as she knew her own voice. But it was something else unearthly. Something more than human, other than human. A demon, maybe, and demons were supposed to know the future and the past. Its words rolled around her mind: *Born wild and died wild. Not fit for this young man...thou wilt love no man never...begone...begone...never...never.*

She didn't want to think about them, but the words kept coming back. She was not only dead, but without love. The dead could not love, or be loved, except in memory. They could not find new love, except through rebirth. When she found tears on her cheeks, she urged the roan into a canter, trying to escape the sensation that a knife was carving a hole in her chest, below her breastbone, a hole that would never be filled. She knew that feeling. It was like when her mother said, "If only you were more like your sister," but somehow much worse. There was no hope in it, no room for change. *Never,* the demon said in her mind, and she pushed the roan into a gallop. But she couldn't out-run that voice. She had just enough sense to steer the roan onto the soft grass verge so he wouldn't be hurt by the jarring pace. He slowed on his own eventually, having enjoyed the chance to stretch out after four days of slow walking.

She forced herself to be calm, to take control.

"Enough," she said out loud. "I won't think about it again. It might be right, it might be wrong. All I can do is live and find out." Her breathing steadied. "Forget it," she told herself. "For-get it. Endure."

ELDWIN'S STORY

T HE FIRST TIME the demon spoke to us, I was just two months out from my seventeenth birthday, from our birthday, my twin's and mine. We were sitting around a table at an inn, the Wide-Mouthed Jug, in Sandalwood, and it'd been a good day for both of us, Ber and me.

We were feeling like men: there was silver in our pockets and a good day's work behind us. And there was no one at home to worry over us, for Mam took our comings and goings with never a hair turned, and our da, what used to worry himself over us, he was dead two months gone.

We just wanted a drink, and maybe a few light words with a pretty girl. Ber found one, pretty enough but a bit wild-looking, with a wolf skin around her shoulder. He took her hand. Then he started foaming at the mouth and spouting demon words, and fainted away afterward. I thought he was dead. My heart stopped its beating for one long space and then I saw his breath bubble the foam on his lips, and it started again with a heavy thump.

When he opened his eyes, they were cloudy, and he remembered nothing. "I was holding your hand," he said to the girl, "and then I was lying on the bench. What happened?"

But I had to take him out of the inn and back to our caravan before I could tell him, for the innkeeper wanted us and the girl out, and she weren't a woman to argue with.

We never saw the girl again. Sometimes, when Ber talks about it all, sometimes I think she's what he thinks on most, even now, like it was her who called up the demon in him.

But I don't think so.

The hardest part, I think, was the way it changed Mam.

She used to be free and easy, never caring where we were or what we were up to, and we'd come home and tell her all about it, whatever it was, and she'd scold us and laugh at us and there'd be no trouble at all. It was Da who worried about us. How that man could worry! From the time we was just walking, he'd take us with him on his tinker rounds, and he'd have us walk ahead of him, "Where I can keep an eye on you." He kept lookout for strange dogs and strange men, for sharp rocks at our feet and snakes in the grass.

He didn't even teach us tinkering till we were nearly thirteen. Then he'd make us do everything twice and three times, and over again under his eye, before he'd let us do it on our own. And Mam would shake her head and laugh at him. He wouldn't hear of us going off on the Road by ourselves, though he had broken from his family when he was fifteen, and married only two years later.

On our seventeenth birthday, around the fire after dinner, we pushed him on it, pushed him for our share of the profits for the summer, for we'd worked long hours and made as much as he.

"Just give us that, Da," I said. "Give us our silver for the summer and we'll be off together."

"I will not!" Da said. "I wouldn't if I could and I can't, anyway—I've spent it already on a nice caravan. It'll sleep all of us, snug and sound. I'm picking it up tomorrow from Oswald the Bodger."

Ber and I looked at each other.

"You had no right to do that," Ber said.

"No right at all," I agreed.

"'Twere our silver, just as much as yours."

PAMELA FREEMAN

"You should have asked us both, and Mam, too, before you did a thing like that."

"It won't stop us," said Ber. "We'll go anyway, with no silver behind us, and trust to luck we'll get work before winter."

"Aye," I said. "We'll go tomorrow."

"No!" Da shouted, jumping to his feet. "You're too young, you're too flighty—the first stranger you meet you'll be fleeced by, I can just see it happening. You're no more fit to be on the Road than when you were babies. I've taken care of you all your lives and I tell you I'm not going to stop now —"

But stop he did, with a look of wild surprise on his face, and he fell down at our feet, the breath gone from his body, tears in his eyes, just like that, dead.

At first, it wasn't so bad. Once the first shock of the grief and the guilt were done, Mam was strong enough. For there was a load of guilt, for all of us, no doubt of that. But after the first time the demon spoke through Ber, she changed. And maybe I did, too.

It was the not knowing when it would happen. Anytime of the day or night—no telling. But it was always in company, so we got out of the habit of going to inns, Ber and I, and we didn't linger with our customers to chat no more.

We knew what they said— "Not like their father, those boys. Why, Griff'd have you there all day, talking about those two, and now they don't give you the time of day ..."

But we were good tinkers, Ber and I, so we didn't lose much custom by it, and we explained the demon away as fits, to them that asked. Maybe we even got more custom—people coming to take a look at the possessed man.

Mam kept a close eye on us, now, and wanted us home in the fire circle by dark; though the demon came in the daytime, too, so what difference that made I don't know. She fussed over Ber,

146

though she used to treat us two so alike, sometimes we joked she couldn't tell us apart. Now it was like I was older, more responsible. And I did it myself, too, like he had a mortal illness and I had to tend to him.

Yet he was no different in himself, nervier, maybe, but sometimes I think it was Mam and I made him so. He had no memory of it, see, no memory of the fire growing dark and the air growing cold, of the hair standing up on your neck, and the flesh crawling on your bones...as that thing used him, used his mouth and his tongue and his eyes...

It never did us any harm direct. When it spoke, it spoke only warnings. Sometimes we didn't even understand what it said, but whoever we were with understood all right. I've seen grown men go white and run from the room at a single word. It might be a name, or a place, and once in Fiton, it were just, "twelve silver pieces," and an old man, white-haired and rheumy-eyed, shuffled out of the inn like Death herself were after him. She caught him later that night, we heard, when he hanged himself in his own barn. We don't go back to Fiton now.

It went on like that for two years. I was thinking about leaving, about just plain running somewhere, anywhere I didn't have to watch Ber every second. But how could I leave him? Or Mam? He was half of my heart's blood, and she was the other. So I thought, *Next time it comes, I'm going to talk to it, ask it to leave us alone. Beg with it. Bargain with it, need be.*

For we'd never had the courage to speak to it directly. It was too hard, it using Ber's voice, and always so calm and reasonable, even when it was accusing some poor soul of murder, or worse. I couldn't bear to look at him when he was foaming at the mouth and blank-eyed. But I had to. Mam was withering away, not eating, not smiling. She'd be sick, come winter, I knew.

So I was waiting, on edge, all that summer. We worked our

way through Pless and Carlion, down the Long Valley to Margarie, then made north to Freewater as the leaves started turning. All that time the demon was quiet, and we kept ourselves to ourselves. It was a beautiful summer—hot days and cooler nights—and autumn came in on a whisper of cold in the early mornings, such that one day we woke to find Ros, our mare, had her winter coat and we hadn't even noticed.

Now we had the caravan, we didn't need to winter over in a town, but this year I wanted to because Mam was looking so thin and frail.

"Back me up," I said to Ber. "She'll get sick otherwise for sure."

He was uneasy with the idea. "Freewater's a big place. Lot of people." He was worried about the demon coming. And I saw he was more pained by it all than I'd known, feeling set apart, like, and not safe for others to be around.

"It'll be all right, twin," I said. "You do no harm, and never could."

"Not I, but it."

I hugged him, feeling suddenly that I knew what Da felt when he worried after us. "What will happen, will happen. And might be there's a stonecaster in Freewater can tell us what it is."

That cheered him, and me too, for it was a good idea and I should have had it before.

So we found a barn on the outskirts of Freewater, and the farmer let us use it and draw water from his well. Ber and I set Mam up good, and that first night we chopped her wood and fetched her water and sat down for dinner with her, and it was like it always had been, she was bright and laughing for once. It was like a gift, and it decided me to act then and there.

"We're going into Freewater," I told her straight after dinner, while she was putting the plates away. "We're going to a stonecaster to see what they say about this thing."

She went pale, standing there, and Ber had to take the plate out of her hand lest she drop it, but she nodded and sat down. "Aye. It's time and past time to face it." But her eyes filled with tears. And the room grew cold. "Oh, gods, preserve us," Mam whispered.

Ber stood up, blank-eyed, shivering, and the light faded. My gorge were rising, like it always did, but this time I stood and faced the demon, eye to eye.

"Do not go to the stonecaster," it said.

"What do you want with us? Why do you come? Why are you tormenting us like this?" I had a hundred questions, but I could barely force myself to speak.

It tilted Ber's head, and on his face was puzzlement; it was the first feeling it had ever shown. It seemed to search for words, where words had always come easily before.

"I help," it said finally.

"You steal my brother's body and call that helping?"

"I...warn. Danger comes, I tell you."

Anger was taking me over; I could feel it, and I knew I had to hold it back or any damage I did would be to Ber. "Why us? Why follow us? Leave us alone! Let us go our own road."

"No!" it howled, foam coming out Ber's mouth. "I've taken care of you all your lives and I tell you I'm not going to stop now—not now, not yet—"

"Griff," Mam said, so quiet, so gentle it would break your heart. "Griff, you're dead, love. Time to let go. Time to say goodbye."

It shook Ber's head, shook his whole body. "No, no, no, no..."

"They're grown men, love." Mam touched Ber's face, looked into his blank eyes. "They can look after themselves."

I was shaking, too, finally hearing Da's voice underneath Ber's. But he wasn't listening to Mam. "Can't you see what you're doing to us, Da?" I said. "You think you're protecting us, but you're sucking the life out of us all, not just Ber."

"I'd never hurt—"

"Every time it hurts! You've got no right. You never had no right to hold on to us. It killed you trying. Let go—for pity's sake!"

"Let go, love," said Mam.

"Love—" it whispered.

"Aye," she said, "aye, I know you do."

He turned Ber's head to look at her, and for a moment he was truly there, looking out of Ber's eyes—my old da, stubborn as ever.

"Love—" he said again, then Ber's eyes closed and he fell over.

Seems to me I watched my da die twice, and both times I killed him. I went to the stonecaster after, and she picked Guilt out, and Death and Love—all lying facedown. But faceup were New Beginnings and the blank stone, which means the future's open-ended, and anything could happen from here on in.

SAKER

THE GODS *had* led him to Connay, Saker decided as he listened to the high, perfect voice of the woman singing. The inn crowd didn't care about her perfection; they banged their tankards on the table in time to the insistent drum and tapped their feet to the flute. After a couple of verses they were shouting out the chorus with smoke-roughened voices.

And Acton laughed!
Yes, he laughed!
He laughed and killed them all!

Verse after verse, the song went through Acton's exploits on the battlefield; a litany of murder, thought Saker, a canticle of death. Then he realized what he was hearing: a map.

When they took a break he fought his way to the small stage. "How many of the old songs do you know?" he asked the flautist.

The flautist was a man of middle years, with intense black eyes. "I know all of them," he said matter-of-factly, using a kerchief to clean the spit out of the flute.

The gods *were* leading him!

"My name is Penda," Saker said. It was a name he used whenever he pretended to be one of Acton's people, the name of one of Acton's companions in Death Pass. Penda was the last one through the pass, just as Saker was the last of the old blood, undiluted. It was a little irony he carried around with him. "I am a student of the old times. I would like to learn the songs, to write them down."

The man shook his head decidedly. "No. The songs must be passed from mouth to ear—never written. If you don't promise this, I cannot help you."

Saker recognized the tone in his voice: absolute certainty. Gold wouldn't change his mind. Nothing would. "Could I write down some of the things the songs talk about? Names, places, what was done there? A history?" he asked.

The man looked uncertain. The singer came and placed a hand on his arm and his hand went up automatically to cover it gently. They smiled at one another, the unbidden smile of long-time lovers, more a softening around the eyes than anything else. Husband and wife, Saker thought.

"The songs *are* the history," the man said finally, and made to turn away.

"But how many people know the songs?" Saker asked, desperation flaring. "How many people have you taught?"

The flautist paused, some pain flickering on his face. "My son. But..."

"But he has left the Road," the woman said, "as he needed to. We are teaching Cypress, here." She gestured to the drummer. Even concentrating on the flautist as Saker was, he noticed the gracefulness of her hand movement, her beauty. Her features matched the beauty of her voice. "It will do no harm for him to write down the names and places, Rowan," she said.

The man hesitated. "It's not the tradition."

"But he's one of us," the woman said. "One of the old blood."

Saker felt himself pale. How could she know? He had dyed his hair red-brown, his eyes were hazel: he looked exactly like any other descendant from the second wave of Acton's invasion.

She smiled at him with pity. "The old blood recognizes itself," she said. "You are driven to find out what happened in the time past."

He nodded.

"I see it. It gives you no peace. Perhaps when you know the total, you will find a way to peace. Help him, Rowan."

She moved away and bent over to talk to the drummer, Cypress.

"If Swallow wants to help you, you'll be helped—one way or another," the man said. "I will tell you the songs and you may write your history. But, Penda, there are many songs and we must travel. You will have to come with us."

Saker nodded. "Of course, of course. And I can pay you—"

"Good," the drummer broke in. "You can start by buying a round of drinks!"

BRAMBLE

BRAMBLE LET THE ROAN travel along for the whole autumn evening, hearing over and over again the ... the what? Curse? Prediction? That demon voice could not be contradicted. *Born wild and died wild. Thou wilt love no man never. No one will ever tame thee.*

The words had hit her like wood because they rang true, because they chimed not only with her feeling of having escaped death, her fate, by a mistake, but with an empty place that she had always known was inside her. She thought that place had finally been filled, by the love of riding and by loving the roan, but she'd been wrong. It was still there, just better hidden, buried deeper. She felt it ache.

She was more disturbed than she wanted to admit to herself by the prophecy that she would never love. Of course, she had wondered, time and again, when the other girls her age had giggled during the Springtree dance as the boys twirled them and smiled at them, when they had gossiped about this one's eyes or that one's hands, why she had felt nothing beyond desire for any of them, and only liking for Wilf, the sweet but ugly boy the other girls ignored.

She had wondered and then let it go, until Maryrose brought Merrick home to meet the family. She could see why Maryrose loved him, but couldn't imagine doing so herself, although she tried and tried hard.

Did she have so hard a heart? She could be kind — her ability to raise orphaned lambs and kids, to gentle them and give them the will to live was well known. She was known, too, as a good nurse for children and old people. "A wild heart but soft hands" was how one granfer had described her. She could be compassionate to young things and old, to the sick and the dying, the unhappy and the mad.

But love…Love for a man was something she'd never been able to come to. Perhaps she never would, now that she was a being of flesh and blood but without feeling. Perhaps she would never love, never marry.

"Is that so terrible a thing, horse?" she asked, and the roan whickered back at her and rubbed his soft nose against her bare leg. She was a little comforted, and hoped to be comforted more by the quiet of the Great Forest.

The road was longer than she had expected and she only came toward Pless as the autumn began to bite down and her money was almost exhausted.

In the late afternoon on a cloudy day, with the threat of a storm in the air, she rode down the main road to Pless, through a valley of pastureland flanked on both sides by deep forest. Halfway down the valley the roan stopped dead in the road.

Bramble sat, surprised, not knowing why he had paused. She clicked her tongue encouragingly, but instead of continuing, he executed a smart quarter turn and trotted through an open gate beside the road. He had never acted like this before, but it was as though he knew exactly where he was going. So Bramble let him go and just tried not to fall off—trotting was the one pace she had not yet mastered. Sensing this, the roan slowed to a walk, and headed toward a fenced yard where a man was gentling a chestnut filly.

The man had dark brown hair and a tall, loose-limbed body

that would have been gangly as a youth. He wasn't exactly comely, not like Merrick, although he had a charm about him in the way he talked to the horse, as though it were a person. But he was at least twice her age, no matter how charming he might be.

She watched for a while, smiling as he tricked the filly by walking away from her so that she followed out of curiosity. He moved quietly and gently, never intruding on her until she felt safe and secure in his hands. When he'd finally managed to slip the bridle on her head, he noticed Bramble at the fence, sitting, as she usually did, with one leg drawn up across the roan's shoulders, no saddle, no reins in her hands, no bit in the horse's mouth, but clearly comfortable.

He smiled at her, with a charm that shone through his gray eyes, with none of the automatic suspicion she'd encountered from most settled people since she had taken the Road. "Bring him in," he invited her. "It'll do the filly good to see another horse so friendly with a human."

She smiled back at him, a little surprised. The easy exchange made her feel more alive. So she touched the roan on the shoulder, clicked her tongue, and sat back as he made his own way to the gate which the man held open.

By the time she'd brought the roan in and turned him around, the man was grinning fit to burst.

"I'm Gorham."

"Bramble."

Gorham looked the roan up and down with a horseman's eye. "Nice conformation."

"Thanks." Bramble nodded at the filly. "Is she yours?"

He shook his head. "No. I'm training her up for a farmer over Sandalwood way."

Bramble was surprised. "That's a long way to bring a horse for training."

Gorham shrugged, as though it were usual. "He wants to run her in the chases."

If Gorham trained chasers from all over this Domain, he must be good at his job, Bramble thought. But then, she had seen that already in the way he handled the filly.

"I'm about to take a break," Gorham said. "Have a cup of cha?"

Bramble was tempted. It was a nice change to talk with someone pleasant. But she needed to keep moving. If she rode hard, they might get to the forest before winter set in. She knew how to survive in a forest, even in the cold months.

"Thanks, but no. I'd better be going," she said. "I want to make Pless by nightfall."

"You have a natural way with that roan," Gorham said. "I'll take you on if you're looking for work."

She shook her head. "No, thanks all the same." Gorham seemed so trusting, like another Traveler, that she felt she owed him an explanation. "I'm heading for the Great Forest. I want to get there before winter."

He nodded understanding. "Wind at your back," he said, the Traveler's farewell, confirming her suspicion that he was, or had been, on the Road.

"Gods be with you," Bramble said.

She touched the roan on the shoulder again and clicked her tongue, but he didn't move, except to shake his mane and stamp his foot in denial. The signs were clear, he wasn't going anywhere.

Bramble jumped off and walked around to look him in the eye. "What is it, lad?" she asked. "You like it here?"

His wise eyes regarded her but gave away no secrets. When she tried to lead him out of the yard he wouldn't budge. Well, she thought, they were partners in this journey and he had as much right as she did to decide where they should go and where they should stay—perhaps more. It was he the gods had kept alive.

She turned to Gorham and shrugged. "Looks like I want a job after all."

He looked surprised but he didn't comment. "I'll show you the lodgings."

The wattle-and-daub cottage, behind the yard and screened by a stand of maple, was more than adequate, with a bedroom and kitchen with a scullery attached. It needed cleaning badly, though, and there was no bed.

Gorham pulled at his lip. "Best you come home with me tonight," he said.

Bramble raised an eyebrow and he smiled, amused by her tacit suspicion. "My wife'll give you a bed for the night," he qualified.

Bramble nodded. "Fair enough."

Gorham mounted his rangy chestnut, which had been tied up on the other side of the yards. "I'm training him up for someone else," he said disparagingly, then looked the roan over. "Nice form, but he's got a bit of temperament, hasn't he?"

Bramble shook her head and smiled. "Not really." Then she went to talk to the roan. "We have to go to town tonight, but we'll come back in the morning."

Gorham hauled her up on the chestnut and they led off. The roan followed amiably, as though he'd never refused to move. Gorham glanced at Bramble with curiosity. "You've got to be boss of your animal," he said.

"Not this one."

As they rode back to town, they tried not to ask each other too many questions, out of respect, but some had to be asked.

"You were a Traveler?" Bramble asked.

Gorham was startled. "How'd you know?"

"The way you looked at me—I mean, the way you *didn't* look at me." She fumbled for what she meant. "No contempt…no suspicion."

Gorham nodded. "Aye, I know what you mean there, lass." He pulled at his lip again. "We *were* Travelers, my Osyth and I, but we came to Pless as crafters and there's no one here who knows what we were. You understand why?"

Bramble nodded. She understood perfectly.

"Osyth has a yen for me to be a town councillor." He chuckled. "I can't see any town voting in a Traveler as councillor, can you? So if you don't mind…"

"I won't mention it." She chuckled in turn. "I'm the opposite—raised crafter, just lately took to the Road."

"Well, it's a funny world," Gorham said comfortably. "We might not tell Osyth you're on the Road, then. What were your parents?"

"A carpenter and a weaver."

"Good, solid, respectable trades." He laughed as she made a face. "Aye, I know, you've had enough of respectability."

"I'd had enough of it in my cradle!"

He laughed again. "Well, then, we won't try to be too respectable out at the farm. We'll keep that for town."

They arrived at the townhouse—a fine, respectable house, she thought wryly—and went through the yard gate to the stables to settle the horses and wash their hands before entering the back door into the kitchen. Bramble hung back a little, suddenly unsure whether she wanted to spend the night inside bricks and mortar, but unable to think of an excuse.

Osyth was cutting carrots at the table. She rose briskly as Gorham came in, and gave him a brief kiss on the cheek. He looked at her for a moment, after she'd turned away, as though he was waiting for something more, then he sighed just a little and turned to Bramble.

"We have a guest," he said.

Bramble came forward. Gorham waited with some trepidation to see how Osyth took to her. The girl had a wilder version of Osyth's own beauty, he thought, that lithe, black-haired beauty, and she looked anything but ordinary. As they confronted each other, Gorham realized that he was also a little nervous about what Bramble thought of Osyth. It made him see his wife afresh, as Bramble might see her.

Osyth was still beautiful: a slight woman with black hair drawn back into a simple roll and small, graceful hands. Only her mouth, with the corners drawn in and the lips a little too firm, hinted at a lack of generosity. It was that and the way she stared at Bramble.

Gorham could see his wife assessing each item and read her reactions as easily as those of a horse to a new companion: narrowed eyes (her coloring, bad—a Traveler), a small nod (dressed like a man, but good quality), a disapproving sniff (no shoes), and arched eyebrows (her saddlebags—a guest for how long?). He remembered when his wife was more carefree, wilder herself. But that was before they'd had the children, before they'd settled. Something had changed long before.

There had been a time when Osyth, whenever they were together, would take his face between her hands and gaze lovingly at him. Over time, the gaze had become more searching, and eventually disappointed. It had leached away his love, that disappointment, as he felt diminished in her sight. But he still missed her looking at him, missed her paying attention to him, even if it brought disappointment. All she was interested in now was silver and becoming powerful in the town. But he wouldn't let her be dismissive of Bramble.

Osyth opened her mouth, but Gorham got in first. "Bramble's coming to work for us. Out at the farm. She'll go back there tomorrow and get the old cottage sorted out for herself. But tonight she needs a meal and a bed."

"I'm happy to sleep in the stable," Bramble said mildly. Gorham raised his hand to protest, but she shook her head at him. *"Really."*

Osyth nodded, satisfied although not happy. "There's not much for supper," she said. "But I suppose I can find you something."

Gorham left it at that. He and Bramble sat by the hearth and talked about the horses out on the farm while Osyth served up supper, a stew with more lentils than meat, but sustaining and tasty.

As they ate, Gorham asked Bramble questions about her family. Osyth listened to the answers, gradually relaxing as all the respectable details came out: carpenter, weaver, long established in their village, grandfather on her mother's side the village voice for twenty years before he died, sister married to the Carlion town clerk's son. She nodded in approval at the news of Bramble's parents moving to town to be with Maryrose.

Finally it seemed that there were no more details to share and Gorham sat brooding while Osyth picked at her food.

"Do you have any children?" Bramble asked.

His face lightened. "Two, then, we have—a girl and a boy, Zel and Flax. They're on the Road."

Osyth got up, her plate still half full, and walked to the hearth, shouting disapproval with her stiff back.

"It's like I told you," Gorham said quietly, "no one here knows we were Travelers. They don't know about the childer, either. They took the Road on their own before we settled here."

"Well, I won't tell anyone," Bramble said reassuringly, pitching her voice to reach Osyth.

"You won't have to tell anyone," Osyth said, turning around, "if Gorham keeps going around saying 'childer' instead of 'children'! That's a give away any crafter could pick."

Gorham flashed her a smile. "Go on, you know I never do it around town folk."

"*We're* town folk now—and don't you forget it." But she was smiling back at him for the first time, and Gorham saw her as lovely as when she was a girl, when she'd been less critical and more loving.

"I'll say goodnight then," Bramble said, picking up her saddlebags and heading for the door.

Osyth nodded at her; Gorham smiled and raised a hand. "Goodnight then, lass."

As Bramble shut the door behind her, Osyth looked at her husband. "Why take on someone who looks like a Traveler, for goodness sake, when we're trying so hard to start over?"

"But she's not a Traveler, love," Gorham said. "You can tell everyone that—drop in a few hints about her being the town clerk's niece-in-law and there'll be no trouble at all."

"Talking mills no corn—they'll still wonder. They'll wonder if you're shagging her, too."

He was still. "*You* don't think—"

She looked away. "Oh, no. I see how you treat her, just like Zel. Besides, your tastes don't run to young and dark, do they?"

He didn't know how to reply, there was so much bitterness in her voice. There was satisfaction in her eyes as she saw his discomfiture. She pushed her advantage.

"They'll all think she's a Traveler, with that hair and eyes."

"They don't think that about you."

"Of course they do! I've been asked who my folks were, where I come from. Not all of them believe what I tell them, either. Not by a long shot."

He hadn't realized that. They lived such separate lives now, he and Osyth. He was out on the farm, she was in town, absorbed in town doings, gossip and alliances, births and marriages, and getting fish for the best price, buying in bulk to save silver. He knew what they said about her: "Counts her change three times, she does." Maude had told him. But they'd not gone hungry since the day she took over the finances, and without her management he'd never have saved enough to buy the farm. He'd done it to please her, but now he realized that she'd known him better than he'd known himself; the farm was where he belonged. And he liked staying out there because he was away from the accusation in her eyes. Love, regret, shame and annoyance mixed equally in him, and hot. He needed to escape it.

"I might just go out for an ale..." he said.

She looked at him. He saw the anger rise in her, and saw her tamp it down with iron-hard control. "You can't go out with that girl staying here," she said. "You're her host. It wouldn't be fitting."

He was flummoxed.

"You wouldn't be back before breakfast," she said. "You never are. What would I tell Bramble?"

It was the first time she had ever alluded to his overnight absences. He thought resentfully that she'd use anything against him, but what could he say? They were skating on thin ice, here, neither mentioning where he'd really be going, neither prepared to acknowledge the truth. If the truth were ever said aloud, they couldn't go on as they did, getting through their days with at least a little dignity and calm. Besides, he couldn't bear the fight that would erupt. He just wanted some comfort, some easygoing laughs and a cuddle or two. With Osyth, everything was so intense. Everything mattered, everything was life-or-death. She was too much for him, and that was the real truth. That was why she had always been disappointed when she looked into his eyes.

She was standing rigid, clutching a wiping cloth in both hands, with knuckles white. Waiting.

"Well, then, I suppose you're right," he said slowly, and he saw her relax, watched triumph curl at the corner of her mouth.

He let go of an image of Maude snuggling down with him on the rug in front of her fire, and managed to smile at Osyth. He wasn't strong enough to be what she wanted, but that wasn't her fault. And strangely, there was still love in that curdling mixture of shame and disappointment. So there he was, caught in her eyes and her grace and her fine-boned beauty, just as he'd been caught the first time he saw her juggling and tumbling with her sisters, out on the Road.

He walked over and touched her cheek. "Come on then, love, let's go to bed."

Her face flushed and she turned within his arm to walk up the stairs to the bedroom.

OSYTH'S STORY

THE SUMMER I was seventeen was a disaster. It rained three weeks before haying, and the hay rotted in the fields. More like lakes, they were, so the hay rotted from the bottom up, and stank like marsh gas. It rained for so long that the wheat lay flat and the grain sprouted on the stalk. The fruit swelled and turned rotten on the trees, and the few pieces that were harvested grew mildew overnight. Even the mushrooms washed away.

The grandams shook their heads and prophesied a desperate, hard winter, lean and hungry. Farmers decided which of their animals to kill, for they'd not have enough feed to last them through winter, and it was better to smoke some of the meat now and have enough left to keep the breeding stock going till spring.

The crafters in the town shook their heads and bought in as much as they could—barley and oats and lentils—till the price went up and the town councils argued bitterly over whether they had the right to set a price limit on staples. Some did, and some didn't, and where they didn't, the folk looked forward to a killing winter.

It frightened me. Life on the Road was hard enough in the good years, when the fields bloomed and farmers were hopeful enough to part with a few coins for the pleasure of seeing me juggle, or hearing my sisters sing. In a year like this there'd be no free food at farmhouse doors, no extra firewood for the price of a juggle and a tumbling run. And in the towns it'd be just as bad, with no prosperous farmers to commission work and no happy merchants with spare silver looking for ways to spend it; the crafters would be sitting idle. Even the innkeepers would have a bad year, for the barley was looking to be twice last year's price and hops worth their weight in coppers.

In high summer I looked forward to a cold, hungry winter, and it frightened me as naught had ever done before.

Me and Rawnie and Rumer had been on the Road for four years on our own, since we'd cut loose of our mam and da in Foreverfroze, way up north. Da had taken a liking to the cold air and white sky of the north, and Mam had a mind to try fishing the way the Foreverfroze women did it. She was ever a good angler, was Mam, with a passion for whitefish and yellowback, which none of us could understand.

So my sisters and I took the Road and did pretty well, all told. We were Road children, after all, and all our life'd been spent following the drum on Da's back, along the high roads and the back roads, with Mam whistling behind to keep our spirits up on the long stretches.

I was the youngest and was used to being looked after. But it didn't take me more than two months to realize that neither Rumer nor Rawnie could handle silver without letting it slide through their fingers like water, just like our da. I was as hardheaded as Mam, and I took that purse out of their hands and doled them out copper like it was gold.

Soon enough it was I who was deciding where we should go and what we should sing, and it was I who made them keep ten silver bits in reserve, even when it meant shagging for our supper. 'Twas better to lie down for ten minutes, I said, and have food where we knew the innkeeper'd feed us for a shag, than find us one day stone broke in an inn with a woman keeper. "I'll not go hungry," I said, "and I'll not sleep in the rain. What's good enough for Mam and Da is good enough for us."

Don't mistake me, I spent time on my back, same as them, though I hated it worse, I think. I hated the blank look in the innkeepers' eyes and the scorn on their faces, the smell of them — the old-man smell more often than not, or else that dirty stale beer smell, and the leather smell from their jerkins — for it wasn't often they'd bother to undress, not for the price of a supper.

Rawnie and Rumer were even-tempered girls, light as this-tledown in body and mind, as tumblers should be. They prac-ticed as often as I wanted without begrudging it, but they were more interested in the young men than anything else. Once they earned their place for the night, if they had to, they washed and brushed their hair, put on their bright performing smiles, and sang and tumbled like nothing had happened. But they seldom had to, no more than once every two or three months, with us taking it in turn as we did. But I remembered every forced time like it was my right hand I'd lost, and I brooded on it, even though it was my idea.

Jugglers don't have to smile — it's better to pretend frown-ing concern to heighten the tension: will she drop a pin, will she catch on fire? In the town squares, sometimes I would send flam-ing batons up into the summer night sky, like distress beacons or warning fires, but to whom, I didn't know. On those nights the copper rained into our hands, and sometimes silver, too.

Rumer reckoned it hurt me worse than them because I'd never done it with a sweet young man, a douce young man with long fingers and soft lips. My first time'd been in Mickleton with a fifty-year-old innkeeper, who had two daughters older than me, and wanted me to call him "Da" all the way through it. Rawnie and Rumer hadn't known till it was over and they found me puking hard behind the horse barn, my fingers blue with cold and clutching onto the barn wall for balance. They'd have taken my place, wanting my first time to be soft and sweet, like theirs'd been, but I wouldn't let them. It wouldn't have been fair.

I remembered that time, and others, as the fruit rotted on the trees that summer, and the prices rose steadily in the towns. I could see a long winter ahead, and I couldn't face it.

We was in Carlion in the late days of summer and it was warm and dry and beautiful now, though it was too late to do any good. Among the townspeople worry bred a need for entertainment, and they walked the streets of an evening, and stopped in the green near the well to watch me juggling the shining silver-painted balls, and to hear Rumer and Rawnie sing sweet songs. "Keep it happy," I'd said. "They want to be taken out of their cares, and they depend on us to do it. They'll give us more that way." But even so, copper was scarce and silver was as rare as balls on a gelding.

There was one evening like that, no different from any other, when I saw a young man, a comely man, watching from the back of the crowd while the three of us tumbled and rolled, balanced and spun.

The crowd applauded. Panting, I saw the young man grin at us and clap heartily himself. Brown-haired, he was, with gray eyes like agate and a tall body that was only just free from the gangliness of youth. He had a pack on his back and he was clearly a Traveler, like us, but he was dressed as well as any merchant, and he had muscle, the kind you only get with regular food and work.

His name was Gorham. He came over to us at the end of the performance, after we'd finished collecting the few coins from the ground. That moment, his eyes rested on all three of us with equal pleasure, I think, but I moved forward to greet him. Rumer and Rawnie smiled at each other and slipped into the background, for, as one of them said to the other later, "It was the first time she ever did so much as look at a likely lad, and it's about time, too!" Of course they were thinking, the both of them, that me taking pleasure with a man would make their lives easier, and mine.

Gorham was a horsebreaker, so his pay didn't depend on how generous an audience felt: he set his prices and the owners paid. No one killed off a horse because of a bad winter; they just sold them to someone who could afford them. And young though he was, Gorham had a reputation already. He'd traveled all his life with his mam, who was a horsebreaker of great fame. Even Rumer had heard of Radagund the Horse Speller, who was said to use enchantments from the Western Mountains to bind the horses to her with chains of affection.

Gorham laughed at the stories. "Aye," he said, "it looked like that, with my mam. Come to that, it looks like that sometimes with me, though not so often. See, I reckon my mam was half a horse herself."

"That makes you a horse's grandson," I said, grinning.

"Aye," he said, "that's me."

He laughed, as he often did, then kissed me. That was his way, to laugh and then reach for what he wanted, as a man reaches who's rarely been refused anything. Radagund had reared her son the way she'd reared horses: with endless kindness and a firm hand on the reins. At nineteen, he was as honest and comforting as bread, and he smelled to me of safety and harborage and solace. I wanted him.

Not in the way Rawnie and Rumer wanted their young men, with a light lust, a giggle in the hay at the back of a barn, and a "wind at your back" the next day and off again—no one the worse and everyone better for it. No, I wanted Gorham the way the winter wind wants to get indoors, moaning at the cracks and crevices, rattling the panes of the window. I could see that after a week or so in Carlion he'd be off to his next yearling, and maybe he'd remember me with a smile in the long winter nights. Or maybe not.

"Oh, he's head over ears in love with you," Rumer said, pushing me on the shoulder as I stretched and warmed up for practice, so I fell over on my backside. "What's he like, eh?"

I shook my head and blushed, and that was enough to give Rawnie and Rumer the giggles. They got on with practice but, truth be told, I didn't know what he was like; I had been playing a teasing, waiting match with Gorham, knowing all too well that to keep him in Carlion a few days more was life and death to me, and knowing how often the young enjoyed and left.

So I went to the stonecaster, but not for a casting.

"A spell I want—" I said, my hard-won silver clutched in my hand.

The stonecaster laughed. "To make a young man fall in love with you," she said with certainty. She had a strange voice, strong and precise, not like a Traveler's lilt, nor a town dweller's burr.

"Aye," I said, without shame. "Love and need, I want, and certain sure and no wearing off."

"Don't we all?" Her voice was mocking and, underneath, pained. "But you won't find that here, girl. The tanner will help you—if it's help you call it. On Leather Street, where the juniper bush grows."

I nodded and made to rise, but the stonecaster stopped me.

"Wait. You interest me, girl. Let's see what the stones have to tell you. No charge." She laughed again, bitterly, drew five stones from the bag, and cast them across the blanket. I watched them fall with keen interest. "All facedown," the woman said. "Unusual." There was no trace of laughter in her, now, she was

170

all serious eyes and pursed lips. She turned the stones over, one by one. "Magic—there's your spell, girl. And Pain. Silver. Children. Frost." She was silent a moment, then raised her dark eyes to mine. "A mixed blessing, you get with your spell, and all facedown, which means secret."

"Aye," I said. "Secret and sure. Silver and children."

"Pain and Frost."

"Nothing's without pain, dam, thou knowest that. Frost... well, with enough silver, you can protect yourself against frost. This'll suit me fine."

The stonecaster watched me out the door with a foreboding frown, but I shrugged it off. It was Gorham I wanted and Gorham I would have.

The tanner was more businesslike and much less pleasant. He stank like his tannery, and his spell powder stank even more.

"Give it to the young man in his cha, and sugar it well," he said. "He'll never notice if you're touching up his leg the while he drinks." He sniggered to himself and his hand brushed my breast as he handed it over. "Hope you treat him well," he said. "That stuff'll bind him to you for all his breathing days, and no mistake."

"It ought to," I snapped. "It cost enough."

Gorham drank it down like it was sweet cider, while I slid my hand up his leg and whispered in his ear. He was sleeping in the hayloft of a livery stable in return for grooming and cleaning tack, and later that night we snuggled in the hay and I opened myself to him body and soul, sure of him at last. For there was no doubt that his eyes were resting warmer on me than they'd ever done before, and his hands were more urgent and his words were all of love and staying together, forever. I had no doubt it was the spell. I drowned happily in the scent of him, the clean, rich smell of horses and hay, and if there came a moment or two when the memory of the old innkeeper slid between us, it was soon over and forgotten.

When he went on to Sandanie at the end of the week, I went with him. Rumer and Rawnie wailed like cormorants as we left, but it may be they were not so unhappy to see me go, when I'd given them two-thirds of our silver and left them free to go where they pleased and sing where they liked, without a baby sister scowling disapproval at them.

And with Gorham, Rawnie had said that I'd be safe and well looked after: "For he worships the ground you walk on, and has done since he laid eyes on you that first day!"

"He'll learn," Rumer grinned. "First time he tries to spend his silver for something she don't approve on. He'll learn."

I turned my nose up at her and we laughed.

But it seemed he never did. It seemed he liked the way I organized our lives, bargained with his customers, insisted on earning as much of my own keep as I could in the inns and on the town greens. I traveled with more pleasure than ever before, and I rounded out with good eating and warm living until I could only juggle, not tumble no more, for tumbling needs you thin and wiry.

The first babe was a girl, Hazel, that we called Zel, and the second, a boy. The years they were born, Gorham took on with a horse dealer for two whole seasons and we stayed planted in one place longer than either of us had ever done in our lives. Mitchen, that was, both times, where we lived in half a cottage that belonged to the horse dealer. The other half was rented by the dealer's farrier, Flax, who became the second child's namesake and taught Gorham all he knew of farriery in recompense, not having any young ones of his own.

I loved the long winter nights by the fire in a good sound cottage with food on the hob, and Gorham's big feet stretched to the blaze. Gorham teased me that I loved the cottage more than him, more than the babies, which wasn't so far from the truth, for I was never a motherly girl, not even when I was nursing. But I treasured those babes, for they were two more ties that kept Gorham bound to me, and not by no spell. For it seemed to me that the spell had worked too well, and had trapped me, too.

"Look at me, love," I'd say to him, and turn his eyes to me. I'd search his face over and over, holding him between my palms. I didn't even know what I was looking for, and was sure I never found it.

How could I? I was looking for real love, for love that wasn't called up by spells, for love that settled itself on me and not just on the girl who'd served him that cup of cha. Even if it had come, would I have seen it? Would it have been any different from the spell-wrought tenderness I'd seen on his face that first night? Surely it would be, I thought. Surely years of living together, loving together, would breed a truer kind of love than that.

But all I saw on his face was the same look he'd had that night in the stable loft.

We brought up the two young ones like true Travelers, to know the Road and love it, to walk uncomplainingly through cold winds and sweltering sun. Later, when times were good, we bought a cart and horse. It was a wild pony from the marshland, who'd been called unbreakable, but Gorham whispered him to sleep and gentled him awake until he was tame as a lovebird, and nibbled gently on Gorham's ear while he was being harnessed.

I taught my young ones singing and juggling, and as much tumbling as I could manage in those days. Zel was the spit of me, dark hair and dark eyes with a strong mouth, and no nonsense about her. Flax was sweet as honey, with a voice like a meadowlark that earned us good takings by the time he was waist-high.

"Look at me, love," I still said, from time to time, but I'd given up hope of ever finding what I was looking for.

Once, when we was back in Carlion, I tried to find the tanner again, to have the spell taken off. He was gone, the neighbors told me, murdered by a customer who hadn't liked the consequences of his spell. I felt a sweet shaft of satisfaction mingle with my disappointment; I knew how the customer had felt.

When Zel was fifteen and Flax twelve, they took to the Road by themselves, wild to try their wings.

Gorham didn't like it. "They're not old enough," he complained to me. "They'll get into all manner of harm."

"How old was you?"

"Fifteen—"

"And I was thirteen. They've traveled all their born days—they'll be fine."

He gave in, as he always did to me, but with a frown. I didn't care: he was mine again, it was just the two of us, and without the young ones to feed and clothe, we were riding high.

The night after they went I lay in his arms. "You don't look in my face no more," he said suddenly. "You've given it up, haven't you? Given up hoping you'll find whatever it was you were looking for."

My heart swelled and I kissed him and murmured, "No, don't be silly." But I had no real answer for him. He was right: I had given up hoping for real love.

That year we went to Pless for the horse fair. Our pony was getting old and we'd more than enough put away to buy a new one, perhaps, Gorham hoped, even a horse.

"No," I said definitely, "just a pony. We can't afford a horse."

"You've got enough silver to buy a whole string of horses, woman," Gorham shouted at me. It was a new thing, him shouting.

It stung me and I stung back. "We'd have no silver left at all if I let you spend what you liked when you liked! That silver's against our old age, man, against the year we'd freeze to death if we didn't have enough to pay our way."

He quietened and shook his head. "It may be that year'll come, and may be not, woman."

He went out of the horse barn where a friend of his was letting us stay, and I didn't see him again that night, though I stayed awake and waited all the night through, my heart knocking hard in me at every step, but it was never him. And that was new, too.

I went looking for him the next day, though I didn't tell anyone that I'd lost him, and that way I got to talking to a score of townsfolk. I came back to the horse barn bubbling with excitement, and found him sluicing himself down at the trough. He straightened hurriedly, with an apology on his lips, but I waved him silent.

"The farrier's dead and he's got no child!" I blurted out.

"What?"

"The horse dealer, old Tinsley. He died last week."

Gorham looked shocked. "I was planning to visit him this morning. He was only my da's age. What happened?"

"Stroke. Isn't it wonderful?"

"Wonderful? Woman!"

"Aye, I mean, of course, it's bad that he's dead. But he's got no child. And his widow's looking to sell the farm."

Gorham stared at me blankly. "Sell—"

"Aye! We've got enough, Gorham. Only just, we'd have nothing behind us, but we could do it. Sure and certain, we could settle here and be set for the rest of our lives."

I was ready with all the arguments but he didn't argue. He went thoughtful like, and quiet. "Let me think on it," he said. "A few days."

175

At the end of the week the bargain was made and we moved into the cottage out by the farm. It was just a few acres then, with a rickety stable and a couple of yards for training the horses. Tinsley's widow moved in with her sister, and the townsfolk nodded approval. Pless wasn't a town we'd been in much over the years, and it was clear that most folk didn't know that we'd been Travelers—with our good burghers' clothes and our solid cart. Crafters we was taken for, and I was pleased, having no wish to see contempt in anyone's eyes. For Travelers, there is no doubt, are scorned and mistrusted, and that's not good for business. We already knew how to talk like townsfolk; we'd done it for fun, pretended, but now it was real. I kept at Gorham until he agreed to leave our Traveler talk behind us.

I expected to be as happy as sky is blue in that sturdy cottage, with my trivet and my cupboards, and my pots and pans hanging from the hooks above the fire. So far as fire and clean water and a soft bed could make me happy, I was. But Gorham was away from that fire entirely too much. I didn't understand it at first; it'd seemed he wanted this move as much as me.

"Look at me, love," I said to him one night when we was in bed, when he was home for once at a reasonable hour, but he turned his face away as if I'd see something shameful there. I let it drop, but cold crept up my spine and my heart started thudding like it would shake the bed. I lay awake too long that night, and he was gone again when I woke up.

In the morning light I went to watch him in the yard with a new two-year-old, and found him humming at his work. He grinned at me but ducked his head out of sight. Too late. That grin was different from any he'd ever given me.

Of course, it was a woman in the marketplace who told me, the thin fishmonger with the buckteeth, "for your own good," she said, and "I think you ought to know." Gorham had a fancy woman.

Her name was Maude and she was a seamstress for the clothier, one of Acton's people, with fair hair and blue eyes, and not even younger than me—a year or two older. She'd been respectable up until this, the fishmonger said, but now it was all over Pless and no wonder, shameless as they both were about it, laughing in the inn together until after the late summer dark, walking back to her place bold as you please.

I believed it straightaway. Gorham would laugh and reach for what he wanted with no thought of consequences, just as he'd done with me. But I searched his face when he ate at my table, while he slept. He had changed toward me, no doubt. Had the spell worn off? Or worse—had the spell never worked at all? Had Gorham's love been real all this time? Had I found a lie, even while he was showing me the truth? If I'd known, could I have kept his love, worked for it, instead of believing it was mine no matter what?

I was filled with rage…at the tanner, at the stonecaster who'd sent me there, at my own young self for being so foolish, so ready to believe, at Gorham, for not making me see—all these years—that I was really at the center of his heart, where Maude was now. I was murderous with rage, but I held it back. I was never no fool. Without Gorham, I had nothing: no house, no food, no fire. Without Gorham, it was back on the Road again, back into the desperate winters. I was too old for that.

Gorham never mentioned Maude's name. Nor did I. I accepted his absence from my bed without a word. I even turned toward him in the night, when he occasionally reached for me, hesitantly, thinking that maybe the day would come when he'd tire of his fancy woman and come back home to stay. I wanted him to, wanted another chance to make him love me real and true.

But it was too late, even when we did well enough to buy more acres next to ours, even when we prospered enough that we could move into a big house in town and give up the farm cottage altogether. It was bitter for me, that day. Everything I'd worked for, saved for, had come true, and all it meant was that he'd now find it even easier to slip along to Maude's and leave me alone.

When he was gone, in the dead of night, when he was sleeping warm and cozy with his fancy woman, I shook my bag of silver out onto my bed and counted the pieces, over and over, listening for his step. But all I heard was the clink and repeated clink of falling coins, and I wished the tanner was still alive so I could try his spell one more time.

ASH

A SH WATCHED Doronit carefully the few days after the Ghost Begone Festival, but she gave no sign that anything was amiss. She was quiet, but somehow pleased with herself. The whole city was quiet, recoiling from the shock of festival night.

Even the ghosts were quiet. They skulked in corners, and looked at passersby out of the corners of their white eyes, with half-smug, half-fearful smiles. Ash ignored them and they seemed happy to cooperate with him. No one suspected that he had set the ghosts loose to hag-ride the town.

Ash couldn't stop thinking about the girl he had killed. He wouldn't let himself think about the warning she had given, but he was ashamed that he hadn't gone back to the alleyway three days after he had killed her, to help her ghost move on, as he had with the two men who had tried to kill Martine.

That had been his responsibility, and he had failed. He had acted as though her ghost wasn't...wasn't *worthy* of being helped, as though she were not really human, just a doll in a game of Doronit's. He was black-burning ashamed of that, remembering her clear ghostly eyes and her wry mouth. He should have gone back to acknowledge his guilt in her death, paid the blood price and set her free. Instead, he was in her debt, no matter what Martine said. According to his mother, the debts he couldn't pay in this life must be paid in the next. He and the girl would meet again—somewhere, somehow—in another life.

He had avoided that alleyway since the night he had killed

her, but now he found himself passing by on that side of Acton Square, glancing down the narrow, winding lane as if he might see her there. It was stupid. It was worse than stupid, it was now a habit, the kind of predictable behavior that safeguarders should never set up, in case anyone was looking for a place to waylay them. But he did it anyway.

A couple of weeks after Ghost Begone Night, Ash and Aelred were set to guard the gates of a select and seemingly endless party in one of the restaurants in Acton Square. After the party guests had gone home, Aelred slapped him on the shoulder with a quick "see you in the morning" and made off downhill toward the boardinghouse behind the Sailor's Rest, where he lived. Although the restaurant was on the other side of the square from the alleyway, Ash found himself drifting over there rather than setting out for Doronit's.

There was no one about at this time of night. His boots rang out in the cool air and he changed his footfall so that he walked silently. It had been a long time since he'd heard silence. He was used to it, out on the Road, but it was a rare thing in Turvite. He slowed his steps, enjoying it, but was still, compulsively, making his way to the alleyway. He knew she wouldn't be there. He knew there would be no clear-eyed ghost waiting for him near the wall where he'd killed her. But he was drawn there anyway; he would take one look, and go home.

He looked, and saw the girl's death reenacted. There she was, up against the wall. There he was, knife in hand, blade glinting as he drew it back for the second strike, the kill strike.

"NO!" he yelled, and leaped forward, reaching for that hand. He realized his stupidity as he leaped: he couldn't touch a ghost, couldn't touch a haunting, he would go straight through...

And he cannoned, instead, into a solid, muscular body, much larger than his. His mind stopped thinking altogether, but his body knew what to do. The months of training had taught him reflexes he hadn't known existed. *Keep the knife away, get rid of it.* In a single swift action, he grabbed the man's hand and slammed it down on the cobbles. The knife skittered away and they both rolled to their feet, and were now facing each other, wary.

He was a big man, stronger, no doubt. But Ash's first blow had done some damage: the man favored one leg, as though his ankle were twisted, and he winced as he put it to the ground. He saw Ash notice it and rushed forward, his big hands out for Ash's throat. *Under and up.* Ash ducked under the attack and used his opponent's momentum to throw him up into the air, across his back, so the big man landed heavily on the cobbles. Ash drew his boot knife. The knife in his hand, in this place, brought his mind back to life, put him in control of his reflexes. He didn't want to kill anyone else.

"I don't want to kill you," he said. He heard the sincerity in his own voice, and the complete belief that he would be able to kill this much larger man. The man heard it too, and scrambled up from the cobbles and then backed away with one hand raised in surrender. He pulled himself around the corner and Ash could hear his footsteps echoing fast across the square.

It was only then that Ash turned to the girl.

Of course, it wasn't the girl. Wasn't even *a* girl. It was the little jeweler with the big mustache. As soon as Ash helped him up from where he had fallen, he began babbling with gratitude and shock.

"Oh, gods, if you hadn't come, if you hadn't come, he was going to *kill* me, actually *kill* me . . . He had a knife, did you see, he had a knife, he was going to k-k-*kill* me . . ."

"It's a popular spot for that," Ash said, and then realized the man was shaking. "It's all right, it's all right, he's gone, he's not coming back... You're all right now." His words seemed to also calm himself down: he was a safeguarder with a client now, not a fool reacting to a ghost who wasn't even there.

After some time the jeweler finally swallowed hard, and seemed to pull himself back into something close to his normal cynical self-assurance. But his hands were still trembling. "I have to go back to my inn... It's down near the docks..." He peered fearfully out of the alleyway at the empty square. "I don't suppose you..."

"I'll come with you," Ash said resignedly. They walked together across the square, the jeweler looking over his shoulder at every second step. "What were you doing in that alleyway in the first place?" Ash asked. "It's not the safest place in the city."

"I wasn't in the alleyway!" the jeweler said indignantly. "I was just walking back to my inn, through the square, after dinner at a client's house and that... that *thug* grabbed me."

"You should hire a safeguarder if you're going to walk around the city at night," Ash scolded.

"I'm going home tomorrow," the jeweler said with obvious relief. "Back to Carlion. It's a lot safer there."

They walked in silence until they reached the Fifty Friends, a middlingly prosperous tavern with an extra house next door for guests.

The jeweler paused under the torch that helped guests climb the steps without falling over their drunk feet. "I'm in your debt," he said.

Ash shook his head. "No, really, you're not."

"Yes, yes, I know I am. I pay my debts." He scrabbled in his pouch and drew out a soft leather bag, about as big as his palm. "Here. You liked this the other day. Have it with my thanks."

Then he darted up the steps and into the door, closing it firmly behind him.

Ash stared at the bag knowing, from the size and the weight, what he would find inside. He drew it out slowly. It glinted warmly in the torchlight, intricate and beautiful. It couldn't possibly be Acton's cloak brooch. Not truly. But something in its heaviness, its undoubted age, told him differently.

To get back to Doronit's house he had only to climb the hill. But his feet took him south from the docks, around the older part of the city, as he thumbed the pattern on the brooch. He walked past the black stone altar and heard, deep in his mind, the susurration of the local gods calling his name. They called whenever he came to this part of town, whenever he passed the altar. He tried hard to ignore them, but the brooch seemed to grow cold in his hands. He walked more quickly.

It was late. It didn't matter if it was Acton's brooch. But he had to know, beyond doubt. Martine would probably be asleep. It would do no harm to go and see. Stonecasters often worked late, their clients preferring the privacy of darkness.

There was a light on in the main room of Martine's house. He hesitated outside. Tonight there were no ghosts waiting for entrance, just the door, plain oiled wood. It was anything but portentous, that door, but it felt like the entrance to somewhere else. It was like the magic circle the Ice People believed in, which takes you to the world of the gods. The local gods whispered his name more loudly, and he raised his hand to knock on the door.

Martine opened it and greeted him without surprise. "Come in."

He sat down on the new fleece rug and she sat opposite him with her bag of stones in her lap. He spat on his palm and held it out. She spat on hers and they clapped and grasped hands. With his other hand he held out the brooch.

"Was this Acton's?" he asked.

She blinked in surprise, and looked at the brooch. Then she smiled, a strange, sideways smile, and reached into the bag.

Only one of the five stones she scattered was faceup. "Certainly," she said softly. "It was his." She turned the others over. "Betrayal. Blood. Murder. Guilt."

"Acton's all right," Ash tried to joke. His insides were churning; he was half nauseous, half excited. He dropped the brooch beside the stones. The fire flickered light over its intricate design.

"There is a story here," Martine said. Her eyes were unfocused while she listened to the stones. "But it is not our story to hear. Nor to tell." She shook her head and let his hand go. "That is all the stones have to say."

They both looked at the brooch. *Acton's.*

A visible shiver went through Martine. "This has seen its share of blood."

"He slaughtered thousands," Ash said slowly, "but I don't get any sense of evil from it. Do you?"

Martine shrugged. "It is just a thing that has passed through many hands since he last touched it. Maybe they have wiped it clean."

"Maybe."

They stared at it until Martine suddenly laughed. "Look at us! Entranced by a bauble! Come, sit up and I will make us some cha."

Ash smiled shamefacedly and sprang up to help her swing the kettle over the fire. They sat companionably in silence until the kettle boiled, and then drank the cha together.

"What am I supposed to do with it?" Ash said suddenly.

"You could sell it. I will give you a warranty that it's genuine. There are many among the old families who would pay well to have a thing of Acton's."

Deep in his mind the local gods whispered, *Keep it*. Martine's face changed, and he knew that she heard them too. It made him feel better.

"Or maybe I'd better not," he said drily.

She laughed. "There *is* some advice it is wiser to take."

"Will you keep it here for me?"

He was reluctant, very reluctant, to take it back to Doronit's, where he would have to conceal it. She would only see profit in it, and he knew she took no account of the local gods. He suspected she even took no account of the powers beyond them.

"That's a great trust," Martine said slowly.

He was surprised; he had taken it for granted that he could trust her, but he had no reason for that, after all, except that she had heard the gods speak to him. Or maybe there was something in her that was the opposite of Doronit—a lack of interest in profit beyond what was necessary to live—which he had recognized because he shared it.

"It's just a brooch," he said.

She smiled that sideways smile that told him she saw right through him. He couldn't help but smile back.

"All right," she said. She picked up the brooch and rose to place it on her mantelpiece. "It will be waiting here for you when you come back." Her words seemed to echo, as though they were part of a prophecy.

"When I come back," he confirmed.

In the silence that followed, the ease between them vanished and he became too aware of his feet and his hands. He reddened and got up.

"I...I'd better—"

"Yes," Martine said. "Go, but be careful of who you trust."

Ash blinked. "I'll try."

She closed the door behind him with a definite thud, as though she was glad to see the back of him, but when he looked at her window she was standing there, watching him, and she raised a hand in farewell as he turned the corner.

He felt lighter, walking home, and not just because he had left Acton's brooch behind him. Martine was the first friend he had found on his own, outside Doronit's control. Perhaps he could craft a life for himself in this city after all.

SAKER

Each night, Rowan, Swallow and Cypress found a place to perform, usually in an inn. Where they were known from past visits they were welcomed, and got beds in the stables. "But no lights, understand," the innkeepers said. "We don't want any fires."

Most of the time, Rowan would make sure they performed at least one song from the distant past, usually about the invasion of the area or town they were in. The customers loved them, banged their tankards on the tables in time with the drumming, and slapped Rowan and Cypress on their backs afterward. While Swallow and Cypress sang, Saker would take notes.

In the vale of Wooding, in the forested valley,
six hundred were slain by the sword-wielding few.
Aelred, he led them, through clearing and coppice
Through river and rushes to victory sweet.

"Six hundred in Wooding," noted Saker. "Near the river."

By ford of the Sprit where water sprites lurk
great-hearted Garlok gathered his men,
led them to raven's nest, glade in the woods.
There were the enemy ranged up against them,
There were the enemy, mighty and strong:
Seven and forty the enemy fallen
By Garlok's strong blade and the blades of three
friends.

"Spritford," wrote Saker. "Forty-seven. Raven's Nest Glade."

On nights when they were not performing, in between villages, Rowan and Swallow would perform some of the history songs that were not popular with Acton's people. Some had been written by Travelers. Saker prized these the most as they often contained detailed information about the victims of an attack: ages, burial and battlegrounds. Rowan's flute cast a high lament into the night for those songs.

Sometimes Rowan would sing in a firm, mellow voice, and Swallow would drum quietly on her knee, showing Cypress the rhythm. Cypress listened as hard as Saker, but Saker could tell that all he really cared about were the rhythms and words, not what they meant.

Each night was precious to Saker because each song brought him closer to his goal, but other things were precious, too. Swallow's calm grace called up long-buried memories of his mother, who had been neither calm nor graceful, but who had shared Swallow's coloring and litheness.

Saker wept quietly into his pillow on the first night a memory returned to him. He saw his mother rushing around the house with a broom after his older sister, threatening retribution for some chore, he couldn't remember what, left undone. His sister shrieked with laughter as she scurried around the table, and his mother was trying not to laugh, too, but shouting, "You're lazy! What are you?" His sister answered breathlessly, hiccuping with laughter, "Lazy!" and finally his mother flung herself down on the settle by the fire, and giggled. He remembered laughing, too, laughing so much his eyes watered. But he couldn't remember when it had happened…how long before they were all dead. But it was a happy memory, and after the tears he went to sleep peacefully.

There was only a handful of memories, and each new one

was priceless. To remember his father hale and strong and whole again just fed his resolution. He had only been able to remember his father after the attack, his head half crushed by a sword blow and the flesh ragged on his shoulder from the spur.

One night, after six long, sorrowful songs, Rowan stopped. "That's all," he said. "You have heard all of them now."

"*All* the old songs?" Saker asked, feeling strangely bereft.

"All the history songs. The others aren't of interest to you."

Saker sat quietly with his notebook on his lap. He looked at its fat pages, almost filled. He looked at Rowan and Swallow, then Cypress.

"Thank you. Then... I must be leaving you soon."

"We'll be in Carlion in a few days," Rowan said.

Saker nodded. The future looked curiously empty, despite all the work he had to do. He would need to go back to the enchanter's house, his house, and work on the map... There were to be no more companionable nights by the fire, no more buried memories surfacing like flowers in a cesspit. Over the last six months he had grown accustomed to being Penda, the student, one of a traveling group. It would take a little time to remember how to be alone again.

"It's been good, having you with us," Rowan said. "Like having our son back."

Swallow frowned. "Nothing like it!" she said sharply, but then smiled at Saker. "But good, nonetheless."

"So your work's over then, cully," Cypress said.

Saker looked at his notebook again, and slowly shook his head. "It's just beginning."

BRAMBLE

GORHAM TOOK HER out to the farm the next day early, after a breakfast of thin porridge, which wasn't half as good as Maryrose's. She turned out the roan in a small field next to the cottage, and set to work.

Cleaning out the cottage took most of the morning. They'd brought an old bed, which Osyth had produced from an attic somewhere, to save having to buy a new one. It was creaky with woodworm, but Gorham lashed it tight with greenhide strips, and with the new ticking (which he'd insisted on) stuffed with fresh straw, it was comfortable enough.

Bramble and Gorham had sat at the kitchen table the night before and made a list of the things she'd need at the cottage: cooking pans, bed linen, dishes, broom, scrubbing brush... Osyth sniffed as they wrote down each item but a few moments later she would appear with a tattered or half-broken or *almost* worn-out version. Bramble had to suppress a fit of the giggles. The shagging woman never threw anything out—not even a badly chipped chamber pot! It'd cut your bum to ribbons if you chanced to sit on it.

"Thanks," Bramble had said when she'd offered that, "but I think I'll buy one of my own."

So the cart had been packed with almost everything she'd need, even if most of it was in poor condition. Gorham fixed a broken leg on the table while Bramble cleaned, but she didn't want to waste too much time with the cottage. Maybe she would get around to prettying it up later.

Sitting on cords of wood at the newly mended table, she lunched on cheese and pickles with day-old bread ("No sense wasting it on the pig," Osyth had said). Gorham had fresh bread, and offered to share it, but Bramble shook her head; she didn't care much anymore. Her sense of taste was dull. She wondered, sometimes, if she would ever really enjoy anything again.

"No need. Besides, you want to be able to tell her that I ate it all up." She tilted her head sideways at him with no smile at all, careful to keep her face straight.

Gorham nodded.

That set the tone for all their exchanges about Osyth: tacit acknowledgment that she was, well, difficult, but never discussing it.

In the afternoon Gorham introduced Bramble to her new job.

She had never been employed before; she hated the idea of taking orders, of being subservient. She wondered if the fog that had surrounded her since the roan's jump would deaden her resentment of being bossed around. But Gorham didn't bark orders. Arriving in the morning, he might say, "I thought we'd see if the chestnut will eat from the hand today." Over those first two days he explained everything that had to be done to keep the farm operating, and what her part would be. And then he generally left her to it.

There was only one exception. She learned to wear boots because Gorham insisted on it. "If a sixteen-hand stallion trod on your bare foot, even accidentally, you'd be off work for weeks." With a stout boot it was merely temporary agony. The first time it happened, the pain cut through the fog all right, although only for a few moments.

She also learned to keep to a routine after she realized that animals thrived when their lives were predictable. She even learned to bite her tongue when clients tried to talk as though they knew one end of a horse from another, when clearly they had never really looked at their own animals.

It was a life they could bear, she and the roan. It made no demands on her that she couldn't fulfill, even with the cloudy glass of death between her and the world. Maybe the sense of detachment made her less restless. What did it matter where she was, after all?

She and the roan explored the countryside each morning before work, and in her time off—usually in the middle of the day—she roamed the forest that bordered Gorham's land. It was a remnant of the old forests that had covered the land before Acton's time: oak, mainly, and pockets of beech and elm, alder and willow along the streams, holly and rowan in thickets where old trees had fallen. She found much of her own food there, trapping rabbits and birds, searching out greens and berries in summer, nuts, acorns, mushrooms and truffles in autumn. She had always helped to fill her family's table and it had satisfied her deeply to sit down to a full meal of her own providing. She'd lost a certain sense of that satisfaction, but it was still good. She supposed that gardeners felt like this about fruit and vegetables they had grown, but why garden, she thought, when the forest did all the work for you?

Besides, what would she do if she didn't roam the forest? Sit in the cottage and knit? As she'd received her pay week by week, she'd replaced most of the broken-down things that Osyth had given her (giving them back punctiliously). Beyond utility, she had done almost nothing to the cottage: there were no curtains, no special plates or dishes, no rugs except one made from rabbit fur that she'd tanned herself. She had never cared about indoor things, and finally she didn't have her mam nagging, "Make your room look nice." Aside from housekeeping, she left the cottage alone and found a new kind of freedom in the unadorned walls and paucity of possessions. She felt light and almost free whenever she thought about how little she owned.

Gorham made her responsible for the physical care of the horses that were brought to them from all over the country for gentling, and mostly that meant becoming very well acquainted with manure and currycombs. But Gorham was a generous man and the day after she arrived, he began to teach her his craft. He was a renowned horse trainer, although by the end of the second year after Bramble joined him, he acknowledged that she was his equal. She might have taken the Road before that. She had certainly intended to. But that was before she saw the chases.

Pless was a famous center for chase races, and they were run at the Autumn and Spring Festivals—after harvest, and after sowing. That first autumn, Gorham took her to see a horse that he'd trained race in the biggest chase of all, the Pless Challenge.

She'd never seen a chase before, didn't even know the rules. The area around Wooding was too hilly and the gullies and chasms too frequent for chases. But she knew, of course, the superstitions.

The Autumn Chase was the oldest, the tradition going back since before Acton came over the mountains. The Kill, who led the chasers over the course, represented the death of the year, her grandam had told her once, and the chasers were the hunters who harried the year to its death. The red scarf the Kill carried was the symbol of its blood.

The Spring Chase was much younger, only a hundred years or so on horseback, although there had always been a footrace in spring to celebrate the new year. The Kill in spring represented new life and it was considered very good luck for one of the riders to actually catch the Kill before the finish line and grab the red scarf. If someone could do that, they became the Kill Reborn.

Although now it was more a sport than a ritual, many still believed that a rider who grabbed the red flag from the Kill in the Spring Chase was someone special, someone marked by the gods. But it was very unlucky for someone to catch the flag in the Autumn Chase. Then it was said that he or she was marked out for death within the year.

Bramble stood with Gorham on a hill a mile from Pless, along with the rest of the spectators, half the town at least, and watched as the riders gathered at the town gate. Among the swirling crowd of horses and riders, each with a brightly colored handkerchief around his neck, there was one, on a stocky gray, with a red scarf tied to a lance.

"That's the Kill," Gorham said. "He sets off before the others, then there's a count to fifty, and then the eight riders go. They have to follow his path exactly, over the obstacles he picks, and the first back to the finish line wins." He pointed to a fence a mile or so on the other side, where there was a small group of men waiting.

"That's it?"

"That's enough." Gorham smiled. "We're looking for Golden Shoes—his rider's wearing a blue kerchief."

She picked out Golden Shoes, a sprightly chestnut shying sideways, away from the Kill's red scarf. It had energy enough, she thought.

The Kill set out. The spectators on the hill spontaneously started counting in unison as the rider set his horse to the first fence, and at "...forty-eight, forty-nine, FIFTY!" the horses at the gate surged forward, fighting for position. They took the first jump over an easy post-and-rail fence, but as they scrambled up the hill toward the crowd Bramble caught her breath. She hadn't realized how fast they would go.

The Kill swept past in a gust of wind, red scarf fluttering, and after him the pack of horses came. She could hear the rumble of their hooves on the ground, then felt the ground start to shake.

The pack went over a stone wall and then a fallen tree. By now the best four riders were out in front, and Bramble was beginning to realize that it took more than a fast horse to win.

"They have to go over the same obstacles as the Kill," Gorham said in her ear, "but they can go over them at any point. The good riders take the straight line, even if it's more dangerous."

She could see that the leaders were not jumping their horses at exactly the same place as the Kill. They cut corners even if it meant setting their mounts at a higher section of a fence, or worse, a stone wall, where they couldn't see what lay on the other side.

The pack thundered up and flashed past them too fast for Bramble to take in more than a confusion of colors, shaking ground, flying dust and riders' shouts.

Bramble realized that she was shouting, too, that all of the spectators were urging on their favorites. She wasn't yelling for any horse in particular, she wanted them all to go fast—to go even faster. Her heart was pounding, her fists were clenched, and her body was leaning after the pack as though she could fly across the fields with them. For the first time since the jump across the chasm, she felt alive.

"Golden Shoes was second, did you see?" Gorham's hand gripped her shoulder. "There she goes!"

Bramble could just see the blue kerchief around the neck of

the second rider. Coming downhill, the pack picked up speed. The next jump was over a stream. It looked deceptively easy, but it was muddy with autumn rain on both sides, and with the extra momentum the footing was treacherous. The first rider made it across safely. Golden Shoes slid a little on landing, but her rider gathered her nicely and she kept her feet. The third rider went down sprawlingly, and the horses behind were coming too fast to stop. Two riders managed to wrench their horses around to jump at a different angle, so they landed on either side of the fallen horse, but two others crashed straight over and were collected by the muddy bank.

The spectators on the hill froze with a collective gasp, except for one woman who cried out "Robbie!" and started running down to the stream. The others took breath and followed.

There were four horses down, three of them struggling back to their feet. The fourth, the bay, which had been the first to fall, was rocking backward and forward, trying to get his feet under him, but without success. His rider had been thrown off to one side, and was sitting with his head in his hands. The other riders were already standing by the time the group from the hill arrived.

The crying woman hurried through the stream careless of the wet and embraced the seated rider. "Gods, Robbie, gods," she said, again and again. "I thought you were dead." It was clear she was his mother.

Gorham had gone straight to the bay's head and helped him up, but it was now walking with a pronounced limp.

Using his mother's arm to stand, the rider came over, his face full of concern. "Is it broken?"

Everyone quieted for the answer. Gorham felt the fetlock carefully, his face grave, and then smiled. "Just a sprain," he said. He looked over toward the finishing fence and the others turned with him, curiosity rising now their worst fears had been allayed.

"Who got the Kill?" the rider asked, but no one knew.

Gorham cupped his mouth with his hands and shouted to the judges, "Who won?"

"Golden Shoes," came back the reply.

Gorham thumped Bramble on the shoulders. "I knew it," he said exultantly. "I knew that one had it in her."

Bramble looked at the four horses that had made it to the finish fence. They were circling, cooling down. Golden Shoes's rider raised the lance with the red scarf attached, clearly the symbol of victory.

She looked back at the riders leading their horses to and fro, checking their legs and their wind, seeming to have forgotten the fall already. One of them had blood coming from his nose, but he wiped it away with the back of his hand and examined his horse's off-hind hoof.

She looked up at the clear autumn sky, felt the thundering pulse in her blood begin to calm down, and smiled. The fog was gathering again, the glass clouding. But now she had a remedy.

"When's the next chase?" she asked Gorham.

"Not until next spring," he said with a knowing grin. "Got you hooked already, have we?"

She tried to seem unmoved, but found herself smiling in a way that was anything but calm, and said, "Next spring. Good. That will give me time to get the roan ready."

He was startled. "Ready for what?"

She gestured to the horses at the stream, to the finishing fence, to Golden Shoes and her rivals. "Ready for this. Next spring I ride."

Once he got over the surprise, Gorham was enthusiastic, although cautionary. "That roan's a good, strong horse, even though he's old enough that you'll only get a few years out of him," he said as they strolled back to the town gates. "He's got the bone for it, and he's got the hindquarters. But some horses aren't jumpers, and some horses aren't chasers, and you can't change that. It's in the blood."

"He can jump when he wants to," Bramble said drily, remembering the chasm beneath her and the jolt as they had landed. The gods may or may not have helped them over, but that first leap had been prodigious.

"Most horses can jump when they want to," Gorham said. "But will he jump when *you* want him to, and where, and at the right speed?"

He went on for some time like that, to prepare her for disappointment, but he could feel his own excitement rising. He'd trained others' horses to chase, but never one of his own. Well, the roan wasn't exactly his, but it would race from his stable, which was much the same thing. He had a brief vision of Bramble handing him the red scarf from the Kill's lance in front of the townsfolk, and smiled inside. Then he sobered, remembering the duties still awaiting him at home.

"I've got to go," he said at the gates. "Osyth's having a special postrace morning tea for the town council and the winning owner and rider." He paused. Osyth wouldn't thank him for inviting Bramble home, but it seemed rude to just leave her standing there.

"Better you than me," Bramble said, grimacing, releasing him from his predicament. She smiled, pleased that he had wanted to invite her, relieved that he hadn't, and knowing he had seen her relief. So they nodded and went their ways.

But later that afternoon Gorham arrived at the farm, rubbing his hands as he approached her, and comfortably back in his work clothes. "Well, no time like the present to find out if you've got a chance. He hasn't had any hard work today, we'll try him over a few small jumps," Gorham said, and Bramble realized that he was as excited as she was.

Yet when she had changed into her oldest clothes and was taking the roan out to the training paddock where Gorham was dismantling the big jumps, to leave small logs for her first training session, he stared disapprovingly at her.

"Where's his saddle?"

"I don't use a saddle. You know that."

"You have to when you jump—at least if you're jumping high fences at speed. You'll fall off if you don't." He watched as doubt crossed her face. "Trust me," he said. "You need to keep your own balance or you won't be able to balance the horse and he'll fall. Do you want him to break his leg because you have a fancy to ride bareback?"

It wasn't the words so much as the tone that convinced her. She realized that he used the same tone with uppity two-year-old colts who thought they could get the better of him, and laughed, but she went and got the saddle. The roan flipped his ears back at her as she put it on, but resignedly, as though he'd always known that the bareback days were too good to last.

That first day of training, the roan had lifted himself over the small logs as though they weren't there. Bramble, solid in her saddle, barely felt the motion. The fog didn't lift as she had hoped, but this was only the first step. She knew that when she was racing she would come alive again. She had to.

"Well, you might be lucky," Gorham said. "Seems he's done this before, and I'd say he knows how to set himself right."

He put up the next level of jumps. The horse dealt with these easily—it was Bramble who had to learn the skills, then, and on the days that followed, as the jumps grew higher.

"Keep your weight over his center of balance. No—*forward!*"

Gorham yelled. "Keep your elbows in—one of the other riders is just as likely to grab one and hoist you off."

She stopped and stared at him, the roan snatching a mouthful of grass when he realized she was distracted.

"What, you thought this was a nice family outing?" Gorham laughed. "They're out to win and some of them don't care how. The winning rider gets a purse of silver, you know."

Bramble nodded, smiling tightly, and fleetingly thought of her foot snapping back that man's head. Anyone who meddled with her was going to get worse than he gave, she thought, then she put it out of her mind and concentrated on crouching in her stirrups to take her weight forward.

"It's not just jumping," Gorham said, over and over, as they cleaned tack or mucked out the stables. "It's strategy, and cunning, and knowing when to push your horse and when to let him take a rest."

Bramble shook her head. "Maybe. And maybe it's just a matter of going faster than anyone else."

Gorham shook his head back at her, but he chuckled as he did it. "If you can, lass, if you can."

Gorham had a long, unfenced stretch of land that bordered the forest: a smooth, rabbit-free length of grass, close-cropped by sheep that were folded each night by the farmer next door. She had tried the roan out there the morning after the chase, just on sunrise.

She had galloped the roan before, of course; how could she have resisted it? But racing speed was to everyday galloping as a full rose was to a bud. That morning as she steadied him, wanting to set off from a standing start, as though they were racing, she thought that she had forgotten what it was like to really look at the world. The fog was still with her, but there was a break in it now, and she could look through it, even feel through it.

The autumn air was rich with loam and mushroom scent, with moisture and the promise of a fine day. It was so early that not even the thrushes were singing. The horse moved like an extension of her, so that she was as strong as he, as fierce and agile and elemental. She sat, poised in a moment of perfect balance, perfect calm, and then pressed hard with her legs and said, "Go!" then, "Faster!" pressing harder, and "*Faster!*" leaning down on his neck, feeling the exhilaration sweep through the roan first and then up into her, the intoxication, the rushing splendor of speed.

When they were forced to draw up by the fence at the end of the paddock, she looked back on that moment of blissful calm before the run and wondered why she had thought she was so happy. It was nothing compared to a flat-out gallop!

She had been grateful for Gorham's training: the discipline of the training paddock, where each jump had to be attempted with calm and precision, was, she knew, necessary for both her and the roan. But on its own she knew it wouldn't help her win. She had to learn to jump at speed, across country, over streams and stone walls and brush fences and wooden rails. And this she had to do alone.

That training took up all her midday hours, the time she had liked to spend in the forest. Although she had loved those rambles, she let them go without a thought, and bought food from town instead. Chases were run in the midmorning, Gorham told her, or at noon, so she and the roan had to get used to racing in the full sun.

She started with the fences around the farm, learning to approach them at increasing speeds. When she could manage them easily at a half-speed gallop, she set out across country, jumping as many obstacles as she could, trying to improve their form in the time they had before the iron-hard ground of winter frost made riding dangerous for the roan.

By then she knew that a chase was to a gallop as a gallop was to a canter: the rush to the fence, the takeoff, the soaring speed through the air, the landing and swift, powerful thrust that got them to full speed again, were like drinking spirits on an empty stomach, like diving into the quarry, like love. And perhaps, she thought, this was what the Love stone had foretold in her casting.

She fell, of course. She fell into mud and onto gorse, pitched headfirst over stone walls and backward into cowpats. She fell, and learned to fall, and learned to keep hold of the reins as she fell. The horse, by some magic of his own, never hurt himself, although he, too, often fell. Always, she realized, it was her fault.

Because the roan was a natural jumper who loved speed as much as she did, it was usually imbalance, hesitation or stupidity on her part that set him wrong for a fence. She berated herself silently after each fall, and apologized to the horse, who snuffled in her hair and never held it against her. Even after the worst fall, standing wet with mud up to her armpits, her head splitting from contact with the ground, her shoulder almost dislocated from being wrenched by the reins, she was full of hope. But the rush of feeling died away when she was off his back and the training sessions were finally over.

She waited for the spring thaw with a little girl's impatience, and as soon as the ground was soft enough she and the roan went out in the early morning and at noon again, getting stronger, growing closer, and building on that wordless understanding that allowed them to act as one. The roan's jumping was flawless, joyful, exuberant; the only thing that concerned her was that he'd had no practice racing against other horses.

"Well, he'll either like it or hate it," Gorham said cheerfully, as they watched the first of the spring foals being born late one night.

"Some horses just take to it, others never do. Try not to frighten him, that's all."

She snorted. "He doesn't know how to be frightened."

Gorham turned his head slowly to look at her, grinning. "That's because you haven't been frightened so far."

At that moment the foal began to slither down the birth canal onto the straw, and it took all their attention.

A little later Gorham continued as though there hadn't been an interruption. "What are you going to call him?"

It took Bramble a while to work out what he meant. "Call him? The Roan, I suppose."

"You can't call an entry in the chases 'The Roan.'" He shook his head decisively.

She smiled at him. "Well, you pick one."

He pulled at his lip. He'd always wanted to do this, to name a chaser. He had all sorts of names picked out: Gorham's Pride, Gorham's Mane, Silverfleet (chosen, he remembered with a chuckle, when he was very young and romantic). But naming a horse for someone else was a big responsibility. He looked at Bramble, her dark eyes and curling black hair, tanned skin and crooked smile.

He smiled back. "What about Thorn?" he said, and she laughed and laughed.

"Bramble on Thorn," she agreed, still chuckling as they walked back to the cottages. She paused at her door. "But that's not his name, you know."

Gorham nodded. "Not around here," he said, and she nodded back, a compact.

She'd never felt she had the right to name the roan. Maybe it was because he came to her through death, or that she owed him her life, but more likely it was because in her thoughts he didn't need a name. He was *the* horse: the others needed names because they were not. And it had to do with his own nature, with his sensitivity to her thoughts, and his courage. It had to do with all the reasons why she was sure they would win.

They arrived two days before the race, to give the roan time to rest. Gorham had registered the horse for the first available chase of the season; he wouldn't be eligible to enter any of the important races until he had won at least one. It was at Sendat, farther north, in Central Domain.

Maude, Gorham's fancy woman, came too. It was the only thing Bramble didn't like about Gorham, the fact that he kept a fancy woman. Not that he tried to hide it—the whole town knew. But having dealt with Osyth, Bramble was a little more forgiving of Gorham than she would have been otherwise.

Maude came up to Bramble at the beginning of the journey to Sendat and said that she had no mind to let Gorham go off on his own. "Not 'cause I'm suspicious-minded, like, lass," she said cheerily. "I just like the outing."

Bramble smiled at her; no one could help liking Maude, who carried her generous nature on her face as clearly as Osyth carried her miserliness. *Still*, Bramble thought, *I wouldn't put up with it. No man of mine would go off with a fancy woman and have me still there to come home to.*

They stayed in a comfortable inn in the center of town. The rooms were bright and smelled of lemon, but Bramble intended sleeping in the stable. In the afternoon she walked through the town to the chase fields. Sendat nestled under a tall hill, topped, as usual, by the local warlord's fort. At the base of the hill, where the smell wouldn't offend those in the fort, was the execution place. Instead of just one gibbet, this warlord had set up three, next to the scaffold and rock press. They were all full, and the bodies, only a few days old, showed the obvious marks of torture: burns, broken bones, scars that hadn't had time to heal. Bramble wondered if the warlord was using the spring chase to make a point; the gibbets were eloquent of power and control.

The warlord was called Thegan, the same name as Acton's son. No one was sure if it was his proper name or one he had assumed. Thegan was a new warlord, from the cold north, and he had married, a local told them, the old warlord's daughter, the Lady Sorn, and taken control. He still kept his old Domain in the north, which a son from an earlier marriage was overseeing for him. That was unusual. Bramble wondered whether the other warlords were happy about it, or if the long peace that had kept the Domains prosperous in recent years was at risk.

The waitress who told them about Thegan spoke with a mixture of admiration and circumspection, careful not to criticize him directly. That and the gibbets told Bramble all she wanted to know about him. She and Gorham had trained all the old warlord's horses, but she suspected they would look elsewhere for custom in the future. She felt vaguely sorry for the girl the warlord had married so conveniently, but her thoughts soon returned to the chase ahead.

Most Kills were experienced chase riders, and it was considered an honor if the warlord or town council asked you to set the course. The Kill could take any route he chose within set boundaries, any combination of fences, any direction, doubling back or straight ahead. Some Kills waited until the chase itself to decide their course, letting whim take over, while others planned obsessively, in secret, to make their course the most challenging.

Aside from the spectacle, the chase was now used mostly as a means of identifying good bloodlines for the warlords' messenger horses, and for gambling. The first Spring Kill was always the youngest person possible, for luck, to represent the new-born earth. And maybe, Bramble thought, always suspicious, to give the riders the best chance of catching the Kill and having a Kill Reborn, bringing luck to the town. But perhaps not. The Kill Reborn was the stuff of fire talk and bedtime tales; it hadn't happened for over thirty years.

The first Spring Chase was often dangerous, as a young, inexperienced Kill could choose the route badly, pick fences that were fine for one riding alone but death traps for three or four horses jumping at once.

She tried to plot all the potential courses, but it was impossible. She decided to follow her instinct: take the roan to the front immediately and stay there. She was certain in her bones that he would be faster than any of the others, and he was used to jumping alone. Staying in front would protect her from the underhanded tactics of the more experienced riders. She was not a cunning person, but she was determined to be very good at winning.

By the morning of the chase she was anxious past eating, almost past talking. The fog still surrounded her and she wanted the chase—the jumps, the speed, the danger—to bring her back to life again, at least for the duration of the race. Gorham counseled her on strategy over breakfast, while she saddled up, while they walked to the starting point. She nodded and didn't hear anything he said. The only thing she was aware of was the roan at her shoulder. She smiled at Maude and Gorham and then went to collect her neckerchief. It was bright blue: a good color, a lucky color.

She tied it on and swung herself up in the saddle as the other riders did the same, jostling and swearing at each other. They eyed her sideways. Women rode often enough in the chases, but none of them had seen this one before, looking like a Traveler with her black hair and eyes. Wasn't strong enough, most of them thought, not enough muscle, not enough guts, most likely, though her horse looked fit enough...too strong for a girl. Some noticed the set of her mouth and felt a momentary doubt, but pushed it aside to concentrate on their own mounts, fresh and restive, eager to race.

The Kill was a young man—very young, very fair—wearing the warlord's colors of brown and gold. He was pale with excitement and shifted his grip on the lance as his hands sweated. "Ride!" the counter shouted, and the Kill set off. "One, two, three..."

Bramble felt the fog lift, the glass clear. The riders counted with him, still jostling for position. Bramble found herself being edged to the back and shouldered the roan forward until she could see the Kill over another horse's head. She counted under her breath, tapping it out with one finger on the roan's neck. They had practiced this, too, the roan growing more and more eager to move as the taps continued. At "forty-nine" she flicked him hard and at "fifty" he was springing ahead, sliding through the gap in front to be among the first group away.

They headed downhill in a helter-skelter flurry of hooves and shouts. Bramble pressed the roan, fixed her eyes on the Kill ahead, and blocked out everything else. The horse was enjoying himself, his ears pricked and muscles springy, having a wonderful time. Bramble laughed under her breath and leaned forward into the first jump.

It was post and rails: easy for all the horses and reassuring to start with. One fell, all the same, at the back. There was a rise up to the second fence and some of the horses slipped back from the first group. Bramble found herself one of three: a chestnut mare on one side, and a dapple gray on the other.

They cleared the low stone fence with equal ease and curved to follow the Kill together. He was over a stream and heading

PAMELA FREEMAN

for a high stone wall. They surged forward, increasing the pace on the flat. The chestnut misjudged the width of the stream and landed in the water. She splashed out but had lost time, so the gray and Bramble were now ahead.

There was a good distance to the wall, and the gray began to edge forward. Bramble didn't even have time to react: the roan surged ahead. She could feel his determination not to be beaten, and his pleasure at leaving the other horse behind.

They were a length ahead at the stone fence and two lengths ahead when they landed. The roan was a marvel, taking off at the perfect moment, and landing with a spring that got them straight back to racing speed. Bramble laughed again and set her eyes on the Kill.

There were two more fences. She and the roan took them alone, just as she had imagined. She was exultant, and so was he. They could both hear the hooves behind them, but nothing could catch them. The practice gallops had been nothing, a canter in comparison. *No one has ever been so fast,* she thought. She could feel the presence of the gods, but only faintly, as though not even they could keep up.

As the Kill labored up the last hill to the finish point, she and the roan flashed past him. The gods had finally caught up. She could feel their presence—the pressure of their attention—just as she had when they leaped the chasm. She reached out and plucked the lance from the Kill's hand, laughing aloud and ignoring the gasps from the crowd at the finish. She waved the lance with its red scarf above her head; she was fully alive again, the fog had gone completely, and she heard the crowd laugh and cheer with her, felt the gods themselves exult.

The roan reared in reaction to the crowd's cheers, the scarf swept out on the breeze, and Bramble was, for a moment, a heraldic figure, the crest for some great warlord: the Kill Reborn.

ASH

DORONIT KEPT Ash busy, training him in the use of poisons. He didn't like the catalog of symptoms, which was gruesome yet compelling.

"Why do I have to know all this?" he protested. "I don't want to poison people."

She smiled at him condescendingly so that again he felt like a child. He was so easy to read, so easy to manipulate; it exhilarated her like a sweet wine. Leading him, step by step, into intrigue and sophistication had become as much her favorite hobby as a way of crafting a useful tool.

"Of course you don't, sweetheart," she said, keeping her voice steady and warm, as to a child. "But others may want to poison you. You need to know what to look for, what to smell for; you need to recognize the effects. With the slower-acting venoms, it's possible to save yourself if you realize what's happened early enough. Come, don't be foolish."

Looking very foolish and rather adorable, he sat down next to her at the workbench in her cellar and examined the herbs she had spread out in front of him.

"Lily of the valley," she said, touching the leaves and red berries. "Yellow leaves are the strongest. They must be kept thoroughly dry, otherwise they grow moldy and lose their strength. This stops the heart, like foxglove. Some use it as a medicine."

And so she went on: meadow saffron, celandine, white hellebore, mistletoe, and rarer plants like yellow pheasant's eye and blackthorn.

"Now with rue," she said, "most use the leaves, but I've found that the stems are just as potent—" She pretended to catch herself up on that and looked at him to see if he had been paying attention. She had to ease him in with nothing too shocking, nothing he would think *unforgivable*. "Not for poison, of course, sweetheart. But... well, you're old enough to know the truth of it, yes? When a young woman wishes to be rid of a child in the womb, perhaps she might come to me, or to another herbalist, and we might give her an infusion of rue. You understand? It's dangerous for her, and certainly uncomfortable, but for some girls it's worth the risk."

It sounded plausible and, if he checked with a herbalist, he would find that rue was used in just such a way. She saw the momentary wariness in his eyes, shifted nearer to him, and laid her hand over his. "What, are you shocked after all, sweetheart? Didn't your roving parents teach you the truth about life? Or didn't they believe in forcing miscarriages?"

He stood up and pulled his hand away, stung. "If they had, I wouldn't be here," he said. "My mother told me that once. She tried to convince my father that it wouldn't be good for them to be burdened with a child, but he said they had to accept the consequences of their actions."

"So, they didn't want you. More fool them." Doronit's heart sped up with excitement. That was it, the cord that would bind him to her: being wanted. Being valued. Belonging. She'd suspected it before, but now she was sure. She stood next to him and slid her hand through his arm so he could feel her breast against his elbow. "I know how to value you," she said. "And you belong to me, now."

Ash swallowed down the lump in his throat. It was true. He did belong to her. Who else would want him? He was no good for anything, everyone knew it. Except Doronit. Doronit had taken him from his parents gladly.

"I won't let you down," he said, and for the first time dared to put his arm around her.

"I know you won't," she said. She stroked his cheek kindly then pulled away and sat back down at the bench. "Now, arnica," she said briskly, leaving him standing there feeling foolish, once again. "It's often used because there's no suspicion if someone finds it in your pack. It's used for so many other things..."

The training went on through the shortening autumn days and the chilling nights. Ash was earning money for her now, as a safeguarder at Merchant House functions, but some part of each day was still given over to training: concocting poisons, or their antidotes, singlestave and knife-throwing practice, hand-to-hand fighting, the system of whistles by which all of Doronit's people communicated (oddly enough, he could whistle those two-note signals easily, although he couldn't sing the same notes), and numbers and tallying.

"Never let a client cheat you," Doronit said as she showed him how to use a slate and chalk. "The only way to protect yourself is to be as fast with numbers as they are."

Ash put all thoughts of killing away from him. He was a safeguarder. It was a respectable profession, not important, perhaps, but respectable. He began to spend more time away from the house. Aylmer took him to taverns where the mead was strong and the music loud, and he met young men working for other guardhouses. One of them was Dufe, the safeguarder who had parted ways with Doronit the year before Ash had arrived in Turvite.

Dufe was a swarthy southerner with bright brown eyes and beautiful hands. Sitting next to him in the smoky din of the tavern, Ash noticed the same heart-thumping confusion he felt when Doronit touched him, especially when Dufe leaned across him to take a mug of mead from the waitress, and rested a hand on his thigh as he did so.

Dufe grinned at Ash's flushed face. "How old are you, young one?" he asked.

"Just turned twenty."

"You look younger. Doronit likes to get them young, doesn't she? The younger the better. She's got no morals at all, that woman."

Ash bridled instantly, his hand going to his dagger.

Dufe laughed at him and lifted his hands. "No, no, I won't fight you over that. She's the perfect woman, if you want to think so." He stood up and drained off his mug. His hand dropped on Ash's shoulder and he bent over. "A word of advice. Have a bit of fun away from the old woman. Find a nice young one like yourself. Doronit will eat your heart out bit by bit, and she'll do it so sly you won't even feel it going."

His grip on Ash's shoulder tightened, then he was gone. Aylmer turned back from the waitress he had been talking to and grinned at him. "Dufe gone? Oh, well, he's got a nice warm wife to go home to. Not that he does that often. He's one that likes to taste life."

"Mmmm." Ash wasn't sure whether to be angry or worried by Dufe's words. He shook them off and ordered another mead.

"Dufe's got a good heart," Aylmer said cheerfully. "That's why he and Doronit never got on. He was already fully trained when he came up from the south. She took him on, but he only lasted a month. He sets strict rules for himself...except when it comes to shagging." He chuckled. "The stories I could tell you about that man!"

212

Ash walked home alone. Aylmer had gone upstairs with the waitress. Ash didn't know if he envied him or not. In the quiet darkness the ghosts stood out more strongly than ever: pale forms clustering near doorways, or walking aimlessly through the night. They nodded to him as he passed, and he nodded back. They seemed as solid as he was. Perhaps they were. Perhaps he was as insubstantial. Perhaps nothing was as it seemed, Doronit included.

On Midwinter's Eve the Turviters shuttered the windows, set covers over the lamps and screens around the fires, so the bright colors of their walls were doused, and sat in pitch darkness, practicing for death. The youngest person in the house, and the oldest, recited together the Midwinter Prophecy, and then the door was set open to the ghosts. The ghosts entered where they pleased. And when they pleased, they set their hand on a man's head here, a woman's there, pointing out the people marked by illness who were to die before the next Midwinter's Eve. They did not always choose to enter.

"It's considered a blessing," Doronit explained to Ash. "It gives the person the chance to put their affairs in order, to say their goodbyes. The ghosts only do it for the people they like."

He looked around the empty room. "They don't come in here?"

She laughed shortly. "Not willingly. Come."

She led him out into the night. The streets were emptier than he had ever seen them.

"Why do the ghosts stay, Doronit?" He had wondered that for a long time.

"Because they're angry at being killed and their killers have not offered reparation. Because they don't want to leave the people

213

they love. Because they owe a debt. Because they're afraid of the dark beyond the grave—as they should be."

"But beyond death is life again." That was what his parents had taught him.

"So *you* think. But who knows for truth? Perhaps there is nothing. Perhaps the spirit…shreds itself against death until there is nothing left."

"Is that what you believe?"

A person who believed that, he thought, would have no reason to live well. There would be no reason for honor or pity or generosity, which, his parents had taught him, were the qualities necessary for rebirth. "These are the things that work against the dark," his mother had said. "These are the only things that can pierce the dark beyond the grave and lead the spirit through to new life."

Doronit stopped. "I think not about it."

She had led the way to the open space where the black rock waited beneath its oak tree. It was the sacred place where, it was said, the gods of Turvite had once lived, before Acton came and drove them all away. Ash knew better. Although nothing called him by name, as it had last time he was there, he could feel the power in the stone beckoning.

They waited. The wind was biting. He felt his nose turning blue with cold. He rubbed it with gloved fingers. Doronit stood still. Gradually, the ghosts came, answering the call. One by one they left the houses and slid into the streets, all of them drawn to the same place.

"They come to greet the dawn at the old holy place," Doronit said quietly. "This will be the last night for those who have paid their debts."

"By giving warning of death?"

"What else can the dead do for the living?"

He thought of the girl he had killed. She had warned him, too, though not of simple death: "Death of the soul," Martine had said.

The ghosts swirled and eddied around the gods' stone. Doronit pointed to one, then another. *"Speak,"* she urged. "Tell me your secrets."

They spoke, reluctantly, one by one, some with sorrow, and some with hatred. They told her all they knew: the silly secrets, of first love and small vanities, and the deep secrets, their own and others'. They spoke of betrayal and murder and heartbreak, of violence, of fraud and lechery, greed and lies, domestic tyrannies and harsh cruelties.

Ash listened. Initially, as Doronit had commanded the first ghost to speak, he had felt elated: at last he knew someone like him, who could not only see ghosts, but compel them to talk. He wasn't a freak after all. But as he heard the stories that Doronit extracted from them, he started feeling ill. Stories flowed out of them of calumny, of rape behind closed doors, of small bribes and large corruption. The ordinary stories were the worst. They filled him so that he was close to tears; they were so full of love and grief, hatred and joy, the secrets of the heart. To listen made him ashamed. But still he listened. Doronit had brought him here for a reason and he needed to know what it was.

He thought of Dufe's scathing remark: "She's got no morals at all..." Was this moral? Was it wrong? Did the dead have the right to keep their secrets? They couldn't be hurt, could they? He tried to convince himself that they were hurting no one, but it was difficult to believe, looking at their faces and seeing how they hated giving up their secrets. Perhaps taking secrets to the grave was the only power the dead had, and Doronit was taking it away.

Doronit's voice was growing weaker. He realized that she

was exerting her will as well as her voice, that it was her strength that was forcing the ghosts' revelations. She leaned against him for support as it continued. Finally, with still twenty or more of the spirits left to speak, she shook her head.

"That's it for me," she said. "Your turn, Ash."

He stared at her, incredulous. "Me?"

"Of course, sweetheart. That's why I brought you. Did you think I didn't know? After Ghost Begone Night? Half the ghosts in the city told me your name."

"I can't —"

"*Can't?*" she said. "What do you think I've trained you for?" She straightened. He could only see her face in the faint light reflected from the spirits, but he knew she was angry. "Why do you think I took you from your fools of parents, who couldn't see what they had in their hands? Why have I housed you and fed and—yes—*loved* you all this time? For *this,* stupid one. And now you say you can't?"

"I..." *She loves me, she says she loves me.* "But—"

She changed tone. "Sweetheart, sweetheart. This is why I'm successful, why I can charge the prices I do. Why the town clerk smiles at me in the street. I know *everything.* I could misuse this knowledge, but I don't. I don't blackmail anyone—I don't reveal any of these secrets. But for my own protection, and for yours, Aylmer's, Hildie's, and all the rest—I must know. I'm exhausted, I have no more strength. I need your help. Now."

He hesitated still.

She drew a breath. He wasn't as well trained as she had thought, but he could still be brought to heel.

"Of course," she said slowly, "if you don't do this, you're worthless to me. I have half a dozen who are better with the knife and singlestave. I'm fond of you, sweetheart, but I can't afford you if you don't earn your keep."

She saw the threat sweep through him, turning him cold. He pictured himself on the streets. He couldn't go back to his parents. He had thought he was doing well with the knife and the stave, but what did he know? Without her...

"*Speak,*" he said, and listened while his guts roiled with shame.

Ash sat on the side of his bed, his hands dangling over his knees. *My room,* he thought, *the first I've ever had. My bed.* He looked around. A cupboard, with several changes of clothing carefully folded, warm red blankets, a lantern on the table, an earthenware jug and mug, two pairs of boots and a pair of evening shoes... All his. The brick walls were painted sea green with a blue trim. The shutters were solid and fit tightly. Even on this midwinter night, it was not freezingly cold. The room glowed. It felt like home.

He thought about being outside, homeless, deserted, and began to shiver. After all, he reasoned, the ghosts were dead. She wasn't hurting them. And Doronit had said that she never used the information for ill. He clung to that even while he knew it was a lie and that she would use her knowledge any way she could, and all for her own good. But he didn't allow himself to think about it, any more than he let himself think about the Deep, or the demons there. He refused to think about how the demons would judge Doronit. This was his home, Doronit was all the family he had; he had to trust her.

He slept badly that night, but in the morning he got up and went to singlestave practice as usual, and smiled at Doronit afterward, while they shared breakfast.

Doronit was very loving to him for days afterward. More, she began to include him in business meetings with Merchant

House, with sea captains who wanted protection for their goods heading for Mitchen and Carlion, with the owner of the Sailor's Rest who had been having trouble with some fishers from Foreverfroze, here to sell a cargo of seal fur and whitefish oil.

Aylmer clouted him on the shoulder and congratulated him the first time he negotiated a deal himself, with Doronit just smiling on.

"So you're the heir, then, eh?" Aylmer grinned over the singlestave, trying to distract him with talk. "She's grooming you to take over, youngling. You'll be worth a warlord's ransom."

Aylmer hit a glancing blow and then doubled it back fast to test his guard.

Ash parried it easily, grinned back and changed from shield to spear, trying to poke Aylmer in the stomach. "I'll be your boss!"

"Yes, sir, no, sir, whatever you say, sir." Aylmer backed out of stave reach and pretended to bow and scrape. "Well, I don't know why she's chosen you, lad, but I suppose you do?"

Ash blushed. It was true, he did know; the memory of Midwinter's Eve was still sharp in his mind, still brought a wave of nausea.

"No need to be embarrassed, lad." Aylmer chuckled. "She's not to my taste, but I can see you're sharper than I ever was — a bit of shagging here and there is a small price to pay for a good business."

Ash grinned halfheartedly. It would be easier to live with himself if Aylmer was right. But Doronit never touched him, except the occasional pat on the cheek or hand sliding down his arm. He had realized, after Midwinter's Eve, that she did it deliberately, to throw him off balance. But that didn't stop him stammering, or the hot wave of desire that swept over him.

He fed the memory of those moments into an attack on

Aylmer: thrust, shield, sweep, spear, parry. He vented all his frustration and pushed his desire into the stave, and for the first time he beat Aylmer back. He rallied quickly but it wasn't enough. They ranged over the practice room, sweating and heaving, with no thought now for anything but the staves and each other's movement. Ash came forward with a step he'd only practiced alone, and took Aylmer by surprise on the back foot, swept his legs out from under him and had Aylmer with the stave at his throat.

"Hah!" Ash shouted, and his opponent threw his stave down in surrender. Ash was jubilant. It was the first time he had defeated any of the older safeguarders, and Aylmer was acknowledged as being very good with the stave.

Alymer grinned, but rubbed his back as he got up. "Trying to make me feel old, boy?" He looked at Ash with fresh interest. He'd always been fast at singlestave but he'd never shown the right mix of aggression and composure that made for a formidable opponent. That had changed; the diffident young man had vanished. Maybe becoming Doronit's chosen heir had given him confidence, Aylmer thought, or maybe he was just growing into himself, as boys often did around that age. It had made Aylmer feel the creeping touch of age. He was old enough to be Ash's father, and he winced as he bent over to pick up his stave.

"Come to the tavern," Ash said, bouncing on his toes, energy undiminished. "I'm buying."

As they walked out into the spring day, into the hawkers' cries and the rumble of carts, into the clamorous bargaining at the market, into the smells and sounds and life of Turvite, Ash felt his heart expanding. He did love this city, loved its energy and its venality, too, the way its citizens were sharp and generous at the same time, openhanded with food or drink, but otherwise kept track of every copper. He loved the sense of being part of something larger, of having his own role to play in the city's life, of sharing fellow feeling with every other inhabitant. He might not have had much to call his own, but he was a Turviter.

He bounded into the tavern and bought Aylmer a tankard of mead, not ale. "You want to get me drunk, boy?" Aylmer protested.

Ash just laughed. "Why not? It's the end of the working day, why shouldn't we get drunk?"

And later he went upstairs with one of the waitresses, the tall blond, buxom one (the one least like Doronit). He was too drunk to do much more than roll in the sheets with her laughing. But they slept, and when they woke up they laughed some more, and sighed, then shagged with satisfying energy until dawn.

He went home in the early morning light and let himself into the house quietly, but not quietly enough. As he walked down the hall, Doronit appeared at the door to her room and just stood there, looking at him. He forced himself to stand still, not to blush or stammer out excuses. She lifted an eyebrow at him and suddenly grinned; it was a real smile, unlike any he'd had from her before. He grinned back.

"I'll be calling you the same time as usual," she said. "You might be better off not going to sleep at all." She disappeared into her room.

He took her advice, his heart lighter, not just because of the night with the waitress, but because he had stood his ground with Doronit for the first time and her smile had acknowledged it. Perhaps he could work his way to some kind of equality with her.

SAKER

SAKER RETURNED to the house he had inherited from the enchanter, in Whitehaven, in the Far South Domain, and finally finished his map. Every massacre site was marked in red, not in blood—as Saker felt would have been appropriate—but at least in red. Every smaller battle site, where fewer than twenty had been killed, was marked in orange. The few individual murders he had managed to track down were marked in yellow. He had to use saffron for that, but it had been worth it. Every death, every desecration, would be remembered.

His walls were covered with scrolls: every account of the invasion still in existence, plus his own notes. It had taken Saker fifteen years to gather them all, once his reason for living had become clear to him. But they hadn't been enough. Only Rowan's songs had allowed him to complete his map. From their words—and from what they did not say—he had colored the Domains to show exactly where Acton's people had killed.

The colors followed the main rivers and the coastline, leaving empty spaces inland. He didn't know what to do about those empty spaces. They weren't empty any longer. In a thousand years Acton's people had spread right across the land, cutting down the forests that his people had left in peace, spreading anywhere there was a stream or a place to dig a well. There were no deaths to be avenged in those empty spaces, but the people living there had benefited from all the other deaths, all the red and orange and yellow. After an hour's brooding over the map, Saker delicately shaded those parts a pale green, for

221

the death of trees. Perhaps the ghosts of the forests would come to join his army. Who could tell? These days he knew that anything was possible.

It was time to try the spell again. There had been something missing, but his Sight knew that it was only a small thing, a twist on what he was already doing...He went over to the cloth-shrouded box near his window and folded back the purple cover. The words of the spell weren't hard, but the concentration required was enormous. He shut out the sounds of the street below, the noise of pots being washed in the kitchen of the house next door, the intensity of his own heartbeat and breathing. Only the bones remained, with their faint earthy scent. He held the knife ready against his palm and made the cut without blinking.

His blood dripped onto the bones as he said the words of the spell, and he felt his heart swell with pain and love as his father's ghost rose before him, looking just as he had twenty-five years ago, in the moment before the warlord's axe had taken him. Saker had been five then. He took in the apparition: broad-shouldered but not tall, dark hair and eyes now pale; his strong, beloved face disfigured by the head wound that had killed him.

His father smiled at him, then raised an eyebrow questioningly.

Saker pointed to the map. "It's finished," he said.

His father moved slowly over to the table and looked down. He pointed to the green areas and looked at Saker.

"The death of trees," Saker explained.

His father nodded. He let his hand trace the contours of the Western Mountains, up to the foothills where their village, Cliffhaven, had been—and still was. He motioned as though to tap the table at that point.

Saker nodded. "I know," he said. "But not yet. We must try somewhere else first."

His father frowned and tapped the table impatiently, although the tip of his finger went straight through.

Saker felt the familiar lurch in his stomach, the desire to please his father tightening his guts. He hardened himself against it. "Soon," he promised. "I don't have enough blood for all the ghosts in Cliffhaven. We have to find a way to share the blood out without killing the spellcaster. We'll try somewhere else first."

His father still frowned.

"We're very close," Saker said. "I promise."

Then his father smiled and made as if to embrace him. Saker said the last few words of the spell, the words he had saved for this moment. His father's arms came around him and he moved happily into the firm hug, feeling his father's hands on his back, the shoulder under his cheek. He closed his eyes and surrendered to being a little boy again, when everything was all right.

The spell faded too soon. Saker covered the dry bones and wiped away his tears. He had to find a way to make it last, and not just for his father, but his sisters and cousins, and all his family. His mother's bones were beyond recovery, but he could call up everyone else...the entire village. And then they would take back what was theirs. Every bit of it.

ASH

A<small>T THE</small> vernal equinox, Doronit took Ash out to the cliffs beyond the harbor, where he had met and scattered the ghosts on festival night. It was a windy, damp night, with thin clouds covering a sickle moon, and the waves below thumping against the rocks.

She stood on the edge of the cliff and told him to stand behind her. Then she whistled.

The melody was a simple one: five notes repeated over and over in a minor key. Ash waited. Nothing happened.

Doronit kept whistling, on and on. He began to feel dizzy, as though he could lean against the wind and into the notes of the tune as he might lean against a breaking wave. He felt light-headed and heavyhearted, sorrowful, almost, distant from his own body, yet sharply aware of the ground beneath his feet. Perhaps she had drugged him.

"Whistle," she said, and dug him in the ribs. He stumbled, almost sending them both over the cliff, but she pulled him back and shook him a little. Then she turned him to face outward over the water. "*Whistle!*"

He picked up the tune from her. Standing there, listening, the notes had wound themselves into his brain so tight he wondered if he'd never get them out. It was the first time in his life he'd ever managed to reproduce a tune. He was making music for the first time! He whistled enthusiastically, and she relaxed, satisfied.

Then he saw the wind wraiths coming, flying across the scudding clouds toward them.

224

He had seen water sprites once, dancing on a waterfall in the high mountains west of Circ. The wind wraiths were like them: sharp features, long fingers and claws, slitted eyes with no pupils, just all black, and hair that waved back from their smooth faces like seaweed under water. But where the water sprites were emerald and silver and blue, the wind wraiths were cloudy white and gray, half transparent, and as much sound as sight, rushing, wuthering, until the back of his head had a line down the middle where it felt like it was going to split open. There were only three wraiths, but they seemed to be everywhere.

"Greetings at the Turn of the Year, People of the Air," Doronit said.

Ash whistled. One of the wraiths slithered past him, beading his arm with moisture and bringing him up in goose bumps.

It faced Doronit, no more than a foot away. "Again, woman?" Its voice was like steam shrilling from a kettle. It pierced his ears.

"Again, honored ones. What news?"

"No news for our enemies." It smiled. Its teeth were square and blunt.

"I am thy friend," Doronit said. "I bring news. Two ships, but a day out from Turvite, bound for the islands. Two *old* ships."

The wraith moistened its lips and slid a finger down her cheek.

She flinched, but stood firm, looking straight into its eyes.

Ash's whistle slowed.

The wraith smiled and set one clawed finger at the corner of Doronit's mouth.

He whistled faster, back to the correct tempo, and the finger was withdrawn. His heart was pounding as though he were running. His mouth was drying out.

"What news for me, friend?" Doronit whispered.

"So sad, so sad..." The wraith smiled. "The *White Hind* gone in a late gale, the *Sunrise* lost its cargo, all jettisoned. The *Cloven Hoof* foundered, all hands dead. The sea is eating woven wool and fine timber, alum and indigo. It will be bluer than ever this summer."

"Ridiculous name for a ship, anyway," Doronit said. "My thanks, honored one."

The other wraiths gathered closer.

The wraith reached for Ash, to pull him over the cliff. Doronit hauled him back. He kept whistling.

"Our payment, friend," it said.

"Not this one. Not this year. I've given you two ships. That should be enough. North and southwest they're riding, with red sails."

The wraiths surrounded Ash, sliding against his skin, trying to disrupt the rhythm of the tune.

"Enough!" Doronit said. "Come, Ash." She pulled him away, walking backward to keep her face toward the cliffs and the wraiths.

"Fondness is foolishness," the wraith whispered to her, but she ignored it and began whistling.

It was a different tune, the same five notes, but in a different order. Ash couldn't stop whistling his own melody until she put a cold hand over his mouth. In an instant they shrieked away, like tattered cloaks streaming across the sky.

She waited for his questions as they walked back to town, but he said nothing. He was thinking about her words, "Not this year." So she had paid them in other years. But what coin had she paid in? Who had gone up with her to the cliffs last year?

That night in his dreams she turned into a wind wraith at the moment of climax, but even as a wraith she was beautiful, and he surrendered his throat to her claws in a kind of ecstasy. He woke, sweating, and lay in the dark, ashamed, but not knowing what he was most ashamed of—helping her with the wraiths, or being drawn to her even if she had a wraith's heart. Because if she had appeared at the doorway to his room at that moment he would have been filled with a fierce desire. He couldn't imagine being without her.

The next day Doronit paid a visit to the merchants who dealt in wool, and purchased a great deal of blue cloth: the blue that only merchants and their servants could wear. She bought up all the blue cloth in the city. A rumor spread that she intended to fit out all her safeguarders in blue tunics. Ash had started it, at her direction.

A week later news swept through port that Beasle's two ships, the *High Flag* and the *Winged Flag*, were lost with all hands and cargo in an unseasonable storm.

The following day Beasle visited Doronit, and that afternoon Doronit gave Ash silver for new spring clothes. When he went to show her what he'd bought, he saw there was a small coffer in her room, which had not been there the day before: a beautiful, painted coffer with very strong locks.

"How many people were on Beasle's ships?" he asked.

"I don't know. Twenty? Forty?"

"How much were they insured for?"

She smiled. "Quite a lot."

"And was there really as much cargo aboard as the insurers were told?"

She laughed. "Very good. Very good. You're doing fine. Now what have you bought for the Merchants' Banquet?"

The sailors were dead. There was no proof: the ships were old and there had been a storm. There was no doubt about the storm. Perhaps the ships would have sunk anyway. Perhaps the storm would have happened without Doronit. There was nothing he could do. Nowhere he wanted to go. Nowhere he *could* go.

The news of the *Cloven Hoof*'s sinking became known. Doronit "reconsidered" her decision to have tunics made for her staff, and resold half of her blue fabric to the wool merchants at double the price. The other half she kept: "On Ghost Begone Night the merchants give their servants their new livery for the year, so they look smart for the festival. The price will triple before then."

The year turned. The fishing boats at harbor began to stink in the sun. Ash ran and trained all through the summer heat as he had through the winter cold. "The weather won't abate itself because you're uncomfortable," Doronit had said. "What use is a safeguarder who has to sit down in the shade?"

On a gray, airless day in early autumn, before the first chill had come to break the summer stew, he loped into the courtyard with sweat running down his whole body, and found her waiting for him with a cool drink and a towel.

"What's happened?" he asked.

She smiled sideways at him. "Twelve months ago you wouldn't have asked anything. You would have blushed and smiled at me. Come."

She led the way into her room. He toweled off as he went and gulped down the juice.

Her room was cool and calm. Conscious of his sweat, he sat on the edge of the window seat, with his elbows on his knees. She sat next to him.

"We have a problem. I... have an enemy."

She pulled a twist of yellow paper from her pocket: a sweetmeat pouch, with balls of dried apricot and shredded nut meat. They were her favorites, from Perle, the confectioner.

"Smell them."

She held the paper under his nose, and he sniffed. Apricot, nut, honey...something else, faint and sharp, like almonds...

"Bitter almond," he said, shocked. "Not Perle?"

"No, no. I bought these yesterday, had some. I was fine, no? I left them here, on the little table. Today I saw three people here—Aylmer, Eral, from the Merchant Guild, and the stonecaster."

"Martine?"

"After she was gone I went to take a sweet. Something was...not right. I don't know. Perhaps the paper was twisted differently. I was careful. I smelled the poison."

"So Eral?"

"No, why would he? We do good trade together. Ten years, no problems. And Aylmer is loyal."

"Yes...yes, he is. But why would Martine—?"

"She came to warn me against Ranny, to tell me not to go into business with her. 'For your own good,' she said. She hates Ranny, everyone knows that."

"Aylmer said it was Ranny who hated Martine."

"Why not? It's natural to hate someone who hates you. But Martine has always hated Ranny and all her house. Why else would she tell her that she knew the date of her death and then tell her no more? That is something one would do only to an enemy. Place death in her mind, with no relief from wondering."

"I don't—"

"You like her. But she is dangerous."

He remembered Martine's knife in the boy's shoulder, her calm face as she stepped over two corpses bleeding on her own rug.

"Yes, but—"

"She tried to kill me." Doronit's voice was sharp.

Underneath his confusion and the shock of Doronit's near escape, he was skeptical about Martine being the culprit. It was hard to believe.

Doronit had a plan. She would ask to see Martine secretly, for a private reading. She would emphasize the need for confidentiality, say that she was coming alone. Ash would wait outside.

"If she wants me dead, she will try to take the opportunity. If she bears no ill will, I will have a reading and we will turn our eyes elsewhere."

There was a storm brewing, the first of the autumn storms. The Turviters were indoors, waiting for the deluge. Only ghosts roamed the darkened streets, glancing furtively at Doronit and Ash as they went past, melting backward into alleys and alcoves. He nodded at one or two, but they never took their eyes off Doronit. She ignored them.

There was a scurry of dead leaves and dust in circles at their feet. Lightning flashed in the distance.

"Hurry," Doronit said. "But stay back until she lets me in."

He hid in a doorway while Doronit approached Martine's door. The circle of ghosts around it drew back and Doronit went in.

Thunder clapped on the cliffs outside the city, and rumbled backward into the hills. Ash hesitated. Doronit wanted him to stay here, but if he went in the back way he'd be able to hear their conversation. Part of him, the remnant of the boy who had come to Turvite, resisted. Surely he could trust Doronit? But the part that remembered Midwinter's Eve and the ghosts' stolen secrets, the part that remembered the wind wraiths reaching for him on the cliffs, knew better.

He turned and ran for the back lane, jumped up over the bakery flour store, over the roof tiles, and across to Martine's roof. He slid his knife under the latch on the dormer window and dropped soundlessly to the floor. This was how the second assassin had got in. Martine should have nailed it shut.

He crept down the stairs. Murmuring came from the parlor. He froze in the dark as thunder crashed directly overhead. He heard a scuffle.

"Ash! To me! To me!"

He found them struggling with a knife, Doronit's skill almost matched by Martine's greater height and strength. He shouldered into both of them and sent them smashing to the floor. He picked up the knife.

"Kill her now!" Doronit said. "She tried to knife me. Slit her throat!"

The women stood up in a breath, glaring at each other. He was frozen, without words, almost without thought.

"Ash. Kill her now."

"She tried to kill you with this knife?" he asked, keeping a wary eye on Martine.

She stared back at him, her breath slowing. She said nothing, but stood a little straighter, less threateningly. She moved away from Doronit, toward the mantelpiece where Acton's brooch still lay.

"You saw!" Doronit said.

Ash was still watching Martine.

"Ash, sweetheart, I know you don't like killing, but sometimes it's necessary. Knowing when is what makes a good safeguarder. Someone I can trust. Someone I can keep with me. Forever."

It was more disguised than on Midwinter's Eve, but still a threat: do what I tell you or I will abandon you. Panic overtook him, just as it had then. He looked at the knife, at Martine, at the knife again.

"This," he said slowly, "is not her knife."

Doronit stared at him. "What?"

"This is not her knife. Her knife is white."

"Well, maybe she has two!"

"Maybe. Or maybe you set this up. How much is Ranny paying?"

For a moment she almost denied it. Then she laughed. "Ah, you have grown clever, no? Old enough now to be more than an apprentice. Ranny pays well—she pays *us* well, and more to come if we rid her of this thorn in her side."

Doronit was now standing close to him, her hand on his shoulder, her breath on his cheek: a moment of dizziness, of sweet closeness and belonging.

"She is nothing to us, Ash. Do it quickly and we will be gone."

For the first time he read desire for him in her eyes and realized that he would have to be a killer for her to want him.

Martine waited. He closed his eyes. Doronit's scent was around him: warmth, home…

He threw the knife to Martine, hilt first. "She says it's your knife. You'd better have it."

Doronit hissed. "You fool!" She swung at him, her ring scoring his cheek. "I would have made you my partner. My successor."

"Successor to fear and death," Martine said.

"Why not?" Doronit glanced at him. "Why should I care what happens to Acton's people? Why should you? The three of us are among the last of the old blood. Why should we care about the Turviters, who murdered our people and took our land and laughed at our ghosts? Why should I not make myself wealthy at their expense?"

After all the lies, he could still recognize the truth: she was driven by a long, twisted hatred. "So to revenge yourself on them, you try to kill Martine, one of the old blood?" He shook his head. "Your revenge has a mercenary tinge to it, I think."

For the first time, she was shaken. Her certainty quivered like wind on water. Then her mouth firmed. "I know enough to know that I can only look after myself. That is a lesson you will learn, boy, out on the Road with no skills and no guardian. You will remember. You will regret this."

She opened the door and walked into the slanting downpour. The wind blew in and rain drenched the rug.

Martine shut the door and put the knife down on the table, then took him by the arm and led him to the small fire. She built it up until the flame shadows danced on the ceiling.

He couldn't stop shaking. The sweat on his face was drying and it stretched his skin taut. There were raindrops hissing down the chimney and sputtering out. He noticed the smell of lavender, wood smoke, wet wool, cha, for the first time. Martine's long hair swung low as she stooped to the fire. She held a mug to his clenched teeth. Cha. The scent loosened his jaw and he sipped once, twice. She put the mug into his hands and he held it awkwardly.

Martine sat at his feet and cast the stones.

"Foresight. Liberation. Understanding. Pain," she said. "And the blank stone. That means anything may happen from now on."

DORONIT'S STORY

IT'S TRUE my parents were Travelers by blood, but they were as settled as can be by nature. I was an only child, raised outside a small town way down past Turvite toward the Wind Cities. My father was a cowman for the biggest local farmer; my mother acted as evening dairymaid so the farmer's wife could get supper for her brood of children.

It was a happy childhood, I suppose, but a lonely one. None of the local children were allowed to play with me, the "Traveler brat." They threw stones but I learned to dodge them. I wasn't so skillful dodging the mud or the cow dung. If they'd come at me one by one I could have fought back, but they never did. I used to straggle home and just stand in the doorway until my mother saw me. She would get a look on her face. I thought, the first time it happened, that it was a look of exasperation with me, tempered with resignation at the work I made for her. I hung my head, but she chivvied me over to the fire and changed my clothes, speaking gently so I understood that it wasn't my fault, and cheered up.

Later my parents bought their own cow, and a few goats, and I had the keeping of them. I hated it, but what was the alternative?

The spring I was sixteen, I was walking down the lane toward our cottage, bringing watercress and some young nasturtium leaves from the stream nearby for supper. I was brooding over my life, the way you do when you're sixteen and think you're unhappy, and I didn't hear the horse come nosing up behind me

234

until it was too late. I heard soft hoof noises on the gravel and then a snuffle and I turned, but the warlord's man was off the horse already and had hold of me a moment later. I knew him by sight and by reputation—violent, crazed almost, but one of the warlord's favorites. His name was Egbert, but they called him Fist. He was grinning at me.

What's the point of describing it? There aren't any words for the terror, the despair, the loneliness of it. He pushed me facedown into the spring mud until it was in my mouth and my nostrils, until I could hardly breathe, and took me from behind. Both passages. Grunting, "Traveler bitch, scum, whore, turd, filth..." And when he'd finished he got up, kicked me once in the ribs, got back on his horse, and rode off.

All I wanted to do was lie there and die. Then I started to vomit and I had to get up on my hands and knees to retch.

But you don't die, that's the worst of it: you have to stand up and stagger back home, walk in and see the look on your mother's face. I'll never forget her face that day. It was like the look she had given me each time I had come home covered in dung, but now I was old enough to read it. It wasn't just her immediate comprehension and the horror. There was a kind of humiliation, as well, and a giving in, a submission to our situation, to the position of Travelers in the Domains, an acceptance that nothing could be done, no justice could be expected. I knew in that instant that someone had once forced my mother facedown in the mud. Strangely, I was angrier about that long-ago violation than I was about my own, and that anger stayed with me and kept me from crying.

She stood for a moment, frozen, then came and cradled me and stripped me, and heated water and made it scalding hot, too, and made me sit in the bath, and drink the small amount of applejack my father kept behind the oats crock, and chew on some rue, while she washed my hair and my hands and crooned over me and urged me to cry, to let it out, let it go. I couldn't, though I wanted to, if only to make my mother feel better. I knew what she was trying to do, with the heat and the herbs and the liquor. But hot water and rue don't always work, and there wasn't enough applejack to make a squirrel sick, so three weeks later I knew I was pregnant.

"It's your own fault," my da said. "You shouldn't have been walking down that lane alone. You know that the warlord's men think Traveler girls are fair game."

"What's she supposed to do?" my mam said. "Never move out of doors?"

Her voice was gentle, though, and I couldn't be angry with him, either, for I'd seen him weep all the tears that I could not on the night it happened, standing, staring at the fire for hours, his hand clenching and unclenching, and that look on his face, too, the one that says: "I need to do something about this but there's nothing I can do that won't make it worse."

I hated the thought of the baby, of course, hated it with nausea and headaches and not eating, but it was a strong one and it clung onto life. Then one day I was out combing the goats for their fleece and I felt it move. I'd been dreading it, that moment, knowing it was coming, knowing I'd feel this product of rape inside me. I'd been waiting for it in horror. But when it came the touch was so soft. Tiny. Innocent. Completely innocent. How could I hate it?

My mam had said, "If you hate this child he will have ruined two lives." And I knelt in the straw of the goat shed and cried, remembering, accepting, coming to love. And I did love her, my darling, when she was born, loved her with all there was in me to love, my sweet-skinned, milk-scented, beautiful black-haired Larch, loved every bit of her from her fat wrists with the crease across them, to the incredible softness underneath her toes. Is there anything softer than feet that have never felt the hard ground? My parents loved her too; Da took a while, resenting her on my behalf, but when she held out her little hands to him and grinned, how could he resist?

So it went on for seventeen months, and the only change was that now the women in the market spat as I passed and said "Traveler whore" out of the sides of their mouths, even though my da had told the story abroad, and they all knew where the baby came from. I grew a shield on my heart, in that time. Inside were Mam and Da and Larch, outside were all of Acton's people, all the rest of the world. But it was only for protection, so I wouldn't care about the spitting and the curses. I didn't hate them, then.

In the early spring the warlord and his men raided the territory of the Wind Cities, in retaliation for raids they'd made on us the year before. It happened every year or so, and people had forgotten who had started it. I loved the spring raids—it meant all the warlord's men were away and I could go wherever I wanted to. It was the only time of year I was really free. But this year they brought back a fever with them, a plague they said was striking all the Wind Cities. Of course the warlord's men brought it back, but there was a Traveler family that had come to town from the north at the same time, a young tinker and his wife and twin baby boys, and the townsfolk blamed them for it. One of the babies had a fever, they said.

It went through the district faster than any other disease I've ever seen: whole families died in a couple of days. It was a swelling sickness, with great black boils under the arms and in the groin, and those who were stricken couldn't keep anything down. The district battened down and people huddled indoors, praying to the local gods (but when had they ever cared about humans?). We did the same, but it was too late. The farmer came down with it after an imprudent trip to market in the next town (he was hoping it hadn't reached there yet, but he was wrong). He came by on his way home to discuss the sale with my father. Da got sick two days later, and Mam that night. Then Larch.

I couldn't care for them all myself, but I tried. Larch didn't have it too badly, at first, and I hoped, gods, I hoped, that she would come through, as some had. Mam and Da needed more than I could do for them. They were bleeding at the gums, and the boils had started under their arms. It happened so fast. One hour I thought they'd be all right and the next they were screaming, begging for water, sweat pouring out of them as though they were water sprites hauled onto dry ground.

We got our water from the farmer's well, and I dared not leave them long enough to fetch it, but finally I had to. When I got to the farmyard, the gate was bolted shut against me. I put down the buckets and yoke to undo the bolts, and the farmer's wife appeared in the doorway, red-eyed, with a pitchfork in her hand.

"Get away from here, you Traveler bitch! It's 'cause of you and your kind that my man's dead and my children like to die! Get away from our well!"

I was aware of the fine summer morning, the sweet air, the chirp of starlings, a rustle in the grass…and the woman, staring at me with a hate that had always been in her, sleeping, until now. That was the moment I found out who I was and what I could do. I didn't care what she thought, or felt, or said, or did: I needed the water and I would take it across her dead body if I had to.

I climbed the gate, with her still screaming and waving the pitchfork, and opened it from the other side, picked up my buckets and moved to the well. She came at me with the fork. As if I'd practiced it all my life, as if I were one of the warlord's men,

I stepped aside and hit her in the midriff with the bucket yoke. She folded up onto her knees and started to cry, but I ignored her. I filled the buckets, picked up the yoke and took the water back to my family.

By the time I got back Mam and Da were dead. I blamed the farmer's wife, and I still do, not for them dying, because they were bound for death, but for robbing me of their last moments, for making them die alone. If she hadn't bolted the gate it would have taken me only a few moments to fetch the water and maybe I'd have been back in time to ease their passing.

But my Larch was alive. She was hot, but she wasn't bleeding at the gums or pouring with sweat. It was the first stages. Sometimes, I'd heard, if the disease was caught early by the healer it could be eased — for those who didn't develop the pus-boils it was the fever that killed. I knew there were herbs that could lower fever. I didn't know what they were, except for feverfew, and we'd used all of that we had.

I decided to go to the healer in town. I carried her in, three miles and a bit, her body burning against mine, her little arms trying to hold on around my neck. Oh, that is the true feeling of motherhood, those little arms around your neck. I could feel her grip getting weaker and weaker and I hurried in response until I was running.

Every shop and house was barred and shuttered, even the healer's. I banged on the door and shouted for help until a window opened above me and the healer leaned out.

"What?" he said.

"My little one's just got the fever," I said. "No pus, no bleeding gums. Can't you help her? Bring the fever down so she's got a chance?"

"There's not enough herbs to go around for our own people," he said, and closed the shutter.

I thumped on the door again and again, but he ignored it. So I carried her back home, giving her as much water as I could along the way, and looking for feverfew beside the road, but there was none left anywhere. I took her out to the goat shed, away from the death inside the cottage, and I nursed her there. I bathed her body with cool water, spooned it into her mouth, and fanned her to keep her cool. But it was no use. She vomited the water up as soon as it went down, and the sweat started to stream off her as the sun went down.

If I'd had the herbs, help from a healer, she might have lived. Since then I've seen others live with fevers just as bad. She was dead before morning, in the still time when the tides of night change and the stars burn more brightly just before they begin to grow pale. She died with her little hand clutching at my shirt. When it loosened and fell away, it was like the world fell away too, or I fell from it, into darkness deeper than the sea.

I don't remember those first hours. My next memory is of standing next to the graves I had dug and filled in. The other dead of the town would lie in the burial caves, but I knew better than to ask that for Traveler scum.

It was getting on for sunset, three days after my parents had died. I hurried back to the cottage so I could be there when they quickened. I closed the shutters so I could see them better when they arrived. I'd always been able to see ghosts, like my da, but it didn't happen too often, apart from the ghost of the draper that haunted the well in the town square. I'd never been to a quickening, but my parents had described them to me. So I waited in the dark room, my heart beating fast, and they came. Their forms gathered on the beds where they had died, their faces still contorted with fever and thirst. Then they moved their heads, looking around, looking for me. I came forward and they saw me and smiled.

I'd thought my heart was numb, but it wasn't. It was full of heat and tears and acid. Yet I couldn't cry. "You are dead," I said.

Mam nodded, Da looked surprised, then saw Mam, misty and frail, and he sighed noiselessly. They reached hands toward each other and turned back to me. I couldn't cry. There was something I had to say.

"Look after Larch," I said.

Grief flowed into their faces and Mam reached out a hand to me. I felt for the first time the touch of a ghost on my cheek, that chill drift just under the skin. Then they faded.

A day later I sat in the goat shed and waited for my baby to come back to me. I made sure I was sitting in exactly the place I had been when she died. She came gently, her little body seeming to nestle into mine as it had so many times. She tried to clasp my shirt, but her hand passed right through. Then she sat up, surprised, and tried to touch my cheek, but her little hand slid through again. Then she got frightened and her face crumpled into silent tears.

"Oh no, little one, don't cry," I said, "please don't cry, talk to Mam instead."

"Mam," she said. "Want Mammy!" And she tried to grab hold of me and couldn't and cried out— "No!" —and her voice was the terrible voice of the dead, the stone-on-stone grating that the rock on the burial caves makes as it's rolled back. I'd just wanted to comfort her, to stop her soundless weeping. I didn't know then that it was possible to make ghosts speak. "Mam!" she cried, and reached for me again and then she faded.

I ran. I ran from the sound of that voice coming from my sweet girl's mouth, its emptiness and pain. I ran out of instinct to the forest, as though being hunted, until I was exhausted, until I could no longer hear the desolate voice, until I sank down and passed out.

I woke desperate for water and found a stream. I knelt and drank. A new beginning, that moment was. I had thought, waking, that the center of my heart was now empty, but kneeling, with the water cupped in my hands, I realized I was wrong. It was cold and numb and full of hate, but still dangerous. I would take payment for what Acton's people had done to me and mine. Revenge was all I had left.

SAKER

SAKER AWOKE from a dream of his mother calling his name and realized how stupid he'd been.

"Alder, arise," he had said. The one difference, the *only* difference, between the spell he had used on his father and those he had tried on other bones was his father's name. He needed names, not just bones.

But the names of the slain had been forgotten. The killers had not recorded the names of those they killed—they hadn't known them. How could he recover the names of those lost forever?

It was a cold night, but he was sweating with excitement. He got up and paced around his room, trying to work it out. Perhaps a spell? A divination spell? But the enchanter had never taught him those. He went down to his workroom and worried the problem all night, walking, talking it over with himself, consulting his scrolls in the hope that somewhere a name had been recorded. Nothing.

Then, as the sun edged over the low hills to the east of Whitehaven and lit the tops of the trees at the edge of town, he realized afresh how stupid he was. The people he wanted to raise were of the old blood. They would have followed the custom whereby the first living thing the mother sees outside the birthing room gives the child its name. It was considered good luck to see a bird; his own name, Saker, was a kind of falcon. In any large group of the massacred, there would be those named after

243

birds, trees, flowers, animals...All he had to do was try some. Surely he would know when he had the right names—his Sight would tell him.

He stopped short as he realized what this meant. It was time to raise the dead.

BRAMBLE

As BRAMBLE grasped the red-scarfed lance, she felt the fog being ripped away by a wave of sensation: life was coming back, her spirit was returning. It hurt, as birth always hurts, but she welcomed it with astonished joy.

"Kill Reborn!" the crowd shouted, and she brandished the lance in triumph. She *was* reborn. The sights and sounds of the crowd, the other chasers, the vivid green of spring all around her were overwhelming. Gorham ran to the finish line and thumped her leg in congratulations, panting too hard to talk, grinning madly. She laughed back.

She followed him up to the counter and received the winner's bag of silver, still too dazed to speak. She just smiled, and smiled, and sometimes grinned, but everyone seemed to think that was quite normal.

The party that followed was long and loud and exuberant. Sendat was celebrating the good luck of being granted a Kill Reborn, and it was determined to celebrate thoroughly.

If she'd wanted to, Bramble could have got drunk ten times over without spending a copper. Everyone wanted to buy her a drink, clap her shoulder, smile into her eyes. Quite a few wanted more than that. She suspected that if she'd been clubfooted, squinty and with breath like a banshee she would have still had all the men after her. Good luck, they say, rubs off, and where better to rub it than onto a man's privates? She could see them reasoning that out.

After the fifth fumbling attempt to seduce her, she slipped

245

out to the stable to talk to the roan, her blood bubbling with delight. She was alive again, aware of the pleasure of taking each breath: the glass was broken, the fog dispersed. From the moment she had grabbed the lance with the red scarf, death had retreated from her. She was truly reborn.

The waitress found her and hustled Bramble back into the common room. "The warlord's here! Come on, come on, don't keep him waiting, it's an honor," she said, picking bits of straw off her clothes and reproving her under her breath. She pushed Bramble forward to the hearth where the warlord stood with the inn's best tankard in his hand.

Thegan was a tall man, tawny-haired and blue-eyed, a bright cornflower blue, with a firm mouth and long, strong hands. He was dressed in dark brown, a good serviceable color, which was made luxurious by the cut and pile of the fabric and by the emblem stitched in gold on his shoulder: a spear and sword, crossed. Laughing at something one of his men had said, his face was alive with pleasure. Bramble could see why the waitress was blushing and fidgeting, hoping for him to notice her. He was comely enough to make any woman blush.

Then he turned his eyes on Bramble and she saw, without surprise, that they were cold as stone behind the cheerful facade. He had a mouth, in repose, that was joined to his nose by long lines that ran down to the corners, deeply etched: the mouth of a man with strong desires, who kept them under tight control. And hard eyes.

A woman moved forward beside him, a lady. There was only one person this could be. The warlord's lady, Sorn. She was like a picture of autumn in a tapestry, with rich auburn hair and green eyes, in a dark green dress with a border of embroidered claret and gold leaves around the hem, neck and cuffs. Her pale skin was fine-pored and delicate, showing the blue veins at temple and wrist. A lovely woman, Bramble thought, wrapped in femininity and assured grace. Only the nose was out of place, a man's straight nose, which gave her face strength but left it looking a little lopsided. But young—much younger than Thegan. Sold to the highest bidder, most like. She smiled at the woman companionably and Sorn smiled back.

"So this is our Kill Reborn," Thegan said. A cheer went up around the room and he smiled more widely. "It was well done."

No doubt she was expected to curtsy and blush and call him "lord." Bramble didn't know how to curtsy and she wasn't about to learn. "Thanks," she said.

His eyes narrowed. It was the same reaction she'd had from the warlord's man, but with a difference. The warlord's man didn't know how to control his anger; this one did, and that made him more dangerous.

"It was a good race," he said, testing her. Next to him, Sorn stayed perfectly still, watching Bramble intently.

Bramble nodded. "I enjoyed it."

They stared at each other for a moment, acknowledging enmity. Sorn bit her lip as though to hold back a smile. Then the innkeeper came up with a tray of drinks and food, and slipped between them, breaking the stare. And just as well, Bramble thought, making her way out to the stables again as the others clustered around the drinks. There was no way that could have ended well.

Gorham and Maude were happily ensconced in a corner talking horses with a bunch of chase enthusiasts. He raised a glass to her as she walked by and they smiled twin smiles of mutual congratulation. It helped her shake off any unease left from the encounter with Thegan. She slipped into the stable and laid her cheek against the roan's side. She was full to the brim with happiness and so was he, she could tell. He pricked his ears as though he heard again the cheers of the spectators and snorted as if he wanted to race again.

She patted him, fed him carrots and promised him they would race again soon.

They rode twice more that year, in different towns, and won each time, making them eligible for the Pless Challenge in autumn. She never overtook the Kill again—they had learned caution. Besides, she didn't want to take the risk: stealing the scarf and lance from the Kill in autumn was the worst of bad luck. She was reborn; it was best to leave well enough alone.

Thanks to being the Kill Reborn, Bramble was immediately as well known among chasers as the most experienced rider. She was offered more horses to ride than she could ever have taken, but she refused them all. She wasn't interested in chasing with another horse. She grew to enjoy the claps and calls as she mounted the roan before a chase, to relish the cheers afterward. But it was the ride itself that kept her at Gorham's, kept her from the Road—the chase, and the feeling of having escaped death. Perhaps she could escape the demon's prophecy as well. Perhaps, now she was alive again, she could love and be loved.

The Pless Challenge was the most prestigious and hotly contested chase in the Domains. No horse and rider combination could enter unless they had won at least three consecutive chases, so the competition was tough. Bramble studied the racecourse for days before the chase, although it was off limits to horses until race day. She saw other riders doing the same thing. Most she knew from the other chases, although one was new: a young man with long blond hair drawn back in the ponytail sported by most of the expert riders. He prowled the course with long, rangy strides as though he had to stop himself from breaking into a run. His ponytail bobbed along behind him and it made Bramble chuckle, although she couldn't have said why. His hearing was excellent. She was on the other side of a field, but his head went up (just like a horse, she thought) and he whirled around to see her.

He grinned and started to walk over to her. "The Kill Reborn!" he shouted halfway across the field. "I've heard about you!"

He sprang to a dead stop in front of her and examined her. "Ah, yes, a good native type, excellent conformation, not too much bone, though, may have trouble in heavy going."

Was that a joke? She couldn't quite tell, couldn't read him, but she decided to act as though it were. She examined him in turn. He was dressed as she was, in rider's leather trews and a loose linen shirt, nothing fancy, but good quality, with well-stitched boots. A red-fringed kerchief around his neck added a touch of flamboyance. He looked like a caricature of Acton's people: hair so blond it was almost white, pale blue eyes, fair skin, and a tall, loosely connected frame. He wore small gold earrings that drew attention to his long neck.

"Hmmm," she said. "Thoroughbred. Pure bloodlines, but a bit long in the back, and those pedigreed animals can be very nervous types. Waste a lot of energy. Expensive to feed, I'd say."

He laughed aloud, throwing his head back. She smiled involuntarily. "Gods, you're right there!" He grinned at her, showing crooked teeth. "I'm Leofric. Leof. Come and have a drink with me."

It was those teeth, she decided later, that threw her off balance and made her accept his invitation. They were so unexpected in such a beautiful man, and they got under her defenses.

249

It was like Wilf back in her home village—sweet but plain—and imperfection somehow always made her gentler than she would be otherwise.

They walked back to Pless across the fields.

"So, the Kill Reborn in Sendat..." he said.

"That's me."

"How many chases had you ridden before that one?"

His intentions were obvious—size up the opposition. Fair enough.

"None." His eyebrows went up.

"But you've been riding a long time?"

"A few months." She saw with satisfaction the shock on his face.

"Gods...and you just decided to start chasing?"

"Yep."

"So, what, you've found some spell to make you win?" His face was suddenly intense, as though, if such a spell were possible, he would move heavens and earth to get it.

"That's me. An enchantress."

He dissolved into laughter, as though the intensity of the moment before had never happened. "Absolutely!" he said, batting his eyes at her. "I came under your spell as soon as I set eyes on you."

"What makes you think I'd bother putting a spell on you?"

He stopped and grasped her shoulder to turn her toward him, then tilted her face up toward his with a finger under her chin. She was torn between wanting to slap his hand away and wanting to rub her cheek against it. She kept still. He leaned closer to her until she could see the sapphire glint in his eyes.

"Wouldn't I be worth putting a spell on? They say that in the Wind Cities the women have a spell that turns men into love slaves. Wouldn't you like to use that one on me?"

His voice was low and intimate, practiced, assured. He was all too used to being irresistible, she decided. "Then I'd be responsible for feeding you — I can't afford it."

He chuckled again and let go of her chin. "Now that you mention it, I am famished!"

They went to the first inn they came to, the Shield, the most expensive inn in town, right next to the river.

"I'm staying here," Leof said. "It's not bad."

The taproom looked more like a restaurant than an inn, with the walls painted the green of spring beech leaves, and the frieze patterned with autumn leaves in russet and tan. There were long cushions on the benches and the tables shone with polish. It was a far cry from the inn nearest the farm, where she sometimes went with visiting grooms, or the alehouse in her home village.

They sat at a bench near the window and looked across the river to the chase grounds. Leof waved to the barman and he came over. Not quite a man, Bramble thought. He was no more than sixteen, a lithe boy who might have been good-looking without a disastrous case of pimples. He was trying hard to flirt with Leof, smiling, smoothing his brown hair back and standing as close to him as he could.

"Ale, maybe, and some new bread and cheese?" Leof suggested. She nodded. "Your best ale, now," he said to the boy, and winked.

The boy blushed and scurried off to the kitchen. Bramble raised an eyebrow at Leof. He laughed.

"No, no, I prefer women. But there's no need to be rude about it, is there? He seemed like a nice young lad."

She thought he just liked admiration, and didn't much care where it came from.

While they waited for the food and drink, Leof cross-examined her on the chases she had been in since the Kill Reborn in

Sendat. Two could play at that game, she thought. He tried to shrug off her questions.

"Oh, I've ridden in a few chases, I suppose. It's not a bad inn, is it?"

"I asked how many," she said with a smile.

"Twelve," he said, smiling back.

The boy hurried back with a full tray and set everything out on the table. He lingered until Leof smiled at him again, then tucked the tray under his arm and strolled off, trying to be nonchalant.

"How many wins?"

He hesitated, pretending that he was deciding how much cheese to cut.

"If you don't tell me, someone else will."

He looked up and chuckled. "Well, that's true. Ten. Here, have a drink."

He passed her a tankard of ale and bit enthusiastically into the bread and cheese. Bramble watched, amused. He did everything enthusiastically. She was aware of her body and her immediate surroundings in the same way as when she was riding: the softness of the cushion under her buttocks and the hard edge of the bench against her calves, the smell of the beeswaxed table, aged cheese, and horse and hay from Leof and herself. All around them people were drinking, talking, eating, but those sounds seemed to disappear, leaving them in a quiet space, so quiet she could hear him swallow a gulp of ale. Everything seemed more alive, the colors were stronger, the sounds sweeter, the smells more evocative. He'd had that effect on the bar boy, too, as though Leof carried some music around with him that made life more intense.

"Why haven't I seen you before?" she asked.

"I'm from the north. I haven't raced in Pless before."

"And do you always take the opposition to an inn the day before a chase and try to get them drunk?"

"Only if they're as gorgeous as you."

Bramble felt the base of her spine tingle. She wanted to turn her arm over as it rested on the table, to expose the soft skin running from wrist to elbow...just to see if he'd notice, look...touch. It had been a very long time since she'd wanted to show anything of herself to anyone. She took her arm off the table and tucked her hand under her thigh.

Leof noticed and took her other hand from around the tankard. He stroked the ball of his thumb around her palm. She felt warm down to her toes, from the inside out, and her breath came faster. So did his.

"I tell you what," he said. "How about a wager? If I win, you make love to me. If you win, I make love to you."

She laughed. "What if neither of us wins?"

"Impossible! But if we don't, we make love to each other."

She pretended to consider it, nodding thoughtfully, bottom lip thrust out. "That sounds fair."

He clinked his tankard against hers, still keeping hold of her hand. "To victory!" he said.

"To victory!"

They finished the meal talking comfortably about chases and horses and riding, but his hand and hers were never out of touch for long, fingers entwined or brushed against each other. It was a match and Bramble played along, as familiar with the tactics as he clearly was, but a little off balance and uncertain underneath. She didn't quite like the feeling, but gods, he was gorgeous...

After lunch they walked back to the course.

"Come around with me?" Leof held out his hand, but Bramble shook her head.

"So you can watch my reactions and ask more questions about my strategy? Don't think so."

"Well, it was worth a try," he said, and winked.

She couldn't help but smile, but was glad enough to get away from him and feel normal again. She couldn't let a pretty face interfere with a chase. The familiar discipline of examining each potential jump and working out what her approach should be calmed her, and she ignored the occasional glimpses of Leof in the distance.

Bramble smiled as she walked toward Gorham's house, where she was staying that night. If he thought he'd distracted her from the chase, he was in for a surprise. But she was still smiling as she went to sleep that night. Win or lose tomorrow, her bed would be sweeter...

She dreamed all night about the demon that spoke from the boy's mouth in Sandalwood: *Thou wilt love no man never... Never...Never.* The words repeated themselves over and over, and when they stopped she saw her foot slamming into the face of the warlord's man. It was much clearer in her dream than in her memory, so that she could hear the ugly sound of the bone breaking and a kind of squelching noise as it shafted back into his brain. He raised his head from the ground, dead and deformed, and the demon's voice came from his mouth. *Not fit for this young man.* She woke, sweating and nauseous.

She sat for a few minutes on the side of the bed with her hands hanging between her thighs. "It's just guilt," she said out loud. "It doesn't mean anything." Her voice echoed in the dark room and she shivered.

She got dressed in the starlight from the window and went down the stairs, treading quietly so as not to wake Gorham and Osyth, to spend the rest of the night in the stable. The sight and smell of the roan calmed her. Until she laid her head on his warm side, she hadn't realized that she was still trembling. He nosed her hair and her pockets, looking for carrots, and she laughed a little. This was where she belonged. She found a carrot for him in one of the feed bins and lay down on his blanket in a corner of the stall. He lipped her shoulder and went back to standing with his head just out of the stall, and then slid back into horse sleep with his weight resting on his off hind. She slept more deeply than she had expected to, and didn't wake until the sun was fully up and Gorham appeared at the stable door, calling her to breakfast.

The weather had turned while she was asleep and it was a true autumn day: cold and windy with a lowering sky. It was a bad riding day, with poor visibility in hollows and streams filled with low-lying fog. The dull tan of the oak trees and the scarlet of the hawthorn berries were the only colors apart from the bright kerchiefs of the riders.

Bramble had brought out the roan early to warm up, along with the other riders, including Leof, who was riding a big bay mare. They all wore their lightest shirts and boots, because even the weight of a jacket could mean the difference between winning and losing. Leof smiled and waved at her, but they were both too focused for more.

The crowd soon assembled and the Kill was given his standard. As the riders jostled for position, Bramble found herself trying not to get near Leof, and she wasn't sure why. Perhaps she just didn't want to humiliate him by getting away from him at the start. *Too much overconfidence, my girl,* she thought sternly, *he's won ten—you've only won three.* But with the roan springing with energy at every step, it was hard not to be optimistic.

"Keep him steady, lass," Gorham called.

She raised a hand to him and concentrated on setting the roan straight for the start.

And then the Kill set off. The crowd counted out fifty—the number of men in Acton's first war band—and the riders were away in a thundering, determined mob of black and roan and bay.

The route was the hardest Bramble had faced yet, over high stone walls and water-filled ditches, through narrow paths between trees with low-hanging boughs. The second jump was a difficult stone wall with a small gap flanked by blackberry bushes. Bramble was well placed for the jump, but Leof, she saw out of the corner of her eye, was heading for the bushes. She heard him yell "Hah!" and his mare surged ahead to take the middle ground, forcing a chestnut straight into the blackberry thorns. The chestnut took the jump but its hind legs caught in the bushes and it tumbled over. Bramble and Leof took the jump together and he grinned at her as they landed.

By the third jump it was clear that the race was between Bramble and Leof. The bay was strong and a canny jumper, and Leof rode her with skill and sensitivity—there were no whips or spurs in sight. The mare had a tendency to jump a bit higher than she needed to, which lost her time. But she was a shade faster than the roan on the flat, so they were evenly matched.

They stayed neck and neck over the last jump and started together up the long hill that led to the finish. It was punishing at the end of a tough chase, and the horses started to show the strain. The mornings of practice paid off now, with the roan, at the peak of his fitness, just having the edge over the bay mare. She began to labor halfway up the hill, but Leof urged her on and she picked up the pace again. It was too late. She had lost too much ground to make it up, and the roan passed the finish half a length ahead of her.

Bramble took the red scarf from the Kill and flourished it, as expected, to the revelers, who were cheering madly to see a local horse win the biggest race of the year.

She escaped the crowd and walked over to Leof, wondering how he would take being beaten by a girl he was romancing. She held out her hand.

He was smiling in disbelief, but he returned the handshake. "Gods, girl, that's a horse and a half you've got."

She smiled widely, patting the roan on the neck. "That's the truth."

"You're a bloody fine rider, I'll give you that, but it was the horse that won that race."

She nodded. "I know."

"If I'd been riding him—"

"He wouldn't have tried that hard for you."

Leof stared at her, giving away nothing. "I don't doubt it." He smiled brilliantly. "We had a wager."

"So we did." She felt laughter bubbling up and let it out, throwing her head back. It was ridiculous to feel this happy.

"The party's at my house," Gorham shouted, and everyone started to move toward town.

Leof and Bramble rode together quietly, letting the horses cool down. She showed him to Gorham's stable and they tended their horses together, in a quiet intimacy shut away from the growing noise of the party in the house. They stood shoulder to shoulder for a few moments, watching the roan and the mare snort at each other and lip at their hay. Leof turned and slid his arms around Bramble's waist.

"Let's not go to the party," he said. He nuzzled the side of her neck. "I have to make good on my wager."

His mouth was soft and warm on her skin.

"Gorham will wonder where we are."

"Let him wonder."

His hands were traveling, then cupping her behind, drawing her against him. Their mouths met, and then loosened reluctantly.

"Let's go back to the inn," he said. "I'm not at my best on a pile of straw."

Bramble laughed, nervously, and went with him, leaving the prize bag of silver sitting on top of the feed bin.

His room at the inn was the most luxurious thing Bramble had ever seen: canopied bed, velvet bed throw, fine embroidered linen sheets. She smiled, thinking that she'd never actually shagged anyone in a bed. Riverside grass and haylofts, yes. Beds, no. She inspected the view from the window and found the river and hills beyond.

"Stop trying to distract yourself," Leof said. He pulled her into his arms. "If I can't make you yield in a chase, I bet I can here."

And he could. He paid the wager in full, with hands and lips and body. For the first time in her life, Bramble didn't try to stay in charge. She pressed into him, against him, around him; she let her mind go for once, and she trusted him.

They made love, slept, woke to evening light and moved again together, caressing and laughing, catching their breaths together like one creature instead of two. Afterward it was full night and the autumn air was chilly. Bramble smiled into the darkness, hoping that the warmth she felt meant that the demon's words had been all wrong. She was on the way to loving, surely?

Leof reached over her and fumbled for a tinderbox. She tickled him and it took three tries to light the candle.

"Stop it, woman! No more of that. I am *starving!*"

"Me too," she said.

He jumped out of bed and hurried into clean clothes from the press at the end of the bed, his pale flesh goose-bumped. Bramble smiled.

"Lots of food," she said.

He pulled on a brown jacket and saluted, his fist pressed to his chest. "Yes, ma'am!" As he took his hand down, a crest on his shoulder caught the light. It was a crossed sword and spear.

Bramble felt stupid, as though her thinking had slowed to a glacier pace. "You...you're a warlord's man."

He nodded, lacing up his boots. "One of Thegan's," he said. "I'm from Cliff Domain, but he's called me down to serve him in Sendat for a while."

"You're a *warlord's* man."

"Well, don't say it like that, love." He tied his boot off and stood up. "A big, big meal, eh? A bit of everything? And some wine?"

Bramble was shivering. She felt unbearably nauseous, wanting to be sick but unable to get past a huge lump in her throat. A warlord's man. She had wanted him. Let him...She wanted to get out of bed, drag her clothes on and run, but suddenly couldn't bear the thought of him seeing her naked.

"Why didn't you tell me?"

He stilled in his movement, searching her face. "What difference does it make?"

"A lot."

"What, you wouldn't have come back with me if you'd known I was one of Thegan's men?"

"I wouldn't have talked to you."

"Why not?" His astonishment was genuine.

"Warlord's men...aren't popular where I came from."

"Ah." He sat on the side of the bed. "It's true, some warlords use their power irresponsibly. And I suppose they attract the wrong kind of men. But we're not all bad, love."

He smiled tenderly at her and reached to brush a strand of hair from her face. She propelled herself backward until her head hit the wall. It was the same reaction that had made her kick the other warlord's man when he had reached for her leg. She couldn't bear for him to touch her.

He sat frozen. "That bad? You hate us that badly? All of us?"

"Warlord's men are thugs and bullies, living off the people like leeches."

"That's not how it is in Cliff Domain. I promise you."

"Really." She was unconvinced.

"Really!" He jumped up, angry now. "Without us, the people would be dead, or worse. We protect them."

"From other warlords! If we didn't have any warlords, they wouldn't need you, would they?"

"Yes they would! We protect them from the raiders, from the Ice King's people. Without us, the whole Domain would be laid waste, just like Cliffhaven was."

"What's Cliffhaven?"

"A pair of villages, up near the mountain pass. Twenty years ago the Ice King's men came down and killed everyone—everyone!—in both villages. I saw—my father took me to see, so I would know what we trained for, what we fought for. It was Thegan who forced them back across the ranges. He's a great man, a great leader. I'm proud to follow him!"

The nausea was dying, leaving emptiness behind. That hollow, dead place was still there, underneath everything. She'd thought that Leof...that the demon might have been wrong. But how could she love a warlord's man? Even one who believed he was doing good? And maybe up there in the mountains they did need protection, but he was still someone who dealt in blood and turned to fighting to find solutions. And he worked for Thegan, who had seemed so cold...She felt very tired.

"Go and get your dinner," she said. "Maybe I'll see you at another chase someday."

"That's it?"

"That's it."

"You can't see past the sword?" He gestured to the corner.

There was a sword in a leather scabbard leaning against the wall, an unobtrusive, unadorned weapon made for killing, not show. It seemed to grow larger as she stared at it, realized it had been there all along. She imagined the edge on it, the cutting blade, and shuddered.

"Well?" he said.

She stared back at him.

He turned and walked to the door.

"Leof." He spun around to look at her. "Don't trust Thegan. I've met him. He may be a great man, but he's not a good one."

His face hardened, as it hadn't done before. "Thegan is my sworn liege. You will not speak of him that way."

Their first recourse was always a threat. Even Leof. "Or what? What will you do to me?"

His face softened again and he suddenly looked like a boy of sixteen.

"Oh, Leof, just take care of yourself."

He went out the door silently.

She dressed and shuffled through the streets to Gorham's house where the party, incredibly, was still going. She went to the stable and sat between the roan and the bay mare, wanting to cry, but feeling that empty place expanding under her chest until there was no room for tears.

From then on she avoided socializing with the other riders, although sometimes, to her disgust, she dreamed of being in Leof's arms, dreamed of his lips and hands and warmth. Her own bed seemed colder when she woke, but she wouldn't let

261

herself weep over it, nor consider running away. She was content, she told herself, to live out on the farm. She tried to ignore the memories of being on the Road, and pushed down the desire to move on, be free, feel the sun on her back as she headed north. There's enough sun here, she told herself. She tried to pretend that she wasn't afraid to take the Road, but she was.

If she stopped chasing, she finally admitted to herself one day, she might stop living, too, and go back to death in life. It was a spring morning and she looked up to watch the migrating birds pass over, snow geese and eider ducks and above, the tall cranes, heading north. She left the tack she was mending and took the roan for a ride in the forest. She couldn't still the sense that she wasn't quite where she was supposed to be. But in the end she stayed with Gorham, and relished the chases even more because of what she knew she was missing.

She took the midnight watches with the foaling mares while Gorham dined with the owners in town, and she was happy to take the yearlings and two-year-olds and gentle them, teach them, love them into willing cooperation with humans. The hard part was letting them go to who knew what kind of master; although, there was many a time when Gorham refused a sale because he didn't like the riding hands of the buyer, or the way they dug in their heels unnecessarily. He wouldn't even talk to one warlord's buyer who wore spurs.

Pless was a free town and a fair distance from that particular warlord's domain, so it was safe enough to refuse, but Bramble admired him nonetheless. Although he did begin to regularly sell horses to the warlord in Sendat, Thegan, despite Bramble's objections.

"No matter how he treats his people, he treats his horses well," Gorham said. "And he pays well, too."

In the late autumn two years after she had come to the farm,

Gorham arrived one morning with a peculiar look on his face, half happy, half worried. He was distracted all day. Bramble stared when he couldn't find the mucking out fork for the third time in one hour, though it was standing there in full view.

"All right, what's happened?" she asked, placing the fork in his hand.

He stood looking at the fork and laughed shamefacedly. "Zel and Flax are here, my kids."

"Well, that's good. Isn't it?"

"Flax's sick. With the marsh fever. In the past they've stayed a few days and then taken the Road again. But with Flax sick, it looks like they'll be here all winter. And Osyth's worried the town will find out about them. They're singers and acrobats, you know, like Osyth used to be—the least respectable kind of Traveler." For a moment his face brightened. "You should hear Flax's voice—he sings like a meadowlark."

She shrugged, not too interested in Osyth's ambitions or Flax's voice. "You'll just have to keep them out of sight."

Over the winter Gorham became more silent and more haggard. He buried his worries in hard work, and there was plenty of that. The winter was too bitter and the ground too hard to let the horses go out to exercise in the fields, which meant snow had to be shoveled from the main yard every morning, pine bark and sawdust scattered. And the horses exercised there on a lunging rein for all the hours that daylight lasted.

Gorham was absent more often than he cared to be, because the town council elections were coming up. Osyth was taking every opportunity to consolidate Gorham's chances, giving parties, attending parties, "dropping in" on people to chat. She was probably bribing people, too, Bramble thought (if she could bring herself to hand over her silver). She shook her head at the idiocies most people were interested in, and concentrated on

263

keeping the roan fit enough through winter so they could start training for the chases as soon as the weather broke.

Then one day Gorham came out to the farm gray-faced.

"Osyth's dead," he said. "Last night. I was with Maude. The catch broke on her window. She died of the cold in her sleep."

He said each sentence separately, as though they didn't follow on from each other. It seemed odd to Bramble: most people woke up when they got too cold.

Gorham noticed her reaction. "She took sleeping drafts sometimes," he said. "When I went to Maude's."

He felt guilty, she could see, but she thought that guilt was stronger in him than grief, and that maybe the guilt was so strong because there was some relief mixed in with the grief.

He went home after an hour; he'd cleaned the same bridle three times. Bramble tried to show sympathy, but she wasn't sure that sympathy was what he needed. Absolution, maybe.

She went to the funeral the next day, of course, and stood by Gorham at the mouth of the burial cave and heard the town clerk speak the farewell words.

"May you not linger on the roads. May you not linger in the fields. Time is, and time is gone," he said.

"Time is, and time is gone," the mourners responded.

"May you find friends. May you find those you loved. Time is, and time is gone."

"Time is, and time is gone."

"Under your tongue is rosemary: remember us. In your hands are evergreens: may our memories of you be evergreen. Time is, and time is gone."

Then they placed her in the burial cave and rolled the stone back over the entrance.

Gorham's children weren't there.

"I told them they could come as far as I was concerned,"

Gorham said. "It was Osyth who cared about me getting on the town council, so people might as well know we were Travelers now. But Flax's still very sick and Zel won't leave him."

Maude was in the crowd but didn't go back to the house afterward for the mourners' honey and salt cakes. Flax and Zel didn't come downstairs, although Bramble saw Gorham go up to them a couple of times.

Two weeks later Gorham was elected to the town council.

"I forgot to take out my nomination," he said, a little dazed, at the election party in the town square.

Bramble smiled widely at him. "You got the sympathy vote, man," she said. "Wouldn't Osyth be pleased?" And that was somehow funny for both of them, that Osyth had got what she wanted, as though she was ordering his life even from the grave.

Bramble never did meet Gorham's children, for they left town as soon as the weather warmed up, by the northwest road. Three months later he married Maude, and became markedly more carefree, despite his new responsibilities as councillor.

At about the same time, Gorham bought himself a Golden Valley stallion with a prize-winning pedigree, a broad-chested palomino with a wicked eye.

The day he arrived, Gorham was beside himself, more excited than Bramble had ever seen him. "This is it," he said. "Now we stop training other people's horses and start breeding our own."

She smiled at him, for she was also pleased. They'd been gradually acquiring a brood-stock of mares, but they'd had to take them to other farms to be covered by a stallion. Bramble didn't like leaving her pregnant mares in someone else's hands, but since they had to be covered again within a month of dropping their foals, there was no alternative. Now the mares could stay home, and she'd have the fun of birthing the foals from the mares other people brought to their stallion.

Gorham had risked a lot on the purchase, but not as much as a Golden Valley stallion usually cost.

"They say he can't be tamed," Gorham said to Bramble as they watched the procession of horses make its way up the road, the blond mane waving in the middle of the pack and trying, again and again, to break to the front. There was energy there and to spare, Gorham noted with satisfaction, although the journey from Golden Valley through the mud and slush of early spring couldn't have been easy.

"They say he's never been ridden, that he'll take a leading rope but not a bit." Gorham snorted, confident, feeling excitement bubble up even more strongly inside him as the horses drew nearer. "As long as I can lead him within smelling distance of the mares, that's all we'll need. The foals we'll gentle ourselves from the day they're born—they'll take the bit all right." He danced from foot to foot. "He's by Gelt out of White Blaze!" he repeated for the fiftieth time. "Gelt!"

Gelt had won every chase in the country for four years straight, until there was no one left who'd take a bet against him. His owners had retired him to stud for two years, then brought him back to racing, but some rival fed him hemlock with his oats, so there were only two years' worth of his get. This three-year-old stallion was one of only four colts born, and his dam was herself a prizewinner.

"He looks well," Bramble said.

He did look well, prancing through the gate at the end of a long day's travel as though he'd just been for a stroll down to the river. He was a healthy, glossy, beautiful animal, with a mad sidestep and bared teeth for anyone who came near him, even his own groom.

Gorham nodded to Bramble and she moved in gently, silently, until she could breathe softly into his nostrils. He stood stock-still at the scent, then shook his head and moved backward, untrusting. Gorham and Bramble nodded to each other, satisfied. There was no malice in him, just mischief and a hatred of being confined and told what to do.

That Bramble understood. She felt his stubbornness—the will to never be mastered, never be compliant—as a kick in her own chest. If she hadn't liked Gorham, she might at that moment have leaped upon the stallion's back and let him race flat out until he was exhausted, using his desire to be free to release her from her own bondage...But she did like Gorham, and there was the roan to be considered, so she pushed down the urge to flight and showed the groom where the stallion should be stabled.

They passed a field where a mare and new foal were grazing, and the stallion broke free and jumped neatly across the fence as though it were only knee height.

"She's not due to come into season for another four days," Bramble said, surprised.

The groom shook his head. "Don't matter. He likes mares. Collects them, you might say, even when they're not in season."

And indeed, when they looked across, the stallion wasn't trying to mount the mare, just sidling around her, whickering, snuffling. He shook his head, the pale mane flying, and Bramble was abruptly reminded of Leof shaking the hair back out of his eyes as he smiled at her. She forced her attention back to the present. The mare was entranced, although she should have been warning this strange stallion away from her foal. They watched her sniffing in turn, smelling that unmistakable stallion musk, and as good as swooning. Bramble held on to the fence and laughed. Gorham stood there, legs apart, arms folded, beaming as though the stallion was his own son.

The stallion looked sideways at the mare, nickering softly, and she rubbed her head against his neck like a coquette. The onlookers shouted with laughter. The sound offended the stallion, who flung up his head to stare forbiddingly at them. That made them laugh more.

"The way he looked sideways at her!" Gorham chuckled, wiping his eyes.

"Like Acton, he is," the groom said, chuckling too.

The legend held that Acton had been irresistible to women. He'd had, they said, a way of looking sideways so that women just melted into his arms. In his own tribe, before the landtaken, they said all a woman had to do to excuse her infidelity with Acton was say, "But he looked sideways at me!" And husbands who followed Acton into battle were mostly hoping that over the mountains he'd find fresh girls to look at. His heir, Thegan, was born of a woman who had no time for men, but had said that if she were going to try it with anyone, it might as well be Acton.

"Like Acton," Gorham said thoughtfully. "So he is, and so we'll name him. Acton it is."

He and Bramble shared a grin, two Travelers making a joke about the old enemy of their people. Even the fair-haired groom smiled. "Aye," he said, "that's the name for him, rightabout."

Then the stallion came up to the fence where Bramble was leaning. He didn't get too close, but stood quietly next to her.

Gorham moved toward him but he flung up his head and moved back. Gorham paused, considering. "Talk him in, Bramble," he said.

So Bramble spoke quietly to the stallion, reeling him in on her voice like a fish on a line. "Here then, Acton, come on, Acton, here we are, come to Bramble, come on, boy."

The words were unimportant, it was all in the tone of voice.

Gorham watched as Acton stepped carefully back to stand near Bramble's shoulder and snort at her, and reluctantly let his plans for schooling and gentling the horse himself slip away.

"Looks like he's taken to you, lass," he said. "Best for you to have the handling of him."

She was astonished and delighted, he could see. Never expected much for herself, Bramble, though she held her dignity so dear. Well, not dignity exactly, he thought. Freedom, maybe, or something like it. She'd never be beholden to anyone, not even for a scoop of oats for that roan gelding of hers. And how had a slip of a girl, as she had been then, got hold of a warhorse?

On the Road you didn't ask those sorts of questions, and even though he'd settled now, Gorham still knew better than to poke and pry where it didn't concern him. Bramble had been a gift from the local gods, as far as he was concerned. He considered himself to be the best horse trainer this side of the mountains, but Bramble, he knew, would outstrip him, or could, if only she could bring herself to truly master an animal instead of working out a compromise, where the beast was a partner rather than a servant.

Gorham loved horses, loved them with a rising of his blood whenever he was near them, loved training, grooming and, especially, riding them, as though their mere scent was his key to happiness. But they were only animals, after all, not people, and no matter how often you felt that wordless sense of accord, or found your horse responding as though it could think in tandem with you, they were still animals and bred to serve humans. Gorham knew Bramble didn't see it that way.

It didn't get in the way of day-to-day business, because a horse that has been bred right and trained right likes to be ridden, likes to have the partnership and even the hard work, so Bramble was happy to prepare them for their owners, or for eventual buyers, knowing Gorham didn't sell to the cruel or the stupid. But it worried him, sometimes, in case they ever came to a parting of the ways over it. And it worried him, briefly, as he put the stallion into her care, but he soon dismissed it. He told Bramble that Acton would have the life all stallions dreamed of: no work and an endless procession of mares to cover.

"Not endless," Bramble protested over an ale that night in the tack room in the stallion's stable block, sitting where they could both see Acton's head poked out over his stall. "Spring to midsummer. You won't get mares coming into season later than that."

"Well, all right," Gorham admitted. "He gets to rest in autumn and winter. But he'll need it by then! I've got twelve booked in for him already, not counting our own seven."

Gorham had built the stallion block big and beautiful, hoping that one day there'd be more than one stallion to house there. The spring wind was always from the east, so they'd put it easterly and well away from the foaling boxes and the mares' stalls, with the width of the breeding pens in between, and a stand of fragrant trees and plants for good measure. Gorham didn't want his carefully constructed stable kicked to bits by a stallion determined to get to a mare.

Acton's bright eyes watched them and his ears pricked forward to listen to them talk. His blond mane shone in the lantern light and his coat was as glossy as an hour's currying and combing could make it. Bramble had sung and whispered to him the whole time and could feel him settle in to the sound of her voice as she did, could sense his satisfaction in being groomed and later, the security of the routine. He might not like being bridled or ridden, but he enjoyed the benefits of human contact. He was too intelligent for his own good, the silly git, she thought, and was surprised to find how much affection she already felt for him.

In the months that followed, that affection grew. She never tried to ride him. Now and then, when Gorham saw how easily Acton came to her whistle, the whistle they used to call all their horses from the field, he hinted at her riding him in a chase. But she sidestepped the suggestion each time. She was happy to groom and lead him, bring him to the mating yard and calm him down afterward, and play games with him. But she felt, down deep in her bones, that if he were ever ridden, something would die in him, and something in herself, as well. Winning a chase, for Acton, would be a dishonor.

Gorham saw it, and sometimes, heading home to Maude, back to the four walls of his townhouse and the responsibilities of the town council, he was glad, too, to know one creature that had refused to be tamed. Acton, he thought, hadn't been gentled, or broken; he just liked Bramble, as all horses did, and went where she went and did as she suggested because he liked to please her. Anyone else, even Gorham, got a swift kick or a sharp bite if they tried to lay hands on him. You couldn't call that tame. So Gorham kissed Maude good evening and went off to his council meetings, but the wildness of Acton lay under his breastbone, sometimes a comfort, sometimes a source of restlessness, and he never tried too hard to get Bramble to ride the stallion.

Bramble developed a lucrative sideline: buying cross-grained, human-wary animals—biters, buckers and bitches, as she called them—and working them until they were safe with children on their backs. Sometimes it took a long time, but it was worth it. She sold them only for children, and only then if the child came to her to be taught to ride and look after it. She took half the profits of that and, as always, a quarter of the profits of the other training she did for Gorham.

She worked, she trained, and she chased. She won the first Spring Chase for three years straight. She'd been glad that the honor of hosting the race went to a different town each year, so she hadn't had to go back to Sendat and risk meeting Leof. She knew that he had taken part in other chases, but he had never raced against her again. Had never even come to watch. She told herself that she was glad of it, but wondered if it meant that he hated her. Her memories of him were so mixed: warm and funny and gentle, and then cold and sharp as his sword. She avoided thinking about him by concentrating on whatever work was at hand.

She trained the roan as usual through winter to be ready for the first Spring Chase, but the week before the entry money was due, she sought out Gorham in the tack room. She stood uncomfortably, fidgeting with a bridle, until he turned around and raised his eyebrows at her.

"What's the matter?"

"It's the roan..."

"Mmmm?" Gorham sat on a bale of straw and looked at her steadily. "What's the matter with him?"

"I'm not sure whether to ride him in the Spring Chase or not."

His eyebrows almost climbed off his face. "Why not?"

"He's lost speed," she said reluctantly. "He doesn't feel as fit as he should be."

"He won the last two chases all right."

"They were poor fields. They were mostly youngsters, entered for the experience. The good horses aren't put up against him anymore. He didn't have to try very hard."

Gorham pulled at his nose and then looked up at the roof, calculating. "He'd be, what, thirteen now?"

"I don't know exactly, but around thirteen, maybe fourteen, I think, by his teeth."

He nodded. "Well, you can't expect him to race forever. Your decision."

She reassured herself: the roan was fit enough, she was worrying unnecessarily, she should give him the chance. She was particularly nervous about missing the Spring Chase, the one where she had been reborn, and she wished that he'd lost fitness in the middle of the season. If she stopped chasing altogether, would she lose herself? It seemed more likely, somehow, if she missed the Spring Chase. She couldn't bear the thought of that fog descending on her again, of looking at the world through cloudy glass forever. So she paid the entry fee and prepared the roan for the race, trying to believe that he would be ready for it.

The Spring Chase was in Pless this year, and as the riders gathered for the start, Bramble felt nervous, sensing something was wrong. Then, as the caller signaled them forward to the start line, the roan stopped. He just stopped, as he had that day in the road outside Gorham's farm. She clicked her tongue and squeezed her legs against his sides, but he didn't move.

Bramble jumped off and moved to his head. He turned away from the start and faced toward home.

"What is it, lad?" she asked, as she had asked then. He looked her back in the eye and unlike that day, he was not calm, but restless, flicking his mane, flinging his head up. She put her hand on his neck and felt him quiet down. When the roan had decided to stop at Gorham's, she had accepted it and had now lived his choice for years. But this... She felt fear under her breastbone, the threat of emptiness and death. Without chasing, it might come back. At that moment, she was sure it would, sure that she would descend, once again, into the fog she had escaped from. She couldn't face it.

"Please," she said.

He let out a great breath through his nostrils, not really a neigh, but a sigh, then turned back to face the start.

It was a strong field and they got away to a quick start. The Kill was the young son of a nearby farmer, who spent every afternoon that he could sneak away from his work at Gorham's, begging to be taken on as an apprentice. He knew every inch of the terrain and had planned his route to get the most out of both horse and rider. It was the toughest course she had ever ridden, and by the approach to the third jump Bramble knew the roan wasn't up to it. He was trying hard, but each jump was an effort, and he had lost the surge back to racing speed after the jump. He began to fall behind.

She had no experience riding in the middle of the pack: they had always led. Bramble found herself jostling for position, trying to see ahead over the other riders, making guesses about the best line to take through a jump. She and the roan were both unsettled. By the fourth jump they were lying fifth, and Bramble was figuring out a safe way to drop out of the race without being trampled by the pack.

The Kill led them at a knee-breaking pace down a half-wooded hillside and soared over a shallow stream that had cut deeply into its banks. There were rocks on the streambed, sharp and unforgiving. The horse in front fell as the bank collapsed beneath it, and the roan had to leap over it as well as the stream. It was a jump that in the past he could have taken with moderate effort.

He took off, but he didn't have the power to get all the way across the stream. For a moment he hung suspended over the gap, then fell heavily, turning as he hit the ground, to shake her off his back, kicking out behind and twisting so she didn't fall under him. She heard his head thwack into one of the rocks and reached for him, but the fall and the current in the stream threw her away. She crawled back against the flow, heedless of the pack jumping over her and thrashing up the farther bank. The noise was deafening, but she moved in a bubble of silence until she reached him and heard his rasping breath.

His head was covered in blood and his ribs were clearly broken, the bones piercing the skin. The stream was flowing red below them and his breath was coming harder and harder. She sat in the streambed and took his head in her lap. He stared up at her with resignation and nuzzled her in between bouts of coughing. "I'm sorry, I'm sorry," she said, over and over. The roan's breath became harsh, settling into the death rattle that meant the end was coming. Bramble put her head down on his to share every shake and shudder. When the shaking stopped, her whole body registered it. She raised her head slowly and looked at him, then gently closed his half-open eye.

She knew that it was her fault. She had known he wasn't fit enough to chase, but had forced him to, out of fear. She had given over to a fear of herself as she would never have to a threat from anyone else. She had sacrificed the roan. Betrayed him.

She was ready, she thought, to pay the price of betrayal. She felt numb, and welcomed the numbness. Then, all at once, her feeling came back. She saw the spring twilight ending with a haze of gold and lavender in the sky. She was aware of it, aware of every dust mote in the air, of the rough streambed beneath her, the texture of the roan's hair, roughened by sweat, under her fingers, the smell of horse, of blood, of leather. She saw the ripples in the stream glow and darken as the sunlight faded. She had passed beyond shock, she thought, to a state where every-thing seemed alive and full of clarity, full of meaning...If only she could understand it. But there was nothing to understand except the dead weight on her lap, and nothing to feel except shame and grief.

Gorham was standing on the bank with a few of the other riders. She eased her way from under the roan's head, but couldn't just put it down under the water. She knew that it was ridiculous—he was already dead. He wouldn't drown, wouldn't even feel the water closing over his head—but she still couldn't do it. Gorham came to her aid by removing the saddle and placing it under the roan's head.

Then he guided her to the bank and hugged her. She endured it, as she endured the other riders' pats of sympathy on her back. She didn't deserve sympathy.

Some of the riders brought shovels, and together they pulled the roan out of the water to a grave they had dug while Bramble had sat oblivious in the stream. She resented that, resented the blisters on their hands that should by rights have been hers, but she endured that loss, too, because a killer can claim no rights over her victim. She allowed herself to hold his head, though, as they dragged him out of the stream, and she filled in the grave herself, shaking her head when the others tried to help. "Come back with Maude and me tonight," Gorham said, but she shook her head and walked back to the cottage alone.

She sat without moving all night, remembering her betrayal. She intended to sit there forever. Looking back later, she realized that she had survived only because Gorham had pulled her out of the cottage the next morning and thrust a newly born foal into her arms. The warm, wriggling body dragged her attention back to the present. She started to cry, then let the foal go to raise her blistered hands to her face, and smelled the roan again. It was the last time she would know that scent.

Bramble worked through the spring foaling and the summer

presentation of mares to the stallions. She worked silently, for the most part, and Gorham let her be. Maude tried a few times to "cheer her up a bit" but eventually realized that she couldn't, and left her alone. Through every day and most of every night, while her hands were busy, her mind went over every moment of her time with the roan, and every moment of his death. For three years she had clutched to the chase to protect her against the fog, against the knowledge that she should have died in the chasm, and for three years the roan had joyfully partnered her. Now it was over.

One day, in autumn, as the wild geese flew over, she suddenly remembered the demon's curse: *Born wild and died wild. Not fit for this young man. Thou wilt love no man never.* That had seemed a terrible curse to her then, and feasible after the chasm. But she had come back to life and, even with the roan's death, life showed no signs of deserting her. There was no fog, no clouded glass. She felt everything sharply, saw everything vividly. She wished she didn't.

Thinking of the light going out in the roan's eyes, she was reminded of the warlord's man's face as he fell, and was ashamed, suddenly, of killing him, and ashamed of not feeling worse about it when it happened. It was as though she hadn't really understood death before—had never felt its finality. Its eternity. Grief and guilt fought for space in her and both won.

She needed...something. Not just to take the Road again. Not just to face her fear of that hollow space within her. Something else. She needed forgiveness. But from where? The two she had injured were both dead. Then she remembered the pilgrims she had met at Sandalwood.

She would go to the Well of Secrets. A real pilgrimage, this time: a pilgrimage to seek forgiveness and absolution. As soon as she had made the decision, she felt better. Just as grief-stricken, just as guilty, but better. She wept again for the roan, gently, and fell asleep.

She left the next day, after a long hour with Acton in his stall. He was getting older, too, had come into his full strength. His sons were adding to the stud's income, now. Gorham had three of his get, from different but equally well-bred mares, and another stallion from Golden Valley: the stallion stable block was finally full.

Gorham was in Pless at a council meeting. Bramble thought she would pack, then ride into town to say goodbye. She took her store of silver—mostly from winning chases—and the three horses she was working with at the time, Mud, Campanile and Trine.

Mud was a bay pony who had figured out early that he was much stronger than any human who tried to boss him around. He didn't bite or kick, just refused to cooperate with saddling and unsaddling by leaning his whole weight against you, or by sitting down on his haunches. His former owner had gelded him, but it hadn't made any difference to his temperament. After a month with Bramble he was grudgingly letting her do up the girths, and he would follow her if she was riding another horse. She used him as a packhorse.

Campanile (stupid name, thought Bramble, and called her Cam) was a flighty chestnut ex-chaser who'd been mistreated as a youngster and was terrified of the whip and even of the reins, if she saw them out of the corner of her eye. Bramble didn't even possess a whip and rode her without reins, as she had the roan. Six weeks after taking her on, Cam was tractable and even eager to be ridden, as long as the rider was Bramble. Given another six weeks she'd have been ready for the reins, and another rider, but Bramble figured she could train her on the road and sell her if she needed extra silver.

Trine was a bad-tempered, intelligent black who'd been sold
to Bramble cheap because her rider had fallen to his death from
her during a stag hunt. The horse had been labeled a killer. And
it was possible she was—she certainly despised humans. She
took every chance to nip and bite, and Bramble had clouted her
on the nose each time, aware that, as Gorham had taught her,
horses were herd animals and she had to establish that she was
one of the older females who would have dished out punishment in the wild.

Gorham had found Trine for her only two weeks ago, in an
attempt to spark her interest in riding again. Bramble's combination of discipline and loving care was just beginning to have
an effect. Of all the horses she had trained, Trine was the most
cross-grained and would take the longest to gentle. Bramble
liked her.

Gorham arrived as she was settling the packs on Mud. He
stood for a moment, taking it in, then silently helped her finish.

"Where are you going?" Gorham asked.

"Do you know where the Well of Secrets is these days?"

"Up north, I heard, in the Last Domain. You heading that
way, then?"

Bramble stilled her hands against Mud's sides, spreading her
fingers out to feel the warmth. It was a clear day, autumn just
making itself felt.

"It's a bad time of year to be traveling north," Gorham
said. "Winter comes early up there. I'd be heading for Mitchen,
myself, or even Carlion, until after winter. Besides, you'd have
to go through the Lake Domain."

"So?"

"The council's worried that war's coming between Central
and Lake. Thegan's looking north, they say. Maybe you'd be
best off taking the long way round, by the coast."

She smiled at him, warmed that he was not trying to persuade her to stay. The boy from the town who turned up every afternoon had been pestering Gorham for months to take him on as an apprentice, and he'd shown that he had a way with the young ones. She wouldn't be leaving Gorham all on his own. Still, he could easily have taken it amiss, she thought, that she was just up and leaving.

As though he read her mind, he smoothed down the pack and said a little regretfully, "It's been too long since I was on the Road myself."

"Maybe I will make for Carlion," she said. "That's good advice. Thanks."

They'd worked together long enough for him to hear all the other thanks in her voice, and the affectionate goodbye that neither of them was comfortable speaking.

"Wind at your back," he said as she jumped lightly onto Cam's back. The Travelers' goodbye.

"Fire in your hearth," she said in return, the Travelers' goodbye to those settled in towns, and he winced, but tried to smile at her in farewell.

She paused at the gate.

She could imagine walking into Maryrose's kitchen, into her welcome. She missed her more now than any time in the last few years and longed to be safe under Maryrose's loving, intelligent stare. Under that stare she felt herself to be just ordinary. Maybe the demon was right, and she would never love any man, but didn't the fact that she loved Maryrose count for something?

The road north led through Sendat, and in Sendat were Thegan, whom she had no wish to meet again, and Leof. Leof. She hadn't thought of him in a very long time, and there was no use thinking about him now. He lived by cold steel and blood, and she wanted nothing to do with him. She definitely didn't want to face the pain she had seen in his eyes. And Thegan, she was sure, even after that one brief meeting, was not to be trusted. It would be foolish to ride straight into his territory, especially with these rumors of war with the Lake People.

Half a mile down the road she stopped. Her stomach was churning. Taking this route, she was doing it again, ignoring her instincts. She needed more than Maryrose's hugs and scoldings. She needed more than anyone normal could give her. Forgiveness. She turned the horses north and immediately she felt better.

At last she was back on the Road. A wood pigeon lifted into the air nearby with that distinctive *slap slap slap* of wings, and her heart lifted with it. There was no sun on her back on this cloudy day, but she didn't care. *The Road is long and the end is death*, she said to herself, remembering one of her grandfather's sayings. *If we're lucky.*

ASH

HE WAS standing by the window keeping watch, knowing what he would have to do if Doronit sent Hildie or Aylmer back to kill Martine. Fight one friend to save another.

"I must leave," Martine said to Ash. "Doronit won't try to be subtle next time—it will be a quick knife as I walk past in the street."

She went to a cupboard and took out paper, brush and an ink block, then sat before the fire to write.

"I'm leaving instructions for my man of business to sell this house and keep the monies safe for me until I send for them," she said, concentrating on the paper.

Ash waited, silently. What could he do? He couldn't go back to Doronit's, not even to pick up his clothes. She would kill him as soon as look at him, he knew. All he had was what he stood up in and the few coins in his pouch. And Acton's brooch. He went over to the mantelpiece to look at it. It glowed in the firelight, larger than life. It seemed more important than he remembered. More alive than he was. It was warm to the touch, but he felt cold, his stomach like lead.

Martine finished writing and waved the letter in the air to dry it. "Call a messenger, Ash, and we'll send this off." The *we* was automatic, and it warmed him a little. He knew he could ask Martine for advice.

He opened the door and gave three sharp whistles to summon a messenger. The rain had stopped for a while, though the sky was green and threatened a storm. Even on a day like this, there were three children who appeared out of nowhere, jostling in the doorway to be the one who took the message. Martine chose the oldest of them, a thin blond girl.

"Here," she said, handing over the letter, "take this to the House of Surety for me. It's next to the Guildhouse. Get their stamp and I will pay you a penny."

"Yes, marm," the girl answered, and then ran up the street. She must have been hungry to run that fast.

Ash latched the door behind her. Martine looked at him carefully.

"I must pack what I can carry," she said. "Back on the Road, when I had thought I'd left it behind me forever. I should have cast my own future that day, not Ranny's." She laughed without humor. "So. I must take the Road, Ash." She paused. "I would welcome the company of a trained safeguarder."

His heart seemed to grow larger, enough to hurt his ribs. "I have no money," he said. "I'd be a burden to you. I'll probably never be able to repay you."

"Well, come to that, I think you just saved my life, so maybe the talk of repaying should be on my side."

He shook his head firmly.

"No..." she agreed, "maybe you and I should not talk of debts and repayment. But it is true I would welcome your company, and I have enough to pay for both of us—at least until we get where I think I need to go."

Ash was too relieved and grateful to even ask where that was. She smiled at him and disappeared upstairs. He sat down by the fire. He couldn't think; he just stared at the flames and let their warmth enter his cold bones. Later he would think about Doronit. Had he betrayed her or had she betrayed him? He wasn't quite sure. All he knew was that she had meant to use him as a tool, like she used the ghosts and the wind wraiths. He would not be a tool. He was sure of that, too. The storm outside began in earnest: lightning, thunder and then an avalanche of rain.

In the middle of it there was a bang on the door. He reacted as a safeguarder, springing up then putting his back to the wall behind the door as Martine came in from the kitchen to open it. She sighed at the knife in his hand. He hadn't even realized that he'd drawn it. But it could easily be Doronit or Hildie, or any of the others out there. He realized that he was ready to kill any of them instantly. It appalled him, but the determination was there, unflinching: he would kill them all before he let them kill Martine or him.

It was the messenger. She came in, drenched and crying, and held out her hand. "I had the stamp, honest, marm. He took the letter, honest. But the rain washed it off."

Martine looked at the hand and then at Ash. If there had been a stamp, it was gone now. "Never mind, child, I'll have to trust you."

The girl's face lightened.

"Come," Martine said. "I'm leaving today. I've packed what food we can carry. You and your friends can have the rest. Ash, would you bring the bag from the upper room, please?"

She took the girl into the kitchen and he went slowly up the stairs, thinking about what had just happened. He had broken from Doronit, but what she had expected from him—the cynicism and control and violence—were part of him now. They would, he suspected, be part of him forever. He *was* a safeguarder.

While a small part of him mourned the boy who had not known how to slit a man's throat or strangle someone with a scarf, most of him felt stronger. At least he had a real trade—the skills were valuable, if harnessed with his own conscience. Perhaps he could get work in another town, somewhere a long way away, where Doronit's influence could not reach him. As he brought down the large backpack from the bedroom, his step was surer and his heart beat more strongly. He smiled at Martine as she came out of the kitchen with another bag packed full. She was followed by the girl, carrying a box stuffed full of vegetables and bags of flour and other things he couldn't see.

"Thanks, marm, thanks, marm…" she kept saying.

"She lives across the street," Martine said to him. "Make sure she gets there with her booty?"

So he went across the street, the rain hitting his skin so hard it stung, and made sure the other children lurking in the doorways didn't rob the girl of her reward. It was a small door in an unpainted house that was much poorer-looking than its neighbors.

"Thanks to you, too, sirrah," she said, and beamed at him from the doorway. "Gods' blessings on you."

It was the first blessing he'd received since he left his parents, and his eyes softened. He lifted a hand to her and went back to Martine a little calmer.

She had the packs ready, together with a storm cape for him. The oiled canvas with hood would keep out the worst of the rain. He hoisted the big pack on his back and fastened the cloak around him, then headed for the door.

"You're forgetting something." Martine nodded toward the mantelpiece. The only thing on it was Acton's brooch.

Ash went over and picked it up. "Why do I feel all this has happened because of this?" he asked, and slipped it into his pouch.

"Perhaps it has. But Doronit wouldn't believe it." They grinned at each other. "Let's go."

They left under cover of the storm by the North Road and saw no one they knew.

Ash was happy, despite the storm and the colder weather ahead, despite his jaw clenching so tight, whenever he thought of Doronit, that his teeth were aching. He had no idea where they were going, and he didn't care. He was relieved to leave Doronit behind him, although he felt a pang for Turvite.

The brooch hung heavily over his left hipbone, but he refused just to be a tool, even of the gods. He was leaving because he'd been betrayed by a calculating, selfish woman—there were songs about that. It happened to men all the time. *Betrayed by a woman, cast out into the storm*...He recited "The Lying Sweetheart" in his head as they slogged through the mud, and he felt grown-up at last.

SAKER

THERE WAS a village on the way to the mountains, in the poor land west of the Lake. Saker had been there often before, as he had made his rounds of the country, drawing his maps and collecting old scrolls. There had been a massacre there, but a small one, just a village. Saker flinched as he realized what he'd thought: "just a village." *Every* death was important. *Every single one* had to be avenged.

The important thing about Spritford, this village, was that the invaders had buried the bodies. They'd learned by then about the stench and illness that came from rotting corpses. They'd gathered the dead and thrown them into a small dell, then shoveled enough dirt over them to keep out the scavenging animals. The dell was named in one of Rowan's songs: Ravensnest Glade.

Which meant that Saker could find the bones.

It wasn't hard for a stonecaster and a mule to make their way from Whitehaven to Spritford in the lengthening days of spring. Everywhere he went Saker mourned: the missing forests, the dead towns without trees where the pale-eyed townsfolk hurried about their greedy business. They had no beauty, no grace, none of the spirit-filled artistry of his own people. Without the Travelers, this land, these Domains would have no culture at all. It was people of the old blood who sang the songs and painted the walls and told the stories and danced the dances. *These invaders*, he thought, *just watch us because they can't do anything else. Maybe that's why they hate us so.*

He found Spritford easily enough, on the shore of the river Sprit, coming to it from the south toward the end of the day. Just as he came in sight of the Sprit, he saw a hawk stoop. It flashed down and struck, both feet extended forward, and then beat its wings twice powerfully to launch again, a ground squirrel dangling lifeless from its talons. As it rose slowly, he could see that it was a saker falcon, and he was immensely cheered by the omen.

"Fly well, brother," he said, and whistled as he rode toward the village.

The land rose beyond the cottages to a ridge that concealed the river Sharp. The Ravensnest Glade, the song said, was on the Sharp side of the village. He wanted to ride on, find the dell right away, but he made himself stop at the inn, take a room, and cast some stones for the innkeeper's sister in return for a meal, as he usually did. He didn't want to attract attention.

He found himself spending the evening casting stones for the villagers, trying not to show how irritated he was by their petty concerns: "Will my girl marry me?" "Does my husband know?" "Will the calf from the red cow live?" "Will I be lucky at dice this full moon?" They were obsessed with the trivial—all townsfolk were, and farmers no better. Never was there a question about truth, or justice, or even rebirth. They were pitiful, pale shadows of the men and women who had lived in this land before the invasion. The land would not miss them.

"I thought," he said carefully to the innkeeper's sister, a thin but red-cheeked woman, "that I would go to pay my respects to your gods tomorrow. Where is the altar?"

"Oh yes, sir," she said, "they'll like that, I'm sure. The rock is in Ravensnest Glade, on the Sharp side of the town. I'll point it out in the morning."

She left him to serve another customer. He sat, feeling his

body grow cold. He'd only asked the woman where the gods were so he'd have an excuse to go off exploring in the morning. The gods were in the actual place of burial. He shivered, appalled. Had Acton's men been insane, to make the gods' place their dumping ground? And why had the gods allowed it?

The woman came sidling back, not sure if he would welcome more chat. She was smiling at him nervously, trying to ingratiate herself as though that would somehow ensure a better result at her next casting. She was one of those women who were excited by magic, by the lure of the stones. He despised them, all of them: they were eager to use the skills of the old blood but contemptuous of those in whose veins it ran.

"The gods used to be by the river, it's said," she offered. "After Acton's people came, they asked to be moved to the glade."

Very good, Saker thought, *the gods had decided it—to be near their dead*. That meant that the gods here, unlike most local gods, cared about what happened to the people in their charge. Most gods were not interested in temporal concerns, and seemed to care more about the beasts of the fields than about humans. Although they did like a sacrifice, so humans were useful to them in some ways.

These gods must be different. A shiver went through him at the thought, but he shook it away. Tomorrow he would raise the dead, feel their bones in his hands, replenish them with his own blood. And their gods would strengthen him when he cast the spell, so the dead could take back what was theirs.

ASH

Ash had grown up walking the Road, and he fell back immediately into that easy, unhurried pace that let you walk all day. He saw that Martine did, too, and remembered that she had said something about being on the Road before. They went on for an hour or so in the sharp rain, heading up over the hills surrounding Turvite. It was a steep climb, and for a long while he concentrated solely on putting one foot in front of the other. The rain lifted as they passed the top of the first line of hills and started down the other side. He hadn't realized how he had been hunched against the deluge, the sound as much as the cold, until it stopped.

"Where are we going?" he asked.

She turned her head and laughed at him. "Finally you ask!"

He grinned, too, and shrugged.

"We're going north, to Hidden Valley," she said. "To visit... well, let's call her an old friend." She looked at him again. "No, let's not call her that. I owe you more than a social lie."

"Elva is the daughter of two people I grew up with. There were the three of us the same age in our village, Lark and Cob and me — two girls and a boy. Lark and I were named on the same day, after the birds our mothers saw following the births — the lark and the house martin. We played together, got into trouble together, were punished together. When I was small it seemed it would always be the three of us. But, two girls and one boy... Of course we both fell in love with him. And when the time came to choose, he chose Lark."

290

She brooded over that for three paces, then went on.

"It was because I was...different. I already knew I could cast the stones—you know how children play at stonecasting?"

He nodded.

"Even before I could read the runes, I could tell what the stones meant. And there were other things...the ghosts, the local gods...When he was small, Cob just accepted it, but when it came time to choose who he'd lie with in the dark of night, he couldn't bring himself to choose someone who spoke to ghosts. He told me. So. Perhaps the gods were listening...because their daughter, Elva, was stranger far than me. The strangest child ever born to our blood."

Martine fell silent.

Ash gathered his courage. "What was strange about her?"

She blinked rapidly, forcing back memory.

"There's no color in her, nothing but white and pink—white skin, white hair, pink eyes. She cannot bear the rays of the sun. I've learned, since, that children are sometimes born that way, but we had never heard of it then. The village voice wanted her put out on the mountain to die, until the local gods spoke to him and said they wanted her to live. But Cob couldn't bear to have her near him, although Lark would have loved her, I think, if he'd let her. Then she started talking to the local gods— almost her first words were to them. Cob couldn't abide it. So I took her to live with me, with their blessing, as soon as she could walk properly."

"And you went on the Road?"

She paused, then clearly decided not to tell him another part of the story. He tried not to feel hurt. She had a right to her privacy.

"No. That came later."

"And then?"

"Then? We wandered. You know the life. I cast the stones, I bought our bread, I laid ghosts to rest, I tended Elva and fed her and loved her, too..."

Ash heard Doronit's echo— *Why have I housed you and fed and, yes, loved you all this time?* —and lost track of what Martine was saying for a moment.

"...and then we were in Carlion and Ranny of Highmark came for her reading. You know what happened. I was a fool, no? After that, it wasn't safe for Elva to be near me. Ranny would have loved to see me bereft and grieving. Elva was a woman by then, and beautiful...though few can see past her white skin. She left me to find her own place, five years ago, when she was sixteen. So. That is where we are going—to Elva."

"Just to visit?" he ventured.

She looked at him in the fading twilight, amused.

"Have you tried to cast the stones, boy? You see further than most. No, not just to visit. The stones have shown me...warnings, about Elva, though it's unchancy to cast for your own needs. A stonecaster rarely sees the truth about those she loves. Still, there are signs that Elva may be glad to see me, and not only because she loves me."

They walked the rest of the daylight in silence. Ash was lost in a daydream about this beautiful white-haired girl, only one year older than him...It stopped him thinking about Doronit, about what she was doing, whether she had replaced him already; it stopped him imagining what it would have been like, if he'd killed Martine and gone home to share Doronit's bed.

Martine said nothing until they reached a stream crossing the road, not far down from a camping place. "Time for fire," she said.

There was a tent in the bag Ash carried, so he set it up while Martine gathered firewood and some dry kindling from under

292

a holly bush, disturbing a lizard, which skittered off into the growing dark. Every movement, every moment, reminded him of the long years of traveling with his parents. It was pleasure and pain, both.

They sat at the fire, ate, and then crawled into the tent, back to back, warmth to warmth. He waited until he could hear her breathing, slow and even, and then he let the tears creep out of his eyes and drip onto his sleeve, so there'd be no mark on the tent in the morning. He didn't think at all, just cried quietly and steadily until the moon set and he slept.

In the morning they packed up and Ash doused the fire while Martine brushed and braided her hair. It was a fine morning after the rain, though the bite of the autumn air in the highland was brisk. The sun caught the shine on Martine's hair. He stared out of the corner of his eyes, not just because she was beautiful, with her brush in her hand, standing and swaying with each stroke, but because the gleam of her hair, moving as the brush went through it, seemed to call his eye, seemed to weave shapes that he could almost make out. It was like sunlight on water, constantly changing, drawing him... The shapes were almost clear... He pulled his eyes away and went off to wait by the road. He'd heard of Travelers having the bright vision, the Sight that shows itself in light, but he didn't want any part of it. Even among Travelers, such folk were thought of as unchancy. He had enough that set him apart from everyone else. He wasn't minded to be any more different than he had to be.

Martine came to the road with her hair neatly braided, the plait hanging far down her back, and smiled at him. "So. Ready to go?"

They walked companionably, enjoying the still, crisp mountain air. "How about a song to pass the time?" Martine asked after a while.

Ash went red in the face and looked away. "I don't sing."

"Everybody sings," she said, surprised by his reaction.

He shook his head.

"Oh, come on. You know 'The Green Hills of Pless,' don't you?"

"I know lots of songs. My parents were musicians. But I don't—I *can't* sing."

She looked at him curiously. "Your voice can't be that bad, surely."

"Yes it is."

"Maybe to your parents, if they were professionals. But I'm just a stonecaster. What do I know about music? Give it a try. My own voice isn't that wonderful."

So, because he felt he owed her so much, he cleared his throat and began to sing "The Green Hills of Pless."

I have wandered the land from Domain to—

Before he finished the first line he saw the look on her face and stopped short. She came to a halt in the road, her face pale. He stopped a few steps farther on and looked back at her.

"It *is* that bad, isn't it?" he asked reluctantly.

She was frowning, as though he were a puzzle she was trying to solve. "It's the voice of the dead," she said.

"That bad, huh?" he said, trying to be casual about it.

"No, really the voice of the dead," she insisted. "Exactly the same."

Ash stared at her, memories cascading over him: the look of pain on his mother's face whenever he tried to sing as a young child; the way his father would turn away, abruptly, or walk out of the room; and, on the day he left them for Doronit, his mother saying "but music is dead to you, anyway," as though to remind him of something he knew already. He had not known. He had not sung since he was small. Not even when he was alone. His mother was right. Music was dead to him.

Strangely, it made him feel both shaken and comforted. To have the voice of the dead was a terrible thing, but it was clearly the work of the gods. It was not his fault that he could not sing; not his fault that music did not spring from him as it did from his parents. To be the son of singers and have a mediocre voice might be shameful, but what the gods visited upon you could not be a cause for shame. Now he could put it behind him and find a new place in the world.

Martine plopped right down in the middle of the road and took out her bag of stones. "Come on," she said, "give me your hand."

She spread out a piece of fabric with a flick of her wrist and held her left hand out to him imperatively. He sank down to the road slowly, but he spat in his hand and clasped hers. She took the five stones out of the bag and cast them across the fabric. They were all facedown.

"The meaning hidden," she said. She turned them over slowly. "Death. Pain. Bereavement. The blank stone, the random one. And here, look—Rebirth. But all hidden. All secret."

She stared at the stones intently.

"I can't make them speak," she whispered. "They know your secret, but they are dumb to me, as ghosts are." She paused, thinking. "Tell them to speak."

"What?"

"Tell the stones to speak."

He shook his head. "No...If they're dumb, maybe I'm not meant to know. Maybe it's better not to know."

"I spend my life seeking knowledge. I don't think it's ever better not to know."

He shook his head again, stubbornly. "You seek knowledge

for those who want to know, who come to you to find things out. This was your idea, not mine."

She let his hand go with a sigh. "So. Maybe…maybe. For now, at least."

Then they'd had to dodge a cart full of cabbages, whose driver swore at them for feckless Travelers, sitting in the dirt and getting in the way of hardworking folk.

They grinned at each other, and kept walking.

They went on like that for days, stopping at villages where Martine exchanged castings for food and shelter. They slept in barns, shepherds' huts, on the floor of inn stables, in the tent. The hedges and trees were full of birds, and at evening and morning the sky was full of flocks making practice flights before their journey south for winter. Ash had forgotten the high, soaring skylark song and the way that, passing through a dell, the grasshopper shrill seems to deafen you.

They grew used to the smell of their own sweat until they didn't smell it anymore. But every Traveler knows that if you don't wash regularly, the townsfolk won't have anything to do with you—which is funny, his mother used to say, for most of them don't wash from one week to the next. But Traveler sweat smells strange to them, and unpleasant.

So they stopped at creeks and pools, thankful that it hadn't been a dry summer, and washed, each taking a turn as lookout for the other, and Ash trying not to think about what Martine looked like bathing when it was his turn to guard. He looked away when she brushed her hair each morning, too, determined not to be snared into the bright vision of the Sight. He filled his head with fantasies about the white-haired girl instead, and refused to think about Doronit.

There was no sign of Doronit's or Ranny's men on the road

behind them, and in the end it felt almost like a holiday, except that Martine was worried about Elva. She didn't say it, but he could tell. She would walk for a while in silence, her face gradually becoming more severe, a frown appearing. Then she would shake her head and turn to him almost desperately, saying, "How about a song, then?"

She'd discovered that even though he couldn't sing them, he could recite the verses of all the ballads, histories, and love songs, though love songs didn't work so well as walking songs. And some of the histories were very old.

"What's the oldest one you know?" Martine asked him one day.

"Oh, that's the invasion song, 'The Landtaken Ballad.'"

"I haven't heard that one."

So he began, although it was a song that always left him both excited—stirred up, as he often was by songs of battle and glory—and angry at how *happy* Acton's men had been as they had killed his ancestors.

Bright in the morning shone the spring sun
Bright in the sun shone the spears of our host
Bright the fierce eyes of Acton the bold
As they took the cold road that led to Death Pass.

Death Pass was where Acton and his men had come over the mountains in the first invasion. They had come at the first sign of spring thaw in the lowlands, plowing their way through chest-high snow, moving as silently as possible so they would not trigger the terrible avalanches that gave Death Pass its name. It was an insane thing to do, which was why they were able to massacre the people living on the other side of the pass. In previous years those people had armed themselves well against the annual summer raids of Acton's tribe, but they had been taken by surprise when their enemy appeared out of the snow and mist, swords and spears in hand.

Bright flowed the blood of the dark-haired foe
Red flowed the swords of the conquering ones
Mighty the battles, mighty the deeds
Of Acton's companions, the valiant men.

No one had been left alive, not even the babies. In the past, the tribe from beyond the mountains had raided, killed some men, raped some women, loaded themselves up with booty and gone home again. This time they stayed. The *landtaken*, Acton called it, the theft of land; it was the biggest theft there had ever been. And when Death Pass cleared in spring, across the mountains came the women and children of the tribe, and they moved into the empty cottages, while the men swept down into the lowlands, killing and keeping what they overran. That first village was renamed Actonston, of course.

Remember their names, and praise them daily:
Acton and Aelred, the boon companions,
Beorn and Baluch, Merrick and Mabry,
Aelric and Asgarn, Garlok and Gabra...

They walked silently for some time after he had finished reciting the song. Ash kept his eyes on the road, not wanting her to see the turmoil the song raised in him.

"So. The world changed in a day," Martine said eventually.

He nodded. "In a day, and a few hundred years. The landtaken took a long time to finish. More tribes followed Acton's people over the mountains, and the Domains are large. It took them a long time to wipe out every settlement."

"Yes," she said. "Longer than you might think."

They made their way gradually north, toward the mountains. Elva lived in a village at the foothills, Martine had said. At first they traveled through farmland, land that had been settled even before Acton came. But as they moved farther from Turvite they came upon more and more patches of wild land—forest, or marsh, or heath.

After two weeks on the Road they were having to walk a whole day to get to the next village by nightfall, and in the evenings their breath clouded on the chilling air. Even though Ash had been on the Road for most of his life, some parts of the country seemed strange to him: moors where the wind wuthered through the gorse; or stretches where granite cropped out from grass that looked as close mown as if sheep had grazed there for a thousand years, but there were no sheep anywhere to be seen, and the granite never took warmth from the sun, no matter how hot the day; or stands of pines where the sun never reached the path, even at midday.

On the fifteenth day, they came late in the twilight to a village set in foothills, and as they came down over a ridge they saw the lights just being kindled in cottages. There was no inn, but a bush hanging above the door of one cottage showed them where the ale was brewed, so they went on down and knocked.

"Come along in," came a man's voice.

"Blessings on this place," said Martine as they entered.

It was a drinking place like you'd find in any village. There were a few tables with benches, a few chairs near the fire for the old men, a couple of kegs against the wall, a shelf of tankards gleaming cheerily in the firelight. Ash felt his spirits rise, and they rose further when the brewer came toward them and smiled, the first smile they'd had from an innkeeper since they'd left Turvite. He was a broad, strong-looking man, though not tall, with wide-set blue eyes and laugh lines at the corners of his eyes and mouth.

"Travelers, then?" he asked. "Singers, storytellers?" His tone was hopeful, the voice of a lover of tales and one starved of entertainment. It was easy to see why he had become a brewer; he relished the company and the talk around the fire.

Martine held up her pouch, and his face fell.

"Stonecaster," he said. "Ah, well, no less welcome for that. I'm Fiske. Come, sit by the fire."

Fiske fed them pea soup, grilled trout, greens, carrots and baked parsnips. The food was good, and they ate hungrily. Fiske sat down and ate with them, asking for the news of the Road. There was a good deal they could tell him about the nearby villages, but he didn't care about news from Turvite, dismissing it with a wave of his hand.

"Foreigners," he said, and asked instead about the horse race in the town they had just passed through. He had a bet on, and he was very pleased when they told him that his horse had won. "Hah! I knew it. With Bramble not riding Thorn last spring, the chases have opened right up again. I knew Silver Shoes could win! Golden Shoes was his dam, you know." He looked at their blank faces and smiled. "You don't follow the chases, then?"

They shook their heads.

"Shame, shame..." Fiske said. "It's a great sport." He realized that he had distracted them from their meals. "Eat, eat."

They returned with pleasure to the sweet crispy-skinned trout and when they were finished, Martine asked where they might find somewhere to sleep for the night.

Conversation around the room seemed to hush.

Fiske pulled at his lip. "Well..." he said, considering.

The crowd of men at the tables and round the fire looked

on, but kept out of it. Ash realized that Fiske must be the village voice, the one who acted as mediator and arbiter in village disputes: not quite a mayor, not quite a judge, not quite a peacemaker, but something of all three.

"I reckon you'd be happiest at Halley's place," he said, finally. "I'll take you."

"I'd better pay you first," Martine said, laughing at him.

He laughed, too, throwing his head back. "Aye, aye, so you'd better!"

So she paid and they followed Fiske out into the dark. He led them to a cottage on the other side of the village, near the southern road.

There was a ghost waiting outside the door. It was pale and wraithlike after the clarity of the Turvite ghosts, but Ash could see it plain enough, though it was clear that Fiske couldn't. It was an elderly man with a big mustache, dressed as a villager. They nodded to it and it nodded and grinned back, gesturing excitedly as if it had something to say. Martine gave it a short nod and tilted her head to Fiske, to show that it should wait until he went away. The ghost nodded.

Fiske, oblivious, knocked at the door. "Ho, Halley, open up! I've got guests for you."

A young man opened the door. He was in his late twenties, maybe, with the fair hair of Acton's people but with dark eyes. The knock had caught him in the middle of getting ready for bed, it was clear—his shirttails were out and he had one boot off.

"Fiske?" he said, in a light tenor voice. "What's the matter?"

"No problem, lad, just some guests for the night—a stonecaster and her boy. Thought you'd welcome them, for your da's sake."

Halley nodded at once and opened the door wide. The ghost

301

slipped in and they followed, into a space that doubled as sitting room and cobbler's workshop.

Fiske raised his hand in farewell.

"Thank you, Fiske," Martine said.

"Welcome, welcome always," he said, and smiled at her, maybe a little more warmly than a brewer would smile at a customer.

She did look very beautiful in the light from the lantern, tall and slender and graceful. She smiled back at him, maybe a little more warmly than a customer would smile at a brewer. Ash raised an eyebrow. He suspected that Martine would not have smiled so warmly if they weren't due to leave tomorrow. In her own way, she was as self-contained as Doronit.

Halley shut the door and gestured to them to sit down on the settle by the fireplace. The fire had been banked for the night and he stirred it up again, and added more wood. Apple wood, Ash thought, by the smell of it. The ghost stood by the fire, waiting, its eyes on Martine and Ash.

"You've had a death in the family recently," Martine said to Halley as he turned from the fire.

He was surprised. "Yes, yes, my father...Fiske told you?"

Martine shook her head. "No. A man with a mustache?" she asked. "Balding on top but with curly hair around his ears?"

Halley went pale. "Yes, that's him. How—"

"He is here," Martine said gently. "He wishes to speak to you."

The ghost nodded urgently.

"H-here?" Halley said, looking around nervously.

"Trust us," she said, and turned to Ash, a question in her eyes. Ash nodded. "My friend here will ask him to speak, but you must be prepared. It will not sound like your father. It will sound...harsh." She held Halley's eyes until he nodded, then she nodded in turn to Ash.

Ash looked at the ghost. "Speak," he said.

"Burn them, burn them!" the ghost said quickly, as though he were afraid the charm would be too brief.

Halley flinched at the grating graveyard voice and looked around the room wildly. He made the sign against evil and backed into a corner near the fire. "That's not my f-father! It's a d-demon! It wants to kill us all!"

"No," Ash said, pitying his fear. "All the dead speak in that voice. Don't be afraid. Nothing will harm you."

Halley calmed a little but wouldn't come out of the corner.

"Burn what?" Martine asked the ghost patiently.

"The stones, the stones, purify them, burn the bag..." the ghost said.

Halley flinched again, and looked for the source of the voice.

"Ah." Martine turned to Halley. "Your father was a stonecaster?" Halley and the ghost both nodded. "He died suddenly?"

"His h-heart."

"And you inherited his pouch and stones. You have been using them."

Again they nodded, the identical gesture marking them as father and son, although in features they were very different.

"Give me the pouch, Halley." Martine's voice was very gentle.

Wordlessly he went to a cupboard opposite the door and took out a stonecaster's pouch, dark blue leather with a red drawstring. He handed it to Martine, who had wrapped a fold of her tabard around her hand.

She walked to the fire and threw the pouch in. "Fire free thee, fire speed thee, fire light thy way," she said, and smiled at the ghost.

Halley protested and moved to the fire as though to pluck it out. Ash didn't understand what was going on, but he trusted Martine and held Halley back until the leather pouch had flared and seared, the smell of burned leather forcing them all to breathe shallowly. The stones fell out of the pouch as it disintegrated and lay amid the wood, their runes glowing white against the dark granite fireplace. The shapes seemed to call his eyes as the light in Martine's hair had done. He looked away.

"Stonecasters," said Martine, "put a little of their soul into their stones and pouch. There's no spell to it—it's just that over the years, with handling, and concentration, and constantly wearing the pouch, the two grow together. The stronger the caster, the more this is so. When a caster dies, the pouch and stones must be purified with fire to cut the tie so that the spirit can travel on. Unknowingly, you have been keeping your father from his journey."

Halley relaxed against Ash's arm, and Ash realized that he had again automatically reacted as a safeguarder, keeping him in a wrestling hold.

When the leather pouch had finally fallen apart, the ghost began to fade and he gestured urgently to Ash.

"Speak," Ash said again.

The voice of death sounded harsher than ever, but this time Halley listened carefully.

"I am in your debt, so I repay the only way I can...The road you are traveling will take you to the dead."

Ash shivered, full of sudden alarm, but Martine just raised her eyebrows. Then the ghost crossed the room and made as though to caress the head of his son, a curving gesture full of love and regret that faded before it was completed. Ash felt his eyes fill and looked at Martine. Her eyes were dark, but not full of tears. He wondered what it would take to make her cry, or show fear.

"He loved you," he said to Halley. It was important that Halley should know it, all the more because he couldn't see his father's ghost. "He wanted to embrace you."

Halley stood, confused, shaking his head in mingled grief and shock.

Martine looked at him with interest. "You are not completely of the old blood," she said slowly. "Nor was your father."

"No...It was his grandmam was a Traveler."

Martine studied the stones glowing in the fireplace. "I'm thinking," she said, "that I might take these stones with me when we go."

"But they—"

"The thing of it is," she cut across him, "you don't have enough of the Sight to make it safe for you to use them. You'll be seeing the wrong things, five times out of ten, or not be able to hear them when they speak."

"Speak?" he said.

That seemed to decide her. "You cannot see your father's ghost, you cannot hear the stones speak—you should not be using them." She softened a little. "It's no disgrace. You have another trade."

Halley sat down in a chair by the table, his working chair. "I used to watch him, and wonder how he knew. The stones...I always wanted to play with them, but he would never let me. When he died, handling them made me feel like he was close to me..."

"He was," she said softly. "But he's gone now."

Halley put his hands in his hair and began to cry, the hard, coughing sobs of deep grief. Martine just stood there, so Ash went to him and laid an arm across his shoulders.

"Out of the dark, new life is born," he said, quoting an old Traveler saying. "The spark flies upward and becomes a star."

He didn't think Halley heard him.

"'The road you are traveling will take you to the dead,'" he quoted to Martine as they spread their blankets on the floor in front of the fire.

"The Road is long and the end is death," she said.

"I don't think that's what he meant."

"What can we do? 'The dead' is not the same as 'death,' of course. But this is a road I must travel." She turned her head and looked sideways at him from under the dark fall of hair she had loosened, as she always did before sleep. "But it's not your road, Ash. You can take another turning anytime you want."

Alone on the roads...A shudder ran through him. "No," he said. "Our road lies together. For as long as you want." He had tried to sound adult and sure of himself, but his voice trembled a little.

She smiled. "You may change your mind about that one day, youngling." She yawned suddenly and stretched. "All right then. We take the Road tomorrow together, and see what comes."

"And if it's the dead?"

She chuckled. "Of all the people in the world, we have least to fear from the dead. They need us too much."

They left in the early morning, with hot porridge warming their insides and Halley's father's stones tucked safely into Martine's pack. The air smelled of hay and ripe apples and they set off with surprisingly light hearts, considering the solemn warning.

They were heading for the ford across the Sharp River, the river that eventually curved around and flowed into Mitchen Harbor. The Sharp divided the Domains into two unequal parts, north and south, with all the fertile flatlands between Turvite and the river. Past it, to the north, was pastureland, heath, swamp and rock. Here there were fewer birds, fewer animals, and fewer insects, except in the swamps. Even the earth was different: much poorer and coarser. The southern curve, as they called it in those parts, was where the people of the old blood had retreated to when Acton's men invaded. They were left alone there for quite a while — the land deemed not worth the trouble — until the invaders ran out of room in the lowlands. Then the push north started, and gradually the people of the old blood were either killed off or forced out and scattered to go where they could. Many became Travelers.

Ash remembered his father teaching him the history of these lands as they walked through. "I say 'people of the old blood,'" his father had said, "because we never had a name for ourselves, not one that suited everyone. We were not a nation, just a collection of villages and towns, each independent but dealing with the others in peace — mostly. *My* father told me that we thought of ourselves as 'Turviters' or 'Plessans' first, and only secondly, loosely, did we see any connection between us and those from other towns. That was one of the reasons Acton succeeded so well — there was no way of bringing the men of the towns together to fight. The towns fell, one by one, to the fair-haired warriors."

That last phrase, Ash remembered, was from one of the long Traveler ballads in the old tongue. He had learned that ballad, and countless others, as his father had learned them, by word of mouth. The people of the old blood had no tradition of writing, just the runes, which were too powerful to be used for anything other than stonecasting.

"Tell me another history ballad," Martine said as they walked.

Ash grimaced. "They're all depressing," he said. "All about death and beheadings and villages put to the sword."

"There must be some lighthearted songs! Something not death. Traveler songs. I know there are…"

"Oh, there's plenty about how wonderful it all was before Acton came. If you can believe the songs, our culture was complex and exquisite—our artisans produced the most beautiful of objects, all that was good was shared, no one went hungry, our poets sang songs of such beauty that no one could listen dry-eyed…"

Martine's mouth made a quirk. "You don't believe them?"

"Well…There are a few songs from that time that survived. They're good songs—that's why they survived, and a couple are beautiful." He paused, remembering his mother's voice soaring into the descant of "Falling Water." "Yes, very beautiful. But they are human songs, after all, not songs from water sprites, whose songs are so beautiful they can steal your soul away.

"It seems to me…" he said with a sudden release of a long-held belief, one he hadn't even known was there, "it seems to *me* that old people always say everything was better in the past. Maybe it was, but what difference does it make now?"

Martine thought for a moment. "Maybe it gives us something to aspire to?"

"Maybe. And maybe it gives us an excuse not to aspire."

She nodded. "Likely. Very likely."

They spent a night camping in a copse of pine trees near the track, and made it to the ford toward the end of the next day.

SAKER

THE GLADE was ringed with scraggly pine trees, untidy, like the raven nests that crowned them. It was not like most of the gods' places, which tended to be beautiful, peaceful, lush. This was just a scrubby glade in the middle of a large pine copse, with brown winter grass waiting for the first snowfall, and a few rabbit burrows at the edges, well away from the black rock at its center.

They were all the same, those rocks, cold even in the summer sun and differing only in size. The gods, it was said, had sent them all to Earth at the same time, at the birth of life. Some said the stones had brought the first life, or they were what remained of the gods' sweat from laboring to create the living world. No matter how they had come, they belonged, everywhere, to the gods.

Saker knelt before the rock and bowed, waiting for the itch under the skin that meant the gods were with him. He felt nothing. Astonished, and a little alarmed, he prayed.

"Gods of field and stream, hear your son. Gods of sky and wind, hear your son. Gods of earth and stone, hear your son. Gods of fire and storm, hear your son."

Nothing.

He sat back on his heels, thinking hard. Did the gods disapprove of his plan? Surely not. Perhaps they had removed themselves so their presence would not interfere with his spell. Yes! *Of course.* His human magic might not work in their holy sphere, so they had left to allow him free rein.

"Thy son thanks you, gods of all."

He began to dig at the far north side of the glade, where Rowan's song had said the bones of the Spritford victims had been casually buried.

He found them easily, for bedrock was only a few feet down. The brittle bones of human skeletons, brown with age and dirt, mingled together; the skulls, with gaping holes, missing jaws, and empty eyes, willed him to work faster. The song had said forty-seven, men and women and children. He found twenty-nine skulls in three hours, and was satisfied. He placed the children's skulls to one side, cradling a baby's tiny head in his palm. He had to stop for a moment, to acknowledge the waste, the crushed bone, the toothless mouth. He laid it down, gently, and returned to the adult bones strengthened in purpose. They would pay. They would pay in blood every part of their debt.

He stood over the skulls, took out his knife, and began the spell.

I am Saker, son of Alder and Linnet of the village of Cliffhaven.
I seek justice. Justice for Wren, for Jay, for Lark, for Sparrow—

There was a little *flick* in his mind at the name Sparrow, and he said it again, but the sensation didn't come again, so he continued.

I seek justice for Falcon, for Owl—

There it was, a strong response this time: his Sight was coming alive and showing him, in his mind's eye, a small man with beautiful hands and angry eyes. He continued with new zeal.

I seek justice for Owl and all of his comrades,
unjustly slain and buried in this place.

He could feel that the one name was enough. The bones were singing to him now, not all of them, but many. The spirits of the dead were listening, finally. The rest of the spell wasn't in words, but images in his mind, complex and distressing: colors, phrases of music, the memory of a particular scent, the sound of a scream...

He paused and looked down at the skulls. They seemed to shout silently for him to hurry. He pressed the knife to his palm and drew it down hard. The blood surged out in time with his heart and splashed in gouts on the lifeless bones.

"Arise, Owl and all his comrades," he commanded. "Take your revenge."

ASH

ASH HAD ALWAYS wondered why the river was called Sharp.
When the road reached the ford, it was easy to see why.

They came down a ridge into a strange world. It was as
though the land had been picked up and turned upside down,
so that layers of rocks stuck up straight into the air, instead of
lying flat under the ground. The wind had worn them into a
maze of razor edges all the way to the water. The road picked
its way between them, zigzagging wildly to find the safest way.
It was hard on foot, Ash thought; taking a cart through would
have been close to impossible.

Ash was nervous. It was an unchancy place, and the ghost's
warning still troubled him. He made Martine follow him, and
he kept his hand on his dagger as they made their way through
the labyrinth. At every turn he expected Death herself to jump
out at them, but other than startling some ravens picking over
a rabbit's corpse, nothing happened. It darkened as they moved
into the valley, and when the sun finally disappeared between
one step and the next, his unease grew.

Only the wind's moan through the rocks followed them; only
the river's rush awaited. The ford was at a wide, hence calm,
stretch of the river, but it was still dangerous: just a series of
stepping-stones joined the banks across the turbulent stream.
Ash went first, testing each rock to make sure it would bear his
weight, careful on the slick, worn granite. He was almost to the
other side when he saw the water sprite, lying between the last
rock and the bank, staring up at him with malice and a smile.

312

"Ware, Ash," Martine called at the same moment.

"I see it," he said, hesitating.

The water sprite couldn't hurt him if he stayed on land. In air, their flesh melted away into smoke. But if he stumbled and fell into the water, or even lost balance for a moment and dipped his foot in, she could pull him under. No one knew what happened to those who were taken by the sprites: no trace was ever found.

But he had a pretty good idea, looking at those long clawed hands and the sharp teeth that smiled at him. Suddenly Doronit's voice came back to him vividly: "Whistle." And it was as though he stood again on the cliffs outside Turvite with the wind wraiths trying to tug him over to his death.

He thrust the thought away from him. He knew if he moved while he was remembering that moment, he would fall. He swallowed hard and strode onto the last rock, then jumped as assuredly as he could to the shore. He stumbled, from fear or clumsiness, but fell face forward and grabbed hard at good, safe land. The sprite laughed at him.

Martine was safe beside him before he had picked himself up. She landed lightly and bent down to him, but he brushed off her hand, embarrassed and angry with himself.

"No harm done," she said, amused.

He grunted and then turned to watch the sprite swim away. It moved like a dolphin, smoothly and powerfully. But it could never leap into the air for joy, he thought, and felt a brief spasm of pity; then he shivered with relief.

The road ahead rose steeply through more of the sharp rock maze, but going up toward the sky, even a twilight sky, felt to Ash like waking up on a fine holiday morning. At the top of the ridge they both paused and looked back. The river spurted and foamed around the ford rocks. It looked perilous, and he shivered again.

The other side of the ridge was different country; they had passed into the sparser, harsher land of the north. Still, it was a kind of country they both knew well. From the ridge they could see the road wind down for miles into a long, broad, shallow valley until it came to a stream, a tributary of the Sharp. Specks of light appeared on the other side of the stream, and Ash realized that the dark shapes he had taken for rocks were really cottages. It was much farther away than it had looked, and he remembered that distances were often deceptive in these wider lands.

"That's Spritford. We'll reach there sometime tomorrow," Martine said. "Let's find somewhere for tonight."

Neither of them felt like going back to the river for water, so they cast about until they found a little pool in the rocks that had enough rainwater to make cha.

"It'll be safe enough if we boil it," Ash said.

There was enough shelter in the rocks to make an autumn night there not too unpleasant, although the ground was bruising to their hips. They drank, ate cheese sandwiches and some plums that Halley had given them, and settled back to sleep.

The next day was unseasonably hot and airless. The land was dusty, with flocks of goats grazing here and there, watched by young boys squatting on rocks who stared hard at them and sometimes deigned to nod when the pair waved. The scent of wild thyme and sage was strong and after a few hours Ash had a headache.

They rounded a low hill and found themselves on the final stretch of track down to the stream, with the village they had seen the night before on the other side.

BRAMBLE

RIDING NORTH, she was riding into autumn. In these parts, the season came in with a biting wind that crisped the leaves on the trees and bent the heavy grass heads flat by the side of the road. The horses didn't like it. It was cold enough for their breath to form plumes in the air. They were fidgety, reluctant to do anything she asked. Bramble wasn't any happier than the horses, and by late afternoon she was more than glad to see roofs above a rise in the ground up ahead.

The village was only a huddle of houses beside a stream. Like most of the country houses in this district, they were two stories: the lower one for the animals to winter in, the upper for the family. She stopped at the largest house and banged on the door with her fist.

"I need lodgings," she shouted. "I can pay."

The door edged open just enough to let her and the horses in, and was slammed shut behind them. The relief of being out of the wind was immediate. The stable felt stuffy, even warm, although she could still see her breath on the air. There were livestock in the stable, a cow and a nanny goat. A couple of dogs, which clearly had been curled up in the straw, bounced around them, sniffing avidly at Bramble's crotch. She pushed them away.

"Gods! It's cold enough to freeze the nuts off a gelding out there!" a voice boomed.

Bramble turned, unwound the scarf from her head and smiled. "It is that."

The voice belonged to a tall blond woman, with strong arms and big hands that she was using to unsaddle Cam. Bramble left her to it and saw to the other horses. Even the relief of being out of the cold hadn't sweetened Trine's temper. She tried to kick one of the dogs and was clouted firmly on the nose.

"That's it," the blond said. "You've got to show them who's boss." She turned and shouted up the wooden stairs. "Lace, put a bran mash on. She's got three poor beasts here near dead with cold."

Side by side they rubbed the horses down in silence until Lace, who turned out to be a skinny adolescent girl in thick orange socks, brought down a wide pan of warm mash and emptied it into the feed trough. The three horses jostled to nose into it. The blond woman watched with satisfaction.

"That'll do 'em. Come on." She led the way to the living area above.

The room was untidy and sparsely furnished with wooden settles and a table and chairs, but softened by thick fleeces on the floor. Bramble, noting belatedly that her hostess had her boots off, took hers off too and sank cold toes into the fleece gratefully. Her feet tingled as the blood flowed more warmly in them.

"I'm Butterfly," the blond said, and jerked a thumb toward the girl. "Lacewing." Bramble didn't show her amusement, but Butterfly grimaced anyway. "They call me Fly and her Lacy," she said. "Our mother must have been crazy, but all the girls in her family were named for things that fly."

Bramble smiled. "I'm Bramble," she said. "With us, it was plants."

Fly guffawed and relaxed.

Bramble sat at the table as she and the girl made cha and cooked bacon and eggs.

"Bad time to start a journey, winter coming on," Fly said, glancing sideways as she turned the bacon.

"I'm on my way to the Well of Secrets," Bramble replied. "Didn't expect the cold to come on so soon."

"Keep going the road you're on, you'll have more to worry about than the cold."

Bramble raised her eyebrows.

"It's shaping up for war, girl, and those horses of yours are like gold around here. Why do you think my stable's empty?"

"The warlord?"

Fly snorted. "Shagging right. He's commandeered every horse within thirty miles. Took both my broodmares—though thank the gods he's breeding them, not using them as troopers. Wants to breed and train a cavalry, for the gods' sake! If it weren't for me being female, he'd have me up at the fort training the horses!"

"I don't quite understand what this war's supposed to be about."

Fly scooped the bacon and eggs onto rounds of bread on wooden plates and slammed them down on the table. "Lace! Eat!" she shouted. "Thegan *says* it's because the Lake People are bleeding us dry with the tolls they charge to ferry our goods across the Lake to the roads beyond, and because they won't let us build a bridge instead, and besides, our Lady Sorn, his wife, has a right to the Domain through her grandfather."

"And what's the real story?"

"Well, look at the map, girl! He's got the Cliff Domain already, now he's married Central, if he takes the Lake he's got the whole middle of the Domains under him, all the way to the coast. He'll have cut us in two."

Bramble considered it. "He won't have a port, though. It's all cliffs along the Central Domain coast."

"If I were Carlion, I'd be feeling nervous."

"He wouldn't invade one of the free towns!"

The free towns had been set up by Acton, and they had *always* been free to govern themselves. No warlord had entered a free town by force in a thousand years. It was unthinkable.

"Who's to stop him?" Fly answered.

The three of them ate thoughtfully for a moment.

The Domain nearest Carlion was South, where Bramble came from. The warlord there was better at encouraging his men to bully and steal than at training them for war. Three Rivers Domain was the next closest, but it was small.

Fly was right. Bramble grew cold from her toes to the tips of her ears. There was no one to stop him. Maryrose lived in Carlion. Perhaps she should turn around right now, go back to Carlion and warn them.

"Someone should warn Carlion," Lace said.

"They wouldn't believe us, honey. If I didn't know Thegan, it wouldn't even have occurred to me. But that one will stop at nothing."

Bramble thought it over. The news of war with the Lake People would get to Carlion soon enough. There were people of intelligence there, not least Maryrose's mother-in-law, the town clerk. They would see the need and recruit help. Few Domains would refuse. It was in everyone's best interests to keep the free towns *free*.

Bramble relaxed a little. "He has to win the war with the Lake People first."

"Easier said than done," Fly said, nodding. "But he's claiming the gods are behind him, because everything has gone so well in Sendat since the Kill was Reborn."

"The shagging bastard! The pox-ridden, slimy little thief!"

Fly's jaw dropped and then she shouted with laughter.

"Bramble! Gods, it was you! The Kill Reborn!" She got up and made a mocking bow. "Well, well, well. So the Kill Reborn doesn't support Thegan. He's not going to like that, girl. Better not go to Sendat."

For once, Bramble was inclined to listen to advice. Following her instinct was what she'd decided to do, and her instinct was to stay well away from anything to do with Thegan. It made her skin crawl just to think of him. He was everything she'd always hated about the warlord system: selfish, brutal, power hungry. He had tainted her by claiming her luck as his own, implicating her in his evils. She had never been so angry. Her blood seethed, hissed in her ears. Like the warlord's man, she wanted Thegan's face under her foot.

But not badly enough to seek him out.

She stayed the night with Lace and Fly, asking no more questions and having to answer none.

She packed early the next morning and was off just after dawn, paying Fly more than the woman wanted to take.

"Saved my life," Bramble said.

"Good," Fly retorted, putting the coppers back into Bramble's pocket. "It's good luck to help the Kill Reborn. I might need me some good luck soon—don't take it away by paying me."

Bramble wasn't comfortable with the gesture, but thanked her and raised a hand goodbye. She had exulted in becoming the Kill Reborn, but carrying the name made her uneasy. It was as though the gods walked with her even when she couldn't feel them, as though some other force used her feet to walk and her mouth to speak. All the more reason to be angry with Thegan, she thought, for using what belonged to the gods.

She turned back on her tracks. Fly had said that there was a minor road—"nearly a track, girl"—two miles back on the right, which would take her in a wide curve around Sendat and up to the top of the Lake, where she could take a ferry across and have an easy ride to the main north road.

It had rained overnight and she rode into a landscape of moving water: drops falling from leaves, streams rushing between hedges of reeds, trickles along the rutted road, and dew-laden sere grasses lifting to the weak morning sun. It was beautiful, musical, magical. Bramble felt the horses detect her stir of blood and lift of heart, and quickened their pace as much as she dared.

Thegan's men saw her just before the turnoff. It was sheer bad luck. As she looked up into the morning glare, she saw six of them, picking their way down the road on sturdy mountain horses that were just bigger than ponies and starting to get shaggy with winter coats. Something about their silhouettes raised a shiver up her spine. She didn't even consider running, the feeling of inevitability was so strong. Besides, she had two packhorses. They'd catch her in seconds.

Bramble was thankful that the sergeant didn't look like either Thegan or the warlord's man she had killed. He was in his fifties, an ordinary looking gray-haired man with the beginnings of a cold. He kept sniffing and turning his head politely to spit out phlegm. It gave a strange rhythm to their conversation.

"Where are you off to, girl?" he asked civilly, and spat.

"Carlion." Eventually, she hoped.

He sniffed, but not in disapproval. "Well, sorry, lass, but you're coming to Sendat today. Warlord's orders."

"I'm on a free road, going to a free town!"

"Warlord's orders. All horses to be collected and their riders brought in for questioning, unless they're on warlord's business. What's your name?"

"Bramble."

He nodded and gestured for her to turn around.

She fell in with them and noted their professionalism: their way of surrounding her without jostling her, the sheen on their weapons, and the good condition of their tack. They all carried the short bows which work best on horseback, and they were slack but ready to be strung at a moment's notice, the quivers full and protected by leather hoods. Thegan kept a disciplined guard, trained and well equipped. It didn't make her like him any more. Trained to kill. Equipped to capture the innocent and steal from them. And what would happen to her once they reached Thegan's stronghold? Robbed and then turned out on the road to survive as best she could?

It took them most of the day to reach the fort above Sendat, on muddy, slippery roads that made the horses uncomfortable and twitchy, and unsure of their footing. They stopped whenever they found a patch of clear ground to rest the horses. When they stopped again to eat their lunch, the men offered to share their bread and bacon with Bramble, "to show there's no hard feelings, like," and she was glad she could show that her own bag was full of food, and refuse without giving offense. She didn't want to eat with them, or be beholden to them, but she wasn't stupid enough to antagonize them unnecessarily.

They talked at intervals about the coming war, which they all seemed to look forward to, especially one man, the sergeant's helper, the only one who kept his bow strung, "in case we see some rabbits for supper." He shot at two in one glade before Bramble had even seen them, the arrows finding sure marks. They all waited for him to gut them, while the horses nibbled lichen from the trunks of the birch trees. Bramble peeled a little of the bark and chewed on it.

The sergeant looked up at her. "Get used to the taste of it," he said sourly. "War in spring leaves the fields unsown and the granaries empty come winter. There'll be nothing *but* birch bark to eat this time next year."

The archer glared at him. "We don't talk about my lord The-gan's business to some Traveler slut."

The sergeant stared at him for a moment, reminding him of their different ranks, but the archer still glared, full of righteous indignation.

"He's not a god, Horst," the sergeant said, and spat tidily into the ditch.

Horst glowered at him but held his tongue.

They reached the fort an hour before sundown, filing up the narrow Sendat streets as the shopkeepers were folding in their counters. The sergeant exchanged greetings with a few of them. They looked at Bramble curiously. One, a middle-aged woman selling candles, let her mouth fall open and then called excitedly to someone inside her shop.

"Father! Father! It's the Kill Reborn! The Kill Reborn's come to join the warlord!"

Immediately others crowded out of the shop and people stared and pointed.

"That true?" the sergeant growled. "You *that* Bramble?"

"So what?"

He smiled. "Well, I don't think you need to worry about losing your horses, girl, ma'am, I mean. You're our luck! Everyone knows that." He paused. "I heard your Thorn passed on. I'm sorry."

He sounded genuine. She nodded.

"I'm Sig." He pulled off his glove and held out his hand.

For a moment she hesitated, not wanting to touch him, not wanting skin on skin with a warlord's man. The feel of Leof's hand leaped to her mind, warm, soft, strong. She reached out for Sig's hand to banish that memory and was astonished to hear the crowd break into cheering, interpreting the simple gesture as a symbol of something bigger, as though everything she did was a sign of the gods' will.

The fort was bigger than the one near Wooding. It covered the top of a plateau, maybe four or five hides of land, with a strong wooden palisade surrounded by a spiked ditch. As they rode through the gate Bramble saw that another wall, stone, was being built inside the wooden one. He's preparing for more than war with the Lake People, Bramble thought. He's making a palace like the kings of the Wind Cities.

The buildings were of stone below and wood above and rambled all over the southern side of the site, angled to the winter sun. The rest of the area was given over to stables and paddocks, with a huge gathering area in the center. That was where the sergeant led them.

"Wait here," he said, dismounting, and strode off into the main building.

Even so close to sundown, it was frantic with activity. The smithies, near the stables, were aglow and noisy; there were coopers hooping barrels in front of what looked like a warehouse; a wheelwright fitted an iron rim to a wheel near its wagon; and some fletchers were using the last of the sunlight to finish a batch of arrows—cloth-yard shafts, Bramble noticed, for the longbow that foot soldiers carried.

The yard to her right was full of horses. She edged Cam over to the railing, dismounted, and looked in. Over the past few years she and Gorham had trained quite a few horses for Thegan. They were all here. And more. He must have been buying up all the good mounts—or just taking them—from the local towns. Bramble recognized most of them in the yard. She whistled softly and they crowded to the rails, recognizing the whistle codes she and Gorham had taught them. She talked to them, deliberately taking a moment of calm before Thegan arrived. They snuffled into her hands, nuzzled her cheek, and shoved each other aside so they could get to her.

"And this," a warm, laughing voice said, "*this* is why the gods have led you to me."

She took a deep breath and turned. There Thegan was at last, slighter than in her memory, but still solid, with the big shoulders of a swordsman. He was welcoming, laughing with cold eyes, playing to the audience of crafters and soldiers who crowded, grinning, to see her.

"Our Kill Reborn!" he said loudly, inviting a cheer and getting one. "Welcome! You are thrice welcome to join us!"

"But I'm not joining you," she said quietly. "Your men arrested me and brought me here. So you could steal my horses, apparently."

His eyes went even colder, but he smiled.

"Following my orders, yes, but following the gods' commands, too, I think. They have led you here."

The crowd cheered and Thegan waved them backward a little so they could speak in private.

Bramble felt her whole body stiffen. She recognized, again, the itch under the skin that meant the gods were present, and she knew Thegan was right. The gods *had* led her here. But for what reason? Not to support Thegan. Of that, she was sure. The gods had their own secret purpose, which they weren't confiding to her. All she could do was act according to her nature—to the nature they had given her.

"But not to join you," she said, still keeping her voice quiet.

"Oh, yes," he said, just as quietly, moving closer until his breath ruffled her cheek. "You will join me, girl. You will train my horses and you will smile. And all men will say the Kill Reborn rides with Thegan and his luck warms his bed."

He didn't even bother to threaten her. There was so much menace in his voice that he didn't need to. She was trembling. At first she thought it was fear, compounded with the fear of humiliating herself in front of him by quivering in terror. Then she recognized it as anger so great that it threatened to rip her apart. It was anger greater than any she had ever felt, and she realized that she was filling with the gods' anger as well as her own. *Blasphemer,* she thought, and on the thought was calm again. She raised her head.

"No. I won't," she said.

For a long moment he looked at her. It was his true face for that moment, without the mask, and she saw the lines from nose to mouth, the deep-set curves at the corners of the mouth, the tracks at the eyes from squinting into snow glare, the pores growing coarser with age. He had a grown son, she remembered, who kept Cliff Domain in his name. He was feeling the sharp breath of the Lady of Death behind his shoulder, and he was reaching for glory to stave off her kiss. He was frightened and refused to know it. She knew that this was why the gods had brought her here.

Then his face was closed to her again, age and fear covered with assurance. "You will," he said.

"You are going to die," she said, "and nothing you do—no war, no conquest, no victory—can stop it. You will die and rot into dust, just like everyone else. That is the gods' message to you from me."

His face turned dark red with anger. "I will unite this brawling pack of warlords," he hissed. "I will create a united country, a great country, the country Acton intended, and I will leave such a legacy of prosperity and splendor that my name will live forever!"

She shook her head. "How many will you kill to ward off your fear of oblivion?" she asked.

He raised his hand as though to strike her, then turned it into a heavy-handed clap on the shoulder. "Let's get you in out of the cold!" he said loudly.

Another cheer went up, but stopped raggedly as the crowd parted to let a woman through. It was the Lady Sorn, shrouded in a cream cloak against the chill air. A young fair-headed maid held the hem of the cloak out of the mud. Sorn looked at her husband and then at Bramble.

The gods were still with her, Bramble realized, but they had turned all their attention to Sorn. They yearned for her, it felt like, but she stood quite still, as though she couldn't feel them at all. Perhaps she couldn't. It was often so, with Acton's people.

"A guest for us, my lord husband?"

"An honored guest, my lady. Bramble, the Kill Reborn."

Sorn smiled. "We are indeed honored. Come, then, my dear." She reached out and took Bramble's left hand in her right.

Bramble felt a stiffness, a piece of paper, pass to her hand before Sorn let go, moving as though to guide Bramble toward the buildings. She palmed it, shoving both hands in her pockets as though she were cold. She and Sorn moved through the crowd, followed by the maid, trying to keep up. There, near the huge open doorway to the main hall, stood Leof. Bramble stopped as she saw his face, saw his eyes go from her to Sorn in puzzlement, raise to Thegan, narrow in apprehension, and come back to her as if to a lodestone.

"Leof, look who has come to be our guest!" Thegan shouted jovially. "Your fellow chaser!"

Sorn, Thegan and Bramble stopped at the threshold beside Leof, who was searching for something to say. Bramble realized that at any other time she would have felt the kick in the stomach, the shock, at his nearness. But the gods filled her sight, darkening it, and there was thrumming in her ears. She felt the gods warning her not to step over the threshold. The maid dropped the edge of Sorn's cloak and held out a hand for Bramble's jacket. She hung back, looking for an excuse, and with gratitude felt Trine nip her on the shoulder. She turned automatically to clout her on the nose.

"Oh, my dear," Sorn said, "we've forgotten your horses, haven't we? Why don't you just turn them out in the yard with the others and one of the ostlers will see to them?"

"A good idea, my lady."

She took Trine's bridle and found Cam and Mud just behind her. She led them toward the yard and nodded to Sig as he swung the gate open for her. She paused and tied the two packhorses' leading reins securely to their packs, so they wouldn't trip over them. The other horses crowded forward, eager to get out, to be near her. She knew this would be her only chance.

At that moment the gods left her, emptied out of her into the sky. She had done whatever it was they wanted, and now they had no use for her. She was on her own. It left her relieved and desolate at once. But the fear rising in her stomach roused her into action: she would not give Thegan the victory of her fear.

She whistled, hard and loud, the code for "run to me," and swung up on Cam's back as the pack of horses turned itself into a herd and came rushing out. She urged Cam into a gallop from a standing start and swept out of the wooden gate in the middle of the herd, whistling "gallop" over and over again.

The men by the gate had no chance to close it, though they tried. For a moment she thought one of them was Beck, the warlord's man from her own domain who had pursued her to the chasm. Then one of the other men was pushed aside by the outside horses and she lost sight of him. She couldn't see if the man had been trampled, but said a prayer to the gods for him under her breath.

Then they were through, in a thundering avalanche of horse-flesh, and heading down the steep streets of Sendat, the shad-ows closing over their heads as they left Thegan's stronghold behind.

FAINA'S STORY

D A CAME ROUND the back of the milking shed in the middle of the morning. I was distracted because the cheese was just setting and had to be watched. If you leave it in the hot water for too long it goes chewy. I hoisted the cauldron off the fire and began to scoop out the curds into the setting basket. He just stood there, fidgeting with his hands in his pockets.

"It's been a bad year, Faina," he began.

I made the sign against ill fortune and splashed some of the hot cheese on my hand, but I bit back my curse. Mam says for every curse the gods add a day to your stay in the darkness before you are reborn.

"Are you all right?" Da asked.

"Aye, I'm fine." I held my amulet for a moment and said a prayer against ill temper.

I kept scooping out the cheese, wondering what he wanted. He's a good man, my da, but women's work and men's work don't mix, he says; and he stays well away from the cheese making, knowing it's unchancy at best, getting the curds to turn, and a man there might set all awry.

"What's the matter, Da?" I asked finally.

"It's been a bad year."

Well, that was no news. What with late spring rains and early frost, and a stinging gale the week before the hay was ripe, it had been a bad year for the whole district. Mam said it was a sign from the gods, but she didn't know of what. That we weren't praying enough, likely.

"We can't pay the taxes, lass," Da said.

I put down the curd spoon and turned to him, drying my hands on my apron. This was serious news. The old warlord, Wyman, was dying of a wasting fever and with no firm hand on the reins, his men were getting out of control. They could take what they wanted in payment of taxes, and they would, too, and a bit over for themselves. We weren't poor, but we didn't have much to spare. If they took the cart, or the oxen, or the boar...it might make the difference between a bad year and a killing year.

"I thought...I wondered...It'd only be for a year. We're short only a bit."

"What do you mean, Da?"

"The Lady Sorn is getting married."

Well, we all knew that, too. She'd been married off to a man twenty years older, from Cliff Domain, where the men were as cold as their mountains. A shame, it was, we all thought, even those, like me, who lived in little villages and had never set eyes on the young lady.

"They need more maids at the fort. I've had a word to our village voice. The tax collector will take a year of service in exchange...Just a year, Faina..."

He was so apologetic, it took me a moment to realize that he was talking about me going into tax bondage. I was shocked, but then I was excited. To go to court! To help with the marriage celebrations! And tax bondage was honorable enough. Even the warlord's men didn't touch the bond servants. I didn't have to worry about rape, well, no more than living in my own village, where a girl who walked down a quiet lane always kept an ear out for the sound of horses' hooves.

"Of course I'll go, Da. It might even be fun," I said, and even if I hadn't wanted to go, it would have been worth saying so to see the relief on his face.

So I went to the court and I scrubbed out rooms that hadn't seen a brush for eighteen years, since the Lady Sorn's naming day. And I washed yellowing linen, carted water and emptied chamber pots, and I did all the work I always did at home, except cheese making and cooking. It *was* fun. There were lots of other girls like me, come specially for the year of the wedding, and our room at night was full of giggles and discussions about the best looking of the men at arms. We worked hard but we ate well, and some of us, I thought — looking at the scrawny ones — better than we'd ever eaten.

The only thing I didn't like was that most of the other girls were unbelievers. They cursed without thought; they had no respect for the gods. They laughed at me for getting up before dawn to go to the altar stone. What did they know?

To kneel by the altar stone in the gray half-light, to feel the winds of dawn and know that the gods woke, to say my prayers, to be in the presence of the gods, to know they listened: that was the center of my day, the center of my life, the calm point that let me work and laugh and eat and sleep with joy, because the gods went with me.

There was always the same handful of people at the altar stone: an old man from the stables, a woman from the kitchen called Aldie, a boy from the blacksmith's, a young woman from the court. We prayed in silence and waited for the dawn, and then moved away with a smile to each other.

It was the third day before I realized that the young woman was the Lady Sorn, and that was only because the old man said, "Tomorrow's the day, then, my lady," and she smiled at him and nodded.

"The Lord Thegan's son will be here at midmorning," she said.

"May all the gods bless you, my lady," he said.

"Thank you, Sip," she said. Then she looked at me curiously. "You're one of the new maids?"

I curtsied low. "Faina, my lady."

"You are very devout, Faina."

I blushed. Mam never thought so. "I like to come to the altar stone, my lady."

"So do I. But I've never had a maid who would accompany me." She smiled wryly, but those beautiful green eyes were warm. "You can't order someone to pray."

I smiled back. "No, my lady. The gods wouldn't like it."

"No, they would not. Come with me."

I followed her to her rooms and from that moment I was her own maid, her special maid. A blessing from the gods. No matter what else has happened, that was a blessing. I think, now, she might be one of those that the gods work through without them knowing it.

We talked often and long, she and I, though not so much that first day as there was so much to do getting ready for the wedding. But over the next weeks, and years, I learned about her life.

She had been cross to be married off without her father even asking, but she'd expected that long enough. The old lord, Wyman, treated his women like dogs and horses — breeding animals were only worth their keep if they bred true. Hah! Three wives he had and only the one ever caught a babe, and then he beat her for producing a girl until she died, lying in the straw still wet from the birth. The gods abhor a man such as he. He will scream at the edges of the dark, but it will be a warm night in hell before he gets reborn.

So he mistreated my lady all her life, for rage and disappointment that she wasn't a boy. And he pampered her, too, for show's sake, for his own pride's sake, so she was dressed in furs and silks and waited on with respect in the court, and then beaten behind doors. And all that time all everyone knew was that my Lady Sorn was beautiful and young and the best catch in the Eleven Domains, because her husband would rule the richest Domain of all when her father died, and he was dying fast from the wasting sickness.

They sent all manner of negotiators, the warlords from the other Domains. They wanted Central for their sons, or for themselves. Arvid, Lord of the Last Domain, was the only one who didn't court her. Central was too far, maybe, although of them all he was the closest in age. Thegan was old enough to be her father, almost. He has a son a couple of years younger, Gabra, who holds Cliff Domain for him, and at first the old warlord said that Sorn should be matched with him. All this happened through go-betweens, my lady told me.

Then Thegan arrived himself, with no warning, riding in large as life and twice as handsome, all gold hair and blue eyes and smiles, as irresistible as Acton himself. I wasn't there, but I can imagine it. I've seen him charm strangers a hundred times, seen that warmth flow out of him like honey, like sunlight. I don't think either my Lady Sorn or the old warlord even tried to resist him. They had the marriage two weeks later, an engagement just long enough to prepare the wedding and for my lord Thegan's son to arrive from Cliff Domain.

The first time I saw my lord Thegan was when he arrived in the hall in his wedding finery, all blue to match his eyes, smiling at my lady as though he had never seen anything so beautiful. And she was. Oh, yes, she was glowing. She believed in him, then. Loved him even.

PAMELA FREEMAN

We all believed in Thegan. After the old warlord died and my lord took the reins, he seemed sent by the gods to lead us. He used the lash and the gallows more than the old warlord, but then things had been let slide a while, and there were lawless men preying on merchants and farmers alike. They deserved the flayings and the hangings they got. At least I thought so—was sure so. After all, the Well of Secrets was Thegan's niece, as everyone knew. Surely that was a family led by the gods.

Just as I met my lady, I met my Alston at the altar stone in the dawn. He is a gods' man, my Alston, pure-hearted, and I loved him soon enough, as he loves me. He follows my lord like a child follows his father, and my lord Thegan trusts him.

About three years after my lady and my lord were married, Alston came to visit me one evening, excited and exalted. My lord had told him great news, news that filled him with hope for the future, our children's future. He explained everything to me, just as my lord had explained it to him: how the Domains were wasting away under lazy and evil warlords, and how they could be—should be—united to form a single great country, just as Acton had intended.

When Acton disappeared, a thousand years ago, he had been in the process of uniting the country. His death interrupted that, but now it was time to complete it—one country, strong and free and prosperous, under one law. Thegan's law. For he would be Overlord of the Eleven Domains. I could see it. It was a wonderful vision. For surely, the warlords cared too much for their own comfort and not much for the needs of their people. If there was an overlord, setting the law, making them abide by it, it could be a great thing for the common people.

My Alston said that Thegan's son in Cliff Domain, Gabra, wasn't strong enough to hold the country together after Thegan's death, but Thegan and Sorn's children would be raised from birth to know their destiny, and Thegan and Sorn's son would be overlord after Thegan. Then he swore me to secrecy, because there were spies from the other Domains who were our enemies, and no one should know for certain what the lord intended. I was so proud that Alston was one of my lord's trusted men. I gave a lock of my hair in thanksgiving to the gods that night, and when my lady asked me why, I told her, for of course Alston wouldn't have meant me to keep such a secret from my lady.

"All the Domains, Faina?" she asked quietly. "And how will he achieve this? He has sent out no letters for a council."

It had been twenty-two years since the last Council of Warlords, since the last attack on the Cliff Domain by the Ice King, where they had all agreed to send men to help drive back the ice warriors. Lord Thegan was one of the leaders of that campaign, along with his father and brother, and was the bravest of them all. That is why his men worship him so, Alston says. He is so driven in battle, but so careful about his men's lives. A true leader, my Alston says.

Looking back, it was after I told my Lady Sorn about the lord's plans that she changed. Stopped looking at him with that dazed, tremulous expression. I knew what that look meant. I'd heard her moaning in his bed, and crying out, and weeping, sometimes, too, but not weeping that needed comforting. For weeks after the wedding, he went around looking like a cat in a dairy and she was soft-eyed and languorous, as a new bride should be, but rarely is. It may be there was too much awakening too soon, for later she resented that her body had betrayed her, that when he called her to his bed she went despite herself, despite her suspicion and her distrust.

"I'm like a bitch in heat," she said bitterly to me one morning as we walked away from the altar stone a few weeks after I told her of the Lord Thegan's plans. "He snaps his fingers and

I go running. And the things he does to me…" She buried her face in her hands, but I could see it was burning red with shame. "The things I do to him…" she whispered.

"But lady, he's your husband," I comforted her. "The gods enjoin us to cleave to our husbands and enjoy them."

"Not like this," she said quietly, then lifted her head and shook back her hair. "Well. He may have my body, but he won't have my mind. And maybe having the body will allay any suspicion of me. He will build his overlordship on the bodies of the innocent, Faina, and the gods cannot approve."

I admit, I was torn at that moment. If my lord Thegan was guided by the gods, then my lady should not be suspicious of him. Nor work against him. I thought, for a moment, that I should tell Alston that my lady mistrusted his master, but then something in me knew, and I thought, no, she told me this for the gods alone to hear. Thank the gods I said nothing!

The preparations for war began, with the blacksmith working noon and night, although nothing was said openly. My lord began to buy all the horses he could, or take them in lieu of taxes if he couldn't buy them. And my lady started to walk all the courtyards and buildings of the fort each day, inspecting the preparations, listening to the sergeants at arms train their men.

Then the night came when the Kill Reborn was found and brought to the fort.

I followed my lady out into the night, intrigued to see the Kill Reborn join with my lord Thegan. Was it a true sign that he was doing the gods' will? Did they want the Domains united into one country, "a great nation" as my lord said, "renowned and strong and free…"?

I saw the Kill Reborn and it was a shock to realize she was

a Traveler. But the gods often choose Travelers to carry their messages, I have noticed. So many stonecasters travel, it cannot be coincidence. Only a few can hear the gods. I've learned to pick them out of the crowd. I cannot feel the gods direct but, at secondhand, I am never wrong. The Kill Reborn travels with them on her shoulder. No doubt. I could feel them around her despite the dark, and the crowd, and the swords and shouts.

She was coming inside — *I might be able to serve her myself,* I thought, and was churned up with excitement — then she leaped upon her horse and whistled, and the whole pack of horses followed her. I felt my lady stiffen in surprise, then relax. My lord Thegan swore and stormed back toward the yard.

"Take her down," he ordered the archer, who was standing nearby, mesmerized by the spectacle.

The archer couldn't believe it at first, but he looked at my lord's face and then nocked his bow and swung it up to take aim. He pulled back the bowstring. My heart was huge in my throat. Blasphemy! Rank blasphemy to kill the chosen of the gods! I couldn't believe it.

"Leof!" my lady said urgently.

My lord Leof, one of the lord's lieutenants, sprang forward and knocked the bow out of the archer's hands.

Thegan rounded on him. "I gave an order!"

"My lord, think!" Leof said. "To shoot the Kill Reborn! The luck would leave you. I acted to save you, my lord."

My lady moved forward. "Not in front of everyone, Thegan."

Thegan stilled, control returning like water flowing into a jug. "Leof. You will find her and bring her back. You will send out men and recapture the horses. All of them. Do it now."

"Yes, my lord."

My lord Leof bowed and made his leave and my lady and I turned to go inside. I could hear the horses charging down the hill and I said a prayer for the Kill Reborn's safety on that slippery road. I stayed, for a moment, just inside the door, to touch the amulet at my breast and say the prayer.

And I heard Thegan beckon the archer.

"Horst."

"My lord."

"You're my man, I know."

"On my life, my lord."

"Follow Lord Leof. If he finds the girl, kill her. If he doesn't find her—she'll probably head north. I sent couriers north yesterday to Lord Arvid in the Last Domain. I will instruct Lord Leof to send you after them if he doesn't find the girl. You can catch up if you ride fast. Tell the Lord Arvid that I would take it as a mark of friendship to have the girl returned to me."

I stood for a moment, and then ran inside as though the Lady of Death herself was behind me. I knew that if he caught me there, having heard what I had heard, I was dead. And still, when I think of it, it was not the order to kill that shocked me the most. It was the way he talked about her. "The girl," he called her, as though she were nothing. No man with any belief in the gods could talk about the Kill Reborn like that. I realized he was without belief: the worst of all men, because there can be no redemption. Even the evil can be reborn if they repent to the gods in time. But to seek the gods' forgiveness you must first believe.

It was like the world had darkened to winter in the middle of spring: my days shortened, my skies clouded. It had been a golden time since they married, since the old warlord died and the reins came into Thegan's hands. He had brought so much joy and hope and energy to the Domain. He seemed to glow like the sun and we warmed ourselves from him. Now I felt cold. And older. Much, much older.

My lady was right. I prayed to the gods to give me the words to reveal the truth to Alston. I prayed to the gods for help, for comfort, for succor. Only they can guide us.

ASH

IN THE LATE afternoon light, the ghosts stood out surprisingly well, white against the rushing water of the stream, against the dull sage green of the bushes by the track.

"They're strong!" Martine exclaimed.

"As strong as in Turvite," Ash agreed. He felt light-headed, relieved. This was all the warning had meant. A group of ghosts! Then, as he and Martine neared the ford, he realized that these were not like any ghosts he had ever seen.

They were a mixture of men and women, but they all had the same look: an antique look, with strange clothes, dirty and disheveled. They were shorter than most people, with the tallest coming shoulder-high. The men were in knee-length skirts, bare chested, the women in long gowns that fell straight from shoulder to hip to ground without a break. Some of them had tears in their gowns; two of the men had the marks of wounds showing dark across their chests.

They had shawls over their shoulders, both men and women, and all wore long braids: the women, one down their backs, the men a series of shorter braids around their heads, tied down with a headband that crossed their foreheads. There were beads and feathers tied to the ends of the braids. Ash could tell that the braids were dark, and so were their eyes.

Each of them, men and women, clutched a tool, or maybe a weapon: sickles, knives, scythes, wooden rakes. Even ghost-pale, Ash could tell that the metal of the tools wasn't iron. Something about the way the light moved over the surface. Bronze,

340

maybe? The ghosts held them in front of their chests as though unfamiliar with using them that way.

They were terrified—and angry. They stood absolutely still as Ash and Martine approached them, but poised, as though ready to run. Martine held out her hands in a gesture of peace. Their heads turned to follow the gesture, and the beads on the ends of their braids rattled.

Ash felt the blood drain from his head, it seemed from his whole body. That was not possible. Even on Ghost Begone Night—when he had set the ghosts of Turvite free to speak— they could make no other sound, not a clapping of hands, nor rustling of cloth as they ran, nothing. It *was not possible* for the beads on the head of a ghost to clink together.

"Ask them to speak, Ash," Martine said calmly.

He saw that there were drops of sweat starting out along her brow. She had heard it too. That was reassuring, in a way.

"Speak," Ash said gently, not wanting to startle them.

They looked at him, uncomprehending. The man in front, the tallest and brawniest, raised his scythe and made to move forward. There was a stain on the blade of the scythe, like blood. Ash swallowed against the stone in his throat. If the beads could rattle, could the scythe slice through flesh? He thought hard, and fast.

"*Viven*," he said, in the old tongue.

Relief flashed across all the ghosts' faces and they began to speak in a rush, gabbling the old language together. The man in the front waved them impatiently to silence, and spoke urgently, quickly, then waited for an answer to his question.

Ash could understand only one or two words in every six. The grating voice of the dead made it even harder to understand.

"*Keiss*," he said.

The man repeated his question.

341

Ash caught the words for invaders, yet where? He shook his head, dredging his memory for phrases from old songs. There was one, a lament...

"*Sive keiss fardassane, loll parlan marl,*" Ash said. Go slowly from the battlefield, the invaders have gone.

"*Loll?*" the man said, eagerly.

Ash bit his lip. Shook his head. Swept his arm out in a circle that took in the whole country. "*Nurl loll,*" he said. "*Fessarna.*" Gone everywhere. Conquered.

The group set up a wail, the same sound the ghosts from Turvite had made, a keening, echoing wail that set every nerve grating.

The sun touched the horizon and, as one, the ghosts turned to look at it, to raise their hands in gestures of homage and farewell.

"Wait!" Ash said, as they started to fade. "Who called you? Why? *Viven! Jli vivel? Se?*"

"*Carse,*" said the man, straining to stay a moment longer. He reached out and touched Ash's sleeve, gripped his arm with a strong and healthy hand. The edge of the scythe came nearer and Ash could smell the blood on its blade. Fresh blood. "*Carse. Sarat.*"

Then they faded.

"What did he say?" Martine demanded. "Who called them?"

"A carse is like an enchanter — but more than that. Someone who guides the tribe, a seer. Like the Well of Secrets."

"And *sarat?*"

"Revenge," Ash said blankly, with the smell of blood still in his nostrils, filling his head. "It means 'revenge.'"

They stood at the ford, reluctant to cross to the village.

"It would be more sensible to go around and find the road on the other side," Martine said.

"There was fresh blood on the scythe," Ash said. "We have to find out what happened."

"Why? Why us?"

"Because they spoke to us." Until he said it, he had not realized how strongly he felt about it. It was as though the ghost's words had put a yoke on him, a leash that pulled him to the village, to further knowledge, perhaps to greater responsibility. He didn't like the feeling. It was too much like walking past the black rock and oak tree in the center of Turvite and hearing the local gods call his name. Like watching the sheen and gleam of Martine's hair and knowing that if he just *concentrated,* he would see more...He shivered in the dusk, looking at the stream gurgling happily through the shallow rocks. But he could not turn away.

"I'm not sure I want to know," Martine said.

He stared at her. Her face had closed in, like the carvings of the dead the southern villagers sometimes did at the mouths of burial caves.

"I have seen enough blood," she said.

"What if this is the same thing that's threatening Elva?"

She shook her head, not in denial but as though to clear her thoughts. "You're right," she said. "It would be...that's the way the gods work."

So they crossed the ford and went up the slope to the village.

It was not a large place—a crossroads with some outlying streets that petered out into the woods on the far side. It had two inns, though, and a livery stable, and a couple of the houses on the ford side had notices on their front doors, drawings of a pillow and a plate, the standard sign for lodgings. Ash noticed that the drawings were done beautifully, elegantly sketched by brush rather than scrawled with charcoal, as they had been in other villages.

Every door was barred. There were some signs of disturbance: an overturned water barrel had made the dusty street mud halfway up, and there were broken windows with boards hastily nailed across them. From one cottage came the high, wailing sound of grief, rhythmically, as though whoever cried rocked to and fro in time to her keening. The shadows of evening seemed to lengthen in response.

Martine knocked on the door of the biggest inn. There was no answer, but a scuffling inside betrayed listeners behind the door.

"They've gone," Martine called. "They've gone."

"Who says so?" A voice came from behind the door.

"Flesh and blood."

"Stand by the window where we can see you."

They moved to the window. Between a crack in the shutters an eye stared out at them.

"Prove you're flesh and blood, then," a high voice said.

Martine shrugged, drew out her knife and pricked her thumb with the tip. A rich drop of blood welled up. The door opened cautiously.

"They're shagging Travelers!" Ash heard a voice say. "They probably brought the—the others..."

"Maybe not," the high voice said. "There's only two of them."

The woman in the inn door was bandaged across her cheek and around her head, and her arm was in a sling. She was thin, with lank blond hair, and had small hectic patches of red high on her pale cheeks.

"What do you want?" she asked, holding the door ready to close.

"To help," Martine said. "To find out what happened."

"We'll help our own," she said. "What do you think's happened?"

"We saw the ghosts, by the ford," Ash said. "What happened?"

"You *saw* them? They didn't attack you?" Her voice had sharpened into suspicion.

Behind her, a crowd of men and women shifted weapons more firmly into their grasp. Ash felt the hairs rise on his neck.

"They were going to," he assured her.

"But then they faded," Martine cut in, "as the sun set."

The crowd relaxed a little. Ash bit back his explanation of talking to the ghosts. Martine had more experience of people than he did; he would take her lead and ask questions later.

"Then they might be back in the morning," the woman said thoughtfully.

"Who knows. What did they do?" Martine asked.

The woman moved out of the doorway and indicated the room beyond. "Look for yourself."

Ash and Martine moved into the taproom. There were the normal long tables set up, but no one was sitting at them. Four shrouded bodies lay on them instead, the shrouds faintly marked with blood from the wounds underneath them. One of the bodies was a child. A woman sat by it, head on her arms in exhausted sleep, one hand still clutching a fold of the shroud.

Martine shuddered. The woman nodded, as though Martine had passed a test, and allowed them farther in. Ash found himself holding his breath. He didn't know what he was feeling.

"They came at noon," an old man said suddenly. "Right on noon, out of nowhere."

"Out of the forest," a woman said. "I was taking the vealer

to butcher and they came out of the forest. I saw them in time and I hid in the stable."

"You couldn't stop them!" said a young man with deep cuts down his bare shoulders. "I had my hayfork and I got one right through the chest, but it didn't stop him!" He hesitated. "I—I ran," he admitted, and began to weep. "If I'd stayed..." He turned aside.

"They're dead already," the innkeeper said. "What could you have done? All that stops them is solid wood and stone. They couldn't get through the doors." She looked at the biggest of the shrouded bodies. "My brother tried to stop them. *He* should have run." She moved toward the table slowly, until she stood by the corpse. "*Why didn't you run?*" She hit her brother's body with a closed fist, and began to sob.

Friends closed around her and a young man, patting shoulders, proffered hot drinks. Ash and Martine withdrew to a corner and sat down on a couple of stools.

"We need to know if there have been any strangers here," Martine said softly.

"The enchanter?"

She nodded. "It's a risk to ask, but we have to know. And then I think we leave these people to their sorrow. Before they turn on us."

She rose and moved to the innkeeper, who was calmer than the others.

"I think my friend and I will not trespass on your hospitality in these circumstances," she said gently. "You will not want strangers here now."

"Strangers, no..." The woman's face was suddenly stricken. "The stonecaster! Oh, gods, he was going to the forest yesterday and he hasn't come back! They must have found him..." She wept anew, although more quietly.

"A stranger?"

"No, no, he's been coming through here for years, now and then. Saker, his name is. He'd have no chance, he's only a thin little thing."

"We'll keep a lookout for him," Martine said, nodding to Ash.

They moved to the door and the young man with the wounded shoulder glared at them suspiciously. "You're going out into the night? With them out there?"

"We saw them fade as the sun went down. To tell the truth, my plan is to travel all night and be well away from here when the sun comes up. Just in case."

There was a murmur around the room.

"Good idea!" an old woman muttered. She turned to a younger woman by her side. "You go, too, Edi. Be away from here before daylight."

"Oh, no, Mam! I couldn't leave you. Besides, what if they're everywhere?"

Martine and Ash slipped through the door and it closed behind them as the argument went on.

"Why would they be everywhere?" the old woman said. "They were *our* ghosts!"

"Wait," Martine breathed. "Listen."

They stood in the full dark outside the door and listened.

"Other places have their own ghosts, Mam," the daughter replied. "They'll be just as bad as ours."

"How do you know they were Spritford ghosts, Mardie?" the innkeeper asked.

"Oh, lass, didn't you see the way they looked when they came into the town? The way they were dressed, the way they acted? Pointing at everything, looking up at the mountains to get their bearings and then looking at our buildings like they couldn't believe their eyes? They were ours, all right, from the old days. From Acton's time. Come back to take their revenge."

"But why have they come back *now?*" wailed the daughter.

"We'll go to the gods tomorrow," said the innkeeper, "and ask."

"Let's go," Martine said.

OWL'S STORY

I COULDN'T STOP them. I didn't even realize the village was being attacked, until they burst the latch like it wasn't there. There were three of them, tall like Acton's people always are, redheaded. And the biggest going straight for my Sparrow, ripping her gown right off her breasts. Oh, Sparrow, I tried, I tried, but they were so many, so strong. All I had was my hands. They had swords, axes, clubs. I tried to get to you, beloved, but they were... They held me, made me watch as they violated you and then slit your throat. Then they beat me to death with their hands and feet. Enjoying it. The blood and the pain. Monsters.

I died cursing them, promising revenge, and after death I brooded on it, locked in the cold dark with nothing to warm me but rage and a thirst for their blood. I yearned to be reborn, but the gods betrayed me and kept me there, waiting...

I don't know how long.

Then the enchanter came and set us free. So few of us, only nine: me, Marten, Squirrel, Hazel, Moth, Beech, Juniper, Cat and young Sage. Only nine of us had kept our anger strong enough to be called back from the dark. But not my Sparrow. Oh, that is the hardest thing, that Sparrow didn't wait for me, didn't cleave to me in the dark behind death. She has gone on and I have truly lost her. Forever. The killers took all the years we might have had together, and more, they took the rebirth together, which we had planned, had prayed for. They took our unborn children, and grandchildren, they took everything we

349

could have had, should have had, but for them. I will never stop hungering for their deaths.

The enchanter was one of our blood, you could tell: dark and slight, though his eyes were lighter than ours. He spoke to us in the old tongue, but stiffly, as though he'd never spoken it before: "Take your revenge," he said. He pointed out of the glade toward the village, and we went, the weapons in our hands that we'd died holding.

We were ghosts. White and silent. I thought that I should feel cold, or shaken, but I was already cold, as cold as endless time.

Then the enchanter reached out and touched my arm. Touched it! My arm was as solid as his. He said again, "Take your revenge. Then go to the river."

As I realized what he was offering us, I was full of rage. And hope that my rage would be sated. I grabbed Sage's scythe—I knew I could make better use of it—and headed for the village. The others followed.

"Kill them all!" the enchanter shouted behind us.

I would.

The village made me understand how long I had been curled in the dark. First, there were no trees—not for a mile or more around. The land had had its bones laid bare, had been raped as my Sparrow had. There were brick and stone houses where our earthen cottages had been. Many more of them. They had prospered on our blood, and they would pay.

At the first house, I reached out my hand and opened the door. It moved. It was true, I could touch. I could act. At last.

Inside were a man and a woman, sitting at a table. Acton's people—pale-haired and blue-eyed. I swung the scythe before they realized what was happening. I made him watch her death as they had made me watch Sparrow's…The blood spurted all over him: hot blood, their blood, blood of the invaders, the rapists, the marauders. I was filled with holy exultation. I tried to shout my joy, but the dead cannot speak. So I swung the scythe again.

He was kneeling by his woman, cradling her head. Yes! Mourn as I mourned. I brought the staff of the scythe down on his neck and heard it snap.

How wonderful a sound.

SAKER

HE WAS still bleeding. Saker sat on the ground next to the bones and shook. Too much blood lost. He tried to bind the cut with a cloth he had laid ready, but his left hand trembled too much. In the end he put the cloth over his hand and clenched it between his knees until the bleeding stopped.

Part of him had never really believed it would work. His father, yes — that had worked — but that spell had been fueled by his deep grief, a need to hold his father again in his arms. Part of him had believed that his grief was the important ingredient in the spell. Part of him still believed it.

Then he remembered how he had lamented over the baby's skull just before he had cast the spell. Perhaps sorrow at the waste, at the shocking disregard for life, was enough. Compassion for those cut down without mercy by the invaders. Perhaps his heart was bigger than he had known.

When the shaking had stopped and he no longer felt faint, he got up, picked up his pack and followed the track the ghosts had left. It made him laugh. A track left by ghosts! Who would believe it? He was light-headed with blood loss and a growing euphoria. He was the master of the dead! No one had done it before — not even the enchanter of Turvite, who brought the ghosts back but could not give them strength.

The door of the first house was open, but there was no sound. He looked in cautiously. It smelt bad, of offal and dung.

Then he saw the woman, her guts oozing over the wooden

floor. That was the smell. The man lay beside her, seemingly without a wound, but dead.

They were dead.

He groped his way outside and along the wall until he came to the corner of the house, where he turned his face into a breeze. He felt sweat cooling on his forehead, and tried to stop himself from vomiting. The bile rose in his throat and he fought it. And lost. The breeze blew some of the vomit over his boots, and he grabbed a handful of grass and frantically tried to rub it off...so his father wouldn't notice, wouldn't despise him for a weakling.

It was the smell, he told himself. He wasn't expecting that.

Enchanter training had taught him how to control errant thoughts and concentrate. He took the image of the dead couple and pushed it firmly to one side. Then he drew a deep breath.

"The first revenge," he said sonorously, as though his father were listening. "There will be more."

He skirted the village, in case someone had connected him with the ghosts' rising, and came out the other side, near the river, and waited in the shade of a small juniper tree. It was appropriate, he thought. The smell took him back to his early childhood, before the warlord's men had come...

There had been a juniper tree outside their house and his auntie used the berries for cooking. He had been forbidden to climb the tree because it was so old. "Older than Acton's people, that one," his father would say, patting the trunk fondly. "You stay away from it, boy."

Saker couldn't remember his father ever calling him by his real name. Saker was *boy,* or *you,* or, in a good mood, *young'un.*

He hadn't minded. He had liked being called boy. His father had not much time for girls. He barely noticed Saker's three older sisters, or the baby.

He had tried hard to please his father. Everyone did, in the whole village. And not just because his father had been strong and liable to prove that strength on anyone who challenged him. He had been clever, too, known to be clever—known for his wit and guile. Saker had heard the other villagers say such things, usually when his father had got the better of one of Acton's people in a bargain.

That juniper tree...Its branches were so inviting, its trunk just right for holding as you climbed. From the top, he had thought, you would be able to see out of the valley and all the way to Cliffhold, where the warlord lived. He battled with himself for weeks, but one day, when he had thought his father was out in the fields with the new ewe, he climbed it.

He had been right, you could see right out of the valley, although not down as far as Cliffhold, which was a day's ride away. If he had looked the other way, if he had turned around to look at the sheer mountains behind, he might have seen them coming...

Over and over in the years since, he had played that scene in his mind, but this time he turned, this time he saw the warlord's men coming over the rise behind the village, swords out. This time he yelled and yelled and yelled so that the women had time to hide and the men had time to pick up weapons, and the children had time to scramble away into the underbrush...

Would it have made any difference? As an adult, he told himself that it wouldn't have. The warlord's men were soldiers who had known their job, and their job that day had been to kill. Everyone. From eldest to youngest. Old Auntie Maize to Saker's little sister, still at her mother's breast.

Everyone, except him. Because when the screaming had started and he *had* turned around, finally, too late, he froze where he was, had been too scared to move, too scared to help his father fight the men who were chopping down at his sisters with short, efficient strokes of their swords. He had been too frightened to jump on the back of the captain of the troop, although he had sat on his horse right below him, and maybe, maybe, he could have pulled him off into the dirt...

And what would he have done then? He scolded himself. He had only been five summers old. Five. The warlord would have batted him away like a fly. And he'd have been dead, like all the others.

Saker began to tremble with the effort of pushing aside *that* memory, the worst one, the one that came after the warlord's men had dragged the bodies away and the sun had gone down. He had stayed so long in the tree that he had wet himself, but he couldn't stay there any longer. His hands had started shaking with fatigue and he nearly fell. So he had made his way down slowly, cautiously, looking both ways at every step to make sure.

He had walked through the village that he knew, even at night, like his own home, but there was no one left. Just empty houses. And him.

The bodies had been piled up down the slope a little way. He avoided them, blocking his mind to the smell rising already, glad they had been hidden from him by the darkness. It had been strange, the way dreams can be strange, to be the only person there, it had reminded him of something. Then he had remembered. The songs and the stories about the first invasion told how Acton had ordered his men to kill the people but not burn the houses, so they could be used again.

The invasion had gone on almost a thousand years, Acton's

people gradually pushing back farther and farther into the land, but that original order had always been followed. The last push from the fair-haired warriors had been less than two hundred years before. Saker's grandparents had talked about it as though it had been yesterday. In that last wave of the invasion, they had herded most of the people of the villages into the forest and killed them there. The remnants of those original people had come to live here, in Cliffhaven, on the poorest land in the Domains, the land that no one else had wanted.

Up until that day.

And, alone in his father's house, the young Saker had known they would come back. They would live in their houses and farm their land and milk their ewes and eat their food.

It had filled him with a vast, wavery anger that seemed larger than himself. It had gone beyond the shock of having seen his family killed. It had gone past the desolation of the empty village, to a mature, burning sense of injustice.

He would go to the gods.

He had seen his family dragged out and murdered in front of him. So he had found the house as it always was. There had been no corpses or blood awaiting him. The soldiers hadn't taken anything. As an adult, he had wondered about that. It wasn't usual. In every invasion song he'd heard, the villages had been preserved, by Acton's order, to give shelter to the old people and children who would follow the warriors across the mountains, but the warriors had stolen any loose items they could find, as battle spoil. But not here. Twenty years later, he still didn't understand why.

It had made it worse for the young Saker, to see every accustomed thing in its rightful place, without the people who used them. He had put his spare clothes and some food into his father's pack, feeling a twinge of guilt as he had taken it ("put that down, boy, it's not yours!"); but he had resolved to survive. He had taken his father's money from the brick under the hearth, his auntie's earrings and his biggest sister's bracelet, and a blanket and a kitchen knife, which he clenched in his hand. It was a black rock knife that his father had made, chipped from the black stone near the altar stone, with the gods' permission. His father had talked to the gods. He would talk to them, too.

He had slipped through the back window, just in case, and made his way by starlight to the gods' place. He had always been able to find it, no matter where he was. It had always called to him, but he had been considered too young to talk to the gods directly. That was for adults. Now *they* would have to talk to *him*.

The stone in its clearing had seemed to drink the light in. He had gone to it and had placed his hand on the cool surface. He had known the words.

"Gods of field and stream, hear your son. Gods of sky and wind, hear your son. Gods of earth and stone, hear your son. Gods of fire and storm, hear your son."

They had risen up in his mind, like pale shadows with dark eyes, whispering his name. He had ignored them, still angry.

"Why did you let this *happen?* How could you?"

The answer had come in a whisper through his mind, not his ears.

Human evil is outside our control. Accept. Live.

"NO!" he had screamed. "I will NOT! I WILL NOT!"

With relief he had erupted into a genuine tantrum, of the kind he hadn't had for over a year, since his father had beaten him for it. He had thrown himself full length and beat his fists on the stone and his feet on the ground. The unfairness of the world had swept over him and he had howled and cried and sobbed, pushed beyond the point where he could stop.

The gods had let him cry, soothing him with whispers.

Little child, little child, there is nothing you can do.

Having exhausted his passion, he had lain bereft on the grass.

Sleep, little child, the gods had whispered. *We will keep you safe tonight.*

He had no reason to trust them, but they were all he had left.

"I won't always be little," he had said, and fell asleep.

Under the juniper tree, Saker shook his head free of memories. It had been a long wait, but the ghosts were finally coming down the road toward the ford. He picked up his pack. Before he had a chance to move, he saw two strangers approaching on the other side of the ford.

Even at this distance, he could see that they were dark-haired and walked with the ease of long practice. Travelers.

He hesitated.

Would the ghosts harm them? Surely not. They were of the old blood, too. The ghosts would recognize that and welcome them. He could not be found with the ghosts. He had to remain hidden.

The ghosts seemed to talk with the Travelers, but he knew that was impossible. Then, the leading ghost, the strong-looking man, turned his head to watch the sun going down below the mountains.

The ghosts faded.

Saker stood, astonished and dismayed. This hadn't happened with his father. Although...he thought back. He had never raised his father's ghost close to sunset. The spell had always finished well before then. What difference did the sun make?

He would have to go to another village and wait for news of what had happened at Spritford. Find out how many had died, how thorough the revenge had been. And then work on the spell. Night was a good time for killing, he thought, turning away from the ford and threading his way back through the trees. He couldn't afford to lose the night...What if he started the spell at night...?

And next time, he thought, remembering his sister's scream as the sword came down, *I will use a bigger massacre site.*

BRAMBLE

THE HORSES surrounded Bramble in a great stampeding cloud. She kept her head as low as she could and urged them forward. They clattered through the cobbled streets of Sendat and were onto the road beyond in a matter of moments.

She felt the same exhilaration as when she chased: speed, horses, danger...She laughed aloud. The darkness made it more exciting. But more dangerous for the horses.

She slowed Cam after they left the town and whistled the other horses to slow, too. They did so reluctantly, and stopped when she stopped, milling around her in a loose herd. She called Trine and Mud and loosened their leading reins from where she had tied them, thanking the gods they hadn't come loose and tripped them up. She turned them to the north, then patted the necks of the horses she could reach and whistled the code for "stay."

They didn't want to let her move off without them, but she was firm. "Go on with you, you big softies, back to your yard and your stables and your dinner."

As they hesitated, she toyed for a moment with the idea of stealing the whole lot of them, depriving Thegan of the chance of going to war anytime soon. But there was no way she could hide such a thundering crowd anywhere in the settled farmlands around Sendat—and it was getting colder out here. She'd lose some of them for sure. So she whistled "stay" over and over until they stopped trailing her up the track, and turned to follow a big stallion called Sugar, which Bramble had trained her-

360

self. Sugar moved off, the others behind him, then turned his big head to look at her.

"Tell you what, Shoog," she said. "See if you can break his neck for me."

Sugar shook his mane and nickered at her.

Bramble nudged Cam. "Let's go, my friends," she said, "and let's go fast."

They were lucky. Half an hour after they left Sendat the clouds cleared and a half-moon shone enough light so that Bramble could see the road between its ditches. She pushed the horses hard, knowing that, while Thegan might assume she would head toward Carlion, he wasn't foolish enough to neglect other possibilities. There would be men after her, and soon. They would be mounted on their best horses, and they'd travel much faster than she could, with three.

She had to put as much space as she could between her and Thegan before sunup. Her only hope lay in reaching the Lake Domain before Thegan's men found her. Once she had crossed the border to another Domain, Thegan couldn't touch her. There was supposed to be a process where a warlord could request that a fleeing criminal be arrested and handed back to justice, but in practice it rarely happened. Besides, the Lake Domain didn't have a warlord, just the Lake and its people and Baluchston, its free town. In the Lake Domain, she knew she would be safe.

It was a wild ride. Clouds scudded across the moon and the wind was high. She was lucky it wasn't the freezing wind of winter; but it was chill enough to cut at her face and make her lips bleed. They rode past farmhouses, past mills with their locked mill wheels groaning against their rain-filled millraces. Through increasing patches of woodland, darkly threatening, she slowed the horses, although they wanted to speed through the gloom, fearing ancestral wolves. Each time they broke through to the moonlit road, the horses picked up their pace.

Bramble began to fret that they needed rest, but she didn't dare limit their pace. Once she stopped them for a few moments, and walked them around until they were cool enough to drink from the rainwater in the ditch by the road. She swapped Mud's burden to Cam so she could mount him, and give Cam a spell.

They started off refreshed, but not long after, all the horses began to tire and they had to slow to a walk.

The tidy farms around Sendat were long past, and the fields on either side of the road were given over to pasture or trees. The patches of woodland were wilder, not tamed by charcoal burners and coppicers. The undergrowth was heavy by the side of the road, though Bramble thought she could force the horses through it if Thegan's men caught up.

The wind dropped as she passed a lone farmhouse where a small light shone, the candle of a farmer getting ready to milk, and she knew it must be near dawn. She had no idea how far she had come. If she were a *real* Traveler, she would know the roads and the borders, but she didn't even know how far it was from Sendat to the border of the Lake Domain. More than a night's ride, that was certain.

At the next forest, she rode in a little way and then slowed the horses, looking for a track leading in deeper. The moon had set and the sky was not yet paling, so it was difficult to see. She tried three false trails before she found one the horses could manage in single file.

Beyond the heavy undergrowth near the road, she found the going easier. This wasn't the kindly wood of her childhood—it was a conifer forest, dark as pitch and smelling sharply of pine. The tall, scraggly trees creaked menacingly as the dawn wind picked up, and high above she could hear the ominous cawing and squabbling of rooks. Below, there was silence, the horses' steps muffled by the thick blanket of pine needles. Nothing else grew but the pines.

She dismounted to lead the horses, fearing they might walk into a branch in the gloom.

For the first time in her life, she was truly afraid. She feared nothing real—not Thegan's men coming after her, nor sharp branches or wolves. Yet it was deep in the marrow, like the terror brought by the gods. But if this was the gods' gift, they were darker and more terrible gods than any she had faced. She stood, trembling in the dark, and felt the urge to run, blindly, wildly, as fast as she could, to anywhere. Her legs twitched and her shoulders trembled with the strength of that desire. She fought it, but could feel herself losing...She felt a sharp pinch on her arm.

Trine had bitten her!

The pain brought her back to herself and she turned, from reflex, to clout the mare on the nose. Then she hugged her, tears on her cheeks, burrowing her face into the warm sweaty hide. Trine snorted astonishment and that made Bramble laugh.

"Yes, you're right, then, aren't you, I'm acting like a fool. Well, come on, then." She led the horses farther on and felt the panic recede, though it left her with a bad taste in her mouth, a distaste for the person she might have become without the horses. Fear diminished further as the dawn light swelled in the gaps between the trees, until she could see a good length in front of her. She hesitated as the trail petered out in the middle of nowhere, between two trees just like any other two they had passed.

"All right, it's up to you now," she told the horses. "Find us some water."

She mounted and relaxed the reins on Trine and sure enough, after snuffling the air for a moment, the mare headed off decisively, the other two following. They went straight, and soon Bramble could hear, under the sough of the wind, water chuckling.

It was only a small brown stream running over rocks, but it was life itself. Bramble didn't let the horses drink too much at once because the water was cold. She put on the horses' feed bags and then went through the packs to see what she had left for herself. Not much. Fly had packed her cheese and scones, but who knew how long they had to last her. She ate half of them, reasoning that she needed the energy. They would rest now, and then get going again in the late afternoon.

At last she had enough light to read the note Thegan's woman had given her. The parchment had been folded twice. Inside, the writing was formal and delicate, the writing of a court scribe—or a lady.

> To the leader of the Lake Dwellers, greetings from Sorn, Lady of Central Domain.
> Against my wishes, Thegan, warlord of Central Domain, will move against you on the first full moon night of spring.
> Be prepared and beware. He comes with fire.
> Sorn.

Bramble let out a long breath. *Oh, dung and pissmire. So much for staying out of things. So much for keeping my head down and disappearing. Thanks a lot, Sorn.*

She knew she had to deliver the message. The Lake. She had to cross it anyway, and at least there she'd be out of Thegan's Domain. Well, if she was lucky, she thought, this forest might stretch all the way there. Perhaps she could avoid the road altogether. Then she looked around. The pines grew so thickly, there was barely any sun on the forest floor. There were no living branches within reach; the lower branches had all died as the higher ones blocked out the sun. In this deep shade it was impossible to tell direction. She would have to climb tree after tree to find north. And as for that old tale about moss growing on the north side of trees—bah! Moss grew on *every* side of the trees. Who knew how lost she was already?

Well, better lost than dead, or a prisoner of Thegan's. She felt almost cheerful. She curled up in her bedroll on a soft patch of pine needles and went to sleep?

When she woke she peed behind a rock and laughed at herself for hiding from the horses as she did so. Then she climbed the nearest tree. It was a matter of nerve and hard hands rather than difficulty, as the branches were frequent but sometimes rotten and the harsh bark scraped her hands raw. Near the top, though, she could see the sun beginning to wester, and realized that her little stream ran west of north: the direction she needed to take to get to the Lake.

Hopefully it would take her the whole way.

They progressed easily enough at first, while the light lasted, following the stream down a gradual slope. Then it joined a larger stream, still heading roughly west by north. There was just enough space between the trees for the light to reach the banks and give life to the undergrowth; they were choked with the thorny stems of blackberry, the long canes of raspberry, and roots and remnants of other plants. In high summer, Bramble thought, she'd have been able to pick a nice salad along here: young dandelion greens, rocket, fennel, nasturtium, flat-lobed parsley, maybe even some tender young strawberries. As it got darker she dismounted and led the horses to keep warm.

The stream grew wider, fed by another stream of equal size, and the undergrowth grew bushier, with evergreen shrubs crowding the banks. Thickets of holly were interlaced with the long horizontal branches of firethorn, their crop of vivid red berries just beginning to ripen. Riding near them could scratch your eyes out. Bramble was forced to walk parallel to the stream about ten yards back.

Moving away from the stream meant moving away from the faint moonlight. Bramble waited until her eyes could adjust. Trine raised her head suddenly, reacting to something Bramble couldn't hear, and widened her nostrils, ready to whinny. Bramble reached up and nipped her nostrils closed just in time. Trine snorted softly, annoyed, and tried to bite her. Mud and Cam had ceded to Trine as herd leader, and waited for her to greet any strangers. As she stayed silent, so did they, their ears pricked forward. Bramble listened with them.

At the very edge of her hearing, she could make out *something*. Whispers? She tied the horses to a tree and went on. If Trine made too much noise and someone came to investigate, at least she wouldn't be there. It was a risk, but she had to know what had made the noise.

Moving silently through a forest at night is not a skill to be acquired in a hurry. Bramble had roamed the forests of her childhood, and those near Gorham's farm, night after night, watching badgers, finding the nests of owls, following bats to find the best fruit, high in the wild fig trees. This forest, with its needle-quiet floor, was child's play. But to follow the sound, she had to move closer to the stream for cover, and moving silently through holly and firethorn was difficult and painful.

She slipped through, never breaking a branch, going low under the firethorn branches and sliding around the dense pyramids of holly. The sounds grew louder, and then she could see the flicker of a small fire on the opposite bank of the stream. That would have been what Trine had smelled—that, and the other horses. There were two of them, dark in the shadows beyond the fire. There were two people sitting in front of it, their backs to her.

Bramble found a place where she could see their faces. They wore Thegan's uniform. She looked closely. Their horses' heads drooped from hard riding, and they themselves seemed very tired. Had they ridden after her from Sendat? She realized that they were camping at a ford; a road ran through the stream right here.

They seemed settled for the night. She could get back to the horses and lead them in a wide circle around the ford, and find somewhere else to cross the stream. Then she heard the sound of horses coming from the north, three or four of them, walking in the dark. The men at the fire stood up and took out their swords. One of them slipped back into the trees behind the fire, near the horses.

Four horsemen came into the clearing, splashing easily across the ford.

"Be at ease, Hodge," the leader called to the man at the fire. "Sully, come out of there."

It was Leof's voice. As he swung down from his mount she noted that he wasn't riding his mare; this was a bay gelding from Thegan's yard. So they'd got their horses back all right. The fire lit his pale hair and caught the metal around him—sword belt, hilt, dagger, boot buckles, earring—so that he walked, for a moment, in a constellation of stars.

Then he moved forward to the fire and she saw his face. He seemed tired, very tired, and something underneath that, something hard that hadn't been there before. *Thegan has tainted him,* Bramble thought with grief. *He has turned him into a killer.*

The other men were busy unsaddling the horses and letting them drink and eat. Sully came out of the trees to help them.

Hodge moved forward to take Leof's horse as he swung down. "Is it war, sir? Are we recalled?" he asked.

"Not yet, no. Your orders stand. You have the letter for Arvid?"

Hodge patted his breast. "Safe."

Leof nodded. "Well, you have extra duty now. You're to keep a lookout for a woman named Bramble. You may remember her—she was the Kill Reborn."

Hodge smacked a hand flat against his thigh. "Bramble on Thorn! I saw that race, saw her take the Kill's banner—as neat a thing as I've ever seen. What's the matter with her?"

Leof paused and weighed his words, then spoke slowly. "She's defied my lord Thegan. He wants her back to train his horses. If you find her on your way to the Last Domain...take her somewhere safe and send word to me. I'll be riding the border until she's found. If you find her on the way home, bring her back with you."

Hodge whistled. "Wouldn't like to be in her shoes, eh, if Thegan's got it in for her."

Leof frowned sharply. "Who?"

"My lord Thegan, I meant, of course, sir."

Hodge's back down was complete, but unconvincing, Bramble thought. *He* seemed to have Thegan's measure, at least. By the horses, Bramble saw that Horst, the archer who had helped bring her to Thegan's fort, was whispering to the other men. He was probably telling the full story.

"She might be making for the border," Leof said.

The archer returned to the fire and eased a log farther onto the blaze with his toe. "She's cunning," he said dispassionately. "She's disappeared off the face of the world."

"That's a good trick," Leof said, smiling tightly. "There's times I wouldn't mind trying that myself."

Hodge grinned at him with easy familiarity. "Aye, we'd all like that now and then, sir."

"I've checked the other roads leading to the Lake," Leof said, "and no one's seen hide nor hair of her. We'll rest here tonight. The Lord Thegan wanted Horst to go after you and ask the Lord Arvid to return her if she makes it that far. But there's no need for three of you to go. Hodge, you can deliver that message."

Horst spoke up. "My lord Thegan told me to take that message, lord."

They stood in silence for a moment, each of them weighing his words.

"Yes," Leof said slowly. "All right, then. You and Sully can take the message to the Last Domain. Hodge and I will go on to the border tomorrow. She has to cross it somewhere."

Hodge scraped a thumb down his cheek, rasping stubble. "She's the Kill Reborn... maybe she has ways we don't."

"She's just a woman, sergeant," Leof said. "I've... raced against her, I know. But she's a woman with three horses, so if we can't find her, Thegan will have our thews for bowstrings."

"Aye, he will at that."

The men chuckled and settled down at the fire. Bramble waited until they were eating and slithered backward until she was completely screened by the undergrowth. Then she picked her way back to the horses. It was the firelight, she told herself fiercely, that had made her eyes ache as though she wanted to cry.

HORST'S STORY

THIS IS how it happened. The old warlord, Wyman, was weak. I'd served him since I was ten, when my granda's wife sold me into tax bondage for five years, to pay off the debts my parents had left. The fever had got them, both at once, and me and my sisters were sent off to Granda's house. Might have been different, I reckon, if my grandam were still alive, but she weren't, and the new wife couldn't see any percentage in looking after young ones who were no blood of hers.

That's what she said, "There's no percentage in it, love," winding her arms around his neck, and my granda, old fool that he was marrying a chit half his age, just nodded and did what she wanted.

So I was sent to the old warlord's fort and my sisters, older than I was, were sent to be chambermaids and drudges at one of the inns in Sendat. One got pregnant by the ostler and married him; she did all right, seems happy enough. The other died of a cut that went bad. The shagging innkeeper didn't even get a healer in for her. Too tight with his money. I got him, though. I got my lord to fine him for losing me her wages, because by then I was a man, sixteen, and what she earned belonged to me, not to my granda. My lord backed me full and the innkeeper didn't argue it.

I gave some of the money to my other sister, though she had no claim to it under law. But then, our mam never liked that law. Said a woman's wages were her own in other Domains. That Central was the worst place for a woman to be. Da just laughed and said, "You do all right," and she'd look in the direction of the altar stone as if to ask the gods to witness his foolishness. But I reckon she did all right, too. Da never laid a hand on her unless she answered him back, and he never had a fancy woman. He kept a roof over her head and food on the table, most nights. But farming's a hard business when the rain is scarce and the taxes are high, and after they were dead there was nothing left.

So I went to the fort and was put to be the fletcher's boy. Making glue — gods, the headaches I got! — and plucking fowls. It wasn't just chickens, but the big birds, too — ravens, hawks when we could get them, grouse, pheasants. But never owls. Owls are unchancy birds and should be left alone. An arrow fletched with an owl's feather can't be trusted. That life wasn't too bad. I was fed and had somewhere to sleep, on the floor of the fletching shed. And old Fletcher didn't thump me unless I made a mistake.

After a couple of years Fletcher put me to making arrows, and that's where it all came apart. My eyes, now, they don't work so well up close. I can tell a hawk from a kite a mile off, but anything closer than my outstretched arm's a bit blurry. Arrow making, it needs good eyes for near work. So I got thumped a lot until they figured it out, and then, as I had my growth early, they put me to be boy to the warlord's men.

Looking back, I can see it was a bad time to be put there, but then I didn't know any better. The men were drunkards — rowdy, slovenly, no discipline, no pride. No purpose. I wasn't big enough to stand my ground, so I got what any young one got from them, and not just the shit work. The casual thumpings, the being pissed on, the insults. I didn't know then that the drunkards were the ones who should have been shamed by all that. I didn't know how real men should behave.

Then came the day my lady Sorn got married. I hadn't even seen her husband, just heard he was a lot older than her, and from the mountains. All it meant to me was that the men were drunk for days after the wedding, and I had a lot more vomit to clean up than usual.

But a week after the wedding, he came into the guardhouse. My lord Thegan. He stood at the door, with the sun behind him. One of the men had just emptied a chamber pot over my head and I stood there with the piss running down my face. Just piss, thank the gods. They were all laughing. He stood at the door, all clean and neat and...perfect, like, and looked around at the men. Half of them tried to straighten up but the other half were laughing so much they didn't even notice he was there.

He looked at me. I was cherry red, expecting him to laugh, too, and feeling like I couldn't bear it if he did.

He smiled at me. A real smile. "What's your name, boy?"

"Horst," I said.

He nodded. "Is this the way they normally are, Horst?"

I shrugged. But he kept looking at me and smiling as though we were friends, as though he understood everything that had ever been done to me. And I think he did. So I nodded. "Mostly. A bit worse than usual, because of the wedding drink."

"The wedding was a week ago," he said softly.

And just from the note in his voice, suddenly all around the guardhouse men were standing up, trying not to fall over, trying to look sober.

"The wedding was a week ago," he said again, and the scorn in his voice was like acid. "I am ashamed of you." He spaced the words out slowly, and looked each man in the eyes as he said them. By the end of it, we were all looking at the floor, ashamed of ourselves, too.

Then he came over to me. *To me.* And he clapped his hand

on my shoulder and he said, "But not of you, lad. None of this is your fault. Go and get cleaned up."

I turned to leave, lifted up by his words. My heart was flying.

"And Horst," he added, remembering my name as though I were someone who mattered. "Tell the sergeant at arms to get down here now."

That was the first order he ever gave me. I ran to do it.

Now I'm his man, and part of the best disciplined, most skilled, most dedicated force in the Domains. He made us. Like he made me. He was the one who saw that my long-sightedness made me a good archer. But he had the real long sight. He's the only man I ever met who sees past the next meal and the next woman. He's the one with the vision to see how the Domains could be united, made one country the equal of any—*better* than any in the world.

He's a great man, my lord, a great man. He'll take us all to greatness. And I'll be one of his men helping to bring his vision to life. Following him, no matter what. Because on my life, I am Lord Thegan's man.

BRAMBLE

SHE FOUND the horses again half by chance and half by smell: as she got closer she could trace the faint scent of fresh horse dung. The relief almost brought her to tears. This place, so different from the forests she had known, sapped her strength. She had never felt so alone, as though she had been traveling among the creaking pines for weeks instead of days. The earlier panic had left her, but a deeper sadness grew in its place. The elements closed in around her: dark forest, heavy pine scent, the soughing of the branches above her as a wind picked up, the still, foreboding air hanging quiet below, surrounded by enemies, nowhere that was home. Again she thanked the gods for the horses. Without them she might have handed herself over to Leof and his men, just to have someone to talk to.

She shook her head briskly and gathered up the leading reins, murmuring softly to the horses, "come on then, come on then," to reassure both them and herself.

They headed west, as far as she could reckon it. She planned to move back on Leof's tracks and cross the border halfway between his resting place and the next border post.

She fondled Trine's nose and pulled her hand away before it could be bitten. "With luck, we'll be across before morning."

Four hours later, with dawn filtering down through the dark branches, she cursed herself for having said it out loud, positively inviting the forest spirits to lead her astray.

Well, maybe it wasn't that. Closer to the Lake, the forest was crisscrossed with streams, small and large, some of them sluicing noisily through deep defiles. She had been forced to detour around two of them for some way before she found a ford, and she had lost her direction. Dawn would allow her to climb a tree and find out which way she was heading.

She tethered the horses, put their nose bags on, and went looking for a tree to climb. It took longer than she had thought. These trees were real giants, so big around the trunk that three men holding hands couldn't have circled them, and their first branches were far out of Bramble's reach. She kept looking, getting more anxious, until she spotted light ahead. One of the giants had fallen and created a clearing. The branches of the trees on the edge of the clearing swept the ground, luxuriating in the light.

She climbed up one of the low-hanging branches wearily. It had been a long night. Her hands still hurt from the last time she had done this, and her thighs were shaking with fatigue. Worse, when she got to a branch from where she could look out, she realized they had been heading northwest instead of west, and were probably far too close for comfort to the border post Leof had spoken of.

But she could see the Lake—or at least the huge beds of reed that covered it at her end. It lay only a couple of miles away, which meant that the border had to be almost at her feet.

The scrape of her boots down the trunk was too loud.

"What's that?" she heard below her.

She froze against the trunk. The voice had come from the clearing. Two men stood up, coming out of the shelter they had formed under the dead tree's roots. Wonderful. She had chosen a tree right next to the border post. As the men moved forward, she realized it was worse. One was Leof. He must have left the campsite last night and come back here to rejoin his men.

Even in the dull early light, Leof seemed to glow, golden and energetic. He *was* gorgeous. She found it hard to hate him, even if he was a warlord's man. But his face was more serious than she had known it. He was concentrating, working, looking for her so he could take her back to Thegan to be enslaved. This was his work, to hunt people down, to obey the orders of a killer...She thought of the full gibbets outside the fort at Sendat and her heart hardened inside her. She could feel it tighten, feel its stone under her breastbone. She clung to the trunk and prayed that the horses, thankfully out of their sight, wouldn't whinny or move.

There were four of them. Leof signaled to two to take the other side of the clearing. They slipped into the trees, swords in hand. Leof and the other man came toward her. It was an archer, she saw, the one who carried a bow instead of a sword. The same man who had been with Leof the night before. Leof sent him farther down, toward the Lake, away from her horses. Then he came, slowly, through the trees toward her. He leaned against the trunk of her tree, casually, and brought his boot up as though to get a stone out of it.

Her heart was thumping so hard she thought he would feel it, like a drum, through the trunk.

"Bramble?" he said quietly. "Don't answer me. Just in case Horst comes back. Are you all right?"

He glanced up at her, like a man judging the time by the sun. Their eyes met. She nodded.

"He—Thegan...tried to kill you as you rode away." The words came out with difficulty, as though torn from him. "Why?"

"I defied him," she whispered.

"That can't have been all!" He pushed away from the trunk and began to pace back and forth, pretending to examine the ground. "There must have been another reason."

"He threatened me," she whispered. "He said I would train his horses and warm his bed whether I wanted to or not. I said no."

He stopped, staring at the ground, his shoulders hunched, his hands dangling. He looked like a young boy.

"Found anything, Captain?" Horst called from the clearing.

Leof turned, instantly strong, full of purpose and certainty. "Nothing here. Go and call the others back, Horst. I think we're chasing a forest sprite."

"Aye, maybe so." Horst turned and disappeared into the trees on the other side of the clearing.

"Stay where you are. I'll move them out straightaway. Which way are you heading?"

"To the Lake."

"And then?"

She hesitated. Right now his sympathies were with her. But back under Thegan's eye, who knew where his loyalties would take him?

"Who knows?" she said, reluctant to actually lie to him.

He stood for a moment, then tilted his head back to stare at her. "I could have loved you."

She nodded. "I know."

It was all she could give him. What could she say? That maybe, if he hadn't been who he was, she could have loved him, too? That if he hadn't pulled on that uniform, they could still be curled up together, making love? The uniform *was* him.

"Take care," she said. "Don't trust him."

He made a gesture as though warding off her words, and moved quickly into the clearing.

"Right, let's get going. I want to make all the border posts today, starting with the west."

They went through the business of packing up and load-
ing their horses, which, it turned out, were tethered down by a
stream north of the clearing.

Leof was the last to leave. He didn't look back, but raised a
hand as if in salute as he rode out of sight. She could deal with
that. It was the sight of his ponytail bobbing up and down in
time to the horse's movement that filled her eyes with tears.

ASH

Dawn broke in a prodigal outpouring of rose and gold across the pale blue sky and the tops of the far mountains lit like beacons. The mountain air coaxed the first faint tendrils of scent from the scrubby herbs and flowers: thyme, sage, gorse. Underneath the scent was the smell of dry earth, and the dawn wind brought a thread of cold air from the west. Skeins of snow geese took off from a long, narrow lake as the sun rose, wing after wing of white birds with black wing-tips lifting into the wind and turning south, away from the autumn chill. Their calling deafened Ash, and the wind from their wing beats buffeted his face. He and Martine stood still to watch them go out of sight, although their calls drifted back for some time after they had disappeared.

Back to the south on the back of the wind
At home in the uplands of the air
Wild as the seal that springs from the ice
Are autumn birds free from care.

"I don't know that one," Martine said.

"It's from Foreverfroze. A song from the Seal Mother's people," Ash said. "That's a loose translation."

"Nothing is truly free from care," Martine said. "Not on this side of death."

"Or on the other. Those ghosts. They wanted *revenge*. A thousand years later! How can the need for revenge last that long?"

379

"'Old revenge tastes sweeter,'" Martine quoted.

"That's an Ice People saying. Not one of ours. How was it that *none* of those from the landtaken were reborn?" He prayed that she would have an answer. Because if none of the ghosts of the landtaken had been reborn, that would mean—surely—that rebirth was only a story, a hope for the hopeless in the dark times.

"Perhaps some were. Do you know any songs about the taking of Spritford? About how many were killed?"

Ash thought for a few moments. Fragments of songs played in his head, about the taking of the Sharp River settlements, and working west toward the mountains. But these songs were only a few hundred years old, he realized by their phrasing, as this part of the land had been taken late in the invasion.

"Well, it wasn't a thousand years ago," he said, almost reluctantly. "There is a song." He paused, remembering, saying the words under his breath. "Seven and forty, the enemy fallen," he said at last.

"Forty-seven?"

Ash nodded.

"But there were only nine ghosts. Only nine had enough hate in them to resist rebirth, to turn away from it in search of revenge. The others were reborn—count on it," Martine said.

He felt cheered by that, but underneath the lift in his spirits was terror: the oldest terror, the fear of the dead, of the dark beyond the grave, of something out there.

Something was out there.

"Is there anyone we can warn?" Ash asked.

"Spritford will send messages out."

"We know more."

"We're Travelers."

Ash nodded. Travelers were automatically suspect, automatically disregarded. Even stonecasters. Try to tell the local warlord about talking ghosts and evil enchanters and they'd be lucky to escape a beating. Or the warlord would decide *they* were causing all the trouble and a quick solution would be a couple of garrotings.

They rested for a few hours. Ash slept fitfully. The voices of the dead echoed through his dreams and brought him awake, time after time, repeating invitations in the old tongue: "Revenge! Join us and revenge yourself! Take back what was yours!" He couldn't remember anything else, just the sound of the dead speaking to him, only to him, and the cold and dry feeling as though ghost after ghost had passed through him.

Then he fell into a deeper sleep and was caught in a dream that seemed infinitely worse, for the ghosts here were his parents. They looked like they had when he had last seen them, but pale, dead pale, and they came to him in his room at Doronit's, the only real home he had known, and laid solid, dead hands against his chest and on his cheek and whispered, "Join us." And although he knew, in the dream, that they were dead, still he reached out for them as if still a little child, and laid his head on his mother's cold breast and sobbed.

He woke with wet cheeks and stared at the ground for a long time before he rolled over to face Martine, knowing she would have heard him crying. She was sitting with her back to a rock, casting the stones on their cloth.

"I dreamed my parents were dead," he said. "Maybe they are. Maybe the ghosts have risen everywhere at once. Will you cast for me?"

She nodded and held out her hand. He spat into his palm and took it. "Are my parents dead?" he asked, then waited while she cast.

All the stones were faceup, except one.

"Life," Martine said immediately, finger on one stone. "They live. Work, or a task to be done. Travel. Music. So, all as usual, no? And the hidden stone..." She turned it over. "Responsibility. Hidden responsibility. That may be you. I'm sorry, Ash, this is a true reading, but the stones are not speaking to me. Perhaps I care too much what the answer is, for your sake. The stones do not like the caster to care too much."

He smiled, so relieved by the first stone that he had hardly heard the others. "It doesn't matter — they're alive. We should go."

They started off again through the thyme-scented scrub and the goat-browsed heather. They turned from the main road around noon and headed north by east, climbing with aching legs toward a high ridge, which stood back from the cliffs that now began to rim the horizon. The cliffs looked closer than they were, taller than seemed possible, and got taller slowly, very slowly, as they climbed.

It took them two full days of walking to reach the top of the ridge. Below was a valley the likes of which Ash, for all his wandering, had never seen before. The Hidden Valley lay in a deep, wide cleft in the hills, protected from the mountain cold by the steep-sided ridges on either side.

They stood still on the chill ridge, Martine smiling at Ash's astonishment, and saw, far below them, deer in still green glades, squirrels bounding from branch to branch, and even, farther off, an elk dipping antlers to drink at a stream. As the valley moved into shadow, birds settled, quarreling, into their roosts. Farther down, where the hillsides were terraced, cows and goats threaded their way along to be milked; and a group of women, seeming tiny at this distance, balanced jars of water on their hips as they climbed up steps set into the bank of the river, which ran through the center of the valley.

It was the most beautiful place Ash had ever seen. The dying light, gold and purple, seemed heartbreaking, as though the precious valley were slipping away from them, sliding beyond reach into the dark.

"Let's get down before nightfall," was all he said, but his voice wavered.

They climbed down into shadow and sunset. Darkness fell before they were halfway to the village, but it was a night of clear skies and blazing stars, so they could see just enough to follow the road.

Martine stopped at a field by the side of the road, with a small hut next to a black rock. Mist was rising from the stone and Ash felt the itch under his skin that meant this was the place of the local gods. But unlike the altar stone in Turvite, no one here was calling his name. These gods were satisfied by their worshippers.

A girl was sitting by the rock. She rose as they came nearer and ran across the field to them, despite being heavily pregnant.

"Careful, love!" Martine scolded, running to meet her. "Not so fast!"

"Mam!" the girl cried.

They embraced.

So this was Elva. Ash felt his stomach clench in disappointment, and then found grace to laugh at himself. So much for his fantasies! She *was* beautiful, her eyes darkened by the night and the starlight picking out the fine bones of her face. And she was *huge* with child. Martine wasn't surprised by it. She might have mentioned it, he thought, annoyed, then shook his head at his absurd expectations, and moved to greet Elva.

"This is Ash," Martine said, not looking away from Elva's face, one hand on the great curve of her belly, the other stroking Elva's cheek.

Ash found he had to look away from them. It was disturbing to see Martine's face naked with love.

"Welcome, Ash." Her voice was light and high, a soprano, but without much range, he judged.

"Blessings be," he answered.

"So. Come, come along in. I told Mabry you'd be here tonight, so they've got dinner going, and the girls are excited. They want you to cast the stones for them."

A prophet? Ash wondered. Or was she a stonecaster like Martine and the stones had told her? Or perhaps—a shiver ran across his skin and he knew this was the right answer—the gods had told her.

They followed her across the field and down a steep track to a homestead solidly planted on a terraced outcrop. There was light coming in stripes from behind the shutters, smoke rising straight from the chimney in the still air, a yap of dogs from a shed, which quieted as Elva shushed them, the soft sound of rustling wings as they walked past the dovecote. It was, as the valley had seemed from the ridge, a picture of peace and plenty. Ash thought of the blood on the ghost's scythe, and shuddered.

The door opened as they walked across the yard. A tall man stood there, as tall as Ash and more solid, curly brown hair haloed by the light inside.

"Elva? About time, love." He gathered her into the warm room with an arm around her waist, nodding to Martine as he did so. "Come away in and get warm. Gytha, shield the light."

Gytha—a tall woman some years older than Ash, with curly hair like Mabry's pulled back into a plait—had already moved to put small embroidered screens in front of the candles. Elva smiled at her and Gytha smiled back.

"Drema made the screens for me," Elva said to Martine. She turned to Ash. "To shield my eyes from the light." He nodded, astonished at how the strangeness of her pale skin, white hair and pink eyes shrouded the beauty he had seen so clearly by starlight.

Drema was sitting by the fire, embroidering a tiny felt coat clearly intended for the new baby. She was older and had a sterner face than her sister, Gytha. She got up and pushed Elva down into the chair.

"Sit you down, we'll manage, just you sit." She turned to Martine. "She does too much, outruns her strength. Maybe you'll be able to get her to slow down."

Martine smiled. "I doubt it. She always was a stubborn little lass."

Drema and Martine considered each other for a moment, and then both nodded slightly, confirming something, before they turned away, Drema to the fire where something was simmering, Martine to put her pack down by the stairs. Ash put his next to it. They smiled at each other, a mere softening of the eyes, acknowledging their success in making it here, then moved back to the fire and sat on a settle cushioned with a thick felt mat.

Sometimes, out on the Road with his parents, huddling in a tent while the wind howled outside, or picking leeches off his legs when they went through the swamps outside Pless, Ash had dreamed about a place like this. It was nothing fancy, just solid, strong walls and a rainproof roof, a warm fire, meat roasting on a spit, bread baking in an oven in the ashes, friends and family gathered around talking, laughing, sharing news. Of course, in his imagination there had been music, too; intricate but lively music from flute and pipe and drum, a melody he'd never heard except in this particular daydream.

Well, he could have the music in his head, at least. He stretched out his legs to the fire and listened to Martine and

Elva talk, about the coming baby, mostly, about women's matters. The music ran underneath their words, filling in spaces and
lifting his spirits even further.

Ash gathered from the conversation that Elva and Mabry
had been married no more than a year, and before that she had
lived in the little hut near the black stone altar. Mabry had been
village voice then, and had been urged by the villagers to move
her on, get her out of the gods' field.

"That was when we met," Mabry said. "I guess that was
when I started to fall in love with her."

"You were just too soft to kick her out," Drema said. "But
maybe that's why *she* started to fall in love with *you*."

"Has to be," Gytha teased him. "He hasn't got anything else
to offer, now he's not village voice anymore."

"Now Mam's dead, I leave that to someone who really wants
to do it," Mabry said comfortably.

Elva touched his hand, lightly. "Your mam is proud of you.
They tell me so."

"They" were the gods, Ash realized. He wondered how
it would be, to have the gods in and out of your head all day
and night. Uncomfortable, he figured, but Elva seemed happy
enough and Mabry was the most satisfied-looking man he had
ever seen.

They ate at a big table in the corner. Ash was sorry to leave
the fire, but glad for the food: roast kid and baked vegetables,
gravy and spinach. He looked longingly at the new bread, fresh
from the oven, but Gytha shook her head at him.

"You'd be awake with stomach pains all the night, if you ate
it as fresh as that! Wait until breakfast."

It was like having older siblings suddenly, for that was
how Mabry's two sisters treated him. And Mabry, after a few
moments weighing him up, had done the same. He felt envel-

oped, welcomed, taken inside, where he had always been on the outside, and it overwhelmed him. He blinked back tears and concentrated on the fine, meaty texture of the goat. Travelers didn't develop many friendships with the settled; his parents had actively discouraged it. So this was his first experience of generous hospitality. But he was sure there was more to their welcome than hospitality. Martine was Elva's mam, more or less, so they were family.

He thought again of the blood on the ghost's scythe and grew cold, and then hot with determination. He would not let those ominous figures hurt this family. Never. No matter what it cost him.

"Hullo! Are you with us, Ash?"

Gytha waved her hand in front of his face and he started, recalled to the present suddenly. They all laughed at him.

"You were miles away," Mabry said.

"Yes, a long way away. But I'm glad to be back!"

They smiled at him, even Martine, although her eyes speculated on what thoughts had distracted him so thoroughly. Gytha and Drema were clearing the table so the others moved back to the fire.

"Give us a poem, lad," Martine said.

He nodded, seeing the women turn eagerly and Mabry sit forward on his chair.

"This is called 'The Homecoming,' " he said, smiling. "It's a song from the far north coast, about a sailor coming back from a fishing trip where he was nearly killed.

From the black eye of the storm
From the keen knife of the wind
From the long sharp fingers of the sprites of ice
From the pressure of the deep

From the terror of the waves
Seal Mother has delivered me...
And I am sailing home...
I am sailing home...

In his mind the music broke into the joyful swell of the song, and beneath it he could hear the creaking of the mast, the slap and thud of the waves breaking against the bow, the *crack* as an iceberg calved. Though he had never been that far north, and never been on a boat with sails. The song delivered the world of its maker sharp into his mind, clear as a memory of his own.

The songs had never come alive before, and he wondered why it was happening now. Because he had chosen the song to suit his own mood, and not to please someone else? He couldn't remember ever having done that before. But then, he'd only just started reciting the words of songs at all, with Martine.

"Oh, that was wonderful!" Gytha said, breathless. "It was like I was really there. Do another, go on!"

So he chose another, a song from the south, a ballad about a girl searching through the forest for her brother, because he felt he was searching for the truth to something, and this song fitted his mood, too. And, like the sailing song, as he said the words he heard the wind soughing in the pines, smelled the sharp scent of a fox as it flitted past, tasted the salt in the girl's tears as she cried in loneliness and despair. Then he felt the extraordinary surge of thankfulness and joy as she found him.

They applauded again and asked for more.

This time he chose songs he thought they would like; and nothing gave flight to the words but his own voice.

He tried to think it over later, alone in his blankets by the fire. Martine was in the only guest room, no more than a cubbyhole formed in the passage that used to lead to the back door. The door now led to a new room in the farmhouse that Mabry had built for Elva, the baby and himself. "So we won't be kept awake all night with the young one crying," Drema had said, in a stern voice, but with her hand gentling Elva's hair.

It was the first time since they had left Turvite that Ash had had time and solitude to think, and he knew that he should carefully go over everything that had happened. But his tiredness, the evening, the fellowship, the warmth, had left him swimming in a soft fog of comfort, and he decided not to spoil it. Instead, he curled up with his back to the solid warmth of the banked embers, laid his head on one of Gytha's felt cushions and slept dreamlessly all night.

Almost all the night. In the very early morning, in the gray light before dawn, Martine and Elva woke him and they went to see the gods.

Ash was familiar with the gods, of course. Every Traveler visited the sacred stones on their journeys, made sacrifices, prayed. His father had been very devout, but his mother less so.

"They don't really care much about people, you know," Swallow had said once, as Ash's father had prepared a gift for the local gods outside Carlion.

Rowan had shrugged. "But they are there, and deserve our worship."

"Maybe."

As a child, Ash had imagined that he heard the gods talking to him, but their voices were so faint that he could hardly hear them. That was until Turvite, and the black stone under the oak tree. He wondered, following Martine across the dew-soaked field, what he would hear now.

As they approached the stone he felt the hair on the back of his neck lift. They were here.

"They are always here," Elva said to him, as though replying directly to his thought.

Her eyes, colorless in the gray light, had lost their focus. She lowered herself awkwardly next to the stone and laid one hand on it, then her head dropped back and came up again.

Her voice, which had been high and a little thready, was now deep and sure. "We warn you," it said. The gods.

The gods were speaking through Elva.

Martine was pale, but it was obvious that she had seen it before and had expected it. "About what?" she asked.

"There is evil," said the gods. "Human evil. Great."

"The calling up of the dead?"

"The wall between living and dead may not be breached without harm to both. You must stop it."

"Us? Why *us?*" Ash cried.

Elva's sightless eyes turned toward him. "She will tell you."

"Elva?" Martine asked.

"The Well of Secrets."

"We must go to the Well of Secrets?" Ash asked.

"When the first thaw comes."

"Why not now?" he demanded.

But Elva's head had fallen back again and when she raised it her eyes were her own again.

"Oh, bugger," she said comfortably, as if just a little annoyed. "I wanted to find out if it's a boy or a girl."

"What?" Ash said.

"I thought they might stay a little bit longer so I could ask them about the baby."

He was speechless. The whole world was in danger and she wanted to ask the gods questions about a *baby*.

Martine was amused. "Elva can't change the future or the past, Ash," she said. "She's used to being the...the instrument through which the gods speak. And she really did want to know about the baby."

He shook his head. There was something here about the difference between men and women. He wanted to *act,* to *do* something immediately. The women seemed more interested in the coming birth than in the fate of the world.

When they went back to the farmhouse they told Mabry and his sisters the story of the ghosts and what the gods had said.

They heard the story quietly, then Mabry nodded. "We'd better tell the village voice," he said, "so she can warn everyone."

That was all.

Then Drema and Gytha simply went quietly about their business again.

Over the next few weeks, as winter settled into the valley, it began to really worry Ash that the others didn't want to discuss what was going to happen.

"They told us to wait," Martine said. "It's hard, but no good ever came of disobeying the gods."

Only Mabry, when Ash was helping him around the farm, would talk it over, and then just to ask Ash questions about the ghosts and what they could do. Half the work they were doing, Ash realized, was not ordinary farmwork, but Mabry's preparations in case the ghosts came.

"They couldn't get through the doors, you say?" he asked Ash, and went about repairing and putting up the heavy storm shutters. Others in the village were doing the same, but not all. Many villagers still thought Elva unchancy and wanted nothing to do with her or the family.

"They only had bronze weapons, you say?" Mabry asked, and he sharpened his steel knives and scythes and his axe, and kept at least one weapon to hand no matter where he was.

"You might not be able to kill them," he observed, "but if they're solid you ought to be able to cut off their arms."

Ash nodded. "If they can't hold a weapon there's a limit to the damage they can do."

Hesitantly, Ash offered to teach Mabry singlestave and fighting, and he was grateful for it. Soon there was a class in the small barn most afternoons, with a few friends of Mabry's joining in. Ash was surprised to find how much he knew; watching Mabry, a strong, able man, fumble with his stick and hit himself over the head with it made him realize that he was, in fact, quite accomplished. Although he still wouldn't have backed himself in a serious fight against someone like Dufe, or the Dung brothers.

The best of the village bunch was Mabry's tall dark-haired friend, Barley, who wielded the singlestave with ferocious determination and had shoulders like an ox.

"I used to be a ferryman," he said briefly, when Ash commented on his strength. "But I'm a potter now."

Barley turned back to his practice, squaring up to his opponent, one of the boys from the farm next door, half his size but quick as an eel.

For the first time Ash felt part of something; it was the first time, he realized, that he'd ever *been* part of a group of just men, working together. It was a solid, comforting feeling and he relished it all the more because he knew he'd have to leave come spring.

BRAMBLE

BRAMBLE MOVED along the branch until she had a better foothold. She waited until Leof's party had had plenty of time to move off, and then scrambled as fast as cramped legs, tired arms and sore hands would let her. She went back for the horses. She had considered leaving them behind, just letting them loose to forage, but it would have felt like Thegan had beaten her in some way if she did, so she took them, despite the risk. Besides, later on she'd need them, she figured, to get over the pass into the Last Domain, the most northerly of the Eleven Domains, where the Well of Secrets was living.

She took their feed bags off and led them to water, which was not hard to find so close to the Lake, as all the streams converged. Every moment made her dance with impatience, but she knew that fed and watered horses were less likely to be noisy or troublesome. Finally they raised their dripping muzzles from the stream. She led them across, and made straight for the Lake, heading into a surprisingly thick mist.

It didn't take long. They came to the first reed bed, which emerged spikily out of the mist, after only half an hour. That meant they were safely across the border. She couldn't relax, though. The forest came right down to the shores of the Lake here, with pines perched on the few rocks, and a variety of trees growing where the sun could reach, with their roots in the water. The leaves of willows, alders, laurels were turning every color imaginable, flaming defiance to the cold wind. Bramble took it as a sign of hope.

She took stock, too. There were three ways across the Lake, if you didn't have a boat. There was a ferry at the neck of the Lake, where it emptied itself into the river that ran to Mitchen. The ferry was surrounded by Baluchston—founded by Baluch, one of Acton's fifty companions—and the second of the free towns, after Turvite. It was small, for a free town, existing mostly to provide the needs of travelers and traders operating on and around the Lake, and, of course, to charge a hefty toll to use the ferry. Baluchston could charge the toll because the river fell two trees' height into a narrow canyon, and was impassable.

It was a prosperous little town and Bramble wouldn't have given a copper for its chance of staying free once Thegan had taken the Lake Domain. But since it was still a free town, Thegan's men were as safe there as she was, and would be watching for her.

The second way to cross the Lake was to swim it. It had been done, once or twice, out of bravado or greed or sheer desperation. But for every man who had made it across, twenty had died in the attempt. The worst thing was, no one knew why. It *looked* safe, the Lake—once you were past the reed beds around the edges it was unruffled, shining water. The lake current was strong, of course, but men had also swum the river itself.

But Bramble had heard the stories of swimmers setting out in high hope and full fitness, simply stopping halfway across and disappearing. Sucked down, pulled down, who knew? The local gods would only say that there were no water sprites in the Lake, which in itself was worrying, when everyone knew they were everywhere in the Sharp River, which fed the Lake. So what kept them out? Something nastier than water sprites. Bramble shivered at the thought. Swimming was one risk she wouldn't take.

Which left the third way: the Lake Dwellers. And she had to head there anyway, to deliver Sorn's note.

Bramble had always been fascinated by the Lake Dwellers. When she was small she had pestered her grandfather to tell her all the Travelers' tales about them. They were the same people who had lived on the Lake in Acton's time: no invasion, no land-taken, had ever dislodged them. If they were threatened—and they had been threatened, time after time—they simply disappeared to the hidden islands in the vast reed beds that covered the northwestern end of the Lake. And anyone who went after them disappeared also.

Camps or towns set up around the edges of the Lake went up in flames. Farms were flooded as the Lake waters mysteriously rose over dry fields. Fishermen washed up on the shore, occasionally alive, and talked about monsters from the deep. And any attempt at building a bridge failed spectacularly, usually in flames and with a lot of screaming. The dwellers believed the Lake was alive, a being of some kind, and she didn't like being shackled by bridges.

Baluch had negotiated with them for the free town and the ferry. The ferrymen were all from two families. When the town was set up, their ancestors had been taken away into the reeds by the Lake Dwellers and brought back a couple of days later. They refused to talk about what they had seen, but they began to refer to the Lake as "She." At puberty, both boys and girls from those families were still taken into the reeds by the Lake Dwellers, and they still returned closemouthed about what they had seen.

She would have to go farther west and north to find the Lake Dwellers. Or, she could ask the Lake for help...

Horsetail, bulrush, nalgrass, birdgrass...Along the edges of the Lake there were a dozen different kinds of reeds. She looked through the hardening autumn stalks to the cold mud beneath. This was not going to be pleasant. She considered removing her boots, but once, in her forest near Wooding, she had tried to climb through a reed bed to get to a stream, and had cut her feet badly. So she put her booted sole firmly down in the squelching mud and forced her way through the reeds.

She was waist-deep and beginning to turn blue with cold by the time she reached a patch of open water. She took great gulping breaths and rubbed her arms, trying to jump up and down to keep the blood moving. She almost lost a boot.

"Oh, shag it!" she said. Then she laughed. Could she have looked more ridiculous, standing waist-high in freezing water, swearing blindly, waiting for—what?

She laughed again, feeling exhilarated, as though she were setting off on a chase, soaring over fences and streams. Her laughter bubbled up and spread out over the water. There were no solemn words, no invocations to the gods that would help her now. All she had to offer was the truth.

"Oh, Lake, Lake, here I am, come to ask for help. Come to give help if I can. Please send the Lake Dwellers to me before I freeze to death."

She laughed again. Was there ever a less elegant prayer? But around her the wind was rising, the mist was lifting, and she felt again the sense of freedom and joy rising in her, as it had when she rode the roan. It was not like the presence of the local gods, not steeped in holy terror, but it had the same *breadth*, as though her emotion were larger than she was—as her anger at Thegan had been not only hers, but also the gods'. Here, she shared her exhilaration with the Lake.

She was not surprised to hear the soft clucking of water beneath a boat, or to see the high black prow curving through the mist, or to feel hands under her shoulders pulling her up over the tightly bound bundles of reeds that formed the sides of the boat. She was, however, surprised to find that her three horses were already on board, huddled in a nervous group in the center of the boat's flat bottom. She turned to the men who had lifted her aboard.

"The Lake told us where to look," one of them said, and there was general laughing. "She likes you, that Lake." He added a comment in his own language, and at that the whole crew—eight of them—dissolved into backslapping mirth.

Bramble laughed too, sitting on the deck with her back to the strong, tar-smelling reeds, a pool of water gradually seeping out around her.

They were tall men, and lean, and they all wore odd hats woven out of split reeds. They weren't exactly hats, just rims that sat on their hair. Their hair and eyes were as black as Bramble's own. Their skin was darker, though, and she thought that all Travelers must once have had skin like this, before interbreeding with Acton's folk. It was like looking back through time, to before the landtaken. But these were real people, not noble relics from a distant past. One had acne scars all over his face, another had several teeth missing. One had the bowed legs that meant he'd had rickets as a child. That one looked at her the way most men looked: body first and face, a very late second.

The men went about their tasks single-mindedly, attending kindly to the horses, steering with the long pole that also moved them through the water, or busy with nets and craypots in the stern. Which left one, the oldest, to talk to her.

He was not that old—fifty, maybe. As he stood at the prow he looked stern and proud; her grandfather had talked about the Lake Dwellers' legendary pride. His eyes were so dark they seemed unfathomable, but he turned to grin at her and a web of laughter lines sprang up around his eyes and mouth.

"She told us to come and get you, but She didn't say why," he said conversationally, a faint accent softening the ends of his words. "I am Eel. I speak your language. The others, not."

"I'm Bramble," she said.

The Lake had led these people to her. Presumably, She trusted them. Bramble reached inside her jacket for Sorn's note and handed it to Eel. Maybe he wouldn't be able to read it, anyway.

But he did, his eyebrows moving up. "So," he said, and called out to the steersmen in a different language. The boat immediately began to swing around in a big curve, turning west.

"Um…" Bramble said. "I understand you want to take this to your council as soon as you can, but I need to get to the other side of the Lake."

Eel nodded. "We are going to the other side."

She settled back. They might end up a long way west, but at least Thegan's men wouldn't be looking for her there. *Let the Lake lead us,* she thought.

The journey lasted all day, with the steersmen taking turns at propelling the boat along. They had headed straight for the middle of the Lake, so far that the southern shore disappeared and the northern shore was only a line in the distance. Bramble had heard about how large the Lake was, but being out on it — in what seemed, in that expanse, a tiny boat — was sobering. Astonishing. And exhilarating. It seemed to her that the freedom she had been seeking all her life, had sought on the Road, might be here, on this wide stretch of water. When the wind picked up from the east, pushing them faster against the westerly current, she laughed, and the boatmen laughed with her.

The horses weren't amused. Bramble spent most of the trip soothing them. Trine alone was unconcerned.

The day was fine as the mist burned off. Autumn sun was warm on their faces and turned the Lake into slabs of polished steel. The boatmen shared their lunch with her: smoked fish, flat bread, dried fruit and sweet water drawn up from the Lake in a small bucket. Before they drank the water the men dipped their forefingers in their cups and drew a circle on the back of their hands. Bramble hesitated. Should she do likewise?

Eel saw her poise her finger uncertainly and shook his head, smiling. "Not yet," he said. "When you have been properly introduced."

She smiled back at him and drank. The water was clear and cold and tasted of snow, and something else, not quite a muddy taste, but a little bitter, like weak tea.

"The taste of the reeds," Eel said. He patted the side of the boat.

It was made of very long bundles of reeds lashed together and then covered with bitumen on the outside to make it waterproof. Inside, the floor and the crevices between floor and side were tarred as well. It made the whole boat smell, but she could see that the combination of lightweight, buoyant reeds and water-proofing made the boat practically unsinkable. It was, however, like tinder waiting for a match. Worse: it would flame up faster than tinder, faster than wood soaked with liquor, faster than straw. Bramble thought of Sorn's message: *Beware. He comes with fire.* She blanched, imagining it all too clearly. Thegan would smile as he set the boats alight. If he could find them.

Toward the end of the day they came to the northwestern reed flats. There was some talk between the men, with a couple of them gesticulating aggressively.

Finally, Eel came over to her reluctantly. "It is our custom not to let outsiders see the paths through the reeds. I know you are a friend of the Lake, but—"

She smiled and held up her hands soothingly. "It's all right. Frankly, I'd rather not know. Then I can't be a danger to you."

He nodded with satisfaction and spoke over his shoulder to the others. They, too, nodded approvingly at her. One brought over a scarf, which they tied over her eyes. It smelled of fish. She leaned back against the solid bulwark of reeds and listened to the soft sounds of the boat: the gurgles from the steering blade, the bare feet of the men on the floor, the horses whickering as they caught the scent of land and fodder. The sides of the boat scraped gently against reeds, and the sounds of wind rubbing stalk against stalk and the squawking and flapping from ducks or geese disturbed by the boat surrounded her. The music of the Lake continued for a long time, while the light seeping under the edges of the scarf faded away. When she could see only a deep golden glow under the scarf, frogs began to call, a few at first, and then more and more, until the boat vibrated with the noise. It filled the world.

Eventually, the prow of the boat scraped against earth and Eel removed the scarf.

Bramble stood up, blinking her eyes. It was almost dark, with just faint tracks of gold and rose far down on the flat horizon that seemed to curve away. Every distance here was filled with the reeds, rustling, swaying, singing with the almost deafening frog chorus. There were houses built out of reeds, half circles seeming to cling to the ground, some the length of a small field. All the buildings were on stilts at the edges of a thin island, like a lace hem on a petticoat. There were boats everywhere, being poled along, tied up, repaired, some as big as the one she was on, others tiny, just big enough for one person.

The island—precious, arable land—was the domain of cattle and crops. Goats were being folded in for the night by young boys. They called to one another in high, carrying voices, and shouted instructions and, if tone was anything to go by, insults at their charges. The smell was rich and complex: reeds, mud, manure, smoke from the fires the boys were lighting near the cattle pens, and something bready cooking somewhere. That smelled delicious.

Bramble turned to look back up the channel they had come down—nothing but reeds and the faint tip of another island. As she looked, a boy came down to the edge of that island and leaped into one of the small boats, crying aloud in a rhythmic shout. He pushed off from the land and began to pole toward them. He was followed, in single file, by huge big-horned gray cattle who stolidly walked into the water and began to swim, only their heads and horns showing. Astonished, Bramble watched as the boy arrived at the closer island, beached his boat and then led the phlegmatic file of cattle up into a yard.

"There is grazing over there," Eel said, laughing at her expression. "Come away from the mosquitoes. Come inside."

Underneath the drumming of the frogs was another, nastier thrumming: thousands of mosquitoes. She slapped a few away without being bitten and stepped up out of the boat onto a platform outside one of the long buildings.

"My horses?" she said.

Eel shouted back to one of the men in the boat and he waved in acknowledgment. "Pike will look after them," he said. "Come."

He led her into a dim, receding tunnel of reeds. At intervals, the huge bundles of reeds supported the roof, arching high overhead. Nearby, a lamp picked up the color of the reeds and gave it back again, so they were bathed in golden light, slightly hazy with reed dust, and smelling sweetly of the lamp's scented oil. Roses, she thought, and musk.

It was the most alien place she had ever encountered. The great curved ceiling made her feel small, which she wasn't sure she liked. And yet...how peaceful it seemed, how warm and welcoming, and alive. She saw more of Eel's people, all men, wearing little felt caps with side flaps to cover their ears, beautifully embroidered in patterns of flowers and plants. They were dressed in loose cream shirts, some over trews, some just over loincloths. They looked at her curiously, and she wondered what they saw. Someone of the old blood? Kin? Or just an outsider, and not to be trusted, like all outsiders?

A young man came in with only a loincloth on. He smiled brilliantly at her, then turned away to put on a long shirt.

Eel smiled with relief. "This is Salamander. He is better at your language than I. He lived with the ferry people for a while."

"I thought I was in love with the blacksmith's daughter," Salamander explained, with practiced charm.

One of the other men made a quick comment and the group chuckled.

Salamander threw up a hand in acknowledgment. "Yes, yes, I was very stupid and she wasn't that good-looking, I know." He leaned toward Bramble and lowered his voice conspiratorially. "She *was*, actually, but what a shrew! Complaining all day and all night—not about me," he added hastily, seeing the amusement in Bramble's face. "At least," he winked, "not at night."

He seemed so young and was so transparently trying to impress her that she laughed.

"Come, come," Eel said. "It is time to do what you came for."

The three of them walked down the long, dim room, between two lines of rugs that were set out against the wall. Eel carried a lamp, so that as they passed, the colors in the rugs leaped into life and then fell back into darkness again. Some of the dye they had used Bramble recognized: the orange of onion skins, deep pink of rose madder, tan of yarrow, yellow of clematis. But there were deep blues as well, and a pale green like the sky just before dawn, and a deep yellow like the sun. Beautiful. Each one of them was beautiful in its own way, alive with images of birds in flight, of vines and water lilies, and the patterns of reeds.

Salamander saw her looking at them. "The weaving gives work to the people who do not have cattle. They must do something to live."

"They're beautiful."

"Yes?" He looked surprised, then nodded. "They are very old, those designs. But weaving is for the worthless. And for women."

His tone indicated that the two were the same. Bramble wondered wryly if all the people of the old blood had felt like that about women. The people in the Wind Cities, who resembled Travelers, also thought poorly of women, it was said. Property. Cattle. So much for an ancient paradise.

They came to the end of the room, into another pool of lamplight. A woman and a man were sitting there, side by side, not looking at each other.

Eel indicated the man. "Our steersman," he said. "And this is the listener."

The steersman was a tall, craggy-faced man with hard dark eyes surrounded, incongruously, with laugh lines. He was dressed like the other men, in cream shirt, felt waistcoat, and cap. He had tucked the side flaps of the cap up behind his ears. He was impressive and impassive. But Bramble's attention was drawn to the woman. She was young, perhaps younger than Bramble, and as ugly as anyone Bramble had ever seen who was not actually maimed. It was not an ugliness of deformity; it just seemed that her features didn't belong together on the same face, that her big nose was stuck on, her eyes were not quite level, her mouth went a little awry, and her ears were far too large for her head. And yet, her eyes were merry, and she smiled at Bramble and Salamander and Eel as though life was always joyful.

Bramble smiled back involuntarily, a guileless, warm smile, the kind of smile she reserved for Maryrose.

Eel handed over the letter from Sorn to the steersman. He glanced at it, then gave it back to Salamander, who read it aloud in the Lake language.

The steersman's head went back at one point and he hissed through his teeth. The mention of fire, Bramble thought. The steersman turned and spoke to the listener.

Salamander translated quietly into Bramble's ear. "What does the Lake say?"

"The message, and the messenger, can be trusted." The listener spoke in Bramble's tongue.

The steersman looked hard at Bramble, and then nodded.

"It will be soon," Bramble said. "He's calling in all his resources."

They nodded.

"Our thanks," the steersman said. "You are our guest."

He gestured to Eel to take her away, but the listener held up a hand.

"Wait." She spoke directly to Bramble, the mismatched eyes steady and serious. "You are going to the Well of Secrets?"

Bramble nodded.

Part of her felt that she should have been surprised that the listener knew it, but she was slowly realizing that that part had come from Acton's people. Her Traveler blood understood that this woman was connected to the gods. And then she bit back a smile, because the thought reminded her so much of the old ballads her grandfather had liked to sing.

The listener smiled as if in response to Bramble's musing. "We are all in a story now, but what the ending may be, no one knows. Not even the Lake." The men looked worried. "You *must* go to the Well of Secrets, and you must go tomorrow."

Bramble nodded, but a little wearily. She had been looking forward to at least a couple of days' rest and the opportunity to explore this strange world of reeds. "Tomorrow," she said.

"Sleep well. The Lake rocks you in her bosom," the listener said.

The steersman nodded at her and Bramble, Eel and Salamander turned to walk back to the other end of the house, where there was food set out, and a kind of wine she'd never tasted before... and more men and more lamps.

"Only men?" she asked Salamander when they had settled down on a rug to begin their meal.

"Would you prefer to eat with the women?" he said anxiously. "Their food is not so good. But I will take you across to their house if you wish."

She shook her head, suddenly exhausted. "No. I just want to have something to eat and then go to sleep."

"We have a house for you alone to sleep in." He was proud of himself. "I told them that the town dwellers like to sleep alone."

It seemed like a great boon to Bramble, to lie down alone in safety and peace. "Thank you," she said sincerely. "Thank you very much."

Exhaustion swept over her as she sat on the rug with Eel and Salamander and ate from a common dish of braised kid and flat bread. It was good food, warm and fragrant, but it was strange, with spices she wasn't used to turning the familiar taste of goat into something alien. The golden glow, the voices of men all around, strange men at that, combined to make her uneasy.

She had never been in a room with *only* men before, except for cleaning tack with a couple of the grooms who brought

405

mares to Gorham's. But that was different, on home turf. And there were only a couple of grooms at a time. As the meal went on, the house filled with more and more men, all looking, and even smelling, strange, and with the dark hair and eyes which were so rare elsewhere. Although she knew she was perfectly safe, she was also tense, unable to read the faces of the men, who talked and laughed and shouted as the wine went around, but whose eyes studied her, openly, with deep and serious interest.

She wished that she had gone to the women's house after all. She was too alone here. When Salamander touched her on the shoulder, she jumped, and was ashamed of herself.

He smiled at her. "Come on, now," he said soothingly, as to a child. She flushed. "I'll take you to your house."

That meant another trip in a smaller boat, with Salamander standing in the stern to pole it along. There were clouds, but the moon was up, half full, and wind raced the clouds across its face, sending flickers of silver across the waves, like fish leaping, over and over again. The Lake seemed alive with movement, even in the channels between the islands: a place that seethed with life.

She could hear the cattle and goats, smell the smudge fires they lit to keep the mosquitoes away from the herds, hear the whine of the mosquitoes themselves, the voices of women as they passed smaller houses, murmuring to children, singing lullabies, scolding. A child's cry of protest rose up into the night and sent goose bumps down her back. Then the mother's voice came, soothing, gentling, finally speaking firmly. The mother said the same thing several times, and then they were out of earshot.

"What did she say?" Bramble asked.

"'Listen to the Lake, she will hear you,'" Salamander said. "It is what mothers say here when their children are complaining and they've heard enough. Listen to the Lake. It means, if you are quiet, so that you can hear the Lake lapping under the house, then the Lake may grant your desires." He grinned. "But it really means 'No.'"

She smiled back. "Does the Lake never give a child what it wishes?"

He nodded. "Oh, yes, often. A lost toy floats back, the child catches a fine fish...many things. The Lake loves children and cares for them."

"And adults?"

This time, his smile was rueful. "The Lake will give an adult what he, or she, desires, but only once in a lifetime, so you have to be very sure of what you ask for. Some people go to their graves never having asked, for fear of getting it wrong and wasting it. Others ask too soon for things which are worthless and must live the rest of their lives with that mistake. Like me."

She looked at him questioningly.

He shrugged, his mouth wry. "I asked for the daughter of the blacksmith in the town. Well, I got her!" And then, irrepressibly, he threw back his head and laughed.

Bramble had to laugh too, although she wondered how much hurt hid behind his laughter, and how much the laughter of the other men had pushed him into making a mockery of himself. He needed to forget about it and find some way of proving himself to them so that they would stop laughing. She sobered. No doubt Thegan would give him plenty of opportunity.

"'She gives us all we need and requires obedience in return,'" Salamander said, clearly quoting.

Bramble raised her eyebrows. "What if She doesn't get obedience?"

"She takes what is her due, either in life or through death. Only a fool disobeys the Lake. They say the fish pick your bones

407

very clean, but I'd rather have my body burned, as it should be. After a peaceful death from old age."

So much for the Lake's universal benevolence. Perhaps it was just as well. She would need to be ruthless to protect Her people from Thegan. Salamander brought the boat smoothly to moor against a small reed house, barely bigger than a room.

"Your sleeping house," he said. "Sleep well. Listen to the Lake and she will soothe you. Who knows? She may speak to you."

"I'll listen. Goodnight, and thank you."

Her packs were already inside, on reed mats, and there was a thick rug, which was clearly the sleeping place. Salamander had not left her a light, but the sliding shutters were pushed back from the windows and the fitful moonlight showed enough to let her find the chamber pot and use it, and then retrieve and curl up under her favorite blanket, with a bag as pillow. The autumn night was cool and she was glad of the blanket. She wondered where the horses were, but she had seen enough of the way Eel's men handled them to be sure they would be fine. She watched the moonlight and listened to the Lake, but all she heard was the low sound of water lapping at the stilts of the house until she slept.

She dreamed that Maryrose's voice called to her to get up. She stood up and went to the window where the voice had come from. Even as she walked, she knew it was a dream, because outside the window shone a full moon, where it had been only a half-moon when she went to bed. And the Lake water lapped at the sides of her hut, higher than before, as though it were spring and the Lake had risen with the melting snow. A warm, light breeze fanned her face.

Outside, she couldn't see any of the huts or the islands she and Salamander had poled through that night. Only the Lake, stretching endlessly in the moonlight, the waters shining silver so brightly it hurt her eyes.

Maryrose's voice came again.

"Will you help me?"

She didn't sound distressed, but calm, gentle, with even tones. But underneath the familiar, beloved voice was something else, another note that resonated with Maryrose's voice as the wind played across waves. Even in the dream, Bramble knew it was the Lake talking. But whether it was the real Lake or just her own dreaming of it, brought on by the strangeness of the place and Salamander's tales, she didn't know.

"Of course I will help, if you need it," Bramble said.

After all, wasn't that why she was here? She found that she was breathing hard, as she did when she rode in a chase. She had the same feeling of recklessnes, of exhilaration, that she got when she was a stumble away from death.

"Will you give me what I need?" the voice asked.

Bramble's heartbeat increased even more and she felt that one wrong word would shatter the dream, and perhaps shatter more than that. It was like talking to the local gods, she had that same feeling of being on a precipice, of pressure that threatened to take your breath if you said what was unwanted.

"You could take what you need," she said, finally, knowing it was true, that she had nothing the Lake could not take, including her life.

Maryrose's voice laughed, softly. "Never without asking. That is the compact. Will you give?"

"Yes."

"Ah." It was less Maryrose's voice now and more a shifting slide of sound—less human, more beautiful. "And will you become one of my children?"

She shook her head without thinking, knowing in her bones

409

that she did not belong here and never would. The Lake was absolutely still, waiting for her answer. The waves against her hut were still, the breeze dead. The whole Lake waited. Bramble cleared her throat.

"Although it would be an honor, Lady, I think I belong elsewhere."

The waves began again, the breeze lifted her hair gently.

"So think I. Wise child, you have far to go before you reach your journey's end."

Then suddenly it was just before dawn, and Bramble was lying under her blanket in the clear gray light, with the air outside so cold that the tip of her nose ached. She lay for a moment, wondering, then heard Salamander call her name as his boat bumped at her doorstep.

"Time to go, beautiful rider," he said, poking his head through the door. "Your boat is waiting."

ASH

WINTER CAME, in a rush, in a matter of days. The last leaves fell, frosts hardened the ground, snow drifted down steadily and the animals were moved into the big barn, crowded by the fodder Mabry had stored there this year, instead of in the small barn. "We need to practice," he had said to Gytha, when she complained of having to squeeze through the hay to feed the chickens.

Three weeks after they arrived, at breakfast, Elva began to have birth pains. Ash was sent to get the midwife from the cluster of houses down near the river.

"Second on the left, no, right—the yellow house," Mabry gabbled, then raced back to the bedroom.

Ash ran, as fast as he could in the snow, slipping and sliding down the steep path in flurries of snow. But when the midwife heard why he'd come, she just nodded and went calmly about putting the things she needed into her bag. Ash hopped from one foot to the other impatiently. She shook her head at him tolerantly.

"First birth, just started the pains—she'll be hours yet, young'un."

So it proved. He followed the wiry legs of the midwife up the path and waited in the main room for hours. Gytha was the messenger, coming out to get fresh towels or a hot brick from the fire for Elva's back, and each time saying, "Don't fret, it's all going well."

It was dark before the midwife emerged. "Well, it didn't take

411

as long as I thought, after all." She smiled at him. "Go on, then, go see the little lad."

Ash rushed into the bedroom and stopped at the door. It was like an image from an old song: the new parents, the mother holding the swaddled babe close, the proud father bending over them. He hardly saw the others. He was struck through with envy, with a desire for what Mabry had: a wife to love, a child to raise, a home to live in and work for, a place in a village where he was known and respected. They were things he would probably never have. For a moment, he hovered on the brink of hating Mabry for that, but he remembered Doronit, her face contorted by hate for Acton's people, and he turned the yearning into an even stronger determination not to let anything harm this family. Or, he thought for the first time, others like them.

Elva looked up from the child. "A boy. With dark hair!" she said. "I must look out the window. Draw back the shutters, Mabry."

They had discussed this, too, in the nights before the fire, and Mabry had agreed that Elva could name the baby the Traveler way, by the sight of the first living thing she saw outside after the birth. But Mabry was prepared to go with Traveler customs only so far, and he had laid plans with Ash. He nodded to Ash now, before he touched the shutters, and Ash ran outside to where they had potted up and hidden two small trees: a cherry for a girl and a tiny cedar sapling for a boy. He positioned himself by the window and called out to Mabry, who then opened the shutters.

"What are you doing, Ash?" Elva asked, and Mabry explained.

The two girls laughed, but Elva and Martine were silent. Ash peered in. They didn't look happy.

"Fine," Elva said. "I can see why you did it. But you have

to take the consequences. The first living thing I saw was Ash. We'll call the baby Ash."

Mabry expostulated, but Elva held firm.

"The gods guide us in our choice of names," Martine said. "You think you're the first father who's tried to cast only the stones he wants? It never answers. It's bad luck."

So Mabry agreed, to Ash's delight. He wasn't interested in babies, but it was as though the gods had heard his yearning to be part of this family, and had given his wish to him backhandedly, as was their habit. An Ash, of Traveler blood, would grow up in this warm and loving spot, cherished and happy. *If they could stop the ghosts.*

The days shortened. This far north, so close to the mountains, the winters were long and very cold. The valley was protected from the worst of the winds, but even so, there were few days when they could walk out comfortably into crisp air. On those days the sky was deep blue and the air tasted sharp and bracing on the tongue, and the women came up from the village, to see the new baby and surreptitiously assess the strangers. A couple of men from the class in the barn came too, awkwardly, and Ash realized that they were courting Drema and Gytha. Gytha grinned and flirted with her beau, but Barley, courting Drema, had a harder task. Still, Ash thought, watching the way her eyes softened as he gingerly held the baby, he might have a chance.

The evenings were spent marveling over the baby and talking, with Ash reciting almost every song he knew. At Drema's request, he began to do it chronologically, working his way through the past, from the very earliest Traveler songs to the ballads of the landtaken and the love songs and nonsense songs of the present.

It sobered Mabry and his sisters a little. It was clear that, like most settled folk, they had never heard the full story of the landtaken: the full toll of the dead, the raped, the enslaved. The songs told of the ceaseless expansion north, which pushed back the old inhabitants to the poor, marginal land, and from there, pushed them onto the roads, to become Travelers.

The ballads were from an earlier, more robust age, where battle was a source of glory and the tally of those killed added to a warrior's renown. Acton's people had delighted in bloodshed. But Mabry's people were farmers, and it was too easy, with the ghosts perhaps gathering, for them to imagine the terror and despair of those attacked.

Holmstead fell! Giant Aelred, shield of iron
Mighty sword arm for his chief.
Down came Aelred, fierce with battle cry
Sweeping all before his blade
Sweeping all before to death.
The dark people leaped to battle
A hundred strong they leaped to battle
Wielded weapons in weak arms.
Mighty Aelred led his warriors
A score of warriors came behind him
Faced the hundred.
Killed them all.

"Do we have to listen to all this blood and death?" Gytha asked.

"I think we do," Drema said, and Mabry nodded.

"Yes. Better to know the truth. Better to understand why the enchanter the ghosts spoke of is seeking revenge."

"Keep to the history, Ash," Drema said. "We must start with the earliest and work our way up."

There were kinder songs, too, and they turned to those with relief. Ash dredged his memory for early songs that were not about battle. Several times he remembered songs, or fragments of songs, that he had heard his father sing at night near the fire, but never his mother. "Useless songs," she had said. They never performed them, because they were in the old Traveler language and would have been unpopular with audiences. But they were haunting, all in a minor key. Although it was difficult to figure out what they meant, even after Ash had translated them.

The gods' own prey is galloping, is riding up the hill
Her hands are wet with blood and tears and dread
She is rearing on the summit and her banner floats
*   out still*
Now the killer's hands must gather in the dead.

"It's not a very good translation," Ash said apologetically. "The original's better. It's a tricky rhythm."

"'The killer's hands must gather in the dead,'" Martine mused. "It sounds like a prophecy."

"Oh, gods, not a prophecy!" Elva exclaimed. "I hate those things. They never say what you think they mean and then they come up behind you when you least expect it and shove you into something horrible."

She scowled. Everyone but Martine looked surprised.

"Oh, it's not that bad, love," she said, and smiled. "It was only a little prophecy."

"Tell us," Mabry said.

Elva shook her head stubbornly, but Martine laughed. "One of the old women in our village foretold when Elva was born that she would live with the gods. She's never really known what it meant."

"But you've already done that, sweetheart," Mabry said.

415

"When you first came here, you built a cabin next to the gods' stone and lived with them."

Elva's pale face went still for a moment and then broke into a wide smile. "I did, didn't I?" She laughed in relief. "All my life I've had that shagging prophecy following me around and it came true without me even noticing it! You see, that's what I mean, it's just typical of prophecies. You can't trust them."

"All right," Martine said soothingly, "we won't worry about some prey of the gods."

"After all," Ash said, "that song was written a thousand years ago. If it is a prophecy, it's not likely to come true right now."

"Enough songs for tonight," Drema said firmly. "Let's go to bed."

Rolled comfortably in his blankets by the fire, breathing in the warm scent of apples from the drying rack over the ashes, Ash drifted off to sleep immediately, but was woken in the middle of the night by little Ash's crying. He lay in the darkness and listened to Elva murmuring to him, and to the funny hiccup he always gave as he was put to the breast. Then there was silence, except for the slow creak of the roof under its burden of snow, the very faint hiss from the banked fire...and his own breathing, slow and steady.

Something about that rhythm brought back a memory from a long time before: he clung to his father's back as they walked a road, somewhere, sometime, when he was little enough for Da to carry him most of the day. His father was singing. His father's voice wasn't beautiful, like Mam's, but he liked its deep resonance, coming up through his back as Ash clung to his shoulders. Mam pushed their handcart behind them, and the rumbling of the wheels was even deeper. His father was singing old words, very odd words. Snatches of it came back to Ash, "knife cleansed, blood flows, memory calls, past shows, the bones beneath it all..."

"That's a song better forgotten." His mam's voice had come sharply.

"No song should be forgotten," his father had said.

Yes, Ash realized, this was why the incident had stayed in his memory, although he had been so tiny at the time. It was the first, one of the only times, he had ever heard his father disagree with his mother.

"No song should be forgotten," his father had repeated. "You remember that, Ash."

So he had. He remembered them all.

They had little Ash to thank that the winter did not seem endless. The few weeks before he was born had dragged out, but afterward the days flew, crammed from morning until night.

Ash would never have believed the difference one little baby made. None of them got enough sleep, except Gytha who could ignore his nighttime cries. They walked around during the day with dark circles under their eyes, and drank too many cups of cha to stay awake. Elva was the worst, of course, but she at least felt no shame in curling up with the baby for a nap. The others had chores to do, even in winter: animals to be fed and mucked out, thatch to be replaced on the barn roof, water to be carried, chamber pots to be emptied and cleaned, cooking, cleaning, felting, sewing, spinning, weaving, chopping wood.

Then there was the nappy changing, the clothes washing, the baby bathing before the fire, the walking and the soothing and the rocking to sleep. And just watching the changing expressions on that tiny face—it was a full-time job for all five of them, which was ridiculous. Perhaps not quite full-time, Ash conceded. They did have some time for other things.

Mabry was also a skilled woodcarver, and made delicate designs of flowers and plants on all sorts of items. He had made the baby's cradle before Martine and Ash arrived. The day after little Ash was born, he set to work to carve the traditional flower for Elva's child necklace, which all the women of Acton's people were given who had borne a child to their husband. Cornflower was for a boy, daisy for a girl, and carved and painted by the father—that was the tradition. A stillborn child's flower was left unpainted, to show the life unlived. When the woman died, she was buried with the necklace. The cornflower Mabry carved and painted for little Ash was a marvel, complex and delicate, almost alive. Through the long winter nights he worked at a pair of dinner plates, rectangles of wood on which he etched the spare outline of reeds.

As the days grew noticeably longer, Gytha spent nights out in the barn in case of early lambing.

Then came the first sign of spring thaw—a warm wind from the south. The five of them stood together outside, with little Ash in Martine's arms, looking south down the valley and watching chunks of ice break away from the riverbanks and be carried away.

"Time to go," said Martine.

Ash couldn't tell if there was sorrow or anticipation in her voice. Perhaps both.

So they packed up that day, saying little except to plan their route. "Down the valley's your best way," said Mabry. "Right to the end and then come up into Cliff Domain and strike east. The roads aren't good, but you'll get there in a few weeks. Then north through the Golden Valley and Quiet Pass into the Last

Domain. They say the Well of Secrets is there now, in Oak-mere." He paused. "It's a long trip."

Martine patted Mabry on the shoulder reassuringly. "We're Travelers, born and bred."

"The road is long and the end is death," Ash said cheerfully.

Mabry smiled. "If we're lucky." He had learned the Travel-er's answer from Elva.

As they were packing, each of them came to give Ash and Martine a parting gift, things they'd worked on all winter that Ash never suspected could be for him. Gytha had woven a big goat's-wool blanket that would cover both of them. Drema had made them felt coats, beautifully embroidered, and far warmer than anything Ash owned. Elva had dried half an orchard's worth of fruit over the fire, "for the lean, hungry times," she said. And Mabry gave them the plates.

"A bit heavy to carry, but lighter than pottery," he said shyly.

Martine kissed him. Ash, embarrassed, pounded him on the shoulder.

The next morning, early, Ash, Mabry, Drema and Gytha waited outside while Martine and Elva said goodbye in the house.

"Take care of yourself," Mabry said to Ash.

"You too. All of you."

Mabry tried to smile. "Don't worry. We'll be ready."

Ash nodded. "Keep your guard up, then."

Then Martine came out, and Elva followed with tears streak-ing down her face. Martine's face was set, as he had seen it dur-ing the attack at her house, when she held the white knife to the young man's throat. He knew her better now, and it was a face that was holding back fear and sorrow.

There was kissing all round, and then they simply turned and walked away.

As they picked their way down the slushy path, Ash felt worse than when he had left his parents behind to go to Doronit's. This time he was leaving people who valued him, who had a place for him. *But only for the winter,* he reminded himself. *It was only ever just for the winter.* It wasn't where he really belonged.

But the winter's contentment had given him a new standard to measure life against. He wouldn't be satisfied, ever, until he could create a home as warm, and a life that meant as much.

"Oh, gods," he said aloud, thinking of what might lie ahead. "Why us?"

Martine glanced sideways at him. "Shagged if I know." She grinned at his surprise. "Look on the bright side, lad. We've full packs, a long road and a reason to walk it. What more do Travelers need?"

He smiled back, reluctantly, and settled his pack more comfortably on his back. She was right, they had a long way to go.

BRAMBLE

BRAMBLE'S HORSES were already loaded in Eel's big boat and were very glad to see her. They almost knocked her down, butting her side with their heads, nickering in her face, moving closer to her, even Trine. Eel waited patiently for them to settle down, smiling so hard his eyes almost disappeared into their laugh lines.

"They missed their *sisgara*," he said. "Their herd leader. They were lost and lone without you."

"I was a bit lost and lone without them," Bramble confessed, absurdly uplifted by their greeting.

She rubbed their noses, clouted Trine on the shoulder when she tried to step on Eel's foot, felt herself surrounded by the familiar warmth and horse smells. She was no longer traveling alone in a strange land.

They came to bind her eyes again and she asked for just a moment to take in the dawn breaking over the Lake. The sky was streaked with clouds, which picked up every color imaginable: green and rose and gold, magenta and heliotrope and violet. All were reflected in the still water. It was a kaleidoscope of color, changing rapidly as the sun rose and the sky settled into duck egg blue, the pale clear blue of winter. Bramble took a great breath as though she could inhale the colors.

"All right," she said.

She closed her eyes and was blindfolded, then settled back against the side of the boat and listened again to the Lake.

They poled out slowly from the narrow channels, leaving the

myriad noises of the village behind until there was nothing to be heard but the calls of birds and the rustle of the reeds and the lap of the Lake water. It chuckled against the prow, happy, but also urgent, as though it were pressing them to hurry. Whether Eel heard it like that she didn't know, but when they came to a larger channel, he picked up the pace and they were now moving much faster than they had the day before.

After some time, he came to unbind her eyes and give her water and cheese and bread. He shared the food with her, sitting cross-legged on the deck. They had drawn up in a small cove surrounded by willows and, standing farther back, elms. The willows had dropped almost all their thin yellow leaves, the elms were already winter bare. There was an autumn scent, of moss and drying earth, just perceptible over the pitch-tar smell of the boat. As they ate, Eel's men put out two gangplanks and led the horses, scrambling, onto the shore.

"We have taken you to the northern side, but a long way west of the town. There is a road, farther up, that you can join to take you to the Golden Valley, and from there over the Quiet Pass into the Last Domain, where you will find the Well of Secrets."

Bramble nodded. "Thank you." She wondered if she should tell him about the dream.

"Remember though," Eel went on, "the road is in the Cliff Domain—Thegan's son's Domain, the one Thegan ruled before he married the Lady Sorn. You must be wary."

Bramble went cold. She had hoped to cross the Lake as close as possible to Baluchston, which would have kept her out of Cliff Domain.

"He's going to come at you from both sides," she said.

"Yes. But do not worry. It has happened before, with men as greedy and blood hungry as he, and we are still here. We will

422

always be here. We are the Lake's children and She cares for us, the way She cares for you."

She was surprised, and showed it.

"You think She does not care for you?" Eel asked, laughing. "Then ask yourself, how can you spend a night with open windows and come out the next morning without a single mosquito bite? She's never done that much for me!"

Bramble looked at her arms, and was astonished that it hadn't occurred to her before. Not *one* bite. Even though, as she and Salamander had poled toward her house, she had heard the insistent whine of the mosquitoes everywhere.

She opened her mouth, but didn't know what to say.

"I am honored," she managed finally.

Eel smiled at her again, and patted her shoulder. She suddenly felt very young and silly. It wasn't unpleasant.

"Then you will understand and forgive her," he said. "She takes only what she needs."

"What do you mean?" she asked, but he smiled and shook his head and gestured to her to follow the horses.

She looked at him for a moment, annoyed that he wouldn't explain, then followed the horses ashore. They came to nose into her shoulder, Trine shoving the others aside to get closer to her. She spent a few moments saddling up and securing their packs, trying not to think of the journeys she had taken with the roan. The hot ball of grief and guilt was never far away, but it could be lived with. She took a deep breath, pushing the memories aside, and decided to ride Trine again. This new affection should be nurtured.

As she was preparing to mount up, and wondering what to say to Eel, Salamander appeared from between the bare willow withes.

"Hallo!" he said cheerfully. "Are you ready?"

She looked at Eel.

"He will show you to the road." He looked at Salamander sternly. "Don't get yourself killed and don't fall in love with any drylander."

The men in the boat laughed.

Salamander sighed. "Uncle, I will try to avoid both."

"Good!" Eel smacked him between the shoulder blades in a gesture of affection and farewell, then turned to Bramble.

"Take care of him. My sister will use my guts as her fishing lines if he gets hurt."

"Oh, I think he can take care of himself," Bramble said drily. Salamander shot her a look of gratitude. "Goodbye. Thank you."

"No," Eel said. "Our thanks are to you for risking so much to bring us our warning." He bowed, formally, his hat in his hand. "The gods go with you."

"Blessings be on you and yours," Bramble replied.

She turned and led the horses off, Salamander by her side.

"I hate goodbyes," Salamander said happily. "This is the way."

He led her along a slender path she might easily have missed on her own, through an arch of bare elm branches. Dry leaves crunched under their feet and a cool breeze lifted off the Lake, as though to bid them farewell. As they walked through the arch, she felt a shiver, some kind of anticipation. Was it fear? she wondered. She ducked her head to avoid a low bough and when her head came up she almost bit her tongue off in surprise.

The elms around them were in leaf: bright yellow-green new spring leaves. The sun was higher in a sky patched with cloud, the air was rich with the heady, full smell of the earth after fresh spring rain. The breeze was warm, now, and looking back she could see that the level of the Lake was much higher, just as she had seen in her dream the night before.

Salamander turned to smile at her uneasily, half apologetic, half scared. "It's only a little bit of time She has taken," he said placatingly. "Just a few months."

Her breath was coming as fast as though she had been running. *Then you will understand and forgive her,* Eel had said. This was what he had meant. *She takes only what she needs.* Bramble breathed in slowly, willing her heart to slow. She grinned suddenly. It answered her questions about whether the dream had been true. She felt again the rush of adrenaline and excitement from the dream. *Magic.* She'd never experienced real magic before, just the presence of the gods, which was part of her blood and bone. No, it couldn't be magic—that was something humans did. To move two people and three horses through time was power of another kind.

Salamander regarded her anxiously.

"You've lost your time, too," she said.

Salamander seemed pleased not to be shouted at. He smiled, immediately relaxed. "Oh, I volunteered," he said. "Who minds missing winter? The road is this way."

He led her up a winding path and she followed, the horses completely unperturbed by the sudden shift to spring, although their nostrils were wide, drinking in the full, living scent.

She looked over her shoulder at the Lake, expecting something, anything, a sign, an omen...But there was just the flickering of sun on the ripples and an empty cove that had last seen a boat in late autumn. Bramble turned in her saddle and stared resolutely ahead. Why had the Lake needed Bramble to be here, now? Right at this time. What was so special about *now?*

Nothing, it seemed, for the moment. Salamander led her

down a winding path, through thickets of willow and alder. There were streams crisscrossing their track, bubbling with snowmelt and forcing them to turn aside several times before they found safe places to ford. All the streams looked alike, all the clumps of willow seemed the same. She would not have found the way by herself.

After a couple of hours they emerged onto pastureland where cows were grazing. These were a different breed from the Lake cattle, big bony black-and-white animals, and only a couple had calves. It must be very early spring. The land was dead flat and the sky was wide above them. It was as though they had been picked up and put down somewhere a world away.

"The road's over that way," Salamander said, pointing north. "Follow it east and take the first turning to the north. That'll lead you up to Golden Valley. It's a bit longer, but it'll keep you off the main track."

"Thanks. I hope you get back safely."

Salamander grinned. "Who'd want to hurt me?" He darted in and kissed her on the cheek before she realized what he was doing. "Had to do it," he said. "Couldn't resist."

Bramble's laugh made Trine toss her head at the end of her leading string, blowing loudly through her nose.

"Exactly," Bramble said. "Couldn't have put it better myself."

She unclipped the leading string and jumped up onto Trine's back. "Wind at your back," she said.

"Smooth water," Salamander replied, then turned and slipped into the cover of the willows.

Bramble rode away and had to resist the urge to turn around and wave at him like a child saying "bye-bye." But she rode away with a smile.

It was good to be on horseback again. She found the road

easily, just a double cart track through the short grass, and followed it without meeting anything more alarming than cows. When it branched, she took the overgrown northern track, which led toward the foothills nearby.

She calculated that she had two days' riding to get to Golden Valley. She would be safe there. Golden Valley lay between Cliff Domain and Far North Domain. It was terrible country for farming but it bred wonderful horses, with stamina and bone and heart. In the past, the two Domains had fought over the valley so often that trade from the far north, from the Last Domain and the Northern Mountains Domain, had almost stopped. About thirty years ago, just after he'd come into his inheritance, the previous warlord of the Last Domain had brokered a peace, and his son, Arvid, now safeguarded that peace. The Golden Valley was now a "free valley," as Carlion and Turvite were free towns. It belonged to no one and was governed by a council elected by its inhabitants. It was neutral territory and Thegan—and his son—could not touch her there.

The track wound higher into the foothills. Bramble felt lighthearted. The spring sun, the clear sky, the clarity of the hill air combined to buoy her spirits. She was across the Lake, had delivered her message, and was on her way again. The Well of Secrets would keep until she got to the Last Domain, and Oakmere. She whistled as she rode and talked to the horses, to Trine especially.

Her good mood lasted until dusk. They had climbed well into the foothills, and the mountains soared above them. She was looking for a place to camp for the night when she heard the howl of wolves.

Early spring, she realized immediately, as the horses whickered in fright and Cam reared up and tried to bolt, reverting in an instant to the flighty animal she'd been when Bramble first took her in. Bramble tussled with her and with the other two, talking to them, and regretting, for the first time, not putting a bit on Trine. They shuffled and twisted a good way down the path before she got them under control. *Early spring.* It would have been a long, hungry winter, and the baby calves and kids had not yet arrived. *No easy prey except us.*

She looked around frantically. There was no shelter here on the bare hillside. She would have to ride on, to a cave, a niche in the rocks, anything where the horses could have their backs protected while they used their front hooves to defend themselves. But it was getting dark, and the footing underneath was growing more and more treacherous. She clicked her tongue at the horses at the same moment the wolves' howl came again, and she had to hold them in hard to stop them galloping off down the uneven track.

"There now, just a little faster, that's it, you're all right, no need to worry, just pick up the pace a little, that's all," she crooned, calming them and herself at the same time.

She had the wolf skin around her shoulders and wondered if that was a good omen or a bad one. *Gods, aid your daughter,* she prayed, but there was no sense of the gods at all up here on the bare hillside.

They went on as fast as she dared through the darkening night until the track curved around a ridge of fissured granite. There were gaps in the rock as though someone had sliced a knife down a cake. She dismounted and led the horses up the hillside, slippery with loose rock, until she found a gap that was big enough for the three of them. It wasn't big enough for her as well, but if she had to, she resolved, she could lie across their backs... She tried not to think about sliding off the horses backward, in the dark, onto cold rock, to be trampled by thrashing, panicked hooves. The wolves might not come. *And spring will follow autumn next year,* she thought. *Of course they'll come.*

There was no wood up here to start a fire. She gave the horses a small drink of water, but not too much, then grabbed some of the oats from a saddlebag and fed them quickly. They'd need the energy if they had to run. She drank some water and ate the dried apricots and flat bread that Eel had given her. That seemed a long time ago. She laughed softly, and the horses shifted in response. It was a long time ago. Months. She settled down to wait, knife in hand. It was the same knife she had slit the wolf's throat with, back in Wooding. It didn't look very big.

They won't be long. Wolves liked to hunt at dusk, not at midnight. *They'll be here soon.*

They were.

They came from all directions at once, even from above the fissure, leaping down to swirl and growl and snap at the horses' hooves, trying to panic them into running. But the horses' instinct to run was overcome by another instinct — to stand and fight. They struck out with hooves flailing, the three standing together, with Trine a little to the front. As their hooves landed, sparks flew from the rocks. The night was full of noise: snarling, neighing, the thud and crack of hooves meeting flesh and rock, and her own shouting. She stayed just to one side of the cleft, out of reach of their hooves, but one of the wolves — the leader, she realized — circled around toward her.

She turned to face it. Here was the image from so many stories: the evil wolf, the northern wolf, sharp teeth bared, claws clicking on the rock, prowling, measuring up its prey. Childhood terror rose up in her. She saw the wolf's muscles tense, ready to spring.

She leaped forward and down a moment before it launched so that it passed just over her instead of reaching her throat. She thrust up with the knife at its belly and dragged the knife down. It felt like her shoulder was coming out of its socket, but she kept hold of the haft.

The wolf yowled in pain and twisted in midair, coming down heavily on its side. She jumped on it with both knees before it could rise. The sound of the air being forced out of its lungs was all she could hear.

And then the world went quiet.

The wolf writhed beneath her, impossibly strong. One claw ripped down her arm. She raised the knife in both hands and plunged it down as hard as she could. The wolf convulsed beneath her and then lay still.

For a moment, Bramble felt nothing but relief, as though it were all over. But noise crashed into the silence and she realized that the fight was still going on around her.

The big brown wolf leading the attack against the horses realized that its leader was down. It flung its head back and howled. Bramble stood up slowly, straddling the corpse, knife in hand, and snarled at the pack. She felt as rabid as she sounded. She would kill them all before she would let them hurt her horses.

There were only three of them left. It had seemed like dozens. One body was lying in front of Trine, smashed and bloody. The brown wolf—a female—stared at Bramble and snarled back. Bramble took a step forward, and the brown wolf broke. She yelped and turned and the other two followed her, only the whites on the undersides of their tails showing up in the almost dark as they ran.

Bramble checked the horses. They had got away with just a scratch or two, and none too deep. She cleaned out the wounds and then cleaned her own, a long ragged tear down her arm that would probably scar. She bound it up awkwardly with one of her shirts.

She dragged the two carcasses away from the fissure before she sat down. Once she sat she'd never be able to get up again, and there would be scavengers after the meat before dawn, and maybe other hunters, like bears. They would be satisfied with the wolf meat and not come looking for more.

Then she sat next to the fissure and let out her breath in a long *houf.* The horses were still fretting and were too frightened to wander off by themselves, and in a way she was relieved, because she didn't have the energy to get their tethers out and find rocks big enough to secure them to.

"Well, cullies, we're safe enough now," she told them. "Settle down, now, settle down."

They did settle down under the spell of her voice, and she even slept a little, sitting up against the hard rock, despite the pain in her arm. It seemed to throb and burn worse as the night went on, and she was afraid it was turning bad. She'd have to find a healer, but where?

In the morning the horses' scratches looked clean and on the mend, but her bandage was showing blood and her arm was hot and red. She fed and watered the horses but there was no water left for her. She had trouble lifting the saddlebags back onto Mud's back.

"Not good," she said to Trine. She was light-headed and not up to jumping on as she usually did, so she led Trine to a rock and climbed on from there. It seemed the wolves had knocked some of the arrogance out of Trine, because she stood still and let Bramble mount her without any objection. She even nosed Bramble's leg gently afterward.

They went as fast as they could on the rocky trail, with stones shifting under the horses' hooves. Mud proved to be most sure-footed, so they followed him and, like Trine, he was unusually cooperative with her. She wondered if killing the lead wolf had cemented her position as head of the herd. It was possible; and possible, too, that this far from their normal life, the horses just wanted the reassurance of someone telling them what to do.

She could understand that.

Just after midday she neared the top of the ridge they had been making toward all morning. She was pretty sure that Golden Valley lay over it. Maybe there she could find a healer. Her arm was getting worse. The trail led to a pass through even higher peaks, sharp and treacherous, with snow on their tops. She threaded her way through a recent rockfall of giant boulders that almost blocked the trail.

She reached the other side and was sure it was Golden Valley before her. It had been named in autumn, her da had told her once, because of the yellow leaves of the poplar trees that grew there. The poplar leaves were a brighter yellow-green now, in early spring, but the valley below seemed lit up with them, glowing in the sunlight. They followed the courses of innumerable streams and circled around ponds. She could see farmhouses and fenced paddocks far below...and horses. She smiled.

She followed the trail with her eye as it zigzagged down the hillside, making a steep way around clumps of bushes and pine trees. They started down carefully.

Two bends down, Trine neighed loudly and was answered by another horse hidden by the curve in the track. Bramble wasn't worried. Here in Golden Valley she was safe. She was just a... a horse trainer, looking for work on her way to the Well of Secrets. Plain and simple. The truth, in fact.

The riders below came around the bend. She was a moment slow in recognizing them. It was the two men Leof had talked to in the clearing—Horst and Sully, on their way back from the Last Domain. They stared at her in disbelief.

"Bramble!" Horst said. "It's bloody Bramble!"

"We're in Golden Valley," Bramble said quickly. "A free valley."

Horst looked up and down. There was no one in sight. "Aye," he said slowly. "But no one knows you're here, do they? I reckon we could have met you just the other side of the ridge."

"You'll be breaking the law."

Sully grinned. "You think my lord Thegan will *care?* Horst, my old mate, he's going to love us for this!"

"Don't take me back to him," Bramble said, her stomach turning over at asking a warlord's man for anything. "You know what he's like."

Sully glanced at Horst. "Aye. He's a coldhearted bastard who'd slit his own mother's throat if it was useful to him. And that's why we're taking you back, lass. Can you imagine what he'd do to us if we didn't?"

They were blocking the trail, but perhaps she had a chance of making it down the hillside to a lower part of the track. She had to try.

She made a feint to turn back up the trail, then, as they surged after her, she turned sideways and bolted across the hillside, dropping the leading reins and letting Cam and Mud follow as they could. She just hoped they wouldn't get entangled in the reins and fall. Trine picked up her pace and slipped across the loose scree on the hill and then turned to slide, dance, and finally leap down to the firmer footing between the trees that masked the lower bend of the trail.

Horst and Sully came after her as fast as they dared, but they kept to the trail so they were a little way behind her. And now it was just a chase. Bramble let everything go out of her head except getting farther ahead. The world narrowed to the track ahead of her, the ground, the way down. She was good at this, better than the men following. She knew how to find shortcuts, how to take risks. Trine wasn't the roan, but she was fast.

She was a fair way ahead of them at the bottom of the hill. The track branched and she swung left, farther into the valley, heading for houses and witnesses...and safety. But she felt increasingly light-headed and hot. Her arm seemed to swell even more, and her heart was skipping its beats.

The track curved back and up the hill, heading for another pass. She had chosen the wrong track. She knew she had to turn back and go down the hillside, but not on the track, that would just head her into their arms. She faltered and turned Trine, her head swimming, but Trine balked at the steep descent and rocky surface, and Bramble felt herself falling, although it seemed to be happening a long way away.

She had just enough energy left to roll as she hit the ground. She wanted to just lie there for a moment. Just a moment. But she forced herself to clamber up. If she could get back on Trine...

Horst caught her as she grasped Trine's mane. He had leaped from his horse and grabbed her arms. She screamed with pain and he let her go in surprise. Trine swung around and bit him hard on the arm. He swore and drew his sword. Sully moved off to the side to stop her running back down the hill. He drew his sword as well.

"Give in, now, lass, give it over and come with us," Horst said gently. "You know you can't win."

Bramble knew he was right. But the same refusal to be

frightened that had stopped her running from the blond, back in Wooding, stopped her from giving in now.

"I'd rather die than be used by Thegan," she said venomously. She drew her knife, and jumped toward Sully.

"Stupid Traveler bitch!" he yelled as he brought his sword down.

THE WELL OF SECRETS

"THEY'LL BE meeting soon," Safred said casually to her uncle. "The other three. But there's no guarantee they'll make it through that moment."

"I'd spit for luck but my mouth's too dry," Cael said.

There was a distant commotion outside in the street. Cael raised an eyebrow. Safred's eyes hazed for a moment, then cleared.

"A healing," she said. "One of the pilgrims fell from the bridge."

"Can you help him?"

"Her. No. But I can save the baby."

And the family'll ask why I didn't foresee the accident and save them both, Safred thought. *I'd ask the same. But the only answer is "because the gods didn't will it" and what kind of answer is that?*

"There's one good thing," she said as she prepared to open the door. "The fifth will be along tomorrow."

"What fifth?" Cael looked at her. "What haven't you been telling me?"

Safred smiled sadly. "Too much. Life and death and destruction and rebirth. Everything, really."

She opened the door before they could knock on it. Three men rushed in carrying the injured woman and placed her on the bed where the Well of Secrets did her healing. She placed both hands on the woman's belly and looked at Cael, noting the increase in gray hairs, the slight blurring of muscle by a thin

436

film of fat: the signs of age approaching, even if it was a long way off yet.

He glared at her as he often did, to remind her that though she was the healing miracle worker to everyone else, to him she was still the child he had raised. And to part of her he was still almost-father, the strong arms that had protected her. But he couldn't protect her from the gods.

She concentrated on the body beneath her hands and began to sing in horrible, grating tones that sounded like the voice of the dead, and the pain left the woman's face.

Cael pushed his way outside through the crowd gathered at the door, watching, worshipping as the gods showed their power.

CAEL'S STORY

THERE WERE fishers on the bank.

When the boat came gliding down the stream toward them, a lantern at her prow and another at her stern, gleaming in the dusk, they thought it was a ghost ship, for surely no craft could navigate this high reach of the river, far above the falls.

There were rocks downstream and rocks upstream, white water churning endlessly, in and out of season. How could a ship come here?

So they ran, throwing down their rods and their gaffs, back to the village crying, "Death, disaster upon us!"

The ship rode the white water lightly, and survived the teeth of the rocks and the smiting of the stream. It smashed to pieces on the high falls—but by then it had served its purpose, and those on board were safe ashore.

I was one of those on board. So I, Cael, tell the tale as one who was there and who knows the truth.

When her time came upon the Lady and her pains drew close together, she called for me and entrusted the coming babe into my care.

"For," she said formally, "though you and I have contested more than once, and more than bitterly, still I know you are honest, and I know you are true. Take the child, and guard her from her father. For I would not travail thus to see her taken and raised at court, a pawn for alliances and treaty making. Teach her the new ways and let her not be seduced into bondage to her father, or to any other."

438

She did travail, indeed, and died therefrom. But the child survived.

I took her, and named her Safred, which means sorrow, for it was true her coming brought little joy. I found a wet nurse, and sent word to the warlord that the Lady and his daughter, both, were dead in the straw. He sent silver for their funeral, and an observer, and we sent two bodies to the burial caves, swathed tightly in the burial clothes, the Lady and a runt piglet.

We hid the child in a cave in the high woods, with the wet nurse and a guard. Later, when it was safe, we brought them back.

I raised the child with my own two. Perhaps I was not as kind to her. There are men who can love any child as though they were true sons or daughters; I am not one of them. When I looked at Safred, I saw her mother's eyes, and though her mother and I had disagreed many times, the lack of her was hard. Sometimes when I looked at her, I saw her father's very look and expression. Then I pushed her out of the house, because I did not like the fear that sprang in me at those times.

It might have been different if my Sage had not died of a fever when Safred was only two. She grieved for Sage a long time, as did my own girls. And I.

But overall she grew up happy enough, and never went in need. I myself taught her the contest, in words and in deeds, as I did my own girls. While March, my elder, took to the word-striving as though born to argue, and while Nim was swift with hands or staff, Safred took no interest in either.

"Your mother was a great striver," I told her often, "you must have something of her in you."

She just looked at me sideways out of those green eyes. I am telling you, and I am telling you true. No matter what she became later, no matter what deeds of argument or arms she achieved, as a child she was slower than most.

Perhaps she practiced in secret; one cannot become a great striver without constant practice. She was secretive—well, all the world knows that. "The Well of Secrets" they called her in Parteg, and lined up halfway to Corpen to confess to her. But I am getting ahead of my story.

She learned quickly in other ways: learned to cipher and scribe, learned herbalry and leechcraft, husbandry and tillage, cooking and weaving. All the village taught her, as though they wished to make up for shunning her mother so when she first came home, big with child, and all knew the father's name. Safred was quick to learn, except when I was teaching her. Yet I swear I taught her as I taught my own, as I taught other village children.

Well, time passes and does not ask our consent. Soon enough my March and my Nim were in their own houses, and Safred and I were left alone. I had more time for her then. I discovered, then, about the gods' power.

At first it seemed no more than skill. When she tended an animal, say a milch cow with hard udders, the cow recovered quickly. So it might be with any skilled healer. The seeds she planted grew fast and strong; so it might be with any skilled tiller. The horses she gentled never kicked at her; so it might be with a beast handler of soft voice and quiet ways. Except that her voice was not quiet. Not usually.

Then Terin, the weaver's son, broke his leg falling from the walnut tree, broke it so the bone was sharp through the skin. And all wailed, for such a wound meant he was almost certain sure to lose his life through bleeding and, if not his life, his leg.

I was nearest the boy when he fell, so it was I who carried him to the leech's house, and Safred followed me. The healer, who must have known, I realized later, put water to boil and reached down the hanging herbs for a poultice, found wood for a splint, but left the tending of the boy to Safred.

That was the first time I heard her sing. Now singing is a bad word for it, as those who have heard it will tell you. For, and I tell you the truth, it sounded horrible. Like a bellows creaking with wind.

I would have stopped her, but the healer laid his hand on my arm and shook his head. Safred put her hands on the boy's shoulders. She looked into his eyes, deep in, with that wide green gaze I remembered from her mother, and breathed these strange sounds. Terin's eyes grew wide, wider, and his mouth dropped like one in sleep. Then she laid hands on his leg and brought the bone back into place as one might put back a hair comb that has fallen out of place—as simply as that. The boy made no noise, and no drop of blood left him.

In all my memory, that is the strangest time, despite all I saw later, and all I learned. The boy's leg was lying broken and white on the covers, his bone showing through his skin like a rock breaking through grass, but no blood, as though he were dead already, though he sat there breathing before me. Lo, that was the strangest sight of my life, and I did not know how to speak to her after—when the leech had bound the leg and poulticed it, and she had stopped singing.

She sat, staring up at me, waiting for my judgment, half resigned to my disapproval, half fearful of it.

"Your grandmother was a woman who walked with the gods," I said. "Your mother told me, once, that her mother was born an enchanter, but her father beat it out of her, for fear she should set a spell upon him or his beasts. For she did not love him, nor should she have."

Safred stirred then, and stood up. She was short, you know, and had to look up into my eyes.

"I set no spells for harm," she said.

"Nor did she," I said. "What's bred in the bone comes out in the flesh. Your mother would have been glad to see this, to see her own mother's gift brought to use. To good use."

She colored, for the first time I remember. After that, I think, we were better acquainted, and she kept fewer secrets from me. But secrets she had to have, no matter what. They were like meat and drink to her.

That was how she discovered the great power she carried with her. It started with a pedlar, a traveling man who had been in our village before: a dark man—not dark of countenance, but dark of spirit. He smiled, but under the smile was pain. Few could bear to talk with him for longer than it took to conclude their bargain, but still we bought from him because few others came our way, and perhaps out of pity.

When Safred was sixteen, the pedlar came to our house to show me new wool cloth from down valley. I was not home. I tell this part of the story as it was told to me by the pedlar. He came, he said, and called out, "Blessing on the house." Safred came out to him, and gazed at him with the green eyes of healing.

"Come in," she told him, and made him lay his pack aside and brewed him rosemary tea and talked with him. I think the man was starved for talk; perhaps that was all the healing he needed. But Safred said to him, "You carry a secret."

That was true. Now, I tell you, I do not know what the secret was, any more than you, for Safred was the deepest pit there ever was for secrets, and after a secret was told to her, the teller did not need ever to tell it again. But tell her he did, and went away a different man. Maybe she laid some blessing on him. Maybe the simple telling was enough. Maybe she forgave him, who could not forgive himself. I never told Safred a secret, so I don't know. I had no secret to tell her, for she had known me all her life. That, I regret—that I had no secrets then to give her.

After the pedlar, others came to her. At first they were just from our village, people who had known her all her life. Margery's neck pains went away; Dalis's breathing improved; but these were not the real miracles. It was the kindness that was true magic. Wherever a secret was washed by Safred's green eyes, that household rejoiced — and was kinder thereafter.

Some people said she laid a geas on them, to tell the secret to the person it most concerned, or to make reparation where reparation was due. Whatever she said, it was done.

Soon people began to come from elsewhere. And sometimes, when pilgrims were in the house with Safred, and I kept guard outside, I heard her singing that harsh song. But I heard no words, ever, though pilgrims sometimes swore they had shouted out their pain.

It was foreordained that her father should hear of it.

Now, I do not know what you have heard of Masil, her father, the warlord. That he was brave and handsome? True. That he was violent? Most true. That he was barbaric, insane, wicked? Perhaps true. But no one ever said that he was stupid.

When he heard of the wonders coming from our village, he sent a messenger to discover the truth, for even then he suspected that this green-eyed enchanter was the daughter of another green-eyed woman, who had bewitched him out of things he had wanted to keep: his heart and his manhood and his children. For they say that after the Lady, Masil could lie with no other woman, and I believe it.

When the messenger came, I knew it was time. For no one has ever called me stupid, either, and I had been preparing for this since the first pilgrim came. The village helped. We showed him Tamany, who was green-eyed enough, but could not have been the child of either Lady or warlord in a year of blue moons. He went away, but it was time to leave.

Safred wanted to stay until she had spoken to all the pilgrims who were waiting to see her. I knew that the train of pilgrims would not end. We argued bitterly. That was the first I knew of her skill at wordstriving, and surprise silenced me. That was my great flaw. I should have overborne her. Everything then might have been different, and I might have children and grandchildren living still.

We stayed an extra week. On the last day, one of the goatherds ran into the village, crying that the warlord was coming himself to see the witch. I called Safred out, but she would not leave her pilgrim, who was crying and wailing fit to die. So I dragged her out by her hair and shook sense back into her.

"Your mother died to give you freedom," I said, in no mind to be gentle. "Will you throw her gift back in her face, will you spit on her grave? Do you want to be a warlord's daughter, a pawn for alliances and treaty making?"

Perhaps part of her wanted to stay and set eyes on her father for the first time, but she came, half dazed, and I took her up the hill path, to the same cave where we had hidden her as a baby, where I had left our supplies. We were not quite fast enough. The scout from the warlord's party saw us, and they followed fast enough.

But I had prepared for this day, too, and for this danger. So I led her into the labyrinth of the caves, which I had spent months learning, months when I could no longer enter my house for fear of hearing another's secret, months when I imagined this day, over and over.

There were others in the village who knew the secrets of the caves. None would guide the warlord. So he put the village to the torch, and all the people in it, male and female, adult and child, and I lost my Nim and my March and their children, too, all three of them. I will never get them back. Nor cease to mourn them.

There is no darkness like the inner darkness of the earth. It lies solid on your eyelids. It is not cold there, nor ever hot, but it can be damp or dry, loud or silent, and all this depends on the waters that run through it. Our caves were formed by water, and water runs through them constantly, dripping, flowing, rushing, pounding. I navigated our way as much by sound as by sight or touch, following my ears as well as the marks I had laid down over many explorations.

There were wonders in that place I can never describe to you. It is one of the differences between Safred and me, that to her the caves were a place of horror and fear, while to me they were a miracle.

We made our way through the heavy dark with a small lantern, Safred whimpering all the way. And deep in the darkest cave, we met the delvers. I was there, and I tell you truth. They do exist, the dark people, the little people, the eaters of rock. Like boulders they seem at first, rounded and heavy. When they move it is slowly, far slower than you or I, yet nothing can stand in their way. They are blind, of course, though they smell their way, and their hearing is like a bat's. They surrounded us before we were aware. A deep grumbling filled the cavern. It was like the harsh sound Safred made when she spelled, but this was a song of anger and distrust. Until she answered them.

All this way, I had been the strong one, unafraid of the dark. But now, when I trembled with fear, Safred stood tall and sang her song of gentleness, of kindness and healing.

It didn't work very quickly. That was something I was to come to know—nothing worked quickly with the delvers. Oh, I spent a weary time there, listening to the two songs contest our safety. But she sang unwearied and finally, for a moment, they listened without singing back, and we were safe.

Or so we thought. In the village, Terin, afraid for his life and promised the lives of his mother and sister, agreed to guide the warlord through the caves. Even at that time, I could not blame him. If I had been faced with Nim and March, knife to throat, would I have had the loyalty to refuse Masil? I tell you the truth, and the truth is that I do not know.

The sound of the singing guided them as well as Terin, I would guess. Sound travels far underground. However that may be, they came upon us when the singing of the delvers had grown sweet and I was finally relaxing. I quenched the lantern, but it was too late. They had seen us. And we saw them. Lord Masil was flanked by two men with torches flaring.

"Greetings, my daughter," he said, and his voice was rich and warm. He did not realize that the singing he had heard came from the delvers. To his eyes they were boulders, dark and rounded. "I have waited long to see you."

It was the only time I have ever understood my sister Perian, when Masil stood there with his red hair shining in the flames and his shoulders broad. She had loved him, once. At that moment I was stricken with sorrow that I had hated her for her disloyalty, called her "the Lady" with scorn like the other villagers when she returned, strove to shame her.

When she died she was only eighteen, younger than my Nim.

At that moment I repented me of my hard thoughts.

"Time to come home, daughter," he said, and held out his hand.

But she said, "I have no home to go back to. You have destroyed it. How many people did you put to the torch before you found a guide?"

And so I learned of my girls' deaths, and learned hatred afresh.

The men behind him gasped at her Sight, but he was silent. Then, "As many as I had to," he said. "You are worth more to me than a thousand lives."

"I am worth," Safred said, "no more than any other. Nor are you."

Anger moved across his face. "I had this argument too many times with your mother. I will not listen to it from you. Take her."

His men moved forward, but Safred sang out a harsh note, quick and sharp. As they leaped toward her, it must have seemed to them that the very rocks had come alive beneath their feet, as the delvers rose and, as formidable as winter, pushed them back, slowly, solidly.

I took her and pulled her away, following a delver who sang softly to us to guide us. Her father shouted after us, "I will find you! I will search until I do, daughter!"

I knew it was the truth, for he was burning with the shame of being tricked out of her once, and he would not rest until that shame was erased. And I knew that they would find a way around the delvers, eventually, for the delvers have no weapons, only strength and surprise.

So I hurried her down the tunnel, through ways I had never been before, until we came, weary miles behind us, into the greatest cavern I have ever seen. And here we could see everything, for there was a glow coming up from a wide lake, a pearly light that showed us the cavern plain as day. There were wonders: shapes formed by the water into statues like people, and animals, and even trees. And there was one shape there I marveled over, for it was as like a ship as any I have seen riding at harbor in the city.

The delver took us to it, singing happiness and escape. For it was a ship, a ship beached high out of the lake, with no sign of damp or rot upon it, though by rights it should have been covered in the stone growth that had created the pillars and statues. Who placed it there? I do not know. There were people who in the past had buried their warlords in boats, but this ship was empty.

Safred laid her hand upon it. "There is a spell on this ship," she said. "A spell of forgetting. It has forgotten the ocean, the river, forgotten the very meaning of water."

Then she went to the lake and, gathering up water in her hands, she poured it over the prow of the ship as you might wash a baby's head gently. The ship shuddered. I would say it came back to life, except it was a made thing only, of wood and cloth and pitch. But it seemed to spring toward the lake as though set free from long bondage, and splashed gladly into the milky water.

Then it waited, quietly, while we said farewell to the delver and boarded, and Safred sang our thanks.

She laid her hand upon the ship and said, "My brother, take us to the light."

The ship turned silently into the current.

We slid down waterways of glowing white. Pale fish swam in the waters, blind as delvers. The whisper of the water against the ship's hull was soothing, and I slept, for the first time in a day and a night and a day, as far as I could reckon time. Perhaps Safred slept too. I did not need to guard her there.

We slid down a smooth current and gathered speed as we went, and we came to an area of sharp rocks and had to be ready to fend the ship off at every turn. We ate twice and slept once more, in turns, before we saw the light in the water growing less. I lit the lanterns at the prow and the stern of the ship. We carried on, an island of light in the darkness, until we realized that in the distance there was daylight.

So we emerged from the mountains into a strange country, onto a river we had never seen. Safred turned into my arms and we wept together as we came into the light again. There were fishers on the bank.

This is the first story of Safred, my sister's daughter. All her other stories can be told by other people, for her life was a public life, and her deeds known to all. But this story only I, Cael, can tell, for I was there, and I swear to you, what I have told you is truth.

ASH

"THE TOP of that ridge, that's the border to Golden Valley," Martine said thankfully.

Ash nodded. He would be thankful, too, when they got out of Cliff Domain. The weeks of walking had been punctuated by bands of armed men riding or marching south, pushing everyone else off the roads and tracks. They weren't just warlord's men. The bands usually had two or three of those in charge, but they were made up of ordinary young men, farmers mostly, by the look of them, and the unpracticed way they held their pikes and shields. The warlord of Cliff Domain was either planning a war or expecting an attack from the south.

"They're taking all the protection away from the mountains," Martine had said a week earlier. "Let's hope the Ice King doesn't hear about it. He'd be over the mountains and raiding in a heartbeat."

"Does that still happen?" Ash asked. "I thought the Ice People had given up."

Martine was silent for a moment. "The last raid was twenty years ago," she said slowly. "It was... bad. Since then, the borders have been heavily guarded. Who knows what would happen if they weren't."

She seemed uneasy whenever they encountered the marching men, turning her eyes back to the high mountains behind them. Fortunately, none of the bands were interested in two Travelers who had enough sense to get out of the way as soon as they heard the tramp of marching feet. The men only whistled at

Martine halfheartedly as they went past, not even bothering with ribald comments. They were tired, not used to walking so far, and not enthusiastic about where they were going.

In the villages, the gossip said the men were going to force the Lake People to stop charging such exorbitant tolls for ferrying goods across the Lake at Baluchston. But that sounded unlikely to Ash.

"Go to war because of tolls?" he said to Martine privately. "Seems a bit of an overreaction."

"Maybe the warlord here isn't planning to actually go to war. Just frighten them."

"Who's the warlord?"

"Gabra's in charge," Martine said, "but the actual warlord is his father, Thegan. Thegan's in the south, now. He married the daughter of the warlord of Central Domain, and left his son in charge of Cliff Domain." She snapped her fingers. "So. There you are. If he takes Lake Domain, he'll have all the middle of the country. From cliff to cove."

It was part of a Traveler saying—From cliff to cove, from sand to snow—that described the extent of the Domains, from the eastern sea to the western mountains and from the southern deserts to the northern ice.

They looked at each other. War. And in the middle would be the remnants of the old blood, the Lake People.

"The Lake protects her own," Ash said.

Martine nodded. "It might not be a bad thing," she said. "If more ghosts arise, it might not be a bad thing to have the middle of the country ready for a fight. With trained men in an organized army."

"You can't kill ghosts."

"No. But we might be able to cripple them. Stop them, as Mabry said. They have solid arms and legs. Without

451

those...how much harm can they do? But that's real fighting and it needs trained soldiers to do it...Thegan might be doing us all a favor."

"The gods said that *we* have to stop them, not this Thegan."

"He might buy us time, though. I suspect we'll be short on time."

Without discussing it, they began to walk longer each day, into the early spring dusk and sometimes, when the moon was bright, into the night as well.

Now, finally, they were leaving Cliff Domain and going into Golden Valley. From there it was only a couple of days' walk to the pass over the northern mountains and into the Last Domain. They were only three or four days away from the Well of Secrets.

"Horses would have been nice." Ash sighed as his legs complained at the climb up to the ridge. "You'd think the gods could arrange a little thing like that."

They came over the ridge and immediately heard horses, several of them, going far too fast for the broken ground. The path below them was obscured by trees. Ash could just make out the shapes of horses coming up the trail—one in front and two following. It looked like a pursuit.

Then the horses broke cover. The first one, a black, was being ridden by a young woman with dark hair. Two men followed on the horses behind—warlord's men, here in Golden Valley, Ash realized, where no warlord had power.

The woman tried to turn the horse downhill, but the black propped and she fell. Ash found himself running down the trail, sliding and slipping on the loose rocks. She was up in a moment, to face her pursuers. They exchanged words. None of them saw Ash hurtling toward them.

The men drew their swords.

She pulled a knife and sprang as the shorter one raised his sword to strike her down.

Ash barreled into him as the sword was coming down, ducking his shoulder so that the blade went over him, and he and the man ended up sprawling, rolling, scrabbling for a foothold.

Ash had no time to think; the man was well trained and came back at him immediately with his sword, but he lost his footing and slithered back a little and his first blow missed. Ash went forward before the man could recover, drawing his knife without thinking, moved in and under the sword arm, stabbing upward.

The man fell, and from the way he fell Ash knew he was already dead. His sword clanged to the ground.

Ash snatched it up and turned to face the other man, who had moved toward him. The warlord's man was brought up short by the woman's knife at his throat from behind. But she wasn't going to be able to hold him long, Ash realized. She was flushed and shaking from fever, or a wound, or both. He noticed she had a wolf skin tied over one shoulder like a cape.

"Drop the sword, Horst," she said. Horst hesitated. "I don't want to kill you, but I will." She whispered the words, but she meant them.

Horst dropped the sword. Ash kicked it away, keeping his eyes steadily on the warlord's man.

The woman stepped back, shakily. "You'd better not take him home, Horst," she said. "Thegan doesn't like failure. If I were you I'd say he died of a fever on the road. I wouldn't mention me at all." Her face twisted a little. "He was going to kill me. It seems the gods protect the Kill Reborn."

Horst spat out of the side of his mouth. "Sully and me go back a long way. I'll not be lying about his death." He turned to look at Ash seriously. "Will you be here for his quickening?"

Ash flushed. They didn't have time... What was one ghost when so many might rise? "I'm sorry. We don't have time to wait three days."

Horst spat again, this time at Ash's feet. "A curse on you, then, and I'll be remembering you. And so will my lord Thegan. You've made yourself a bad enemy today, lad, and all for a Traveler bitch."

"All for a Traveler," Ash agreed.

Horst's eyes lifted, for the first time, to his hair, and Ash saw him realize that he too was a Traveler. It was as though the fact that Ash could fight had blinded Horst to his coloring. A look of horror came on Horst's face.

Ash smiled grimly at him. "It's a bad thought, isn't it, that we might learn to fight back?"

He was filled with fury, a long suppressed fury, born of all the nights sleeping in a stable instead of an inn room, all the times he'd been served last in a shop, all the times Acton's people had sworn at him or spat in the dust as he passed, or charged him twice the fair price, just because they could. For a moment he understood the enchanter, *knew* why he had raised the ghosts. His hand tightened around the sword hilt.

Then Martine's voice cut through. "Let him go, Ash."

The voice was a balm to him, banishing the rage and leaving him empty. He stepped back and gestured to Horst. "Take your friend and your horses, and get out of here."

Horst laid the body over Sully's horse, mounted his own, and led the horse downhill. When he was a fair way down the slope he turned and shouted.

"Don't think you'll find a welcome in Golden Valley. You've murdered here."

"You had no right to stop her here. It's a frcc valley," Ash called back.

"You attacked us unprovoked," Horst said, his face grim. "Who do you think they'll believe?"

Then he spurred his horse off down the track, Sully's horse following.

"He's right," Martine said. "They'll believe him."

"We have to get out of here," Ash said.

The woman was clinging to her horse. "Water?" she asked. Martine gave her the water bottle and she drank deeply, the color coming back a little to her face. "That's better. Thanks." She looked at Ash. "Thanks to you, too."

He nodded acknowledgment. He was saved from wondering what to say when her horse whickered loudly and was answered by two more horses that emerged from the clump of pines above them.

Ash looked at the sword and felt sick at the blood drying on it. But he knelt and wiped it on a tussock of grass, then slid it through his belt. He'd have to find a proper sheath for it later.

"Throw it away," Martine said.

"What?"

"You know the penalties for anyone other than a warlord's man carrying one of those. Throw it away."

It went against all his instincts.

"She's right," the woman whispered. "Cause you nothing but trouble."

Reluctantly, Ash slid it out of his belt and tossed it in the grass. Both women nodded, for a moment looking like sisters.

"I'm Ash," he said. "This is Martine."

"Bramble," the woman breathed. "Help me up."

"Your arm is hurt," Martine said. "We should see to that first."

Bramble shook her head. "We have to move now, before he gets a gang together to hunt us down." She whistled to the other horses and they came trotting forward, nosing her shoulder and cheek. She passed the reins of the bay to Martine and those of the chestnut to Ash. "Help me up?"

Ash hoisted her onto the black's back. She was unsteady on her feet, but rock solid on the animal's back.

"Can you ride?" she asked. They both shook their heads.

"Well, guess you're going to learn," she said, her eyes crinkling with amusement. "Use a rock to mount."

The bay tried to lean his full weight against Martine as she reached for his mane to pull herself up. Bramble scolded the horse and he stood upright. The chestnut skittered a little as Ash approached her and Bramble soothed her—"There, Cam, he's harmless"—and she stood calmly as he mounted.

"Are you a horse speller?" Martine asked.

Bramble smiled and shook her head. "Just a beginner at it," she said. "Let's go."

She led the way, walking first, then, as they reached the firm grass at the valley bottom, picked up the pace to a canter. They avoided the farmhouses and villages, skirting them as widely as possible. Ash and Martine's thighs were soon aching and chapped.

Bramble stopped at a stream to let the horses drink and Martine eased herself against Mud's saddlebags, and sighed. "You had to go and ask the gods for horses, didn't you?"

Ash snorted. "At least we'll get there faster."

"Where are you going?" Bramble asked.

Ash felt that she was pretending interest, trying to ignore the pain and swelling in her arm. She looked very pale. "The Well of Secrets," he answered. No reason she shouldn't know. Lots of people went to the Well of Secrets.

She looked sideways at him, eyebrows raised. Ash realized that she was really quite pretty, under the sweat and the pallor.

"Me too," she said.

They took each other for pilgrims, and no more was said. They started off again, a little slower this time as Bramble was beginning to look more drawn and wince every time her horse moved sharply.

Golden Valley wasn't large. A two-day walk was only a morning's ride at a good pace. They were braced for sounds of pursuit, but they heard no followers. They would hear them, Bramble knew, if their pace slackened any more.

Bramble gestured to Ash to take the lead. She was swaying, but managed to twist her hands tight in her horse's mane and she laid her head down on its neck. "Trine will look after me," she said. "You go ahead and she'll follow."

Martine stayed behind Bramble and came up next to her when the path was wide enough. They moved through green-gold poplar groves and sparsely grassed fields where granite boulders edged up through the thin dirt. They kept as close to the foot-hills as they could, away from the villages and main road.

When Martine found a clump of comfrey, she insisted that they stop to bathe Bramble's arm and put crushed leaves on it. It looked bad. Yellow pus was trapped under the skin and the whole arm was red and swollen.

"If we can't get to a healer here," Martine said, frowning, "the best thing we can do is make it to the Well of Secrets as fast as we can. She's supposed to be a healer."

Bramble chuckled painfully. "Well, if she's not I reckon there'll be a dozen who claim to be in Oakmere."

Martine smiled. "You may be right. Charlatans gather around crowds."

"Let's go," Ash said impatiently, watching behind them.

Bramble climbed painfully onto Trine.

It was late afternoon by the time they reached the end of the valley. They had to come back onto the main road to take the pass into the Last Domain, and Ash insisted that Martine take the lead so that he could guard their backs if necessary.

He was still jumpy from that morning: he didn't want to think about it, but he kept replaying the fight in his head. Could he have avoided killing that man, Sully? Could he have chosen some other way? Was there a moment when he'd decided to kill? He couldn't remember a moment. All he remembered was movement and action and instinct ruling him. But it was a trained instinct, and it had been trained, he realized, to kill. Not to safeguard, but to kill.

He pushed the thought away. He had been protecting Bramble and himself. Sully would have killed her—killed him. He'd had the right to...Did *anyone* have the *right* to kill? That was too hard a question. He dismissed that thought, too, and concentrated on the increasingly difficult task of staying on a horse when his legs felt like jelly.

As they climbed the road to the pass they met a farmer with a bullock cart laden with apples coming the other way.

"Afternoon," he said affably, reacting to the horses rather than the riders. Then he looked again and scowled at them. "Got airs above your station, ain't you?" he said, and spat on the road behind them.

"Afternoon to you, too," Ash said.

He wanted to quicken their pace, but Cam had her own ideas about how fast you climbed a hill, and he didn't know how to persuade her otherwise.

By the time they had threaded their way into the pass, the sun was setting. The pass was a flattened part of a saddleback ridge, sharp as a knife everywhere but here. They stopped for a moment and looked down the long road before them. In the distance they could see a village by a river.

"Oakmere," Martine said, and smiled. "Not far."

"Let the horses take a rest," Bramble said. Her voice was thready.

Martine dismounted, groaning, and then stretched and went over to her. She didn't try to help Bramble down, just checked her arm and gave her water.

Ash climbed off Cam and discovered why Martine had groaned. Every muscle in his legs and most in his back wanted to lie down and die. As for the chafing... He'd wait until he was somewhere private before he found out how bad that was.

"Go faster," Martine said privately to Ash as they mounted. "She might lose that arm if it's not treated soon."

"Next stop, the Well of Secrets," Ash said cheerfully to Bramble.

She tried to smile at him. "And that's supposed to be re-assuring, is it?"

The path was wide enough, so they set off down the long slope side by side.

THE WELL OF SECRETS

"THEY'RE ALMOST HERE, the other three," Safred said to her uncle Cael. "Get them to clear the street so the horses can get through easily. There's no time to be lost if we want to save that arm."

"Whose arm?" Cael asked, but she didn't answer.

She was listening to some other voice again. Then her eyes focused and she looked at him. "What comes after the healing, that's the hard part."

"Well, what comes after?"

"Nobody likes being destined to do something," she said, and he knew how little she relished her responsibilities from the gods.

"It's an affront to our sense of free will," he said mildly.

"Powerlessness without impotence. Purpose, but someone else's volition." She paused. "I must make it their own will if we are to succeed."

"Can you do that?"

She nodded slowly. Her mouth curved wryly. "I will have help. From Saker."

SAKER

H E RAISED the black stone knife level with his scarred palm. The bones of a thousand murdered innocents lay before him. He was at one of the largest massacre sites in the Eleven Domains.

"I am Saker, son of Alder and Linnet of the village of Cliffhaven. I seek justice for Owl, for Sparrow, for Lark, for Ash, for Oak, for Cedar..."

There were so many buried here that every name he spoke brought up an image in his mind: men and women, old and young, beautiful and ugly, strong and frail. But all angry. All thirsting for revenge.

The rest of the spell wasn't in words, but images in his mind, complex and distressing. Colors, phrases of music, the memory of a particular scent, and now, the memory of blood and broken bodies and exultation could be added...

He pressed the knife to his palm then drew it down hard. The blood surged out in time with his heart and splashed in gouts on the bones as he walked over the site, sharing his blood as widely as he could.

"Kinsmen," he said. "Arise."

ACKNOWLEDGMENTS

An earlier draft of this book was my thesis for a Doctor of Creative Arts degree at the University of Technology, Sydney. Many thanks to my supervisor, Debra Adelaide, and to my examiners: Richard Harland, Van Ikin and Sophie Masson. Thanks also to my agent, Lyn Tranter, and to the people who read the manuscript in draft form: Stephen, Rose, Jeremy, Ron, Cathie, Leanne, Patricia, Judy and Jens.

extras

meet the author

Alison Casey

PAMELA FREEMAN is an award-winning writer for young people. She has a doctorate of creative arts from the University of Technology, Sydney, Australia, where she has also lectured in creative writing. She lives in Sydney with her husband and young son. Visit the official Pamela Freeman Web site at www.pamelafreemanbooks.com.

interview

What professions were you involved with before becoming a writer?

I have only been a full-time writer since my son was born, in 2001. Before that, I ran parallel careers as a writer and scriptwriter, university lecturer, educational designer, technical writer, consultant in organizational communications, and trainer. My most interesting work involved researching the effects of reporting misconduct or corruption in law enforcement organizations. We found that the people who reported (the good guys) were much worse off socially, physically, and psychologically than the people they reported about (the bad guys). This research allowed me to help some Australian law enforcement agencies and government departments design programs to support the people who were trying to do the right thing. I still get asked to consult in this area from time to time, and also to design complaints systems that ensure natural justice is achieved. Not easy, but fascinating.

Prior to writing Blood Ties, *you predominantly wrote for children. What made you want to write a novel for adults?*

There are some stories that just aren't right for kids, and the Castings story is one. I have always found that I am moved to tell a particular story, and then figure out what age group it is for. In this case, it was clear from the start that the story was both too complex and too political to really appeal to children—not to mention the violence, which is extreme.

What interested you about the sci-fi fantasy genre?
I have always read speculative fiction and I think my imagination was shaped by early exposure (thank you, Mrs. Wall, my local librarian). If I'm writing a story, quite often it just takes a specific twist without me intending it. I think it's just the way my mind works. As a reader, I love the sense of otherness, of exploring limitless possibilities, of things larger and in some way more real than our normal lives. The sense that everything *matters;* every action, even every thought. And having read fairly widely in contemporary mainstream fiction, I think that spec fic is where ideas are being explored, as well as emotions and relationships. I find a book that combines all those to be the most satisfying.

Who or what do you consider to be your influences?
Probably Tolkien is number one, closely followed by Jane Austen—and for the same reason: every time I read their work I learn something new about writing. Then all the classics: Le Guin, Carroll, Lewis, L'Engle, Heinlein, Asimov, Ellison, etc. I would also include Dorothy Sayers and Georgette Heyer, because their styles are so clean and their dialogue so vivid. And let's not forget the Bible; the rhythms of the King James Version even got to me, and I was raised Catholic, with a different version altogether!

extras

The Castings Trilogy is a wonderfully unique concept. How did you come up with the idea for it?

Um...I can't tell you without spoiling the third book. I can say it was a combination of a lecture by Bishop Desmond Tutu, having a prime minister who has no respect for indigenous people, and the desire to know what was going to happen the night before I auctioned my apartment. That's where the line "The desire to know the future gnaws at our bones" comes from. I was pacing around my living room, just wanting to know if the place was going to sell, and the sentence popped into my head. I thought, "That's a good line, I'd better write that down," sat in front of my computer, and wrote "The Stonecaster's Story" in one sitting.

The ghosts probably come from a poem by William Butler Yeats, "The Cold Heaven," which asks, "when the ghost begins to quicken, / Confusion of the death-bed over, is it sent / Out naked on the roads, as the books say, and stricken / By the injustice of the skies for punishment?" I read that in high school, and it has stayed with me. There's your quickening, and the roads, and the sense of a larger power...maybe the whole story comes from there, after all...

Blood Ties is a very intricately plotted novel. Was it difficult to structure it so that the characters' paths would intertwine?

Yes. It took several drafts to get the passage of time right. At first, I had several more years pass for Bramble than for Ash, but I realized that they needed to move through the same years at roughly the same pace. So although there was some jigging with time to get them to meet in spring, that wasn't because of their paths not meshing, it was to set up a part of the plot for *Deep Water,* the second book.

extras

When you have finished writing the Castings Trilogy, what type of literature do you think you will be interested in writing?

I hope I will continue to write both children's books and fantasy for adults. I do already have an idea for the next story, set in the Castings universe but in a different time and place. Even after three books, there will still be some unanswered questions for me, some areas I want to explore further. I hope readers will feel that they want to know more, too. But don't worry—I'm not planning on leaving the Castings story up in the air in any way. There will be resolution!

introducing

If you enjoyed
BLOOD TIES,
look out for

DEEP WATER

Book Two of the Castings Trilogy
by Pamela Freeman

THE WELL OF SECRETS

"The desire to know the future gnaws at our bones," said Safred, the Well of Secrets. "Or so a stonecaster I knew once told me."

Her uncle, Cael, grunted and kept cutting up the carrots.

Carrots, beetroots, onion and garlic, lemon juice and oil. Delicious. "Are you going to bake that?" Safred said hopefully. She wasn't fond of salad, but Cael loved it.

Cael grinned at her. "The desire to know the future gnaws at our bones."

She threw a cushion at him, laughing, then sighed. "They're almost here. Send out the word. The girl is badly hurt."

"Don't tire yourself out."

"You'd rather I let her die? Besides, you'll like her, this Bramble. She's contrary."

He frowned at her but went out to the street to spread the word, as she had instructed.

The Well of Secrets sat for a few moments more, wondering if she had the strength to bring the Kill Reborn back from her second death. The gods were silent on the matter; she had even asked them, a thing she rarely did. Prophecy was all very well, but then time came to a turning point, where the future could go either way, or it came to a person who held the future in her hands; this was such a moment and Bramble such a person. If the Kill Reborn lived...if the girl, Bramble, survived...Which was more important? Safred thought that not even the gods knew.

What was to happen in this room in the next hour would shape the future of the Domains, perhaps of the world, and Safred was as blind to it as Cael was.

"Gnaws like a rat," she said, and laughed so she wouldn't cry.

SAKER

Oh, it was so easy! There were so many bones here, and not buried, just thrust into the cave like garbage and the stone rolled across the entrance to keep down the smell. No laying out, no ceremony. There had been no sprigs of pine between these fingers, no rosemary under their tongues. Hundreds of bones, hundreds of skulls. So many names responding to his call. He had not needed to bring Owl's skull from Spritford after all, but he placed it with the others anyway. The man deserved to be recalled again from death.

Saker tolled the names with glee: "I seek justice for Owl, Juniper, Maize, Oak, Sand, Cliff, Tern, Eagle, Cormorant..." So close to the sea there were many seabird names, and even fish: "Dolphin, Cod, Herring..." At almost every name there came a *flick* in his mind, and in one out of ten a picture came to his head: men, women, babies, granfers, all ages and conditions, with nothing in common but their anger.

It was the dark of the moon and he had not used light; the risen would be invisible to the inhabitants of the town below them. The brick houses of the harbor town looked more forbidding than they really were. The dead would be upon the sleeping usurpers before they realized what was happening.

"I seek justice for Oak and Sand and Herring and all their comrades."

Saker paused. Here on the hillside overlooking the harbor he could feel their anger building. It was dangerous, that anger, even to him. He remembered when the ghosts of Spritford had met two Travelers at the river. For a moment, there, he had feared the Travelers would be struck down, not recognized as their own. They had been spared. But this was different, a night attack, when Traveler and invader would look and sound alike in the dark, so he had made precautions.

"I seek recompense for murder unjust, for theft of land, for theft of life; I seek revenge against the invaders, against the evil which has come of Acton's hand. Let no Traveler blood be spilled, let no brother or sister fall by our hands. Listen to me, Owl and your kin: taste my blood, recognize it as your own, and leave unharmed those who share it."

The spirits of the dead were listening. The rest of the spell wasn't in words, but images in his mind, complex and distressing: colors, phrases of music, the memory of a particular scent, the sound of a scream...He looked down at the skulls. He pressed the knife to his palm then drew it down hard. He flung his arm wide and blood surged out in time with his heart and splashed in gouts on the bones.

"Arise, Oak and Sand and Herring and all your comrades," he commanded. "Take your revenge."

He watched, smiling, as they streamed down the hill towards Carlion, weapons in hand. Then he followed.

VISIT THE ORBIT BLOG AT

www.orbitbooks.net

FEATURING

BREAKING NEWS
FORTHCOMING RELEASES
LINKS TO AUTHOR SITES
EXCLUSIVE INTERVIEWS
EARLY EXTRACTS

AND COMMENTARY FROM OUR EDITORS

WITH REGULAR UPDATES FROM OUR TEAM,
ORBITBOOKS.NET IS YOUR SOURCE
FOR ALL THINGS ORBITAL.

WHILE YOU'RE THERE, JOIN OUR EMAIL LIST
TO RECEIVE INFORMATION ON SPECIAL OFFERS,
GIVEAWAYS, AND MORE.

imagine. explore. engage.